MW01006040

DARKNESS VISIBLE

A Dungeon horrible, on all sides round
As one great Furnace flam'd, yet from those flames
No light, but rather darkness visible
Serv'd only to discover sights of woe,
Regions of sorrow, doleful shades, where peace
And rest can never dwell, hope never comes
That comes to all . . .

—John Milton, Paradise Lost, Book I

DARKNESS VISIBLE

A Novel of the 1892 Homestead Strike

Trilby Busch

Darkness Visible © copyright 2012 by Trilby Busch. All rights reserved. No part of this book may be reproduced in any form whatsoever, by photography or xerography or by any other means, by broadcast or transmission, by translation into any kind of language, nor by recording electronically or otherwise, without permission in writing from the author, except by a reviewer, who may quote brief passages in critical articles or reviews.

ISBN: 978-0-615-56479-1

Printed in the United States of America
Cover design by Richard Mueller
Book layout by Ryan Scheife, Mayfly Design
First Printing: 2012

16 15 14 13 12 5 4 3 2 1

Published by Steelworks Press

For my grandfather, George W. Busch, who was there,
And for my parents, Edward and Frances, who came after.

I.

. . .there are no limits to which powers of privilege will not go to keep the workers in slavery.

—Mary Harris. *The Autobiography of Mother Jones,* 1925

Thursday, November 19th, 1891

"Homestead!" sang out the conductor as the train began to slow. Emlyn Phillips stood and stretched, then moved closer to the steamer trunk that the porter in Pittsburgh had placed by the exit. The rhythmic clicking of the wheels slackened as the engine's shrill whistle announced its approach to the Amity Street station. The brakes screamed, and the short passenger train halted at the platform.

Emlyn squinted into the smoky autumn evening. Across the tracks he observed the huddle of hotels and commercial buildings on the flats. Beyond them, he could barely see the houses set upon the big hillside, their lights winking through the swirling smoke. Somehow, it wasn't what he had envisioned.

"This is Homestead?" Emlyn asked the porter.

"Yes, sir. Do you need help with your luggage?"

Emlyn indicated his trunk. "Please."

So this was the place he had heard about in so many letters from his sister and brother-in-law.

The station porter and Emlyn wrestled the trunk off the car and onto a handcart. The engine hissed, puffing out small clouds of sooty smoke, while several other passengers alighted onto the platform. Emlyn swung his violin, snug in its coffin case, over his left shoulder, and followed the porter to the end of the platform.

"All aboard!" the conductor shouted. Two toots of the whistle, a great sibilance of steam, and the locomotive engine started to pant with ever-faster gasps. As the train pulled forward and cleared the station, Emlyn jumped when a thunderous boom erupted from one of the huge structures at the east end of the town. The porter glanced at him and grinned.

At the end of the platform, Emlyn peered into the murk. The sweep of the horizon was stained with a throbbing orange glow over vague outlines of colossal buildings. He set the violin on top of his trunk, looking around in bewilderment. He pulled the watch out of his pocket and squinted at its face: 6:52.

A cacophony of metallic sounds filled the hazy darkness. Hisses, shrieks, groans and roars, clangs and bangs emerged from the great black mills before him. It seemed like a hundred smokestacks of various heights exhaled blackness. The air was thick with sulfurous smoke. Emlyn recognized the smell from back home, the odor of burning coal.

As his hearing started to get accustomed to the muted din, he drew back in alarm when a colossal burst of blue-yellow flame erupted into the sky across the river. He relaxed at once when he recognized the source of the eruption—oxygen being shot into the hot belly of a Bessemer converter. He knew because he had seen Bessemer furnaces at Tredegar in the upper reaches of Rhymney Valley in his native Wales.

This was indeed a change from Cardiff, that bustling Welsh port from which he had embarked nearly two weeks previously. He winced as he thought of his father, trembling, face stricken with pain behind the white muttonchops, when he had told him that in good conscience, he, Emlyn, could not follow in his footsteps. How could he be a minister if he wasn't sure there was a God to pray to?

After that confrontation in July, his father could no longer bear the sight of his youngest child, the child upon whom he had rested such high hopes.

That was the end of Emlyn's studies for the ministry. Disowned, almost penniless, Emlyn had been taken in by his college friend, Gareth Morgan. The torture of having to live off the charity of others was at last relieved when his older sister Eirwen offered a solution: Come to work in America. Her husband Gwyn would send money for a second-class passage to Philadelphia. After all, wrote Gwyn, who had a good job in the mill, Emlyn could easily repay them after he landed work in Homestead.

The offer was kind and generous, like Eirwen and Gwyn themselves. Emlyn wired them his acceptance.

During the weeks of packing, saying goodbyes, and the week on board the ship, Emlyn had been besieged with doubts. He dreaded being asked about the reason for his forsaking a university career. He had wandered through each passing day as if in a waking nightmare.

He didn't take much away with him, just a small trunk of clothes, some books, and the violin—his maternal Grandfather Davies' fiddle that he had inherited at the elder's death two years before.

As Emlyn had waited to board the steamer, fiddle in

hand, his small, sad-faced mother and older brother Arthur had suddenly emerged from the crowd on the dock in Cardiff. Arthur had taken him into a brief embrace, and stood aside.

Pressing a small bag of coins into his hand, Mam had pulled his face to hers and kissed him fervently on both cheeks. "Sgrifennu ata i. R'wyn d' garu di. *Remember to write me. I love you.*" Then she turned, and she and Arthur were swallowed by the mass of people and luggage. It broke his heart.

Every day of the crossing Emlyn had stood on deck for hours at a time, leaning onto the railing, watching the dark water slide by. What if he, a former student whose occupation had been reading and studying, couldn't take the tough physical work in the mill? Could he last long enough to repay Gwyn? What if he hated the physical work more than he hated the idea of being a hypocrite?

Now here he was, standing on the platform in Homestead, thousands of miles from Cardiff, wondering to what sort of place he had come. Even though it was night, he knew, he felt, that this valley, the valley of the Monongahela River, was much broader and larger than the valleys he knew in South Wales. The Allegheny Mountains, which he had crossed by train from Philadelphia, seemed immense, sprawling. From what he had seen, everything in America was writ large.

He pulled a well-worn paper from his breast pocket. It was the most recent letter from Eirwen, giving the directions to their house. "714 Third Avenue. Come toward the river on Amity. Turn right. Second block, sixth house on right." He dragged the trunk to the corner of the station platform and looked into the street. A man with a horse cart came over and asked him if he needed a lift somewhere.

Emlyn gave him the address, the trunk was loaded on back, and they plodded off.

The cart swayed along the rutted street, passing small houses, some vacant lots, and a few larger structures—stores and a church.

In several minutes they pulled up in front of a two-story clapboard cottage with a peaked roof fronting the street. As Emlyn climbed out of the cart, he could see the silhouette of a small head between the curtains of a downstairs window. The curtains moved and the head disappeared. He had finished paying the driver when the door opened and a small figure stepped on the porch.

"Uncle Emlyn? Is it you?" asked a small voice hesitantly.

"Indeed it is. And you must be Thomas."

Before either could say another word, a young woman appeared at the door holding a baby on her hip. A woolen shawl with a Welsh pattern was thrown over her shoulders.

"Emlyn bach!" She stepped forward, and he ran up the steps and swept her and the baby into his arms.

"Thank God you arrived safe and sound," she cried, hugging him with one arm while holding the baby with the other.

"You're so big now!" she exclaimed, stepping backwards. "I hardly recognize you as the scrawny lad I left in Treorchy."

"That's right," he grinned. "All grown up, I am. Someone to be reckoned with."

"I see you've already met your eldest nephew. Thomas, help Uncle Em bring his things into the house," she directed.

Handing the violin case to Thomas, Emlyn dragged the steamer trunk through the front door. He found himself in the parlor, the oiled pine plank floor covered with a Brussels rug. By the glow emanating from the hissing gaslight, he saw a passageway at the right going through to the kitchen.

"You can leave the trunk by the door," said Eirwen. "Gwyn will help you carry it to your room when he gets back from the mill tomorrow. He's upstairs sleeping now."

Whirling around, and squeezing his arm again, she exclaimed, "I can't believe you're really here!"

Emlyn replied, "It's you I have to thank."

"We must have a long talk after the children are off to bed. Come, let me get you something to eat. We ate two hours ago, but you must be famished after your long trip."

"Oh, not so bad. I ate a bit waiting for the train in Pittsburgh. Truth to tell, I'm weary of sitting."

"Then come into the kitchen and tell me about your trip."

As Emlyn removed his cap and coat, he saw a small face peeking around the corner. "Dilys, come and meet Uncle Emlyn. Don't be shy, dear." Eirwen took the little girl's hand in her free one and drew her gently into the room. Eying Emlyn suspiciously, Dilys clung to her mother's shirts.

Thomas piped up, "What a big scaredy cat you are, Dil. 'Friad of your own uncle."

"Let her be," admonished Eirwen. "You're a big fellow of six, but she's only three. And David here," she said, bouncing the baby, "is only six months old."

The baby blew bubbles with the drool on his lips.

"There will be plenty of time for getting to know me, " agreed Emlyn.

Thomas bolted to the alcove, yelling, "This is the way upstairs. And this," he added, pointing behind him, "is the kitchen."

Dilys repeated, from the safety of her mother's side, "Upstairs. Kitchen."

"Don't keep repeating what I say, dummy" said Thomas to his sister.

"Thomas! Now, that's not nice," said Eirwen. "Let's show

Uncle Emlyn what a peaceful family we are. And keep your voices down so you don't wake your father."

Glowering at Dilys, Thomas ran to the sideboard, where he pointed out the dishes his parents had brought from Wales. Emlyn nodded approvingly.

A writing desk and a small bookcase shared the long wall opposite the front door in the parlor. "This must be where you write letters home," observed Emlyn, touching the desk with his fingertips.

"I do write letters at that desk, but not to my home, which is here." Eirwen smiled at him. "But I know what you mean. I hope you'll think of here as home soon, too."

Moving to the alcove to the kitchen, she said, "Here's the best room, the room with most activity." As if on cue, David started to wiggle and fuss. "This is where I spend most of my day," said Eirwen, setting down the baby in a blanketed wooden box on the floor.

The kitchen at the back of the house was considerably warmer than the front room. A wood-burning cook stove stood on the back wall between a window and the outside door. A long, well-worn pine table, littered with bowls, utensils and pans stood in the middle of the room. Over the scrubbed floor lay a piece of linoleum, patterned to look like a carpet.

"Mind that you don't tread on David," said Eirwen to Emlyn and Dilys, who followed her into the room.

She went to the stove and moved the big iron teakettle over the firebox. In a short time, steam was issuing from the spout.

"Sit down, Em," she directed, "and I'll make us tea."

"Lovely," he replied, pulling up a chair where he could watch David, who was on all fours, rocking back and forth.

Turning to Thomas, Eirwen said, "It's time you started to get ready for bed. School day tomorrow."

"Ah, Mum, why do I hafta?" he whined. "Uncle's just got here."

"Yes, but there will be plenty of time to talk to him tomorrow and the next day and the day after that." Turning to her daughter, she added, "You, too, Dilys. Here, let me pour some warm water in the basin for you to wash up."

She scalded the teapot, dumped in the tea, and filled the pot with boiling water. Then she mixed hot and cold water in the washbasin and, pushing aside some dirty bowls, set it on the table for the children.

"This reminds me of back home," said Emlyn, "when, during cold weather, we children would wash in the kitchen." He sat back and watched Eirwen work beneath the pulsating gaslight.

Now that he'd had a chance to look closely at her, he was unsettled by her appearance. Of course, he hadn't seen her for seven years, but in that time, how she'd changed! He remembered her as a bride of 20, a girl, really. Her slim figure, her silky brown hair braided with blossoms under a white veil, her mother's simple white wedding dress remade for her. Her pale blue eyes shone with joy as she'd come out of the doors of the chapel into the June sunlight on the arm of Gwyn Jones, stocky and solid in his new black wool suit.

But that happy day was clouded for him, then only 16, because of the realization that his only sister, his Eirwen, would not only be leaving home, but leaving Wales. One of Gwyn's cousins had gone to Pittsburgh and found work making steel. He wrote Gwyn glowing reports of many job openings and good pay in the mills. He urged Gwyn, who already had worked two years in the Iron Works at Ton du, to come to Pittsburgh, a city of opportunity.

Two months after the wedding, the newlyweds boarded

a steamer for America, leaving behind Gwyn's parents and two brothers and a sister in Ton du, and Eirwen's parents and two brothers in Treorchy. When the couple first arrived in Pittsburgh, Eirwen wrote that Gwyn had a few frustrating months working as a laborer at the Jones and Laughlin plant on Pittsburgh's South Side. Happily, on the advice of another Welsh immigrant, he had gone to Homestead, up the river, and landed a better job. There, advancement was rapid for him. After three years, he had worked his way up to a well-paying, skilled position—a roller in the 112-inch mill. Now Gwyn and Eirwen had three children and a house. Life, it seemed, was good in the New World.

Nevertheless, Emlyn couldn't get over the changes in Eirwen. She was still slim, but gaunt. Her blue eyes were underscored with deep, dark semicircles; her once-glossy hair was dull, pulled haphazardly onto the top of her head, a few stray strands hanging onto her neck. As she handled the heavy teakettle, Emlyn noticed that her slender, once-beautiful hands were chafed and red. Maybe he should expect that seven years and three children would do this to a woman.

The next hour Eirwen devoted to getting the children down for the night. She helped Thomas and Dilys wash and change into their nightgowns. Then, picking up David, she herded them upstairs.

Emlyn followed them so he could see the small back room where he would be sleeping. Eirwen showed him the narrow bed against the inside wall of the tiny room. "We've gotten this from the neighbors whose son was recently married," she said. "It should do for now."

The narrow upstairs hallway had four doorways, three to the bedrooms, one with a door to the attic. In the front was the largest room, where Eirwen and Gwyn slept, with the baby's cradle at the foot of their bed. As they passed by the doorway to the master bedroom, Emlyn could hear Gwyn softly snoring.

The children's room was next to his, around the hallway corner. He and Eirwen watched as the two children said their prayers on their knees beside the one bed, then jumped in and struggled for control of the feather tick.

As Emlyn and Eirwen started down the stairs, Thomas yelled twice from the darkened bedroom, "Good night, Uncle Em." Eirwen told him sternly to hush before he woke his father.

Back in the kitchen, Eirwen sponged the baby, put on a fresh diaper, and bundled him in several layers of flannel. At last, she sat down with the baby in her lap. Glancing over at the stove, she exclaimed, "Oh no, I forgot about the tea." As she started to rise, Emlyn reached out and put his hand on her arm. "Don't worry about that. You sit. Let me do something."

She relaxed against the back of the kitchen chair. "Take down that blue tin from the shelf and help yourself to some Welsh cakes. Dilys and I made them just for you."

Emlyn took down the tin, opened it and held out its contents to Eirwen. "Bakers first." She took one. "Brothers next." He grinned and picked up several. "You know how I've always loved these things. Arthur and I always fought over the last ones." He laughed and bit into a cake.

The parlor mantel clock struck ten.

"How late it is," said Emlyn. "You should be getting to bed yourself."

"Oh Em, I want to stay up all night and hear about your journey, about how the family and friends are doing back in the Rhondda."

Emlyn looked into her dark-circled eyes. "You may want to do that now, but tomorrow is another day. Let's get some sleep, and we can talk in the morning."

"You're right," she said. "You get some things out of the trunk and go upstairs to bed."

"What about you?"

"As you can see, I have a bit of work to do here, cleaning up after supper."

"Can't that wait?"

"Gwyn would be upset if he got up at three-thirty in the morning and found a mess. He needs a big cooked breakfast before he goes to work."

"Hmm. What can I do before I go to bed?"

She hesitated.

"Come on, this is your brother here to help you."

"All right. You can go outside and fetch more wood and water."

He put on his coat and cap and went out the back door. As he emerged from the heat of the kitchen, the smoky, cold air stung his face. Again, he was struck by the noises emanating from the huge mill buildings. For a moment he stopped to look over at the mills, wondering what it would sound like inside one. Even here, hundreds of yards away, the sounds were impressive.

The back garden was small and desolate. In the dim light, he could make out a bare vegetable patch, small shed, and privy. After he used the privy, he found the ax by the woodpile and split up a few logs. Then he pumped water into the pail Eirwen had given him.

He brought in the pail and wood to find Eirwen nursing the baby under the woolen shawl.

"Don't mind me," he said averting his eyes, while he bent and kissed her cheek. "I can get to bed on my own."

She smiled and nodded in reply.

Using the children's water, he washed his hands and face. "Nos da. *Good night,*" he said, quietly moving into the parlor.

He pulled a few garments from the trunk, tiptoed upstairs, and stretched himself onto the narrow mattress. It was very cold. He pulled the feather comforter up to his ears and lay there, listening to the omnipresent hum and clamor from the steel works.

Emlyn lay in the bed shivering, trying for the thousandth time to comprehend the sea of changes he was awash in. Within a short time, exhaustion crept up on him, and he sank into sleep.

Friday, November 20th

Emlyn slept fitfully. Strange dreams played across his mind's eye. It was night. He was on a ship. Dark waves rose and fell on the side of the streamer. There was a scream. Someone had fallen overboard. He leaned over the railing, but he couldn't see the person in the water. He looked about for a life preserver, but none was evident. He heard slow footfalls on the darkened deck. They kept coming closer. He tried to shout, but no sound came out.

He awoke in a panic. Then he realized that the footsteps were Eirwen's as she came up the stairs and into the front bedroom. His hands felt under the pillow for his pocket watch. He found it and held it up to the faint light at the window. 12:35.

Shivering, he lay back down and pondered the lateness of the hour. Was Eirwen always up so late? He had probably disrupted their usual routine. He'd find out soon enough. He turned over and tried to sleep.

This time sleep didn't come easily. Emlyn felt chilled to the bone. He pulled his legs up and tried to tuck the comforter under his back, but the cold kept creeping in. Repeatedly, as he'd begin to nod off, he'd be awakened by the thunder of the mill. After an hour or so, he finally fell asleep.

Again, the sound of Eirwen's shoes on the staircase awakened him. It was still dark. He pulled out his pocket watch and stared at the dial in a stupor. 3:25. Eirwen must be getting up to stoke the fire and prepare Gwyn's breakfast. He should go downstairs to greet Gwyn. A few more minutes, and he'd get up.

When he opened his eyes, weak sunlight was filtering through the window. He seized the watch: 8:10. He hurriedly pulled on his clothes and slippers and stumbled downstairs. From the kitchen he could hear Eirwen's and the children's voices. He tentatively poked his head around the corner.

Eirwen was helping Thomas button his jacket. Dilys was at the table, drinking out of a mug with both hands. David apparently was the bundled form in the box on the table.

"Bore da. *Good morning,*" said Emlyn.

Eirwen turned and smiled, "Good morning."

"Hey, Uncle Em," said Thomas, "You musta been real tired from your trip."

"Yes, tired I was." Emlyn excused himself and made a quick visit to the backyard privy.

When he returned to the kitchen, Eirwen was handing Thomas his lunch box and cap.

"Don't dawdle on the way to school, now."

"Can Uncle Em can walk me to school today?"

"Not today," said Eirwen. "Maybe he can come meet you when school lets out."

"All right!" replied Thomas, sprinting for the front door. "See ya later."

"Where's Gwyn?" asked Emlyn.

"At work. He has to be on the job by four o'clock. He'll be back around four this afternoon."

"Right. I should've known that." He paused. "I'm sorry I missed seeing him."

"Never mind. You'll see him when he comes home. He has a few hours before he has to go back to bed." She turned to Dilys, who was sitting at the table, legs dangling over the edge of her chair. "Let's see what we have for Uncle Em's breakfast." Dilys smiled shyly at him.

"Sit down, Em." Eirwen set out a plate of bacon and buckwheat pancakes she had warming on the back of the stove.

Emlyn suddenly felt famished. He pulled up a chair and ate quickly, silently. Eirwen poured tea for both of them, wiped her hands on her apron and sat down.

"Thanks, Eirwen. Da iawn, iawn. *Very good it is.*"

She gave him a tired smile. He looked at her eyes, underscored by bluish half-circles. "You look like you could go back to bed yourself."

"As they say, a woman's work is never done." She smiled again and sipped her tea.

"Mummy," said Dilys in a small voice. "Can I show Uncle Little Bess?"

Her mother nodded, and Dilys struggled off the chair. She padded into the front room and returned with a small rag doll.

"See. This is Bessie. She's three."

"Three, just like you," said Emlyn. He admired Bessie, her homespun smock, and brown yarn hair. "She's very pretty, like you, too."

Dilys giggled, clutched the doll to her chest and ran back into the front room.

While Dilys went back and forth, showing Emlyn various blocks, bits of twine, and marbles from the children's toy box, Eirwen broached the subject of his quarrel with their father.

"It's not likely Tad will accept my decision any time soon, probably never. He's so set in his views. Mam tried to make peace, but . . ." He lifted a tea towel to his mouth and looked down.

Eirwen bent toward him, taking his hands in hers. "Don't worry, Em. Everything will work out, you'll see." She kissed his brow and straightened up. "Mam has sent me several letters—unbeknownst to Tad. She's so upset about this whole business. Tad is very stubborn, as you know."

She turned to the stove. "I see you brought Taid Davies' violin, Em, or rather your violin now. When Gwyn gets home, we want to hear you play."

"How about you?" asked Emlyn. "Do you have any opportunity to sing?"

"Yes." She hesitated. "At chapel—or church, as they say here."

Dilys looked up from the top she was trying to spin. "Mummy sings all by herself."

"A soloist, then?"

Eirwen smiled shyly. "I don't have a lot of time to spare, what with the house and children, but I try to go to practice whenever I can. The choir director, Sarah Oesterling, and I have been working on a special piece for this coming Sunday, the first in Advent. Sarah likes my voice, I think."

"As well she should," replied Emlyn.

"She's Thomas's teacher at the First Ward School as well. She likes to organize musical performances at the school, too. I told her you play violin, and she's hoping you might play together sometime. "

Emlyn looked uneasily out of the window. "Maybe here, or at school. Not at chapel."

"Did you get to play any on the trip?" Eirwen asked, changing the subject.

"Only on the ship. There were some Irish lads on board

that we picked up in Cork who had instruments with them—a violin, a concertina, a tin whistle, a flat drum. Every day they'd clear space on the floor. They'd play some tunes and sometimes some of the other Irish would dance. To them, it was a way to pass the time."

"Did you play?"

"I was so curious about the tunes, one morning I tried to strike up a conversation with the Irish fiddler."

"Tried to. . . ?"

"The fellow didn't know Welsh, of course, and I could hardly make sense of his English through his thick accent. So I took out my violin and played the Llanover Reel. He caught on straightaway, picked up his fiddle and played a tune for me. We kept playing back and forth, until each of us learned the other's tune. After working at it for a few days—there wasn't much else to do on ship—I managed to learn several more tunes. I even played a bit with the other fellows for the dancing the last two days."

Eirwen looked at him in silence.

"What's wrong?" he asked.

"Dancing?" she replied.

"I know. Tad and the holier-than-thou assembly disapprove of fiddle tunes in general and dancing in particular. I myself didn't dance, but I don't see what's wrong with people having a good time."

"Dancing is often the occasion for hard drinking, and it leads to other unsavory activities."

"If so, I didn't see it on ship," Emlyn responded testily. "You sound rather like Tad."

For a moment, neither spoke.

"Let's not quarrel," said Eirwen at last, placing her hand on Emlyn's arm. "I'd like to hear these tunes myself. You'll have to play them for me. I must say I've never heard this kind of music here."

"Aren't there any Irish in Homestead?"

"Oh, yes, plenty of Irish, but they're mostly Catholics."

"I see."

"As in Wales, church and chapel don't mix much socially here. But here the chapel—that is, the Nonconformist Protestants—run the town." She paused to pick up her teacup. "And the mill."

"That's very odd," mused Emlyn, gazing out the window. "It's hard to fathom that, coming from a country where being Methodist or Baptist is a liability."

"It's not the Methodists or Baptists at the top of the heap. It's the Presbyterians, like Mr. Carnegie, and of course the Episcopalians. You'll find very quickly that those who can speak English are the ones who get the good jobs and the political offices. That's why Gwyn insists that we speak English, not Welsh, at home, so the children will be brought up as Americans."

The kitchen clock's tinny bell chimed out ten strokes. Glancing at it, Eirwen pushed herself to her feet and shoved a piece of wood into the stove's firebox. "Today's Friday, baking day. I'd better keep the fire going."

"Shall I chop more firewood?"

"That'd be good, but I don't need you here underfoot all day."

"I can take a hint. I'd like to write a letter to my friend Gareth Morgan, letting him know I arrived safely. Then I'll go out exploring—but first, I'll chop wood for you."

"Good," said Eirwen. "I will post the letter later today with the one Gwyn wrote to his brother John."

After he finished chopping the wood, Eirwen gave him

writing paper. He sat at the writing desk and composed a brief letter in Welsh, telling his friend about his safe passage and arrival in Homestead. He left out the part about fiddling and the Irish dancing on board the ship. The tone of the letter was much more positive than he felt.

He went into the kitchen to get his jacket and cap.

"Tomorrow we'll take you shopping on the Avenue," said Eirwen as she slipped two pans of bread dough into the oven. "Maybe today you'd like to walk to the Monongahela."

"Mo non what?"

"The river. 'River of high banks' in the Indian language."

From the front porch, Eirwen pointed out the way to the river and, in the opposite direction, the way to Thomas's school.

Now he was outside, the cacophony coming from the mill buildings about half a mile away overwhelmed him. Hisses, bangs, clanks, buzzes, and booms echoed throughout the streets. The crazy mix of rhythms and pitches seemed like a song out of the industrial nightmares of William Blake. Dark Satanic mills. That's what Blake called them, albeit metaphorically. But Blake had never seen a mill on this scale, Satanic or otherwise. What would old William think if he were here, Emlyn mused, experiencing Homestead?

Such a benign name, Homestead. Not strange or bleak, like the name of the old iron town in South Wales, Merthyr Tydfil. Tydfil the martyr, first in a long line of poor souls crushed by filth, disease, hard work, dissipation. This place, however, had been somebody's homestead, a farm on the river. Not any more. Andrew Carnegie had bought the Homestead Works in 1881, and invested in the latest technology.

Gwyn had written that during the last decade, the Carnegie Homestead Works had developed into the most advanced steel mill in the country. Homestead had state-of-the-art open hearths producing steel ingots from metal smelted across the river in the Carrie Furnace Bessemers. The ingots were then rolled into finished shapes, such as ship's armor plate.

Emlyn turned to the steelworks to study its silhouette. The cavernous mills were lined up along the riverbank, with many stacks thrusting out smoke of various dusky hues. Nothing stood out in sharp relief. The entire scene was veiled in smoke. Under a gloomy sky, the furnaces throbbed with a hot glow. Emlyn was eager, yet apprehensive to find out what it was like inside those buildings. He'd know soon enough.

In the other direction a few blocks off, he saw two other clusters of smokestacks, those of the Howard Axle Works and Homestead Glass Works. Gwyn's characterization in his letters was correct: Homestead really was an industrious town. And the smoke! It was so dense, perhaps thicker than he'd ever seen in Wales.

Emlyn walked toward the mill and McClure Street, which Eirwen said offered access to the riverbank at the ferry landing. The streets were rutted and full of potholes. The wooden sidewalk, punctuated with broken boards, sagged under his weight. At the corners the crossings were marked with a bed of stones set into the ocher-colored mud. The dwellings were mostly small frame two-story houses or row-tenements. Vacant lots were dotted with piles of trash, some burning.

Everybody out on the street seemed to be on some errand. On the corner of Ann Street, a man in a black overcoat examined a crumpled piece of paper. A dappled draft horse plodded toward the railroad tracks, pulling a wagon holding barrels, while an old woman hobbled along, carrying a pail of potatoes.

Emlyn walked all the way to City Farm Lane, a raw, ugly thoroughfare choked with mud and trash. Toward the river Emlyn caught whiffs of human waste and garbage coming from filthy, ramshackle tenements. He turned right, away from the tenements, following the boundary of the mill. No fence marked where the mill began, but it was obvious. Through the gaps between the structures, the mill yards were visible through the smoky haze. Against the gigantic scale of the mills, workers seemed pygmy-sized. The din emanating from the yards was overwhelming.

When Emlyn reached the tracks, he turned back toward the town. Cheap hotels and saloons were lined up on both sides of the tracks, including some squeezed in between the sets of tracks. Emlyn marveled that anyone could sleep in these places, considering the omnipresent racket from the mill and the whistles and rumble of passing trains.

At McClure Street, Emlyn turned toward the river. Making the turn, he passed a saloon on the corner, then stopped short at the sight of a modest clapboard church. The sign over the door read: 'First Congregational Church.' He stepped back. Now he knew where it was.

He picked up his pace and continued on McClure until he reached the overpass for railroad tracks into the mill. Passing beneath the tracks, he found himself at the ferry landing at the river. From there, in both directions he could see the sweeping curve of the river on which Homestead was built. Across from the town was steep, wooded hillside, with railroad tracks running along the bank. The Monongahela was well named. As far as he could see, the land was buffered from the water on both sides by a vertical embankment.

Emlyn moved to the river's edge. The cold river looked murky, with treacherous eddies swirling in the middle. Where the river disappeared around the bend to the east, Emlyn could see the far end of a railroad bridge spanning the river. Railroad tracks ran along both banks, and along them appeared engines hauling loads of fuel and food for the insatiable black maws of the steelworks.

Through moving clouds of smoke he spotted the long slope of the hillside on which more buildings were spread on a rectilinear grid. He caught occasional glimpses of carts and horses and pedestrians crossing this grid.

As he traced the streets of the town with his eyes, his attention was drawn to the mill, where a steam whistle sounded a loud report that echoed down the valley. He pulled out his watch: 2:32. This could hardly be the time for a change of shift.

Emlyn walked back up the embankment grade to the streets. The scene that unfolded before his eyes astonished him. Dozens of people, mostly women, were emerging from houses and tenements. All of them seemed to be heading for the mill, some at a run. As they hastened by, oblivious to his presence, their worried faces reminded him of those of women he'd seen back in Wales, when a mine cave-in had crushed seven men underground. He knew then that the whistle had announced an accident at the steelworks.

He stood on the corner of Third Avenue and City Farm Lane, unsure of what to do. He didn't know anyone in town except Eirwen and her family. Wasn't Gwyn at work? Hesitantly, he walked to the place where a crowd was gathering.

Emlyn joined the people converging by the mill. He came up to the back of the group, trying to see what was going on. He moved around to the town side of the crowd and stood behind a group of women, but he couldn't see much.

He started as he felt a hand close hard on his left shoulder.

"Croeso i America! Welcome to Homestead, young man," said a deep voice behind him.

Emlyn turned to see what face matched the voice.

"Gwyn!" Emlyn was scooped into a bear hug.

"How are you, Em? A good journey?"

"Yes, although it seemed to take forever. What are you doing here? I thought you were working."

"I was, until there was an accident at a furnace next to the rolling mill. Production was temporarily halted."

"What happened?" said Emlyn.

"I'm not sure," replied Gwyn. "It was almost the end of my shift, so the superintendent said to go home—the next shift would resume work. Let's try to find out what happened."

The tall young man and the brawny older man moved to the one side of the crowd to get a better view. Women of all ages, some with children, some with other women or men, were thronging around the spot between buildings where workers came and went to work. Worry was etched on their faces. Several men were standing at the entry place, stopping people from rushing into the mill.

"These are the ones with men on this shift," said Gwyn.

People were scurrying in all directions.

"Is this the main way to get to the mill? It doesn't seem, well, very official."

"No, this isn't it. The mill gate is nearly a mile away, in Munhall. That's where the mill offices, the company club, and the superintendents' houses are located. This is a more convenient way to get to work for many of the men, myself included."

Emlyn surveyed the crowd, peering into the passage to the mill yards.

"How was your trip? And how is Wales?" Gwyn asked.

"The trip was uneventful, and that's good," replied Emlyn. "Wales is Wales."

Gwyn nodded.

Emlyn examined his brother-in-law as they stood waiting for news. Gwyn was still burly, but more muscular than Emlyn remembered. The muscles of his shoulders and chest pulled against his jacket. Grime and grit flecked the pale skin of his face. His eyes, like Eirwen's, had dark circles. Did anyone in Homestead get enough sleep, Emlyn mused, looking around at the anxious crowd.

A man in rolled-up shirtsleeves pushed through the group of men holding the crowd back. The crowd pressed forward. The man spoke, but he was too far away for Emlyn to make out his words.

A wail of agony came from a woman near the front. Emlyn caught a glimpse of her faded floral headscarf as she sank from view. Several other women bent to help her, as a few workmen came out of the mill and pressed through the throng towards the agitated knot of women. The keening and wailing grew louder.

Emlyn felt vaguely uneasy. A fine introduction this was to his new home.

"Let's go over here," said Gwyn, pulling his sleeve.

They made their way over to a big man with flame-red hair and mustache to match standing at the edge of the crowd.

The man turned to greet Gwyn. "A shame," he said, pursing his lips and shaking his head.

"Do you know what happened?" asked Gwyn.

The man answered in an American accent that sounded strange and harsh to Emlyn. "I guess some water was in the molds in O.H. 2. Three of them hunkies were nearby when the steel was poured. It hit the molds and exploded. One's dead for sure, the others badly burned."

Gwyn slowly shook his head. "The open hearths can be dangerous. How many have been injured there in the last year, do you think?"

"At least a dozen," replied the man. He moved his boot toe back and forth in the dirt. "It seems someone is injured just about every day, someone killed every month. Remember two years ago when the Edgar Thomson works lost Captain Jones, a great man and a good superintendent?"

Gwyn nodded. "It was an accident something like today's, wasn't it?"

The man continued. "Yep. The Captain was killed when one of them new blast furnaces they was installing exploded and blew him into the casting pit. A rotten shame, in more ways than one. The Captain tried his damnedest to keep the shift at eight hours. Now he's gone, Frick and Potter don't care if we work 24 hours a day, as long as the steel rolls out and the money rolls in. For them, that is."

Gwyn nodded grimly.

They all turned toward the crowd at the entrance, where the shrieks of a woman grew louder, then ceased.

Emlyn tried to shrug off a growing uneasiness.

The man turned to face Emlyn.

"Who's the young feller you got with you, Gwyn?"

Gwyn introduced Emlyn to Jim Duncan, one of the members of the Amalgamated Association of Iron and Steel Workers, the union of skilled workers to which Gwyn belonged.

"There's nothing we can do here," Duncan observed. "Let's stop for a quick drink before we go home."

"Sounds like a good way to introduce Emlyn to Homestead," agreed Gwyn.

Emlyn hesitated, recalling Eirwen's comments about liquor and dancing.

"Won't Eirwen get upset if we go to a pub?" he asked Gwyn.

"She usually doesn't say anything if I stop for a beer now and then."

"She's heard many a sermon by Tad about the evils of liquor, as have you and I."

"True, but your father's a long way away," declared Gwyn,

patting Emlyn on the shoulder, "and Eirwen's not much for sermonizing. Come on."

As the three men walked away from the mill entry toward Eighth Avenue, Emlyn turned back to see the crowd part as a man in a suit made his way to the woman lying on the dirty cobblestones. A doctor, speculated Emlyn, as he made his way through the muddy street. Too late for her husband.

The streets around the mill were thronged with Homesteaders buzzing with rumors. Two men stopped Duncan to ask what he knew about the accident.

Across the railroad tracks, they passed three young women in stained satin dresses and blowsy capes. Their eyes were blacked with kohl, their lips and cheeks rouged garishly.

"Hello, gentlemen," crooned one with henna hair. "Goin' to the Avenue? Want to buy us a drink?"

Emlyn slowed to look at them. Encouraged, the woman who spoke hiked up her soiled skirts to show the ankle of her boot and beckoned to him.

"Hey, young sir. C'mon over here."

Confused, Emlyn stopped. The other two women waved and smiled.

Gwyn stepped back and took Emlyn by the sleeve. "Keep moving. You'll have the whole pack of whores on our heels."

Face beet-red, Emlyn moved briskly ahead of Duncan and Gwyn. The only streetwalkers he'd seen close-up were those near the docks in Cardiff. Since he'd been with his family, he was too self-conscious to take much of a look. Then there was the incident with Gladys. Better not dwell on that. That was in another country, and besides . . . He caught a quick backwards glance at the women accosting another group of male passersby.

As they hastened along, images of the dingy buildings they were passing flooded into Emlyn's view: an open door, a broken gate, a slanting porch roof, a window with one cracked pane.

On Eighth Avenue, odors overpowered the images. The smells of mud, horse manure, coal smoke, sweat, grease, oysters, meat, freshly baked bread, all wafted by him as they made their way on the rickety plank walk.

As Emlyn followed the others into a dark doorway, a rush of stale warm air, laced with the smell of whisky, beer, and tobacco smoke struck his face. It took nearly a minute for his eyes to adjust to the dim light. Daylight glinted weakly through the smeared window of the pub. Gaslights flickered overhead. A half-dozen men in dirty work clothes were leaning on the bar; a few more sat at tables.

"How you doin', Otis?" asked Duncan as he bellied up to the bar. Otis the bartender, a sad-eyed, sallow fellow, replied that he wasn't too good, but much better than the fallen workers they were now carrying out of the mill. Some of the others asked Duncan what he knew. Emlyn didn't listen as Duncan recounted the story for the fifth time.

Duncan asked for whiskies to be set up, and they drank to the memory of the worker from O.H.2, even though no one there knew him personally. As Duncan raised his glass, Emlyn noticed that the pointer finger of his right hand was missing. Emlyn stared at the stub.

"Mill accident," said Duncan to Emlyn as he set down the glass. "A chain caught my finger while I was trying to hook on."

"I'm sorry," replied Emlyn, embarrassed.

"Don't be," replied Duncan. "I was lucky. It could've been my whole hand." He laughed.

"Unfortunately, these kind of things happen all the time," noted Gwyn. "This is what happened to me when a bit of molten slag exploded after hitting wet ground." He pushed up his left sleeve to show a quilted red scar covering the outer side of his arm.

Emlyn stared at the arm. Duncan flashed a look at Emlyn, then at Gwyn.

"Hey, is your brother-in-law planning on working in the mill?" Duncan asked Gwyn, as if Emlyn weren't there.

"Yes, I am," said Emlyn before Gwyn could answer.

"I hope we're not scaring you. It's a good job—hard, but good—with good pay."

"It may be good for you tonnage fellows," drawled a dark-haired young man in stained overalls standing next to them. "Not so good for the rest of us."

Duncan turned to the speaker. "Lookee who's here, boys. How's your liver, Virgil? Say, what're you doing here? Aren't you working day shift this week?"

"Yeah, I was working, but got sent away when they shut down part of O.H. 2 for clean-up after the accident."

"Too bad to lose the income."

"Yep," said Virgil sullenly. "It's hard enough to make ends meet even working full shifts."

"I'll not argue that it's hard work, whatever the job in the mill," replied Duncan. "Still, they don't seem to be having any trouble filling jobs, whatever the wages. The pay's better than for most outside work. The foreigners seem to do OK on laborer's pay. Look how many of them take their money and go back to the old country after a few years in the mill."

"I ain't going to argue with you, Jim," replied the man, setting down his glass. "I need to get some shut-eye."

They said goodbye to the man, and talk resumed.

Duncan asked Emlyn why he was seeking work in the mill, rather than as a teacher or other white-collar occupation.

Gwyn answered the question: there were no openings in

the Homestead schools, and even if there were, the pay was so bad no men worked as teachers. One could make more working in the mill as a laborer than as a teacher or clerk.

Emlyn asked what the pay was for laborers in the mill. Gwyn explained that skilled workers like himself and Duncan made between $4 and $7 a day, but they were in the minority. The rest of the workmen made far less, more than half of them less than $1.40 a day. Emlyn did not know what wage he'd be making in the mill, but he needed work fast. The money he brought was almost gone.

Duncan and Gwyn bought another round of whiskies and began speculating on what would happen when the Amalgamated's contract, signed with Carnegie Steel three years previously, expired the next summer. The Amalgamated men were being paid on a sliding scale, their wages linked to the price of steel billets. $25 a ton was the minimum agreed upon. If the price of steel sank below this figure, the company would protect the workers by holding wages at the $25-a-ton level. Duncan and Gwyn weren't worried. With all the Navy contracts for steel plate to build new ships, there was plenty of work.

"As I told you in the letter," said Gwyn to Emlyn, "you should get a job easily. Monday I'll take you in and introduce you to the boss. You'll have to start on a lower rung, but you'll move up quickly, as I did."

"That's true," said Duncan. "Five years ago I started out hooking up dinky engines. After I lost my finger in the accident, I transferred to the slab mill, and now I'm a second helper there."

At that, he ordered another round, and they drank to Emlyn's luck in landing a job. They talked for another hour, downing two more drinks in the process. Emlyn started to feel lightheaded.

The clock on the wall chimed four, and Gwyn slapped his hand on the bar, exclaiming that it was time to go home. "Eirwen will be expecting us soon," he said, placing some coins on the counter.

The whiskies were making Emlyn's head swim and his stomach roll. He struggled to get control of his legs.

As Emlyn slid off the stool, a commotion broke out at the front door.

Three men were standing in the doorway, and one of them, a big man with sandy hair and dirty work clothes, was swearing at someone outside.

"Let me be, you crazy bitch. It's my money and my time. Don't make me hit you again."

He lunged forward. He stopped, and then laughed. The other two men laughed, too.

"I'll be home when I damn well feel like it," he shouted over his shoulder as he came into the bar.

Emlyn's temples pulsed with pain at the sound of the loud voice.

"How ya doin', Bucky?" asked Duncan as the big man passed by.

"Fine, just fine," he replied. "But I'd be doin' better if that old ball and chain wasn't forever draggin' at me." He grimaced, shaking his fist toward the door, and laughed again.

"Time for a drink," he said, as he and Duncan clapped each other on the back.

Emlyn carefully followed Gwyn around a table and to the entrance.

As Emlyn emerged into the cold, smoky air outside, he leaned on the doorjamb, fearing he might pitch into the street. Gwyn took his arm and led him down the avenue to Ann Street, where they turned toward the river. Emlyn's stomach turned over as it had during a rough part of the ocean passage.

"Duw! *Good God!* You're looking green around the gills, Em," observed Gwyn.

They crossed the railroad tracks, passing the station where Emlyn had alighted the previous evening. Beyond the station, through fogged vision Emlyn saw the figure of a woman with three children on a corner a block ahead. Her back was to them. He gazed at the tableau as if it weren't real, only an image in a stereoscope.

As they got closer, one of the children broke away from the group and started running toward them. "Dad! Uncle Em!" Thomas ran up to them, and throwing his arms around his uncle's legs, pitched his head into Emlyn's middle. Emlyn held his stomach and doubled over.

"Why didn't you meet me at school?" he demanded of Emlyn, not seeming to realize the effect of his greeting on his uncle.

"We were on the Avenue," replied Gwyn, pushing back Thomas's cap. "I was introducing Em to some of the lads."

Emlyn nodded and tried to smile. He held his arms protectively across his belly. His stomach turned over again as the woman on the corner came up to them. For a brief instant he glanced up. All he saw was that she had green eyes.

"Uncle Em, this is my teacher, Miss Oesterling." Thomas beamed up at Emlyn.

Emlyn stood as if stupefied for a brief second. Smiling, she extended her hand. But instead of raising his, Emlyn suddenly turned to the side, fell on his knees, and heaved the contents of his stomach into the gutter.

Miss Oesterling, stunned, took a step backward.

"Uncle Em!" cried Thomas, kneeling beside him. "What's wrong?"

Gwyn reached out and drew Thomas back. "It's alright, Thomas. My apologies, Miss Oesterling. I guess we celebrated Emlyn's arrival in town a bit too hard."

"Apparently," she replied, and turning on her heel, walked away, up Ann Street.

His head throbbing, Emlyn staggered the rest of the way back to the house, leaning on Gwyn. Thomas walked alongside, looking up worriedly. When they reached the house, Thomas burst through the front door shouting, "Mum! Uncle Em puked in front of Miss Oesterling!"

The sound of a pan hitting the floor in the kitchen struck Emlyn's ears like a shell-burst. Gwyn half-carried him to the sofa, where he collapsed groaning, his right arm over his face.

"What in the world happened?" Eirwen asked.

"Oh, it's nothing, really," said Gwyn, going on to explain how their chance encounter had led to the excursion to the pub.

"Gwyn, what on earth were you thinking?" Eirwen demanded. "That's a fine welcome to Homestead."

"We need to get him to bed to sleep it off. In fact, I'd like to get a bit of a lie-down myself before supper," replied Gwyn.

Eirwen looked at Emlyn, back to Gwyn, and shook her head in dismay. From the kitchen, the baby began wailing.

"Be a good lad and tend to David," Eirwen directed Thomas. Together, Eirwen and Gwyn hauled Emlyn upstairs, set him in bed and loosened his clothing.

"Wake me for supper," said Gwyn as he lurched into the front bedroom.

That was the last thing Emlyn heard before he lost consciousness.

Dr. William Oesterling stood at the soot-streaked window of his office overlooking Eighth Avenue and contemplated the traffic, both two- and four-footed, below. He pulled out his watch and noted the time, almost six-thirty. He inhaled deeply and coughed.

"Do you want me to lock up, Doctor?"

He turned to his nurse assistant standing by the door, a tall, gaunt woman in her late 40s. She was pulling a short wool cape over her uniform.

"No, Mrs. Cramer. You go on. Cerberus and I will close tonight."

Mrs. Cramer glanced over at the black animal lying under the doctor's desk and her small starched white cap twitched almost imperceptibly—not dramatically, only a little twitch to let her employer know once again what she thought of dogs in a medical office.

"Very well. Good night."

Oesterling heard her boots tapping down the staircase to the street. He walked over to the hall tree and took down his coat and hat. He stood in front of the cracked mirror over the sink. The image looked back at him with tired gray eyes. He smoothed back his salt-and-pepper hair and placed the black homburg on his head. He rubbed the stiff white hairs in his short beard. He did need to stop by the barber's soon.

"Well, Cerberus, are you ready to go home?" The dog clambered out from his place under the desk. He was a middling-large canine, mostly black, with a blaze of white down one side of his face. On the white side, his eye was white-blue; on the black side, it was walnut brown. The dog's coat was long, thick, and sleek.

"OK. Let me get my things."

As he shrugged on his overcoat and closed his bag, the

dog ran to the door, tail wagging. His teeth shone white against his black mouth.

To think that Cerberus came very close to being drowned as a pup! What would he do without his buddy now that Margaret was gone? The doctor shook his head. She was gone three years now. He still could not quite believe it. So sudden. Gone. Gone to her Maker, Reverend Griffiths had said.

As Oesterling extinguished the gaslight and backed into the dark stairwell, the dog ambled down the stairs. The doctor smiled thinking how many people were initially terrified at the sight of his dog. The dog's smooth, stealthy predator's trot was one thing. But what usually took people aback was the one blue-white eye, which gave the canine an intense, maniacal look. Not that he was maniacal, although he could be intense.

The cold, sulfurous air stung Oesterling's face as he opened the door to the street. The dog trotted ahead of him as he walked along the gritty sidewalk planks to Ann Street and turned up the hill. He exchanged brief greetings with the passersby he knew.

The doctor recalled the day nearly three years ago when he had gone out to the MacAleister place to treat the farmer's ailing two-year-old son. As he left the house, he saw the farmer emerging from the barn, carrying a small black object in one hand and a big wooden pail in the other. The farmer's sheepdog, a border collie named Nan, ran alongside, glancing up anxiously at the black object.

"How d'ye do, doc?" asked the man, looking over. "Is the bairn goin' to be alright?"

"Yes. He should be fine. The medicine and a change of diet should help."

The farmer nodded in reply.

The doctor resumed his walk to his horse tied at the fence, but halted when he saw the farmer set down the pail.

"What are you doing, Alec?" he asked, walking closer to the farmer.

"Oh, my collie bitch had pups six weeks ago. Since the father or fathers we dinna ken, I drowned the lot of them. That be too many dogs that might grow up to worry my sheep. Then this morning I discovered that Nan had another one hidden in the barn. So it'll be goin' off too now."

"Wait. May I see it?"

The farmer handed over the wiggling black ball. It was a male, black with a white patch on the face and a white ruff running into white stockings on his front legs. The very tip of his tail had a few white hairs as well.

Oesterling, deep in grief from the death of his wife a few months before, was instantly charmed. So much death in this world, he mused.

"Could I have him?"

He cradled the pup, scratching behind its ear with his index finger.

The farmer eyed him and the pup suspiciously.

"I'll keep him in town, and he'll never bother your live-stock, or anyone else's."

The farmer hesitated.

"You can give me the dog in payment for today's call."

That settled it. The doctor rode back to Homestead with the puppy. He had always loved dogs, always had one, until his marriage to Margaret. Then he had to choose between having a dog and having her. He chose her, and never re-gretted it.

Now he had a dog again.

His housekeeper, Mrs. Sproule, was none too pleased when Oesterling brought the canine into the house, but his daughter Sarah was delighted. That evening he and Sarah had sat in the small study, playing with the puppy and mulling over possible names for their new pet. At Sarah's suggestion, they settled on Cerberus, the name of the gatekeeper-dog of Dante's Inferno.

Since then, he and Cerberus had been virtually inseparable—even though Mrs. Sproule had nearly fainted away when she discovered fine black hairs on the counterpane of the doctor's bed.

His older daughter, Carrie, married to a lawyer assisting Mr. Henry Clay Frick of the Carnegie Company, had views similar to her mother's about dogs. When she came to visit shortly after he got Cerberus, she roundly scolded him for bringing a filthy animal into the house. When Sarah stepped forward to defend Cerberus, she and Carrie wound up having a row— unfortunately, not an unusual occurrence.

Since Carrie had moved to East Liberty, it seemed that nothing in Homestead lived up to her standards. She frequently began her diatribes against Homestead with the phrase, "Oliver says..." Yes, her husband, Oliver Strong, had a lot to say about Homestead, very little of it complimentary. The workers were coarse, the mills loud and dirty, the town rough, uncivilized.

Maybe so. Nevertheless, it was his home, and had been her home since the four of them—Margaret, Carrie, Sarah, and he—had moved there in 1882, a year after the first steel was produced by the Homestead Works. Homestead wasn't Eden, but then, neither were his native city of Brooklyn, nor the city they'd moved from, Philadelphia.

Now that Sarah had returned from two years at Normal School and taken a job teaching music and second grade at the First Ward School in Homestead, the friction between the two sisters had increased.

There wasn't much he could do about that, he thought sadly as he reached for the latch on the iron gate in front of the big frame house on Tenth Avenue. As the gate creaked open, Cerberus dashed up the brick stairs and raced around the house to the back door.

Their entry through the rear pantry was the doctor's conciliatory gesture to Mrs. Sproule. He wiped the mud from the dog's paws and removed his boots.

The kitchen was warm and fragrant with the smell of fresh bread and apple pie. Ah, he loved Fridays, baking day. He thought of taking one of the crullers cooling on the board, but Mrs. Sproule glared at him, saying that the crullers might take the edge off his appetite.

"We wouldn't want that," he smiled. "But that's unlikely. It was a long day at work."

Sarah came bursting in from the hallway.

"Hello, Papa."

She kissed him quickly on the cheek. "And how's my dear Cerby?" She bent down and rubbed the dog's back. Mrs. Sproule sent her, and implicitly, the doctor, off to wash their hands in the little room under the main stairs.

"And take the beast with you. No dogs in the kitchen!"

They retreated into the hall, preceded by a cowed Cerberus.

In the dark, wainscoted dining room, Oesterling sat at his customary place at the head of the table, his back to the charcoal-burning fireplace, Cerberus at his feet under the table. Sarah sat at his left. The doctor thought it rather silly to have just the two of them at the long formal table, but that's the way Margaret had liked to have dinner served. And so they kept the practice.

Molly set out the pot roast, mashed potatoes, carrots, turnip greens and bread, and vanished into the kitchen. After grace, Oesterling, tearing into a piece of bread, inquired about the events of the day. As was family custom, father and daughter exchanged anecdotes about what had happened since breakfast.

"Oh, nothing much," replied Sarah, spooning potatoes on to her plate. "This gray November weather seems to have the kids a bit down. I tried to get them to sing some cheery songs like 'Camptown Races,' but they were so listless and off key."

She made a face.

Oesterling smiled. "Soon Christmas will be near, and the children's spirits will rise. You'll see."

"How was your day, Papa?"

"Long. I was called to the home of one of the workers who had been hurt in an accident at the mill. He's in bad shape, burns all over his legs. I doubt he'll make it. Infection is too likely in such injuries. The man couldn't speak much English, his wife none. His friend, another mill hand, acted as translator."

He paused. "Only another working day in Homestead."

"You do look exhausted, Papa. You should go straight to bed after supper."

Oesterling smiled wanly and nodded. They ate in silence.

"Oh yes," said Sarah suddenly. "I almost forgot. I met Eirwen Jones's long-awaited brother today. That is, sort of met."

"What do you mean 'sort of' met?"

"At school all day Thomas was prattling on about 'Uncle Em this, Uncle Em that.' Thomas was beside himself with anticipation that his uncle would be there to meet him at the end of school."

"He didn't show up?"

"No, it's worse than that. Poor crestfallen Thomas went off with his pals to look for him. Unfortunately, they eventually found him."

She speared a piece of carrot. "What a fool! I can hardly believe this is the allegedly brilliant young man Eirwen's been talking about."

Scowling, she set down her fork.

"Thomas and his friends returned to school to escort me home in hopes of finding his uncle. As we walked up Amity, I saw two men coming the other way. One of the men I recognized as Gwyn Jones, and the other, a tall, thin fellow. Thomas ran ahead when he saw them. When I got to the corner, Gwyn introduced the other man as his brother-in-law, Emlyn Phillips. I extended my hand, but instead of taking it, the wretch fell to his knees and vomited into the street."

She picked up the fork. "Can you imagine?"

"My dear Sarah, unfortunately, I can," said Oesterling as he set down his.

Sarah glanced over at him.

"I'm so sorry to have brought this up during supper, Papa. Please forgive me."

"That's all right, Sarah. After what I saw during the Civil War, it would take a far worse image than that to spoil my appetite. Doctors see a lot of foolery, I'm afraid. What was wrong with him?"

"Why, he was drunk!"

"There are plenty of drunken men stumbling out of bars all along Eighth Avenue at all hours of the day and night."

"Yes, but presumably they aren't 'gentlemen and scholars' as he supposedly is."

"Your Uncle Trevor was an educated man, kind and considerate—until he took a few snoots of whisky. Then Mr. Hyde appeared."

"I know. Mother was mortified the time he did this when he visited us in Philadelphia."

"You remember that?"

"I couldn't forget it. Carrie and I hid in the upstairs wardrobe all evening. We were so glad when he left the next day."

"He didn't exactly 'leave.' Your mother threw him out."

"I wonder if Eirwen threw Emlyn out when he arrived at the house in that state."

"Trevor had only come from Trenton. Emlyn has come all the way from Wales. Anyway, maybe we'll both get to meet him when he comes to church with Gwyn and Eirwen on Sunday."

"I think that it's appalling to see a musician retching into the gutter."

Oesterling brushed some crumbs off the tablecloth.

"It's an old tradition among fine musicians, I hear—retching into the gutter. Especially singers."

"Now you're teasing me. Anyway, Eirwen's brother isn't a singer. He's a violinist."

Oesterling was about to make a crack about violinists when the door swung open and in came Molly with two big wedges of apple pie. The conversation then turned to a discussion of the merits of different kinds of pie apples.

His piece of pie eaten, Oesterling pushed back from the table.

"Sarah, I think I will follow your advice to retire early tonight. Come on, Cerberus. I'll bet you're dog-tired, too."

Sarah went into the parlor to practice the piano in anticipation of her upcoming performance on Sunday. Oesterling took the dog into the back pantry, fed him, and let him out the back door. He stood on the stoop shivering while Cerberus sniffed around the small yard. Tomorrow would be Saturday—only a half day at the office.

When Emlyn awoke hours later, the pain inside his head was almost unbearable. His mouth tasted of bile and sour whisky.

He opened his eyes. The room was dark. Almost worse than the headache was the awful thirst. As he sat up, it seemed like his brain was bumping against the inside of his skull. Groaning softly, he forced himself to stand. Lord, what had led him to this sorry state?

It was on him in a flash: the sidewalk, the figures, the green eyes, the vomit lying in the dusty street. Wincing, he put his palms to his temples. What idiocy!

He started to shake his head, but the pain stopped him. He must get water.

He fumbled around for his shoes and staggered to the stairs. Holding onto walls and furniture, he navigated a course toward the kitchen.

In the kitchen the fiery light from the mill cast grotesque shadows on the west wall. Without bothering to put on a coat, he grabbed a pail and went into the back yard. He stopped at the pump. His head was throbbing; his stomach turned once, twice, and quieted.

It seemed he had pumped a very long time before water gushed from the spout. He filled the pail, set it to one side, and still pumping, thrust his head under the flow.

When the icy water hit the back of his head, a new, sharp pain cut through the headache. He turned his head and gulped in the water. He pumped a few more times before sliding to his knees. The water continued to flow over his head and down the neck of his shirt.

"You deserve this," his father's voice pronounced. "You always think you're so smart, so clever, but you do such stupid things."

The water trickled to a stop, and he fell sideways, knocking over the pail. He lay there in the mud shivering, unable to move.

He heard the back door open.

"Emlyn, what in heaven's name are you doing out there?" a female voice cried out.

He tried to reply, but only a moan came out.

Eirwen came and stooped beside him.

"Lord help us," she said, tugging at his elbow. "Emlyn, you must get up."

Gradually, she pulled him to a standing position, and led him into the kitchen. As she lit the kitchen gaslight, its rays renewed the pulsing pain in his head. Shivering violently, he lowered himself into a chair.

"We must get you out of these wet things. You could catch a death."

He peeled off his soaked shirt and trousers and wrapped himself in the afghan Eirwen fetched from the parlor.

Eirwen quickly kindled a fire in the cook stove and bent to look in the icebox.

"Just what do think you were doing out there?"

"I . . . I was getting a drink," he rasped. "I was so thirsty."

She cast a withering glance at him.

"You are still thirsty, I gather?"

He nodded. She handed him a tumbler of water, and stood back to watch him drink it.

"What time is it, anyway?" he asked.

"A bit after three-thirty."

Emlyn groaned.

Buttoning his cuffs, Gwyn came into the doorway of the kitchen, where he halted in surprise.

"What's going on? What happened to you?" he asked Emlyn.

"Emlyn is suffering the consequences of his overindulgence at the pub. I thought he—and you!—had better sense," she replied. "I saw the back door partly open and went out to find Emlyn drowning himself under the pump spout. Such foolishness! Now I don't have time to make you a proper breakfast before you go to work."

Gwyn looked at Emlyn hunched over under the afghan. "It doesn't matter. I am responsible for this."

"That's true, but so is Emlyn. Sit."

Gwyn sat at the table across from Emlyn, and Eirwen set a steaming cup of tea in front of each of them. She handed Gwyn thick slices of bread with butter and jam.

Gwyn ate and Emlyn drank his tea in silence.

Emlyn finished his tea and started to stand. All he could think of was getting back to his warm bed.

Emlyn wanted to say something to them, but the pain clouded his thoughts. He couldn't manage a conversation in his present state. When Eirwen tried to help him, he raised his hand to stop her.

"Thanks, I can manage," Emlyn mumbled. He turned back. "I'm sorry, Eirwen."

Eirwen stood by the stove with her arms folded as she watched him leave the room.

Saturday, November 21st

By the time he awoke again, Emlyn's hangover headache had abated. When he went downstairs, he found Eirwen and the children busy in the kitchen.

Eirwen said nothing about the incident at the pump. Thomas looked at his uncle's tousled hair and declared he looked like a woodpecker. Everyone laughed.

The rest of the day went better than the previous one. Thomas went to the neighbors' and Eirwen, with Dilys and David in tow, took Emlyn on a shopping excursion to the Avenue. Emlyn got a good look at the business district that lay mostly to the south of the two sets of railroad tracks that ran right through the town. Eirwen exchanged greetings with someone in almost every place they went. Yes, she was at home here.

Later that afternoon when Gwyn got home from work, he cleaned up and took Emlyn on another trip to the Avenue. This time they went to a used clothing store to get something for Emlyn to wear at the mill.

"By the end of next week, these probably will have burn holes and rips in them," said Gwyn, holding up a pair of rumpled woolen trousers. "They won't last out the year in the mill. No use ruining the good clothes you brought over."

On the way back home they approached the entrance to the saloon they had visited the previous day. Many men were crowded inside. A woman with an unkempt knot of brown hair stood peering into the door. A man in an apron appeared and said something to the woman.

"Yeah, well tell Bucky not to expect me to be waitin' around when he gets home," she declared, whirling around and bumping violently into Emlyn.

"Pardon me, fella," she said, pulling her shawl back over her shoulders. She looked at Emlyn, then at Gwyn.

"Say, ain't you Gwyn Jones?"

Gwyn nodded.

"Your son's in class with my boy," She glanced at Emlyn, then back to Gwyn. "I'm Addie Buckman, Bucky's wife."

She turned to Emlyn. "And who is this? I don't recall seein' him around."

"This is my brother-in-law, Emlyn Phillips, recently arrived from Wales."

She stood back and looked him up and down.

"Welcome to Homestead," she said. "Nice to meet you, sir. I hope your family's been givin' you a good introduction to town. I myself would be happy to show you around."

"Pleased to meet you, Mrs. Buckman," said Emlyn, touching his cap visor.

"We really must be going, " said Gwyn, pulling at Emlyn's coat sleeve.

They started off again.

"That's one guide you surely don't need," muttered Gwyn under his breath. "If you think you had trouble yesterday, wait till you see the trouble that woman can stir up, not to mention her bully of a husband."

They walked in silence to Amity Street.

"I'm sorry about yesterday," said Gwyn as they crossed the tracks.

"Me, too," replied Emlyn. "I feel like such an idiot. On my second night here Eirwen has to pick me out of the mud in the back garden. If Tad hears about this, his worst fears will be confirmed. His younger son is a profligate."

Gwyn shook his head. "You aren't a profligate over one indiscretion, and he won't hear about it. Monday you'll start a new job and start bringing in money. It'll work out fine, you'll see."

Sunday, November 22nd

Emlyn awoke to Thomas's voice at the bottom of the stairs.

"But Dad, Uncle Em has to get up now or he'll miss service."

"Never mind, Thomas," he heard Gwyn say. "We'll be going on without him this morning. Come now and get your coat on."

"Ah, Dad!"

"Don't you dare run upstairs and bother your uncle." Eirwen's voice.

"Oh, alright." Thomas's voice, sulky.

Emlyn heard voices at the bottom of the stairs for a few more minutes. The baby gave a brief wail. The door opened and closed shortly thereafter. Silence.

He lay there for a while, idly watching the raindrops stream down the windowpane. It looked like a cold and miserable day. What would the next day bring? Despite Gwyn's enthusiasm, he had many misgivings about laboring in the mill. Yes, he needed the money desperately. But no, he didn't plan on making it a career.

As he had so many times in the past months, he reviewed possible options. Teaching? Journalism? Administration? Perhaps he could find work in one of those fields. However, at the moment, here on this rainy November morning, he could not see his way through to finding this kind of work in this strange town in this strange country.

The streams of water slowly slid down the mill grit on the windowpane. He needed to get up. This was his opportunity to do some reading and writing now that the house was quiet. Tomorrow he'd be starting work in the mill.

He threw off the feather tick and quickly dressed in the cold bedroom.

The house was quiet. Even the noises from the mill were neither as frequent nor as loud. Emlyn visited the privy and returned to the kitchen. It was so warm, so full of homey smells.

Eirwen had set out the teapot covered with a cozy, and a

half loaf of bread was sitting on the board. Emlyn cut himself a few slices, slathered on strawberry jam, and pulled out his worn copy of Thomas Henry Huxley's essay, 'Agnosticism and Christianity.'

The more he told his father about what he had been reading at university, the more disturbed his father became. Huxley in particular brought the older man's blood to a boil.

According to his father, the Reverend Mr. Jeremiah Phillips, Huxley, an English scientist, represented all that was sinful in the world in general and in Britain in particular. To his father and many other clergymen, Huxley was a bete noir, a thorn in the side of Faith.

Even thirty years later, clergy of his father's generation were still smarting from the memory of the debate between Huxley and Bishop Wilberforce over Darwin's *The Origin of Species.* In an impressive display of his skills as a debater, Huxley had demolished Wilberforce's arguments. In more recent years, Huxley had debated Prime Minister Gladstone on the topic of interpreting the Bible. Now an old man, Huxley still was a red flag to many of the faithful.

Indeed, Huxley had written 'Agnosticism and Faith' in 1889 as an answer to those who claimed that agnostics were simply infidels under a different name. Over the last two years Emlyn had come to the discovery that this essay articulated his attitudes as well.

What had angered Emlyn about his father's indignation regarding Huxley was the fact that the man had never read a word the scientist had written. His father's opinion had in fact been based on the opinions of other clergy, who probably hadn't read Huxley either. They were, Emlyn suspected, merely adopting the views of one old codger who'd read a newspaper account of the Wilberforce debate in 1860. It did no good to try to persuade his father to read any Huxley. Tad knew what he thought about the godless scientist.

Emlyn turned to the beginning of the essay, which he had practically memorized in its entirely. Huxley began with a quote from Augustine's *City of God*: 'No one, therefore, should seek to learn knowledge from me, for I know that I do not know—unless indeed he wishes to learn that he does not know.'

Emlyn leafed through the dog-eared pages, seeking one of his favorite passages, where Huxley takes on a moralistic 'Cleric':

> 'Faith,' said this unconscious plagiarist of Tertullian, 'is the power of saying you believe things which are incredible.'
>
> Now I, and many other Agnostics, believe that faith, in this sense, is an abomination; and though we do not indulge in the luxury of self-righteousness so far as to call those who are not of our way of thinking hard names, we do feel that the disagreement between ourselves and those who hold this doctrine is even more moral than intellectual.

This Cleric could be his father, a man who thought anyone who didn't believe what he did was wicked. Moreover, he thought that because these skeptics had no faith, they could have no morals, either. They were damned all way around.

Emlyn bit his lip remembering the escalating arguments between himself and his father during the past year, his second year of studies at Cardiff. How did it come to this sad pass?

British Nonconformists in general and Congregationalists in particular were avid supporters of education and, as a whole, were fairly open-minded. Hadn't they worked tirelessly to build the University of London, and now the university at Cardiff, institutions where Nonconformists, closed out of the Establishment's universities, such as Oxford, could get an education, and a very good one at that?

However, his father, having come of intellectual age during the period of heated debate about religion and science, was not in the vanguard of open-minded thinking.

Emlyn's thoughts returned to that final confrontation in his father's study in the grim, gray-stone house in Treorchy. It had taken Emlyn months to get up the courage to tell his father about his faltering faith. Emlyn had at last broached the subject by showing his father his copy of Huxley's collected essays. His father had riffled through the book without reading any of the text.

"We all have our doubts at times," said his father, sitting back in his chair. "You must ask the Lord to renew your faith, and bring you back to the paths of righteousness."

For a long moment, Emlyn had stared at him, unsure of what to say. In the end, he'd declared simply that he could not in good conscience enter the ministry.

His father looked as if Emlyn had struck him in the face.

"What do you mean?" he asked, aghast. "Why?"

"Father, I've been trying to tell you of my doubts for some time."

"But you never even hinted about giving up the ministry. After all these years of study! After all the sacrifices our family has made to make this possible!"

Emlyn looked down, his eyes tracing the paisley design on the carpet.

His father stood up and looked out the window.

"I'm sorry," Emlyn said in a choked voice. "It's the truth."

The only sound was the ticking of the mantel clock.

His father turned to face him.

"Emlyn, this is unconscionable. I . . . the family and the congregation have had such high hopes. Since you were only a lad, I've dreamed of the day when you would follow in my footsteps. And now this." He paused. "I was so proud of you."

He said the last sentence as if it were an accusation.

"Tad," Emlyn replied softly. "I can't undo the past. I can't forget what I've read; I can't unlearn what I've learned."

His father looked at Emlyn, and then at the Huxley volume on his desk, an expression of horror growing on his face as full comprehension of the situation sunk in.

"So all these years of work have come to naught? We give you an education, and these are its pitiful results—You lose your faith in reading the words of ungodly men. You cast all away."

"Tad, you've never even read Huxley or Ruskin or. . ."

"Don't speak to me of these arrogant sophists who've lured you off the straight and narrow way."

"That's a ridiculous idea that they've 'lured' me, as if into temptation. It's foolish to condemn ideas that you've never examined. Huxley is one of the great thinkers of this century."

"Be careful whom you call a fool. I had faith in *you,* in your intellect."

"Yes, but apparently not in my ability to think for myself."

"Oh! So this is what it's come to. My son studies for years to become a freethinker! And what are you going to do with yourself now?"

"I don't know. I only know I can't be a minister."

His father stood glaring at Emlyn, his face contorted in anguish.

The clock kept ticking away the seconds.

"Very well, then," he said at last, his voice low, angry. "I want you to leave this house, now."

Emlyn stared at the older man, uncomprehending.

"Didn't you hear me? I said I want you to leave *now*."

Emlyn sat there dumbfounded. "But, Father, I . . ."

"Don't call me by that name. You're no son of mine."

Eyes blazing and white mane shaking, his father picked up the Huxley volume and strode to the study door. Savagely throwing it open, he said, "Get out. Get out and don't come back." His voice shook with hurt and anger.

"And take this with you," he added, sending Huxley skidding across the desktop.

In shock, Emlyn took up the book and left the study in silence. As he reached the front door, his mother came rushing into the foyer.

"What's this? Emlyn? Where are you going?"

His father's stern voice from the study door admonished, "Mari, let him go. This freethinker is no son of ours."

His mother grasped Emlyn's hand, her face contorted. His father started towards them. "Go, I say!"

Emlyn squeezed her hand and stepped out of the door. He heard her utter a sharp cry as the door slammed shut behind him.

Emlyn went down the three steps to the street and stood watching the traffic pass by, oblivious to his agony. He turned to gaze at the parsonage. Its dark stone façade showed no expression; its windows were blinded to the street.

He slung his book bag over his shoulder and walked slowly on the short path to the main road through town. On the next block the solid bulk of the chapel where his father was minister cast a shadow across the street.

He started walking, past dozens of identical stone row houses, down the Rhondda, toward Arthur's place in Ystrad.

He hadn't gone a half-mile when a member of his father's congregation driving a cart stopped to ask if he needed a lift. He sat in the back, jostling atop the pile of potatoes, watching the houses and chimneys of Treorchy recede into the monochrome distance.

That was last summer. Now it was November.

Emlyn became aware that he was bolting his food thinking about this last encounter in his parents' house. He took up the teacup and washed down the bread. Think of something pleasant. Last night.

It was so wonderful to hear Eirwen sing again. At her urging, he had taken out his violin and they'd had a fine time, playing the old songs they knew from their childhood. Gwyn even joined in as they concluded with the national anthem of Wales, 'Hen Wlad fy Nhadau,' 'Land of My Fathers.' Thomas was enthralled, partly by the music making, partly by the mysterious music of the Welsh language, which he rarely heard.

After the children had gone to bed, Gwyn asked Emlyn if he'd be going to church to hear Eirwen sing. He now regretted that he had replied so brusquely. Gwyn's generosity, after all, had brought him to Homestead. He had seen the hurt in Eirwen's eyes, the bewilderment in Gwyn's.

Emlyn pulled out his pocket watch: a little after ten. If he hurried, he could make it to the church in time for Eirwen's solo.

For Oesterling, Saturday morning at the office had come and gone with the usual procession of illnesses and injuries to attend to. That evening he fell asleep in his reading chair after dinner, woke up, and decided to go to bed before 9 o'clock. He was too exhausted to do anything but sleep.

The next morning, Sunday, he awoke to the sound of raindrops gently hitting the window by the bed stand. Oesterling stretched lazily and yawned loudly. He glanced at the clock, which indicated the time to be nearly eight o'clock.

Sarah had been right. He had sorely needed a rest after a long week of croups, colics, coughs, cuts, and sundry other ailments, with a mill accident and a tough delivery thrown in for good measure.

It would be a great pleasure to hear Eirwen Jones' lovely voice again. She and Sarah had worked so hard on this special piece for the service today.

As he swung his legs out of bed, he thought of her brother, recently arrived from Wales. Could he be a drunk like his own brother-in-law, Trevor Williams? The Welsh certainly had their share of heavy drinkers—but then, didn't the Irish and Scots and Russians and Slovaks, too—or, for that matter, the Americans?

Margaret, who suffered enormously from the antics of her drunken brother, had made Oesterling promise before she agreed to marry him that he would never drink anything stronger than soft cider. He had agreed willingly, having seen plenty of the ills of liquor from both his service in the Army and his practice as a physician. During the war he'd seen men flushed with 'liquid courage' rush at the enemy, only to be cut down by saber or minié ball. Many patients came to him for treatment of various drink-induced problems from liver failure to injuries from fights in bars. He'd seen children of chronically inebriated mothers turn out to be slow, odd. So much suffering and death.

As he stood up, he heard Sarah's voice from the hallway.

"Are you up, Papa? Come down to breakfast so we can get to church early for rehearsal."

After a breakfast of coffee, rolls, and coddled eggs, they took out their umbrellas and started walking to the Congregational Church on McClure Street below Fifth Avenue. As they picked their way around puddles and broken sidewalk planks, Cerberus trotted beside them.

The Reverend Joshua Griffiths, who was very fond of dogs, would allow Cerberus during bad weather to stay in the anteroom behind the altar with the pastor's own dog, a scrappy terrier. Griffiths had named the terrier Albert after the late and unlamented (by Griffiths at least) English Prince Consort.

The first Sunday that Cerberus had shared the room with Albert, a snowy day the Sunday after Christmas, not twenty minutes into the service the two dogs had gone at each other tooth and nail.

Mr. Griffiths had assumed command of the pulpit and was expounding upon John 5:48 ('Except ye see signs and wonders, ye will not believe'), when all hell broke loose in the anteroom. Griffiths looked beseechingly at Oesterling in the fifth pew back. Chagrined, Oesterling stood and hastened to the anteroom door, opened it and closed it swiftly behind him.

At his entrance, the dogs left off barking and snarling, turning to him with each other's fur in their mouths and wagging tails. Oesterling worried if one or both had been injured, but as it turned out, Albert had suffered only a small cut to the mouth and Cerberus's ruff was wet with Albert's slobber.

Apparently, whatever difference they had was settled that day, for from then on, the dogs either waited quietly together in the anteroom, or sat by the rear entrance of the church until services were over.

However, as he stood outside in the falling snow with the dogs that morning, Oesterling worried about how the congregation would react to this unseemly escapade. He was already an outsider, neither Welsh, nor a Congregationalist by birth. The only reason he had become a member in the first place was Margaret, who was immensely proud of her Welsh heritage, and who had served as the first organist for the congregation.

The doctor wasn't concerned for himself—privately, he cared neither for religion nor churchgoing—but for Sarah and for Griffiths, who indeed looked a bit like a terrier himself. He was relieved to find that when the congregation left the church after the services, people greeted him as if nothing had happened.

One wag, Dai Morris, a patient of his and a first helper in the mill, even came over to Cerberus and patted his head.

"Da ci. *Good dog.* That's the way to liven up a sermon," he said, and winked at the doctor.

However, now, only two years after this incident, the congregation was losing its Welsh identity. Fewer than half of the church members were Welsh, or of Welsh descent. Although they sometimes sang hymns in Welsh, English had become the language of the service. The previous summer, 'Welsh' had been dropped from the name of the church.

"Papa, I know you're tired, but could you please walk faster?" Sarah stood on the sidewalk, holding her skirts up with one hand, the umbrella in another. "I don't want to be late."

"You go on ahead. I'll catch up."

She walked on swiftly while he plodded, Cerberus at his side, through the mud in the last two blocks of McClure Street. He passed by the front entrance and went around to the back. Gwyn Jones, his son Thomas, and William Williams, a mill superintendent originally from Wales, were standing in the shelter of the roof over the rear entrance.

They turned to greet him.

"Good morning, Dr. Oesterling, and you, too, Cerberus," said Gwyn, as Thomas bent to stroke the dog's head.

"How are you, Gwyn? Where are the ladies of your family?"

"Mum's inside with Miss Oesterling, while Dilys watches David," offered Thomas. "Mummy's singing a solo." He grinned broadly.

Gwyn chuckled. "I think it's Mrs. Powell watching both Dilys and David. And I think Dr. Oesterling is well aware of who's singing and playing what today."

Thomas ran out into the rain and kicked a stone into a puddle.

"Yes, Sarah's been practicing this piece for over a month," said Oesterling.

As they spoke, Williams glanced up and down the street.

"Where's your brother-in-law, Gwyn?" asked Williams. "Is he inside?"

Oesterling looked around. "Sarah told me he had arrived and that she'd met him briefly on Friday," he said.

Gwyn took a sudden interest in the tops of his shoes.

"Um, yes, he did arrive safely. Eirwen is so relieved that he's finally here."

Gwyn shifted his weight to the other foot. "He won't be coming to church."

"Why not?" the doctor blurted out, and immediately regretted it.

"I thought he was studying for the ministry," said Williams.

"The truth is he's had a terrible quarrel with his father over the church and the ministry. Last night he told Eirwen and me he'll never set foot in a church of any sort again, not to play music, not for a funeral, not to marry."

Williams' eyebrows went up.

"Ah!" Oesterling couldn't conceal his shock. Was this young man really a wastrel, fled to the New World after disgracing himself in the Old?

"I'm sorry to hear that," he added lamely.

"Eirwen's disappointed of course, but maybe he'll change his mind once he starts his new life here in Homestead."

Thomas, who had been poking in the mud with a stick, looked up and said, "Uncle Em got out his violin and played while Mummy sang last night. A couple of times Mummy and Em sang together. It was really swell. Even Dad sang one song with them."

Gwyn, relieved at the change of topic, nodded in assent. "That was 'Hen Wlad Fy Nhadau.' It stirs the spirit so."

Oesterling agreed. He loved the national anthem of Wales, even though he knew little of the Welsh language.

"There's the prelude," observed Gwyn as the organ started up inside. "We'd better go in."

Oesterling settled Cerberus in the anteroom with Albert and went to his customary pew. Despite himself, he grew increasingly anxious as the offertory approached. He knew that the performance meant so much to both Sarah and Eirwen.

His worries were unfounded. Sarah's accompaniment that she had composed on the hymn tune 'Hiraeth' by Daniel Protheroe was lovely on the organ. Eirwen's warm contralto grew to fill the sanctuary. How could such a wispy thing as she produce such a big sound? Perfect shading, perfect phrasing. He closed his eyes.

Rw'yn edriych, dros y bryniau pell,
I gaze upon those distant hills

Am danat bob yr awr;
and seek Thee ev'ry hour;

Tyr'd, fy Anwylyd, mae'n hwyrhau,
Come, my beloved, daylight fades,

A'm haul bron mynd i lawr.
my sun has reach'd his bow'r.

The words, by the famous hymn writer William Williams, a distant relative of Margaret's, were very fine. But even if one didn't know what the words meant, mused Oesterling, he'd still be moved by the music. If God dwelled nowhere else, he certainly lived there—in the magical, sacred sounds of music.

Back at the house, Emlyn had rummaged through the steamer trunk for his slicker and struck out the back way to the modest church that he had passed on Friday.

After he arrived at the entrance, he paused at the door, cracking it open to hear what was happening inside. He had to wait only a few minutes before Eirwen began her solo.

The soft sound of the rain pattering on the hard earth made a mournful backdrop to her singing. Minor keys always sounded sad to him. He found himself deeply moved by her clear, expressive voice.

At the end of the piece, Emlyn softly closed the door and waited at the bottom of the steps.

Of course, no one clapped at the end, as the performance was given to the glory of God. After the service, many came forward to compliment Eirwen. In about ten minutes, Emlyn saw a short, wiry man with a bristling copper beard and vestments of a Congregationalist minister come and stand at the entrance, talking and shaking hands with people as they came out. Many of the members of the congregation glanced at Emlyn as they raised their umbrellas outside the door, and he retreated to the side of the building.

When the crowd dwindled and the pastor went inside, Emlyn came up the steps to the open door.

Thomas came dashing up the center aisle. He rushed up to Emlyn and peered into the hood of his slicker.

"Uncle Em!" cried Thomas. "It really is you! I hafta tell Mummy."

Before Emlyn could reply, Thomas ran back down the aisle.

In less than a minute Eirwen appeared at the church door. She was so delighted to see him there that she hugged him slicker and all.

"You'll be getting your best dress soaked," Emlyn remarked as she stepped back.

"So happy I am that you came," beamed Eirwen.

"So am I. It was lovely, lovely. After all the singing we did last night, I'm surprised you have any voice at all."

She looked around uncertainly into the sanctuary.

"I'll wait for you here. Don't hurry," said Emlyn.

Oesterling had been puzzled when he had seen Thomas come up to Eirwen and pull on her skirts. At first, she tried to brush him off. However, after listening to a whispered message from her son, she excused herself from the small crowd standing by the choir pews and went toward the back of the church.

What could be the matter?

The doctor turned to see her rush into the arms of a tall figure in a slicker standing outside the doors in the rain.

"Come on, Doctor," urged Gwyn as he swept by Oesterling with the baby in one arm and Dilys on the other. "It looks like you'll get to meet my brother-in-law after all."

Gwyn came to the entrance, David and Dilys in tow.

"Thanks for coming, Em," he said. "It means so much to Eirwen."

Emlyn nodded, but before he could think of anything to say, a stout, tallish man of late middle years with graying hair and a cropped beard came and stood next to Gwyn.

"Do you remember Sarah Oesterling, Thomas's teacher?" asked Gwyn.

Emlyn flushed when he remembered what a bloody fool he'd made of himself.

"I'd like you to meet her father, Dr. William Oesterling."

The two men exchanged greetings and shook hands, one inside the church, the other outside.

Feeling awkward about the situation, Emlyn began to back down the steps.

"I think I'll be off now. It was good meeting you, Doctor. 'See you back at the house, Gwyn."

As he reached the bottom step, he glimpsed a flash of golden red hair in the entryway. The woman looked at him and he noted those distinctive green eyes. Sarah Oesterling.

His boot skidded on a wet sidewalk board and he fell forward. Please, please, no. He clutched at the iron railing as his left knee glanced off the edge of a plank and plunged into the packed gravel. Pain shot through his knee into his upper leg, as he kneeled, once again, in the gutter.

"Are you OK?" asked Oesterling, starting toward the steps.

Emlyn could think of only one thing: Get away. Now.

"Yes, yes, I'm fine," he said over his shoulder.

With an awkward lurch, he pulled himself to his feet and limped away as quickly as his throbbing knee could carry him.

Did he hear Gwyn calling after him? He was almost to Sixth Avenue when he realized he was headed in the wrong direction. As he continued to hobble up McClure Street, he never looked back.

He turned right at Eighth Avenue. All the stores and pubs that had been so crowded the previous day were deserted. Valuable merchandise had been removed from the shop windows, and the bars were shuttered. The foot and street traffic was a trickle compared to that of the previous day, horses and people slopping through puddles of yellow mud.

Limping along the uneven planking, Emlyn looked for a place to rest and gather his wits. He turned toward the railroad tracks and spotted a hotel situated between the sets of tracks. The empty bench under the covered back entrance to the hotel seemed like a good place to stop.

Emlyn crossed the first set of tracks and climbed the steps to the hotel's porch. Both the bench and hotel's creamy clapboard siding looked new. He peered through the frosted window of the door, but could see no movement.

Pushing back his slicker hood, Emlyn lowered himself onto the bench, rested his head against the wall, and closed his eyes. He couldn't believe what a hash he was making of things in his first days in what he had hoped would be the Land of Opportunity. Was all this effort a big mistake?

His musings grew gloomier.

A train whistle sounded in the distance. Emlyn opened his eyes and turned toward the sound. A black locomotive was bearing down from the direction of Pittsburgh. The whistle sounded as the train approached the Amity Street station, but it did not stop. The train roared through the crossing past the hotel. Smoke, steam, and rain swirled around in the engine's wake as it passed by less than fifteen feet from where he sat. As the passenger cars of the express clattered by, the whistle again sounded again when the locomotive approached the Munhall Station. Thirty seconds, and relative quiet returned.

Emlyn pulled up his hood and limped back to the house.

Monday, November 23rd

Emlyn was dreaming he was having tea with his mother. They were in the kitchen at home with Eirwen and Arthur. She was heaping little cakes and sandwiches on his plate and pouring tea.

Abruptly, someone shook him roughly on the shoulder. It was his father, waving the Bible and glowering at them. Was his father going to strike him? He tried to grab the hand on his shoulder, but he couldn't move.

"Psst, Emlyn. Time to go to work."

Emlyn struggled to open his eyes. "Gwyn? Duw, it's still night."

"Come on. We have to be at the mill by four."

In the darkness he put his legs over the side of the bed and stood up. His left knee was sore from the fall the day before, but not real bad.

He pulled on the chambray shirt, baggy wool pants, and worn suit coat Gwyn had helped him pick out at the second-hand store.

Eirwen set out a breakfast of eggs, bacon, toast, tea, and baked beans. Gwyn filled his lunch pail with several sandwiches made of chicken left over from Sunday dinner, a couple of apples, slices of pie, and as an afterthought, the rest of the breakfast beans.

"A man gets really hungry on the job," he said, setting a tea towel on top. "Saturday—payday—we'll have to get you your own pail."

Emlyn looked at the lunch pail with misgivings. Gwyn picked it up, grabbed Emlyn's cap from its peg, and threw it on Emlyn's head at a jaunty angle.

"Come on. Adventure is calling." He laughed.

"Good luck," said Eirwen as she saw them off.

"He'll need it," replied Gwyn, chuckling.

"What do you mean?" asked Emlyn, his voice quavering a bit. He straightened his cap and pulled it down tight.

"Nothing. Don't worry. It'll be fine. As I said, I've already talked to William Williams, one of the superintendents, and he said to talk to the first helper in Open Hearth Shop #2."

Gwyn glanced over at Emlyn. "Don't worry so much. Williams is a member of our chapel, and from Merthyr, a Valley man. Carnegie brought him over two years ago to oversee the construction of O.H. 2, and now he's the superintendent there."

He clapped Emlyn on the shoulder, and Emlyn managed a wan smile.

As they trudged though the darkness toward the black silhouettes of the mill buildings, Emlyn felt the knot in his stomach grow. Other men bearing boxes and pails were walking in the same direction. Emlyn shivered under his light coat. No one spoke. There was only the sound of the men's boots on the dirt and gravel and the increasing volume of thuds and hisses from the mill.

"Mind your step," cautioned Gwyn as they entered a mill yard. The brick-covered yard was much noisier than the street. From a nearby building came a loud metallic crash. Men were shouting to make themselves heard; a few were signaling with their extended arms. In the glow of a furnace, Emlyn could make out narrow train tracks crisscrossing the yard, with big piles of rails stacked in a haphazard arrangement.

"You've been to Blaenavon Ironworks?" asked Gwyn as they walked through a yard.

Emlyn nodded. Blaenavon, at the end of one of the Valleys in South Wales, was the site not only of the Ironworks, but also of Pwyll Mawr, the 'big coal pit.'

"Look sharp," said Gwyn, yanking Emlyn by the arm. A small steam locomotive, constantly ringing its bell, chugged by only feet from them.

"That's a dinky engine," yelled Gwyn. "They're the iron work horses of the mill, but they can do lots more damage than a horse if they run you down."

"Anyway," continued Gwyn as they walked on, "a decade ago Carnegie paid the Blaenavon Ironworks a quarter of a million dollars for the right to use the steel-making process invented by two of their chemists, Percy Gilchrist and Sidney Thomas. Carnegie said that these men did more for Britain's greatness than all the kings and queens put together."

Emlyn nodded again, this time looking around for a dinky. "Rule, Britannia," he muttered.

"Now you'll get to see part of the process of how phosphoric ore, useless before our Welsh brethren's invention, is made into steel," said Gwyn as they went to the gaping entrance to the open hearth.

Gwyn introduced Emlyn to Tony, the foreman, and giving Emlyn his share of the food, went off to his work as a roller in the 112-inch mill. Tony called over another man. Emlyn immediately recognized him as the dark, wiry young worker they had seen at the bar on Friday.

"This here's Virgil," said Tony. "He'll show you the ropes."

Emlyn extended his hand.

"We've already met," said Virgil, ignoring it. "What's your name again?"

Emlyn told him.

"What kind of pansy name is that for a man?" Virgil asked casually.

"It's pretty common back home," replied Emlyn, offended.

"Hmph," said Virgil, unimpressed. "Them English sure have strange names and customs."

"I'm Welsh, not English," said Emlyn.

"Same thing."

Emlyn was about to reply, but thought the better of it.

"Take off your coat and roll up your sleeves. Come on, Emmy. Grab one of them shovels over there. We're going to make front-wall."

"Em-*lyn*," corrected Emlyn, annoyed, but the man had already moved ahead.

Emlyn's irritation with Virgil evaporated when he saw the furnace. Its huge black hulk stretched along one side of the building. Even from the entrance to the mill, he could feel the warmth. When they got to within twenty feet of it, the heat rushed at him with staggering intensity.

Virgil explained that the furnace had already had been loaded with twenty-five tons of scrap iron and heating had begun. They now had to make front-wall, that is, temporarily reline the furnace with dolomite for the next draft of flame.

Emlyn watched as Frank, the man Virgil introduced as the second helper, took up a gargantuan spoon, about fifteen feet long, and Virgil loaded it with dolomite. Using the spoon, the second helper carefully spread a protective layer along the front wall of the furnace through the open furnace door. The heat was withering.

Virgil beckoned Emlyn to come over and help with the shoveling. Emlyn and Virgil kept heaping the spoon full, and Frank carefully placed the dolomite inside the furnace. Sweat ran down the faces of the men as they worked in the searing heat. At least he wasn't cold anymore.

"Yep," declared Frank, finally setting the down the big spoon. "That'll hold 'er."

Turning to Emlyn, he took off his glove and offered his grimy hand. "Welcome to O. H. 2. I'm Frank Schultz. I hear you're Gwyn Jones's kin. Good man, Gwyn. We're in the same Amalgamated lodge."

Frank leaned closer to Emlyn. "Never you mind Virgil. He's just pissed as hell the South lost the war. Even though he wasn't even born yet." Frank gave a brief guffaw.

Virgil grumbled that they needed to tend to the furnace, and then directed Emlyn and another man to load and push wheelbarrows full of materials around the area till Emlyn's arms started to tire.

The other man, named Joe, spoke halting English. Virgil bossed them both around. One time as he passed by Emlyn, he muttered, "Dumb hunkies. Don't understand a damn thing."

Once in the dimness, Emlyn accidentally banged his left knee hard against a piece of machinery. Emlyn secretly chided himself for being so careless as to hit the same knee as he had hurt the previous morning. The knee began to throb, and he pulled up his pant leg to examine the injury. The metal had torn through the fabric, gashing his skin. Blood was oozing out through the grime. Emlyn futilely dabbed at it with his handkerchief.

The longer Emlyn worked, the more his knee bothered him.

After a while, Virgil directed him to return to the furnace door. "Time to make back-wall."

The men on Frank's furnace and the crew from the adjoining one gathered around the closed furnace door. "Grab your shovel and stand here to see how it's done," said Virgil. The men gathered in front of the furnace door. The heavy door was lifted a couple of feet, and the white heat inside blazed forth with stunning intensity.

Emlyn watched as each worker in turn approached the door of the furnace carrying a heaping shovel of dolomite. When a worker reached the door, leaning toward the inferno, he flung his shovelful into the maw of the furnace, then stepped aside to let the next man have his turn. The men walked casually, as if taking a stroll. The operation went like clockwork, each man working as part of a synchronized team. It seemed so effortless.

Frank came over. "We'll have you take a crack at it soon."

Emlyn watched for several more minutes.

"It ain't a job for a greenhorn," said Virgil, stepping out of line after his turn. "You have to pitch the dolomite in a high enough arc to hop off the mound and land high. You have to move in tight and peer in to see where the dolomite lands. You can't just pitch it and run."

Virgil pointed to the mound of dolomite, "All righty, Emmy. It's your turn."

Emlyn flushed with anger. "I told you, my name is *Em-lyn.*"

"OK, Emmy-Lynn."

Emlyn dropped his shovel and lunged at Virgil, clutched his shirt collar, and pulled him nearly off his feet. "Damn you, call me by my proper name."

Virgil seized Emlyn's wrists and they tussled back and forth.

"Whoa, there!" shouted Frank, inserting himself between them. "Stop it."

Releasing his grip on Virgil's collar, Emlyn shoved him away.

"Shit, ya don't have to be so damned touchy," smirked Virgil, smoothing his sooty shirtfront. Emlyn rubbed his right wrist.

"I don't know what that was about, but we'll have none of that here," Frank said firmly to Emlyn. "It's too easy to get hurt even without these kinds of antics."

He turned to Virgil. "What's the matter with you? You should know better."

Frank bent down and picked up Emlyn's shovel. "Now we're almost done, let's have you take a turn at making back-wall. Do you have gloves?"

Emlyn nodded.

Frank handed the shovel to Emlyn. "Fill this and bring it to the furnace."

"Let him step in," Frank directed the next man, who stood back.

"The object is to get the dolomite as close to the back wall of the furnace as possible. Don't look right into the furnace or you'll burn your eyes out. Here, you can borrow these." He took out a pair of spectacles with soot-blackened lenses and handed them to Emlyn.

"The best way to protect your eyes is to throw your left hand high at the end of your swing. That gives you an instant to spot where you threw it. Try to copy what the boys have been doing."

Emlyn put on the glasses and sidled up to the left of the furnace door. The heat was overpowering. He could feel the warmth instantly penetrate his clothes; he caught a whiff of scorched fabric. Standing beside the entrance to the holocaust, he felt as if the skin on his hands would blister at any second, despite his gloves. His injured knee burned with pain. He peered in, but could see only a pulsating explosion of light. Closing his eyes, Emlyn swung back the heavy shovel and flung its contents through the door.

He staggered back and nearly fell over. His watch felt like a chunk of brimstone through the lining of his front pocket. His body was streaming with sweat. As he took off the glasses, he could see smoke coming off the front of his shirt. Virgil and a few of the other men snickered.

"You'll get the hang of it in time," said Frank, taking back his glasses. "Now we'll let 'er cook." The crew went off in various directions.

Emlyn took out his watch and glanced at it. It was still warm.

Frank, noting the watch, said, "If I were you, I'd leave that and any rings at home. They might get busted or caught in the machinery. Either way, it's a bad deal. We'll let you know when the shift is over."

Emlyn limped away from the furnace to get his lunch, when he saw the foreign worker drinking from a dipper at a metal pail. "Here," said the man. "You get big headache without drink and salt." He handed Emlyn a chunk of salt and the dipper.

Emlyn looked at the man's broad, Slavic face closely for the first time. He wasn't as tall as Emlyn, but obviously he was very strong. His well-defined muscles showed through the fabric of his shirtsleeves. He had warm hazel eyes. When he grinned, he revealed a missing lower-front tooth.

Emlyn looked at the water with misgivings. It was murky, with bits of debris floating on the surface.

"Is from river," said the man. "Is OK. You drink." He made an upward motion with the palm of his hand, as if urging the dipper to Emlyn's lips.

The water was lukewarm and gritty, but it went down easily enough. Emlyn drank a half dozen dippers-full and handed it back to the man.

When he went back to work, he saw the first helper passing by the furnace doors with blackened glasses on the end of his nose, peering in briefly through the peep-hole in each.

Virgil came over to explain. "He's checkin' to make sure the bricks don't get too hot. If the bricks are as red as the gas flame shootin' in from the ends, the lining's burning away, and that ain't good."

He pointed to each end. "Both air and gas come in to keep the brew cookin.' The hotter the gas comes through, the quicker it cooks and the more steel—the more tonnage—is produced. Of course, for the tonnage men like your brother-in-law, that's more money in the pocket. For the rest of us, it don't mean a blasted thing."

He spat on the floor. The Slavic worker was passing by with a wheelbarrow.

"Ain't that right, Hunky-Joe?" Virgil asked.

Joe looked at him blankly. "Huh? What you say?"

"Forget it," said Virgil, running his tongue over his upper front teeth.

Shortly after this exchange, the first helper said to Virgil, "Get me thirty thousand pounds." Emlyn couldn't imagine how Virgil could 'get' fifteen tons of molten metal. He watched as Virgil walked down the mill building and climbed to a platform near the blower. Virgil said something to the man on duty there, who blew a whistle.

As Virgil walked back to the furnace, he was followed by a locomotive dragging a gigantic ladle emitting fumes and a soft glow. When the ladle reached the furnace, an overhead crane picked it up and poured the liquid iron from the blast furnace through a spout in the open-hearth furnace. Virgil stood on the floor and directed the crane operator where to pour the incandescent river by slowly waving one hand.

Emlyn was impressed. It looked so easy.

When the operation was complete, Virgil came over to Emlyn and said, "Sometimes she spills a bit over the side, so look out. The sparks fly and the molten iron runs onto the floor by the furnace. Puddles of hell."

Emlyn nodded. This work was even more dangerous than he had imagined.

"Now we let 'er cook," said Virgil.

"How long does that take?" asked Emlyn.

"Oh, anywhere from twelve to twenty-four hours. It's the first helper's job to test the steel by scooping some into a small mold and lettin' it cool. Then he smashes the ingot with a sledgehammer and all the fellers go over to inspect it. The first-helper decides if she has too much carbon or not enough . . . if she's ready to tap, or ain't. If she is, we tap."

"Tap? Like a keg of ale?"

"Yep. Let 'er run out and make ingots. It ain't as simple as that, though. You'll see."

"Right," replied Emlyn dubiously.

"While she's cooking, we'll get ourselves some vittles. 'Gotta find my lunch pail," said Virgil, walking off.

"You take more water?" asked the Slavic man, holding up the dipper.

Emlyn went over and drank his fill again. Lord, it was hot in there. His left knee was throbbing with pain, more so when heat hit it.

"Come, we eat over here," said the other man, heading toward the entrance where several other workers were eating.

Emlyn slumped onto the bricks by the wide entryway. A cold breeze blew through the opening. The gray sky above the yard was streaked with billowing tan and black smoke. He felt terribly tired.

The other worker sat down cross-legged near him and took out his lunch. "I Joe. Joe Galik, from Slovakia." He held out a grimy hand.

Emlyn took it. "I'm Emlyn Phillips, from Wales."

"They speak English in Wales?"

"Yes, and also Welsh."

"Welsh?" The man looked puzzled.

"Cymraeg. Sut ydych chi?"

Joe laughed and bit into his thick sandwich. "That Welsh sound funny." He pointed to himself. "Joe speak Slovak and little bit Deutsch and Magyar and English. Slovakia part of Austria-Hungary. Many languages."

"Wales is part of the British empire, upon which the sun never sets. Empires have many languages." He sighed, and then brightening, added, "Ich spreche ein bischen deutsch auch."

"Sehr gut!" exclaimed Joe, smiling. "Dann koennen wir ja deutsch zusammen sprechen."

Emlyn nodded. "Jawohl."

He and Joe fell hungrily on their lunches and ate in silence till the food was gone. Emlyn leaned back and closed his eyes. He was on the verge of nodding off, when he felt something smack the sole of his right boot.

It was Virgil, standing there with a shovel. "Rise and shine there, Em-Lyn." He pronounced the name with excessive articulation, as if it were two words. "No lollygagging around." He went off into the mill, whistling.

Holding on to the wall, Emlyn struggled to his feet. His sweat-soaked clothing, now cold, clung to his skin. He shivered and rubbed his sore knee.

"No mind that Wirgil," said Joe, grabbing his shovel. "He big horse's ass."

"I see you're picking up the vernacular English very fast," observed Emlyn, placing his hand on the man's shoulder as they headed back into the darkness. "And I couldn't agree with you more."

After they ate lunch, the tedious, backbreaking work

continued with few breaks. After two o'clock the rest of the day was for Emlyn a blur of pain and fatigue. He was hardly accustomed to this kind of labor, and he had to force his limbs to react to his mind's commands.

As he shoveled, pushed and carried around various materials, he began to feel faint. His knee screamed with pain.

By the time Gwyn came by to accompany him home, he was blindly pushing himself through the motions.

At the house he washed up, removing his trousers to try to sponge the dirt off his injured knee, again with little success. During supper, while the rest of the family talked about the day's events, he ate without saying a word and immediately went to bed. He noted vaguely that Thomas seemed to be disappointed at his lack of attention.

In bed, he kept turning over to try to find a comfortable way to rest his aching muscles. When he rubbed his knee against the sheets, pain would pulse from the surface into the joint.

Several hours of this and Gwyn was rousing him to come downstairs and get ready for work. Eirwen and Gwyn looked at each other with undisguised shock as he dragged himself into the gas-lit kitchen. They both asked him several times if he could manage going back to work, and each time he insisted he could. He ate the toast and eggs slowly, in a fog of exhaustion.

In his now-sooty work clothes, Emlyn limped alongside Gwyn into the cavernous spaces of the steel works. As they parted, Gwyn stepped in front of him and seized his arm. "Now you mind those dinkies today. This is a dangerous place even for the most alert man. I don't want you getting mangled or burned on the job."

Emlyn returned Gwyn's gaze and nodded his assent.

"Give me your word on it," Gwyn insisted.

"I give my word."

"Da iawn. *Good*. I'll see you later."

Emlyn tried to keep his promise, but the fatigue was overwhelming. The pain in his knee kept a sharp edge to his consciousness, even as it wore him down.

Virgil took perverse pleasure in Emlyn's pain. He continued to needle him now and then, but since Emlyn didn't react, Virgil got little fun from it.

Frank urged him to try his hand again at making backwall, and Emlyn was about as adept as with his first try—that is, hopelessly inept.

Later that day Emlyn got to see them tap the steel. Before the tapping, they kept shoveling fluorspar into the furnace to thin out the waste slag. The slag drained off the top of the molten metal. They repeatedly made small test ingots through this long, exhausting process.

Finally, Virgil shouted, "Come on, Em-Lyn. Take this manganese shovel and follow me to the gallery behind the furnace."

Emlyn took the small, flat shovel and went around to the rear of the furnace near the tap-spout. He looked down into the pit where the giant ladles were kept. There some workers, the clean-up men, painstakingly were gathering up fragments of spilt or sprayed metal to save for another melting. They suddenly left the pit.

"Yeow!" shouted the senior melter, and Frank, the second helper, came up to the tap-spout with a pointed rod and poked it into the material at the spout.

"Now he's gonna ravel 'er out. Pay attention," admonished Virgil. Frank leaped away as if chased by demons, and the molten steel spilled out, terrible and red. Spitting flame, the concoction fell into the ladle with a great hissing and plopping sound. The first helper and Frank staggered up to the ladle with huge bags of a fine black material and dropped it into the contents of the ladle, with dramatic results.

Emlyn gasped as flames erupted from the cauldron, shooting up to the roof of the pit, curling viciously along the platform where they stood.

"They're putting in fine anthracite," said Virgil. "'Know what that is?"

"Of course. I'm from Wales, where they dig up a lot of it."

"Hmph," responded Virgil.

Frank and the first helper kept dumping in bagsful of coal until they had an enormous conflagration going. Then they stepped back.

"Get ready," said Virgil. "When he gives the signal, we're goin' to shovel manganese—fast!"

Emlyn gripped the handle of his shovel tightly.

The melter gave the cue and Virgil, followed by Emlyn, ran along the gallery to the side of the spout where the molten metal was coming out. He thrust his shovel into the pile of manganese and started tossing it into the ladle. Emlyn did the same, and discovered that the manganese was incredibly heavy. So that's why the shovels were small.

Virgil and Emlyn kept pitching into the manganese and hurling it into the incandescent brew. As the tap-stream was only about a yard from their heads, the heat was overpowering. After a short time, Emlyn felt lightheaded, overwhelmed by the physical exertion in the excruciating heat.

The tap stream stopped, and Virgil moved back from the spout. Emlyn followed. He looked down and saw the ladle was full.

"That's the first. We'll probably get another ladle-full in a bit."

"Ye gods!" exclaimed Emlyn, pulling his sweaty shirt from

his chest. His left knee throbbed from the heat and exertion. "For a minute there, I thought I'd died and gone to hell."

Virgil chuckled. "Maybe you have. 'Sorry you came to this hell-hole?"

A shout from the melter and the furnace tap-stream began pouring into an empty ladle underneath. Virgil and Emlyn began shoveling manganese again.

Just as Emlyn thought his left knee might give way, the stream stopped flowing. Virgil wrapped his hands in wet burlap and picked up a piece of sheet iron, setting it gingerly over the spout.

"There. That'll do it," he remarked, throwing down the burlap.

Emlyn dropped to his good knee and, pulling out a dirty bandana, wiped the streams of sweat from his face and neck. His hair was soaked with perspiration.

"Let's get some water," said Virgil, starting across the platform.

"Coming," said Emlyn, but didn't.

He tried to stand, but his legs were like rubber. The darkness of the mill closed around him, and he pitched forward, his sore knee coming down hard. He blacked out.

He felt water splash onto his head as he lay face-up on the platform.

"Damn it, don't drown him," he heard Frank say.

Then Virgil's drawl, "Ah, that'll feel good."

He opened his eyes, and there were Virgil, Frank, and Joe looking down at him.

"You OK?" asked Frank.

"I think so," replied Emlyn. He tried to sit up, but the black space started to spin. He laid his head back again.

"He ain't OK," declared Virgil. "In fact, he's dead on his ass."

"Let's try to get him up. We can't leave him that way."

Frank bent down and grabbed Emlyn's right arm, and Joe grabbed the other.

"We're going to try to pull you up, so you can walk to a safer place," Frank explained. "One, two, *three*!"

They hoisted him to his feet, and he stood there for a moment, swaying slightly. He took a step, leaning heavily on Joe.

"Ah, my knee," Emlyn moaned. Virgil crossed his arms impatiently.

"What happened?" asked Frank. "Did you hurt your leg shoveling?"

"No, no. On Sunday, I..." Emlyn's voice faded. They half-dragged him to a bench away from the furnace.

An hour later, Gwyn came by to walk home with Emlyn. His smile disappeared when he saw Emlyn sitting there with his left leg up on the bench. Emlyn's wet clothing had cooled, and he was shivering.

"Good Lord, Em. What happened to you?"

After Frank told him the story about Emlyn's collapse, Gwyn suggested that Emlyn go right to Oesterling's office before the doctor left for the day. Emlyn insisted he was all right. He really didn't want to see that particular doctor, although he didn't say so. But when Emlyn couldn't even stand without help, Gwyn insisted that he go to Oesterling.

Since the office wasn't far from his boarding house, Joe volunteered to help Gwyn take Emlyn there. Gwyn helped Emlyn into his jacket and put his own larger one around the younger man's shoulders.

Emlyn thought he saw Virgil smirking as he passed him supported by Gwyn and Joe. What was the matter with that fellow, anyway? The pain in his knee quickly obliterated any thoughts about Virgil as they picked their way through the dark furnace shed.

In the wintry dusk, Gwyn and Joe, holding up Emlyn between them, made their way through the mill yards and along the tracks until they emerged onto City Farm Lane.

The going was slow, but they managed to get to the doctor's office on Eighth Avenue shortly before five o'clock. Only one patient, an old man with a red face, was waiting in the office when Gwyn, Emlyn and Joe came through the door at the top of the stairs.

Emlyn crumpled into a chair as Gwyn thanked Joe, who immediately left to go home.

Dr. Oesterling's nurse came from behind a shirred fabric screen and frowned at them. "You're too late for today's office hours," she said. "You'll have to come back tomorrow afternoon. I mean, Thursday afternoon. Dr. Oesterling does house calls on Wednesdays."

Emlyn sat there, observing her with glassy eyes.

Gwyn said, "This man is injured. We practically had to carry him from the mill."

"He's not in a stretcher, so I assume he can make it home," she replied.

"It took two of us to get him here. I don't see how you expect..."

Emlyn broke in. "Never mind, Gwyn. Let's get out of here."

He was secretly relieved that Oesterling, who had witnessed the fall on Sunday, wouldn't be asking questions about the second injury as well. He was struggling to stand up when Oesterling appeared from behind the screen.

"Hello, Gwyn. I thought I'd recognized your voice."

"Doctor," said the nurse, "I was just telling them they're too late."

"It's OK, Mrs. Cramer. You can go after I see Mr. O'Connor."

She cast a dubious glance at Emlyn and went behind the screen.

The old man followed her with the doctor and emerged several minutes later with a small bottle of medicine. Dr. Oesterling motioned Gwyn to bring Emlyn into the consulting area.

The nurse watched as Emlyn, aided by Gwyn, painfully rose to his feet. She set down her cape on a chair and came over to help. They eased Emlyn into a white metal chair with a leather-covered seat behind the screen.

Emlyn, still shivering under the two jackets, gave a brief description of his two mishaps, the fall on the sidewalk and the cut from the machinery. The doctor directed him to remove his trousers.

As Emlyn pulled off the left pant leg, Gwyn whistled low. "Bloody hell. That looks nasty."

Dr. Oesterling pulled up a metal stool and sat down. "Let's see what we have here."

He looked at the knee, a mess of dried blood, grit, soot, and bruised skin, swollen to nearly half again its normal size. He turned to his nurse and said, "We have to clean it before I can see what is the matter."

Mrs. Cramer mixed boiling and cold water in a basin and brought it over to Emlyn. With soap and clean toweling, she gently washed around the knee and the scab on the gash.

"You should have washed this cut last night when you got home," Oesterling said to Emlyn.

"I tried. I was too tired." Emlyn shivered again.

"It was his first day on the job," Gwyn explained.

The doctor nodded.

"I'm afraid it's infected now. I'm going to open it up again to try to clean out the wound. Fortunately, the knee itself is only bruised. That should heal on its own with no problems."

Emlyn gripped the bottom of the chair as the doctor began working on the wound. The doctor scrubbed at the scab and coaxed blood out of the cut. With surgical scissors, he cut away some of the blackened, torn skin.

"Mix up a solution of carbolic acid," the doctor directed the nurse, who went to a cabinet, took out a white powder and mixed it with boiled water. Oesterling poured the liquid over the cut. Emlyn winced as the disinfectant ran over the cut and down the leg.

Oesterling dabbed away the bloody fluid and the nurse handed him a bottle of tincture of iodine. "Brace yourself," Oesterling said to Emlyn. "This might sting a bit."

As the doctor applied the solution with a glass rod onto the cut, Emlyn threw his head back, closed his eyes and grimaced. "Good God! That stings more than a bit."

Oesterling replied, "It usually kills more germs than patients."

Gwyn laughed, but Emlyn didn't.

The doctor cut a length of wide gauze bandage and wrapped the knee.

"There," said Oesterling, pushing back the stool, and Emlyn relaxed into the chair again. "You'll have to keep off that leg for the next couple of days at least, and preferably through the weekend."

Emlyn straightened in the chair. "I've put in only two days. I must go back to work."

"That is not a good idea," said the doctor. "You are chilled and could possibly have a fever because of the infection. You must give yourself time to recover."

"I'll be fine after I get some sleep. I must go to work."

"Rubbish," replied Gwyn. "You passed out very close to the pit today, and I'll not let you risk further injury—or worse—on the job. Eirwen would never forgive me. And besides, how would you pay me back, then?" He winked at Oesterling.

Emlyn closed his eyes in resignation. Even though he hated the thought of being laid up after working only two shifts, the idea of going to bed and sleeping for a long time was very appealing.

The doctor handed Emlyn his trousers. "Try not to get the bandage dirty. I do house calls on Wednesday afternoons, and I'll stop by to change the dressings."

"But," said Emlyn, "I won't be able to pay you even for today until next Saturday."

"Don't worry about that," said Gwyn. "I'll pay Dr. Oesterling, and you can pay me back. In for a penny, in for a pound, you know."

"Yes," agreed Oesterling. "Don't concern yourself about paying me right away. Rest that leg so you can get back to work in good shape next week."

Gwyn thanked Mrs. Cramer for staying to clean the wound, and they both went down the stairs, he to look for a buggy or cart to take Emlyn home.

An awkward silence ensued as Emlyn and Oesterling were left alone. Emlyn sat slumped over in the chair as the doctor tidied up and packed his medical bag. As he passed by his desk, a dark form emerged from underneath and crept toward Emlyn. Emlyn, who was half asleep, sat bolt upright in alarm.

Oesterling, reaching for his overcoat on the rack, smiled. "That's only my dog, Cerberus. He's very friendly."

Emlyn reached out his right hand, and the dog licked it, wagging his tail.

"He reminds me of a sheepdog on my Grandfather Davies's farm—although he's bigger than any collie I've seen."

He smoothed the wavy black hair on Cerberus's back. "Ci defaid bach."

"His mother is a sheepdog. We don't know who his father was, but from his looks, I'd guess an Alsatian. That would account for his larger size," observed Oesterling, "and his wolf-like shape."

"He might look like a sentry of hell, but he doesn't act like a demon-dog."

Oesterling laughed, then turned serious. "You know, it's no disgrace not going back to work tomorrow."

Emlyn stopped stroking the dog and looked up.

"Many a man hasn't even lasted a full shift in that mill—in one day and out the next. It's tough and dangerous work. You didn't notice any older men in there did you?"

"Now that you mention it, no."

"It's a rare man who lasts beyond the age of 45 in the mill. Either he gets injured or the company lets him go," said Oesterling, extinguishing a gaslight. "Eirwen says you were a student back in Wales."

"Yes. I just finished my second year of university studies when my father and I... er... when I decided to come over here. This kind of work is a first for my family, who are farmers, teachers, and ministers. Unlike the Davies or Phillips families, Gwyn's family has worked in the mines and mills for three generations now. They're a hardy lot."

Gwyn came through the office door. "I found a teamster on the Avenue who'll drop us at the house on his way to the stables."

Oesterling pulled on his overcoat and put out the last light. Cerberus slipped out of the door ahead of the men and ran down the stairs. Emlyn threw his left arm over Gwyn's shoulder for support as they laboriously descended the stairs, followed by the doctor.

In the street an empty wagon with a team of horses waited by the door. Gwyn boosted Emlyn into the seat beside the driver, and Gwyn swung up next to him.

As they pulled away, Oesterling waved. "See you tomorrow. And keep off that leg."

"Thanks again," yelled Gwyn as they rattled off down the Avenue.

At the house, Gwyn jumped down and took out his lunch pail before reaching for Emlyn. The driver came around, and together he and Gwyn hoisted Emlyn down onto the street.

The door flew open, and Eirwen, wearing an apron and shawl, rushed out. Behind her, were Dilys, and Thomas, carrying David. "Where were you two?" she asked. "I was so worried."

"We're O.K.," assured Gwyn. "And," he added with a grin, "nobody is drunk."

Eirwen did not return the smile.

"Where have you been?" she asked, peering into the dark street.

"At Dr. Oesterling's," said Gwyn coming forward as Emlyn leaned heavily on him.

"Oh, no. Uncle Em!" cried Thomas, lugging David to the front steps. Dilys started to cry, then David.

"Please, I'm fine," rasped Emlyn.

A woman, who seemed to come out of nowhere, appeared by the wagon. She glanced down at Emlyn's leg. "Lordy, what's happened?"

"A mishap at work, Mrs. Buckman," answered Gwyn.

"We need to get him inside," Eirwen said brusquely, brushing past the woman.

"Can I help?" the woman asked.

Emlyn glanced over at her and saw she was quite disheveled and had a large bruise on the side of her face

"We can manage, thank you," said Gwyn, pulling Emlyn forward.

The whole family bustled around Emlyn, helping him into the house and onto a chair in the kitchen. The woman followed them onto the porch, but Eirwen closed the door before she could come in.

Gwyn set another chair in front of Emlyn so he could prop up his left leg.

Sitting in the warmth by the cook stove, Emlyn handed back Gwyn's jacket, and shrugged his own onto the back of his chair. At last he had stopped shivering.

"Who was that woman in the street?" he asked. "She looked like she needed help more than I did."

"Could be," replied Gwyn. "That's Addie Buckman, the woman who came up to us on the Avenue yesterday. She and her family live at the end of the next block. Her husband Roy—known as Bucky— is a serious drunk and bully. I got to know him when I worked in the 33-inch mill."

"Yeah, their kid is in my class at school," said Thomas.

"I see," said Emlyn, who, at the mention of school, forgot about the Buckmans and recalled the image of Sarah Oesterling.

"Uncle Em, are you gonna meet me after school like you said?" Thomas asked.

Before Emlyn could answer, Gwyn said, "Now, Thomas, leave your uncle be. He has to work, and before he can go back to work, he has to get better. School will have to wait. Wash your hands and get ready for supper."

The family gathered at the table, and Gwyn said grace. Eirwen set out the food as Gwyn described the events that delayed their arrival home. Emlyn contributed little to the narrative, for he felt faint from fatigue.

"I couldn't imagine what was keeping you," declared Eirwen, passing a bowl of boiled potatoes. "Or rather, I could imagine all kinds of horrible things that could delay you. Thank God you're both in one piece."

When Emlyn nodded, the room spun a little.

"Yes, well, Emlyn here needs some rest, lots of it," declared Gwyn. "And since I have to go in again at four, I'll be turning in as well. I'll send word to the foreman in O.H. 2 that Emlyn won't be coming in tomorrow."

After dinner, Emlyn and Gwyn washed up with the children, and everyone except Eirwen was in bed by eight.

Emlyn lay in bed for over an hour, but sleep did not come right away. Utter exhaustion made the bed feel like it was shaking under him, and his sore, throbbing knee prohibited him from sleeping in any position but on his back.

At last, he slipped into a deep, dreamless sleep.

Wednesday, Nov. 25th

When Emlyn awakened, weak sunlight shone through the dirt-streaked windowpane across from his bed. He felt very hot and threw off the comforter. The cold air in the bedroom chilled him quickly.

He thought of the crew at the furnace in O.H. 2 and tried to imagine what they were doing, and what he'd be doing if he were there. He'd probably be pushing around a heavily laden wheelbarrow, sweating and straining.

His bones seemed to creak as he threw his left leg out of bed and stood shakily. He relieved himself in the chamber pot, pulled a blanket over his nightshirt, and hopped to the top of the stairs on his right leg. He sat on the top step and lowered himself down the entire length of the staircase. He was trying to decide what to do next when Eirwen appeared in the kitchen doorway with Dilys behind her.

"I thought I heard something," she said. "How are you feeling?"

"Ddim yn dda. *Not so good*."

Dilys peeked around her mother.

"Good morning, young lady," said Emlyn. "How's Little Bess today?"

Dilys smiled shyly and held the doll out for him to see.

"Are you OK?" Eirwen asked.

"I will be after I put on some clothes and get breakfast," he replied.

"Dilys, your uncle needs help. You keep an eye on Little Bess and David, alright?"

Dilys nodded and sat down next to the baby on his blanket.

Eirwen helped Emlyn into the kitchen, where he washed off the remaining mill soot and put on a clean shirt and trousers, topping them with a gray sweater his mother had knitted. He started to shiver, so Eirwen fetched an afghan to put over his shoulders.

She held a hand to his forehead. "You seem rather warm to me. You need to drink lots of tea to flush away the fever," she said, scalding the teapot.

He sat in the chair nearest the stove eating the breakfast of biscuits, stewed fruit and bacon that Eirwen set before him. He ate slowly, washing the food down with great gulps of sweet, milky tea.

"It's too bad you're laid up," she said, "but at least we get to spend time together."

"Maybe I'll be well enough to go back tomorrow or Friday."

Eirwen frowned. "Not very likely, I should think. You need to mend before you go back. Working in the mill is hard even on healthy and fit men. It takes time to get accustomed to."

Emlyn sighed. "You're right there. But I'd like to get established and start making money to pay back you and Gwyn. I can imagine what some of the other workers are thinking when I'm out after only two days on the job." The image of Virgil's smirking face popped into mind.

"Don't mind those fellows. They know what it's like to start in the mill. You weren't seriously injured, and that's the most important thing."

Eirwen glanced over at Dilys, who was involved in playing with David.

"By the way," said Eirwen, lowering her voice, "I want to warn you about the woman who was in the street last night. That Mrs. Buckman is someone you should be in no hurry to meet." She refilled his teacup and added milk and sugar.

"Why is that?"

"I do feel sorry for her because her husband beats her when he's drinking—which is most of the time," she said, handing him the cup, "but then she makes it worse by acting like a trollop.

There was a big row between her and Mrs. Sawyer, the neighbor woman behind us, when Mrs. Sawyer discovered she was meeting Mr. Sawyer after work.

Gwyn says she has apparently taken an interest in you."

"Lucky me. That's all I need, to be popular with the ladies," he said, his mouth half-full of biscuit. He thought of his two encounters with Sarah Oesterling and blushed. Yes, he was quite the ladies' man.

He swallowed, drained the last of the tea from the big white cup and set it down.

"Maybe this would be a good time for me to write Mam and Arthur," he said. " I want to let them know I've arrived safely."

"Do you want to enclose a few pages in the letter I'm sending?"

"Definitely not. Tad would see it, and there'd be hell to pay." He smiled. "So to speak."

"How will you manage to send letters, then?"

"Arthur and I have arranged that I'll send any letters to him, and he'll pass them on to Mam."

"Da iawn. *That's good*. They will love to hear from you, I know. Come, let's move you into the front room. I'll make a fire, and you will be very snug there."

She helped him to his feet and to the sofa in the parlor. He put his legs up, and she propped him up with pillows and tucked the afghan around him. She took some paper, a pen, and an inkwell from the desk and placed them on the side table. He closed his eyes, thinking about what to say to his mother. By the time Eirwen had started a fire in the grate, he had dozed off.

—•••—

William Oesterling pulled up the collar of his long riding coat as fitful gusts of wind blew off the river to the north. As his horse Figaro walked on the rutted road alongside Streets Run, his breath emerged in wispy puffs.

Cerberus trotted ahead, his thick black coat ruffled by the wind. The sky was dark and troubled, presaging rain.

After stopping to pay several home-calls in Homestead, Oesterling had ridden out to Hays to see a patient who had been scalded last week. The handle of the cooking pot the woman was lifting had snapped, spilling its contents onto her right hand and forearm. Still in severe pain from the burn, the woman had to cope with caring for an infant and three young children. It was going to be a difficult recovery.

Dead leaves blew about the horse's legs as they trotted into the outskirts of Homestead. The doctor liked doing house calls on horseback, even if meant lugging about his medical supplies in saddlebags. Most doctors who went out of town on calls did so in buggies or other small conveyances, but he preferred to ride.

Dr. Baker teased him that he was trying to bring the Wild West to Western Pennsylvania, but Oesterling didn't mind. He'd never been west of Cincinnati, where one of his sisters lived, and he had no urge to go beyond there. He'd seen enough.

He had always loved to ride. During the summers of his childhood, he'd stay with his paternal grandparents on their Long Island farm. He would ride the pony—and later—horses all around the area. On afternoons sometimes he'd take a ride to the ocean shore, where he'd give the horse his head, letting him run flat-out on the open beach.

His love of riding led to his service as a cavalry doctor during the Civil War. Oesterling was finishing his studies at Bellevue Medical College in New York when the war started. Eager to serve the Union cause, and also get some experience as a surgeon, upon graduation, he had joined up and was assigned to serve under Brigadier General Henry Baxter.

Oesterling had acquired plenty of experience, but this experience put the damper on his enthusiasm for military service. The horrors of the battle at Gettysburg, Pennsylvania, in July of 1863 haunted him still. During and after the artillery barrage on Cemetery Ridge, he and other doctors had worked 'round the clock on the incoming rush of broken bodies that never seemed to end. As the hours ticked by, he had worked as in a trance, mechanically hacking and sawing and cutting, dazed at the proliferating mounds of flesh and bone.

Afterwards, he and two other officers had walked up to the Ridge. There, the carnage was appalling: carcasses of horses, whole and partial, were strewn everywhere. Animals, men, caissons, guns, supply wagons, and other equipment, all blown to hell. Recalling the stench of the battlefield in the summer heat, he began to feel queasy.

The war had forced him to suspend emotions, to detach himself from the present. It had taken him nearly a decade of civilian practice to begin to allow himself to feel anything about those he treated. His marriage to Margaret after the war and the births of their two daughters had eventually thawed the numbness inside him.

He pulled his muffler closer around his neck. He forced his thoughts to Emlyn Phillips, his new patient. What an odd young man. Oesterling could not for the life of him understand how someone could throw aside years of study and go to work in the mill, and to come all this way to do it. It made no sense. And then there was this craziness about not setting foot inside a church.

Perhaps this Phillips fellow was a bit off. Sarah seemed to think so. When he'd told her about Emlyn's visit to the office, she had remarked about his fall in front of the church on Sunday, an event she'd witnessed from the door. He seemed such a nervous fellow, the opposite of his calm, steady sister.

Well, whatever the case, it was no business of theirs. He just needed to check the condition of his patient.

•••

Inside the house, on the sofa, Emlyn was dreaming of his grandparents' farmhouse in Wales. A tapping on the front windowpane awakened him. Groggily, he looked in the direction of the sound.

Through the dusty glass he made out the figure of a woman, shading her eyes with one hand, peering into the house. She was beckoning to him and pointing to the door. Why didn't she knock?

"Eirwen," he shouted, "someone's on the porch."

Eirwen, carrying David, came into the room. "What is it?" she asked. Emlyn pointed to the window.

"Myn cythraul i! *The devil!*" muttered Eirwen. "It's Addie Buckman."

"What could she want?" asked Emlyn.

In reply, Eirwen rolled her eyes.

"Gad hon i fi. *You let me handle this*," she said, going to the door and opening it.

Mrs. Buckman disappeared from the window and appeared at the door.

"Hello, Mrs. Jones," she said sweetly, trying to see around her.

"Yes?" asked Eirwen coldly.

Emlyn could see the woman's face over Eirwen's shoulder, and he was shocked at how haggard she looked. Her dishwater blond hair was pulled back in a knot from which a number of greasy strands had escaped. In the daylight the dark bruise on her left cheek was even more obvious. Her gaunt face was creased with deep lines. He couldn't even begin to guess her age—30? 40?

"I happened to be passing by and thought I'd stop to see how you'ns are doing," she said. "We have this here cane that Roy got when he hurt his foot."

She held up the cane. "I reckoned your brother could use it."

"There's no need for the cane, thank you. He's very tired and needs to rest."

"That's too bad to be hurt in the mill so soon."

Eirwen shifted David to her other hip.

"Yes . . . well, please excuse me, but he mustn't be disturbed, and I should be getting back to my work."

"Perhaps later, I could stop . . ."

"Thank you. Good day," said Eirwen, closing the door firmly.

"O'r Mawredd! *Lord, help us*," she said, leaning back against the door. "I can't believe she's trying to give you her husband's cane. If that hussy comes back, I'll completely lose my patience."

Rocking David roughly in her arms, Eirwen stood with her back to the door, scowling at nothing in particular.

Oesterling dismounted the big red roan gelding in front of the Joneses' house. He patted the neck of the horse as he secured the reins to a post and took the medical bag from its saddle compartment.

As he came toward the porch, he saw a woman turn from the door of the house and walk quickly down the front steps and away. She kept her head down and did not speak, but he thought he recognized her as one of Dr. Baker's patients.

Cerberus at his heels, he came to the door and knocked. Almost immediately, the door flew open, making him step back in surprise.

"Oh!" exclaimed Eirwen, holding the door in one hand and the baby in the other.

"Hello, Eirwen," said the doctor tentatively. "Were you expecting someone else? I've come by to call on your brother."

"Yes, of course," said Eirwen, glancing back and forth out the door. "Someone has just left, you see."

"Ah," said the doctor. "I saw her as I rode up. A Mrs. Buckley, I believe."

He remembered treating her for a broken arm when Dr. Baker was out of town. She had said she'd fallen. Later, Dr. Baker had said that her husband knocking her around had probably caused the injury.

"It's Buck*man*," corrected Eirwen, "but no matter. Do come in, Doctor."

"Thank you," said Oesterling, removing his hat. He turned to Cerberus.

"Wait," he ordered the dog, which obediently lay beside the door. He was about to step inside when he noticed a gnarled wooden cane propped next to the door.

"Did you leave this outside?" he asked.

Eirwen glared at it, apparently annoyed by its presence.

"No. Mrs. Buckman forgot it. I'll take it."

She seized it and hung it on a peg inside the door. She took the doctor's riding coat and laid it on Gwyn's overstuffed armchair.

"If you need me, I'll be in the kitchen," she said as she carried David from the room.

"Hello, Doctor," Emlyn said. He was sitting on the sofa, a thick afghan around his legs. He glanced at the doctor, then at the door.

"How do you feel today?" asked Oesterling, setting down his medical bag and pulling up a chair near the sofa.

"Much better than last night," he replied weakly.

"That's good. Let's see how the knee's doing."

Emlyn set aside the afghan and slipped off his trousers. Oesterling carefully removed the bandage and looked closely at the knee.

"Hmm, the swelling is down by at least half. That's encouraging. How is the pain?"

"It hurts to put weight on the leg," said Emlyn. "Otherwise, the pain isn't bad."

The doctor dabbed on more tincture of iodine and applied a clean bandage. "You'll probably be ready to start work again Monday."

"I hate getting off on such a false start here," Emlyn said, hitching up his trousers. "Nothing has gone as I imagined it would."

"That's not surprising," replied the doctor. "Immigrating to a new country thousands of miles from home is a very big step."

He handed Emlyn the afghan. "When we moved here from Philadelphia a decade ago, we—that is, my family and I—had to make many adjustments. But we had each other, and we had the church congregation to help us through it."

Emlyn silently stared at the floor. In the kitchen the baby began to cry.

Oh no, thought the doctor; he had blundered into the taboo subject of the church.

"So it takes time, but everything works out," he hastily added.

Emlyn nodded uncertainly.

"I hope so."

Oesterling stood and began gathering up his things. Eirwen came into the room carrying a sobbing David. She rubbed a red mark on his forehead.

"Do I have another patient to see?" asked Oesterling, smiling at David.

"The baby bumped his head trying to creep under a chair," she replied.

"There, there," she whispered soothingly, rocking to and fro.

Emlyn took David into his arms and bounced him on his good leg while Eirwen and Dr. Oesterling discussed his treatment. Dilys had climbed up onto the rocker with Little Bess. She was having a hard time rocking because her feet did not reach to the floor.

A thumping noise sounded at the front door. Emlyn stopped bouncing the baby. Please, he thought, don't let it be that strange woman again.

Eirwen went to the door and opened it. A gust of cold air rushed past, chilling Emlyn. A moment later, Thomas and the doctor's black dog bounded into the room, followed by a tall woman in a dark green coat and bonnet, red-gold hair protruding from beneath it.

He almost let David slip from his grasp. The woman was Sarah Oesterling.

A commotion followed as Thomas and Cerberus circled the room twice.

"Please!" shouted Eirwen over the clamor.

Thomas ran over to the sofa. "Are you OK, Uncle Em?"

"Yes, fine. But what's all this? " replied Emlyn, propping David in the corner of the sofa.

"Thomas, you and Cerberus behave yourselves now. No getting the dog all riled up," said Eirwen.

Thomas plopped down on the floor next to the sofa, and the dog sat down between the boy and the doctor, his tail flopping against the floor.

Oesterling stood holding his medical bag, unsure of what to do next.

"Good boy, Cerby," said Thomas, hugging the dog's neck.

"Let me take your coat," said Eirwen to Sarah.

Emlyn got up enough courage to look at the younger woman.

She was quite tall—an imposing figure, really. Her cheeks were red from the cold, her eyes shining from the biting wind. For some reason, she looked different than she did when they had met on the street. But then, he was not paying attention that time.

"No, thanks," Sarah replied breathlessly. "I'll only stay a moment. Please excuse me for barging in like this. Thomas wanted me to come by to meet his uncle today, but I also wanted to talk to you, Eirwen."

She glanced, smiling, at Oesterling.

"You see, Papa has agreed that we should have a Twelfth Night party this year, as we used to."

"That's good news indeed," said Eirwen. "They are always such fun."

Twelfth Night? Sir Toby Belch? Fun? As long as it wasn't a comedy of errors, such as his first week in Homestead had been.

Eirwen came behind the sofa and put her hands on Emlyn's shoulders.

"These occasions have been memorable. When the Oesterlings put on parlor concerts, it's always a grand time. Perhaps Emlyn could tune up his violin for the occasion."

He smiled weakly. If he was in one piece when January rolled around, he thought, maybe he could.

"By the way, Emlyn," said Eirwen, "may I introduce Sarah Oesterling—as you have undoubtedly gathered."

"And this," she said, squeezing Emlyn's shoulders, "is my brother, Emlyn Phillips."

Emlyn struggled to get to his feet. Sarah watched him as if she expected him to fall on his face again.

"Please, don't get up," she said after a moment, moving toward him and extending a gloved hand.

"Pleased to meet you," said Sarah, unsmiling.

"I'm pleased to meet you as well," replied Emlyn, hoping she would not mention their first meeting.

"I hope you'll be feeling better soon," said Sarah politely, backing away.

"Thank you," said Emlyn.

"He's doing quite well," interjected Oesterling, picking up his overcoat from the chair. "Now, I must be getting back to my rounds."

"I must go, too," said Sarah. "Maybe we can talk sometime this weekend, Eirwen, about the music for the party."

"Alright. Emlyn and I will try to come up with some ideas for music by then," replied Eirwen.

As the doctor put on his coat, Thomas jumped up and ran to the window, followed by Cerberus.

"Dr. Oesterling, is that your horse out there?" asked Thomas.

"Yes, that's Figaro."

"Gee, swell. How come you never bring him to church?"

"He's a doctoring horse, not a church-going horse. I ride him only when I'm going out of town."

"Oh," said Thomas, disappointed.

"Did you know that we have another horse as well, a horse Sarah rides?"

"Another horse?" asked Thomas in awe. "What's his name?"

"*Her* name," said Sarah. "It's a black mare called 'Dee.'"

Eirwen and Emlyn laughed. Thomas looked at them quizzically.

" 'Dee' is the Welsh word for black," explained Eirwen.

"We share the horses with Dr. Baker and his family," said

Oesterling. "That way the animals get enough exercise, and we pay only half the upkeep,"

"Emlyn, our brother Arthur, and I used to ride the ponies on our grandfather's farm. We all loved it so," said Eirwen, gazing wistfully out of the window at the doctor's horse. "We'd spend all day riding along the brook and up into the hills."

Sarah looked at Eirwen as if she had a sudden thought. "You must come riding with me sometime!" she exclaimed.

Eirwen's smile faded. "Oh, I shouldn't think so—Not that I wouldn't like to. There's no time, and besides, I'm many years out of practice. I'd probably go tumbling off straightaway."

"But," she added, "perhaps Emlyn would like to."

Emlyn, who had been paying more attention to stopping David's attempts to crawl off the sofa than to the conversation, glanced up. Everyone was looking at him.

"What would I like to do?"

"Go horseback riding," said Eirwen.

"Oh no," he said, taken aback. "I haven't done that for a few years, not since the farm was sold."

He thought back to Grandpa Davies's funeral, the auction. Eirwen had missed that sad episode.

"Horseback riding! Gee, Uncle Em, you're so lucky," exclaimed Thomas.

Sarah gazed at him, apparently trying to assess if Emlyn could manage to stay on a horse.

Emlyn sat there, overwhelmed at the thought. He envisioned himself raising his left foot to the stirrup, pulling himself into the saddle and winced.

"I couldn't even get onto the horse with my knee in its present condition."

"There's plenty of time to go riding," observed Oesterling. "Recovery can't be rushed."

Sarah nodded in agreement.

"That's true," agreed Eirwen. "But, Emlyn, wouldn't you like to ride—that is, when you feel better?"

"I guess so," Emlyn said. "I mean, yes, although I'm hardly in shape to do so at the moment."

He could see himself making a fool of himself yet again in front of the Oesterlings.

"Perhaps later, when your knee improves," ventured Sarah.

"He should take it easy for a couple of weeks," reiterated the doctor.

Turning to Emlyn, he added, "Come by during office hours Saturday and I'll take another look at your leg."

Emlyn rubbed his left knee gently.

"I'll come by Saturday morning."

"Good," smiled the doctor. "Now, this time I really must be going."

"And I, too," said Sarah. "We don't want to exhaust the patient." She looked him straight in the eye.

Emlyn could feel the blood flooding into his face.

"Yes," he said, looking away. "Let's wait and see."

East Liberty, Pittsburgh.
Friday, November 27th

In the gathering darkness, Karl Bernhard trod wearily up the steps to the porch of the small house on Mayflower Street where he lived with his wife and six children. He stood for a moment looking at the door, trying to muster his courage. He pushed it open.

In the parlor the two youngest boys were building a tower out of bits of scrap wood. He greeted them and went through to the kitchen. There his wife Susanna was draining the water from a pot of potatoes, aided by their oldest girl, Kate, 15.

"Hey, Papa," said Kate, glancing over at him, smiling. Her smile faded as she saw the expression on his face. "What's wrong, Papi?" she asked.

Susanna looked up. "Good Lord, Karl!" she exclaimed. "What's happened?" She hastily set down the pot and pulled out a chair, gesturing for him to sit.

He lowered himself into the chair. "I've lost my job," he said, his voice almost a whisper.

"They didn't fire you!" said Susanna, instantly indignant.

"No, no," Karl replied dejectedly. "It's that orders for machine parts have slowed down almost to nothing this fall. The company is shutting down production for a few months, maybe for good."

"That's awful," said Kate. "But you'll find something else, Papa. You always do." She bent over the chair and gave him a hug.

"I'm not getting any younger," said Karl. "It's hard to compete with all the young men out there looking for work. It took nearly three months to find this job, and it didn't last a year."

At that moment, the back door flew open and the two oldest sons, George, 18, and John, 16, burst into the kitchen. They stopped short when they saw the other family members gathered around the table.

"Papa's lost his job," Kate said.

"No!" said the two brothers together.

George came over and took a seat next to his father. "I'm real sorry to hear that, Pa. Don't worry. John and me have our jobs."

"Yeah, Pa," said John. "Our pay will help while you look for work."

"You're good boys," said Susanna. "What would we do without you?"

"Ja, that's the truth," said Karl, nervously smoothing his moustache. He looked at his family gathered around the table and managed a faint smile.

Susanna directed the family to get ready for dinner, and fell to mashing the potatoes violently, taking out her anxiety on the food.

As he watched Kate set the table, fear crept upon Karl. Every day he had seen the unemployed walking the streets, desperation written on their faces. Now, with winter closing in, he was once again among their ranks.

Homestead. Saturday, November 28th

Emlyn set down his teacup and glanced at the kitchen clock. Nearly ten, and he wasn't dressed yet. Emlyn had spent the past two days in bed or on the sofa with his left leg up. Eirwen helped him clean the wound and change bandages, and his knee began to mend. He passed the time by reading and writing, knowing that he would have scant time for these after he resumed work. He stayed up later and rose later.

This morning, he had gotten up as Eirwen was preparing to leave the house.

What was going to happen to him when he had to rise in the middle of the night and go back to work? He dreaded the thought.

Gwyn had left for work early, as usual, when Emlyn was sleeping. Thomas had run off to play with his friends, and Eirwen had gone shopping on the Avenue with the two younger children.

The house was quiet, although he could hear the muffled racket from the mill echoing up from the river and against the hills. Emlyn closed the copy of Thomas Henry Huxley's *Science and Education* that his friend Gareth Morgan had given him after they had had an argument about the value of science in the curriculum.

Emlyn's resistance to Huxley's message was greatly diminished when he learned that Huxley had not only expounded on the value of a scientific education, but also on the application of scientific principles to religion.

Emlyn grimaced as he recalled that last meeting in his father's study. It was yet another example of his father's closed-mindedness. Tad wouldn't even read books whose authors he knew he'd disagree with.

Emlyn knew the Bible almost by heart, especially the New Testament, and so did his father. The difference, thought Emlyn, was that that was all his father knew—the Bible itself (in Hebrew, Welsh, and English) and Calvinist theology.

Emlyn heaved a long sigh and glanced at the clock again. He had told Eirwen he was going to Dr. Oesterling's office, and that he could manage on his own. Initially, he had decided not to go, and tell her he couldn't make it. Now he was having second thoughts. He didn't like lying to Eirwen. She might get worried, and he might be trapped into telling even bigger lies in explanation. He decided to go.

He finished dressing, and went to the front door to get his jacket. As he took it down, he saw a cane hooked over the peg. His knee still bothered him when he walked. Maybe this would help him navigate over rickety sidewalk planks and around potholes in the street.

Cane in hand, he pulled down his cap, opened the door, and started off toward Eighth Avenue.

He passed the Amity Street station, the site of his entry into town, and saw a small cluster of men in cheap dark suits waiting on the platform, large valises set by their sides. Probably drummers—traveling salesmen—heading home for Sunday, Emlyn conjectured.

The hotel where he had rested on a bench Sunday stood a short distance down the tracks. Workers were preparing for its grand opening the next weekend. Men were carrying in furniture, and women were cleaning windows. Two men were testing the electrical lights on the porch entrance.

Gwyn had told him about the recent electrification of Homestead, first the mill, then the town. New houses were being built with electrical service, although some people insisted on dual-fuel fixtures, fearing that electricity would be unreliable. Unreliable or not, Emlyn liked the electrical lights. They did not flicker, hiss, or give off fumes, as did gaslights.

On the Avenue, people were bustling about on various errands. It was payday at the mill. Women were coming and going in the shops on the Avenue, the number of parcels in their arms growing with each stop. The bars were much busier than they were the first, and perhaps only time that he would visit one here.

Emlyn made his way carefully through the throngs on the sidewalk. He held the cane in front of him with his right hand, a guard against something or someone hitting his knee. After walking nearly six blocks, he began to feel confident that his leg would be fine when he went back to work. It was tough work, he knew, but he was young—young and determined to make up for time and wages lost.

He came to a place where the sidewalk was partially blocked by two workingmen, who were looking at a large man wearing a dusty bowler. He was gesticulating and talking; the other men were laughing. As he approached them, it dawned on Emlyn that the men were standing outside the pub where Gwyn and Jim Duncan had taken him.

He made for an opening between the building and the group of men, but as Emlyn got behind him, the large man suddenly threw out both arms and stepped backwards. He bumped into Emlyn and knocked him toward the entrance of the bar.

Clutching at the doorjamb, Emlyn dropped the cane.

"Whoa, Bucky," laughed one of the other men. "'Looks like you've had enough for today."

"Hell, no," roared the large man, righting himself unsteadily. "I'm just a-startin'."

He turned to Emlyn.

"Sorry there, bub," he slurred. "Here, let me pick up your stick."

"That's quite alright," said Emlyn. "I can get it."

The man was already leaning over to get the cane. One of his buddies grabbed him to keep him from falling over.

The man picked up the cane and was about to hand it to Emlyn, when he stopped dead. The smile on his face faded as he stared at the cane.

"What the fuck?" He blinked as he gazed at the cane. "These are my initials—'R.B.' I carved them into this here cane myself."

He turned to Emlyn, his voice a snarl. "How did you get my goddamn cane?"

The blood drained from Emlyn's face.

Abruptly, still holding the cane with his right hand, the man seized the shoulder of Emlyn's jacket with his left. He pulled Emlyn's face to his.

Emlyn felt the man's hot breath, smelled the heavy fumes of alcohol. The man was as tall as Emlyn, but outweighed him by a good fifty pounds.

"How did you get this cane?" he demanded, punctuating

each word with a heavy tap of the cane on the boardwalk.

"I . . . I don't know," stammered Emlyn. "I mean, it was in the house."

The other men moved in on either side of the big man.

"That sounds real likely, don't it, Buck?" sneered one man, a skinny blond.

The big man glowered at Emlyn. "That bitch gave it to you, didn't she?"

Emlyn swallowed and tried to step backwards. "You mean your wife?" he asked in a faint voice.

"Yeaaah!" bellowed the man. "My bitch of a wife."

"Really, I'm not acquainted with your wife."

The men hooted.

"Oh la dee da. He ain't acquainted with the bitch," Buckman mocked, looking around at his comrades.

He raised the cane to Emlyn's eye level.

"Who the hell are you, you goddamn Limey?" he growled.

Before Emlyn could answer, Buckman pulled back the cane and swung it hard at Emlyn's face. Emlyn ducked, and the cane struck a saloon window, shattering it. Buckman lost his balance and fell heavily against the doorjamb.

Emlyn, in a crouch, looked desperately for an escape route. Buckman was staring at a gash in his hand from the broken glass. Keeping his eyes on Buckman, Emlyn, legs shaking, started backing into the saloon.

"You Limey bastard!" bellowed Buckman. "Now look what you've done!"

Buckman lurched toward Emlyn when a figure stepped deftly between the two.

"Hold on there, Bucky," said the man in a cool drawl. "He ain't no Limey."

"He sure sounds like a Limey," retorted Buckman, brought

up short. "Anyway, I don't care what he is. He's been messin' around with my wife."

Virgil stepped back and put his hand on Emlyn's shoulder. "This here's Em-Lyn, and he's a Taffy, not a Limey. Since he arrived here only last week, I doubt if he even has had time to make the acquaintance of Mrs. B."

Buckman blinked at Virgil in a whisky fog, dumbfounded.

"You got your cane back, right?" asked Virgil.

"Yeah, but it's damned strange that..."

"You got your cane back. That's the most important thing, ain't it?"

Virgil, grinning, pressed forward.

"I'm sorry," stammered Emlyn. "If I had known it was yours, I..."

"Shut the hell up," hissed Virgil, as he seized Emlyn's arm and yanked him to the left of Buckman. "Let's go."

Virgil pulled Emlyn past Buckman and the other men, out onto the sidewalk.

Behind them, Emlyn heard a voice from inside the bar yell, "Hey, who busted this window?"

"Don't look back," said Virgil, as he drew Emlyn into the street, behind a large brewery wagon that was parked in front of the saloon.

"It's gonna be ugly now," whispered Virgil, peering around the back corner of the wagon. Angry male voices shouted from the opposite side.

"Yep. Now Bucky and the bartender are gonna have it out over the broken window." Virgil stepped back. "Buckman's such a brute." He shook his head. "Damn fool drunks."

He turned to Emlyn, who was still shaking. "Speaking of damn fools—How *did* you get that cane, anyhow?"

"I'm not sure," said Emlyn. "I think maybe the Buckman

woman left it at the house. She was trying to come inside, but my sister stopped her."

Virgil nodded. "Your sister done right. That woman is bad news, very bad news. Almost as bad as her husband. Come on. Let's get out of here. Which way you headin'?"

Emlyn nodded in the direction of Oesterling's office, and they walked off, blending into the passersby on the sidewalk.

"Thank you very much for saving my hide," said Emlyn.

"Tain't nothin'. I just didn't want to see you so bunged up you wouldn't be able to come to work Monday. And I'd be stuck with Hunky Joe—and nobody to tell what's up. By the way, how's the leg?"

"Much better, thanks. I'm heading to Dr. Oesterling's office to have him check it."

"OK. I'll see you that far, to make sure you don't get into no more trouble."

Emlyn smiled. "Thanks again."

Virgil grunted.

They parted at the stairs to the doctor's office. Emlyn offered his hand to shake, but Virgil just walked away, hands in pockets, whistling.

Peculiar fellow, thought Emlyn as he trudged up the stairs.

II.

The problem of our age is the proper administration of wealth, so that the ties of brotherhood may still bind together the rich and poor in harmonious relationship.

—John Ruskin, *Wealth* (1889)

Saturday, November 28th

"I'm ready to go, Papa," said Sarah, pulling up the hood on her cape.

Oesterling opened the front door of the house and was immediately knocked back by a strong gust of wind. Dead leaves, bits of paper, and dirt swirled around as he and Sarah went onto the porch. Sarah pulled her hood tightly about her throat and went down the steps, her kidskin shoes clicking on the bricks as she descended. At the bottom, Junius from the livery stable was waiting with an enclosed buggy.

"Good evening, Miss Sarah, Dr. Oesterling," smiled the young black man, touching his cap.

"Good evening, Junius," replied Oesterling, helping Sarah into the back seat of the buggy. Oesterling climbed in behind her, and they started off for the ferry landing.

"The weather has turned quite nasty," Sarah observed, peering around the driver. "It would be no fun riding tomorrow. I can't say I'm eager to go riding with Eirwen's brother. Such a strange fellow."

Oesterling nodded. Emlyn's knee, while much improved, was still red and swollen when the doctor had examined him that morning. For some reason, the young man had seemed relieved when he had suggested that Emlyn postpone the horseback excursion.

"How did you and Eirwen get on this afternoon with the planning of the Twelfth Night party?" he asked Sarah.

"I think it's going to be good. Of course, Eirwen will sing, and I will play something. We're also going to ask Melanie and Jack Carstens to sing a duet, and Eirwen is going to try to get Emlyn to play." She rolled her eyes. "I talked to Mrs. Sproule, too, and she is enthusiastic about planning a menu and getting invitations ready. Thanks so much, Papa, for letting me go ahead with the party."

Sarah gave his arm a quick squeeze.

Oesterling smiled. "I'm happy you're happy. I'm looking forward to it as well."

He leaned back in the seat. That was actually a bit of lie. Since Margaret's death, he had dreaded the holidays. The happy memories of past celebrations made the present ones, by contrast, seem sad. Still, he knew it was time to make the effort to set aside his mourning, if not for his own sake, for Sarah's.

As they passed the Amity Street station, he noted that many young workers had congregated for their customary Saturday night trip into Pittsburgh, where they would chase women, get drunk, and generally raise hell. Many of them would blow their entire week's pay (which they had received only hours before) in this weekly effort to compensate for the dreariness of the other six days of work. Groups of young townswomen, couples, and a few families were on the platform as well, many of them headed into the city to take in some music hall entertainment or melodrama.

At the river landing, Junius drove the buggy onto the ferry, and they crossed over to Brown's Hill. A half hour later they were pulling up to the porte cochiere of Carrie's house in Point Breeze.

In August, Carrie and her husband Oliver Thornton Strong had leased the house from one of the Carnegie Steel Company's engineers who had moved to New York. For Carrie, moving to Point Breeze had been the second great event of her life—the first, of course, being her marriage to Oliver, an up-and-coming attorney and legal adviser to Henry Clay Frick, Carnegie's partner.

Carrie and Oliver had met nearly six years earlier, when he was starting with the company in Homestead. Oliver's attention was instantly drawn to the dark-haired, petite Carrie, who recognized a good match when she saw it. They were married a year later, and a year after that, Oliver was promoted to a position at the company's office in downtown Pittsburgh. He and Carrie were only too glad to leave Homestead behind.

Point Breeze, a new, prestigious residential area of the city, was the place where Frick himself had built his impressive new estate, Clayton. The Strongs' house, a two-and-a-half story brick Queen Anne, was modest by Point Breeze standards, but quite luxurious by Homestead's.

As he alighted from the buggy, Oesterling peered into the softly glowing rooms on the first floor. He liked going to dinner parties in Homestead, but at Carrie's, he felt self-conscious. Yes, there was some social status to being a physician, but he felt uncomfortable among the lawyers, company men, society doctors, and their wives that he encountered at these gatherings.

Of course, no one ever said anything, but he caught the message in the subtle sideways glances at his ten-year-old tuxedo and worn dress shoes. He knew that many of Carrie's guests thought of him and Sarah as the poor relatives that had to be included.

Sarah, on the other hand, seemed oblivious to the difference in social rank. Or perhaps, thought the doctor, she was too proud to admit to any discomfort. She always wore the same dress to every party of the social season, the dress that Margaret, before her sudden death three years ago, had hired a dressmaker in Pittsburgh to stitch for her. Margaret justified the expense by saying she wanted Sarah to be 'presentable' at Carrie's social events.

Oesterling never tired of seeing Sarah in the dress, not only because of its association with Margaret, but because he liked the dress itself. The tightly fitting bodice and sleeves were of emerald green velvet; the square neckline was trimmed in French lace. The skirt was of gray-green watermarked silk, and in the fashion of the late 1880s, it had a velvet bustle.

As Sarah handed her cloak to the maid, Oesterling noticed that she was wearing Margaret's pearl necklace and drop earrings.

Oesterling felt a hand on his sleeve.

"Papa! Sarah dear! You're here at last." Carrie slipped one arm around his waist and kissed his cheek.

"You're the last ones to arrive. I was beginning to worry."

"Forgive me," said Oesterling. "I was called out to set a worker's broken leg and. . . ."

"It doesn't matter. You're here now. Come and join the party."

"You're looking very fetching tonight," said the doctor, standing back to admire Carrie's elegant dress of deep crimson velvet with leg-o-mutton sleeves and a skirt of yellow-gold satin. Carrie beamed in reply.

"Oliver had this made for me to wear to the Fricks' party last month. I love it."

She held out her arms and whirled around so they could see the peplum in back.

"Quite lovely," said Oesterling. Carrie then took her father's arm with her left hand and Sarah's with her right, and swept them into the front parlor where the dozen or so guests were talking and sipping punch. Seeing them enter, Oliver excused himself from a conversation and came over to greet them.

"Welcome, welcome. How are you, Father?" he asked, shaking the doctor's hand. "And Sarah?" He pecked Sarah on the cheek, as Carrie went back to circulating with her guests.

They exchanged pleasantries for a few moments, when Oliver said abruptly to Oesterling, "Please excuse us. I want Sarah to meet someone," and led her away.

Oliver steered her across the room to a man in his late 20s. His dark auburn hair was parted in the middle and slicked back on the sides. His wire spectacles and thin mustache made his white skin seem even paler. Sarah was slightly taller than the man.

Standing by the entrance to the parlor, Oesterling looked around and saw one of the superintendents of the Homestead Works, Edwin Cross, and his wife Marian. The doctor went over and struck up a conversation with them.

"Do you know the fellow talking to Sarah?" the doctor asked Cross.

"That's Norton Montague, one of Potter's new hires, allegedly a financial wizard. He works for the comptroller," replied Cross. "He used to work in the company office downtown, which, I believe, is where Oliver met him."

"I see," said Oesterling, giving the young man the once-over. John A. Potter was the General Superintendent of the Homestead Works, and this was apparently a big jump up for the young man.

A few minutes later, a maid called them in for dinner.

At the long, polished table bedecked with fresh flowers in a low crystal bowl, Oesterling was seated between Mrs. Cross and a young Mrs. Parker—the second wife, apparently, of a lawyer who was about the doctor's age. Sarah sat across the table two seats down from Oesterling between Mr. Parker and Norton Montague.

During the first course, the doctor, Mrs. Cross and Mrs. Parker talked about the chilly weather, then about a performance in Pittsburgh of Gilbert and Sullivan's latest opera, *The Gondoliers*—which the younger woman had seen.

Mrs. Cross had recently returned from a shopping excursion to New York City, and she was full of stories of the magnificent mansions and elegant fashions she had seen on Fifth Avenue. Pittsburgh paled in comparison with Gotham, she said, and Homestead was a pathetic backwater.

When Oesterling pointed out that the way of life on Fifth Avenue was hardly representative of the way most New Yorkers lived, Marian Cross smiled at him condescendingly. Of course, she realized that, but what was wrong in admiring the fruits of Progress?

Nothing, rejoined Oesterling, as long as one kept things in perspective. "Have you seen *How the Other Half Lives*?" he asked.

The women exchanged uneasy glances at his mention of the title. The previous year, Danish immigrant and journalist Jacob Riis had shocked middle-class America with his graphic descriptions, accompanied by photos, of deplorable slum conditions on the Lower East Side of Manhattan.

Mrs. Parker had read it, she said, and was disturbed by it. Mrs. Cross replied that she had started it, but found it far too depressing to finish. Oesterling then asked Mrs. Cross what she thought of conditions in the poorest Homestead tenements.

She sat up very straight in her chair. "Edwin is very concerned for the workers, and makes every effort to keep them happy. However, I don't see any need to visit the stews where those filthy, drunken people live."

She looked directly at the doctor and smiled primly. "That's your job, isn't it, Dr. Oesterling? To tend to the sick, wherever they may be? And you must go where duty takes you."

She pointedly turned away and began a conversation with the man seated on her other side.

Smarting from the cut, Oesterling sat in silence for the rest of the dinner—a total of six courses served in the French style. At the end of the dinner, the seven men adjourned to the study for cigars and brandy, while the women went back to the parlor. Oesterling knew that Sarah hated this custom of separating the sexes. At least they wouldn't be staying much longer, as Sarah had to play for church the next day, and they had a long buggy ride back to Homestead.

In the study, while the brandies were being handed 'round, Oesterling had his usual tussle with his son-in-law. Oliver couldn't understand why Oesterling continued to abstain from alcohol now that Margaret was gone. Oliver acted as if the doctor's teetotaling was tantamount to a breach of hospitality.

"Now, Father," said Oliver. "What would a small drink hurt?"

Oesterling stubbornly persisted, finally taking the empty brandy snifter from Oliver and pouring water into it. Oliver threw up his hands in mock surrender.

Suddenly serious, Oliver bent his head towards the doctor's.

"I need to talk to you about a wonderful investment opportunity," Oliver said in a conspiratorial whisper. "I heard about it yesterday from a friend. I could get you in on the ground floor."

Oesterling looked up at Oliver. "I don't have any extra income for speculation."

"This isn't speculation. It's practically a sure thing," said Oliver. He straightened up.

Oesterling looked at him skeptically. Oliver always had some scheme or another that he was hoping to get rich by.

"We can talk about it later," Oliver said, patting Oesterling's shoulder.

Raising his brandy glass to Oesterling, he added, "Cheers!"

As a maid passed around a box of Cuban cigars, the talk turned to the ongoing wage dispute between the Carnegie Phipps Company and its workers. The late 1880s had seen three major confrontations between labor and the company, the most recent occurring in early 1889 at the Homestead mill.

Carnegie, determined to slash costs and raise profits, proposed reducing the workers' pay by 25%, and at the same refused to negotiate with the union collectively. The union had, of course, rejected the cut. Carnegie agreed to collective bargaining, and in the end, had accepted a three-year extension to the existing contract. In so doing, Carnegie allowed wages to be pegged to market conditions, the so-called 'sliding scale.'

"The company has made a tremendous investment in improvements to the plant," Edwin Cross said, clipping a cigar and lighting it. "In the three years since the strike, the company has made ongoing technological improvements: twenty-three additional open hearth furnaces, the armor plate press shop, the fitting shop, and the 40-inch blooming mill." He gestured with his cigar. "And don't forget the #2 Carrie Furnace and the expansion of the Bessemer converters to 10-ton capacity. It's ridiculous for the workers to think that because production has increased, their pay should keep going up. The company is making huge investments, not the workers."

A couple of the men nodded in agreement.

"That's why," Cross continued, "Mr. Carnegie has insisted that the men individually sign an agreement to work under the sliding scale. The Amalgamated has been complaining about this ever since. They don't like the implication that the company is making individual contracts. Nevertheless, Mr. Carnegie has made it perfectly clear: If they strike, he will close the plant."

"And rightly so," agreed Norton Montague. "The mill is company property, built with company capital. The workers wouldn't have jobs if it weren't for the company."

Osterling contemplated Montague with mild distaste. He seemed rather full of himself, but nevertheless cut an arresting figure with his intense dark eyes and ivory skin.

"Do you think the workers would seriously consider striking when the contract expires next summer?" asked John Woodruff, a company metallurgist.

"Well," said Oliver, turning to Oesterling, "you probably know the workers' mood better than the rest of us. What do you think?"

Oesterling swished the water around in his glass. "I can only guess. I'm more involved with patching up their bodies and treating their ailments than with their politics. However, I have heard that the Amalgamated men are very angry that the company is cutting them out of contract negotiations."

Oliver blew smoke into the air. "Let them be angry. They obviously don't understand the reality of the situation. Let them go out on strike. They'll soon learn the hard way."

Woodruff frowned. "You aren't implying that the company *wants* a strike, are you?"

"Of course not," replied Oliver, tapping ashes from the cigar. "Strikes are bad business. I'm only saying that if push comes to shove, the company will stand up for its rights."

"I know that Mr. Potter is committed to doing what's best for the company," added Montague. "If the company thrives, the workers thrive."

"That's true to a certain extent," Oesterling said, "but . . ."

Cross cut him off. "The workers don't seem to understand the extent of the company's investment. The Homestead Works is getting a structural mill next year, a facility that will produce steel beams for the construction of the new high-rise buildings such as those going up in Chicago."

"That shows Carnegie's usual insight," added Oliver. "Whenever we go to visit the family in Chicago, I'm amazed at the new buildings being constructed there, like the Montauk. Steel construction is the wave of the future."

"Definitely," agreed Montague. "I hear Chicago's Masonic Building, planned for construction next year, will be the tallest building in the world, taller than the New York World Building."

"Since the company is apparently making impressive profits on these innovations," interjected Oesterling irritably, "I don't understand why . . . "

The sentence was interrupted by a knock at the pocket doors. A maid slipped in, and whispered to Oesterling that Junius was waiting to take them back to Homestead.

In the hall, the maid held their coats. Carrie was chattering away, while Sarah was quiet and withdrawn. Oesterling noticed that when the sisters embraced at the door, Sarah held herself stiffly.

In the back of the buggy, Oesterling asked Sarah if anything was wrong. She shook her head and looked away.

He waited several minutes and asked her what she thought of Norton Montague.

Sarah gave a short laugh. "He's a big music lover. He had an opinion about everything from Vivaldi to Verdi. He did go on at length. I could hardly get in a word edgewise." She paused. "Actually, I think he's a bit lonely. He told me he grew up in Maryland. Both his parents were killed in a railroad accident years ago, and his only sister is living in California. He's staying at the company club in Munhall. All he does is go back and forth to work and his lodgings—except on weekends, when he goes into the city to take in a concert or play."

Looking out at the passing streetscape, she shook her head. "Carrie's up to her usual tricks. She feels sorry for me and wants to help me find a 'good catch' like she did."

"She means well," said Oesterling. "Now that Mother is gone, she feels that she should play a bigger role as the older sister."

"Well, she's *not* Mother," said Sarah heatedly. "It's quite irritating."

It was past midnight by the time they pulled up in front of the house.

"I wish the party hadn't gone so late," Sarah said, pulling off her cloak in the foyer. "I have to be at church by nine."

"Carrie's parties always are evening-long affairs, it seems," said Oesterling, tugging at his necktie. "At least we're only invited to two or three a year."

"That's one or two too many," said Sarah, her hand on the newel post of the staircase to the second floor.

Oesterling looked at her sharply. "I didn't realize you disliked the parties so much."

Sarah slumped, sitting on the bottom stairs. "They're so tedious, and Carrie seems to think she's a hostess rivaling Mrs. Cornelius Vanderbilt."

Oesterling sat on the stairs beside her. "You know that Carrie's always needed to feel important. Oliver and the house and the parties help her feel that way."

Sarah closed her eyes, and one tear squeezed out and ran down her cheek. "Do you know what has really upset me?"

Oesterling waited for her to continue.

"As we were coming into the hall to get the wraps, Carrie said she thinks my gown looks dated, and that I should get a new, fashionable one. She said she would give me one of hers, but it could never be made big enough to fit me."

Sarah smoothed the skirt with both hands. "After Mama had this dress made just for me!" She started to sob.

Oesterling took out his handkerchief and handed it to her. "That was silly of Carrie—although I don't think she wanted to hurt you. I think it's a very fine dress. I've always thought you look lovely in it."

He put his right arm around her shoulders and squeezed gently. "Carrie's views aside, would *you* like a new one?"

Blowing her nose into the handkerchief, she shook her head emphatically. "Definitely not. What need do I have for another fancy dinner gown?"

They sat there, Sarah softly weeping into the handkerchief. After a few minutes, she gathered her skirts and stood up.

"Papa, I'm so tired. I really need to get to bed. Would you please ring Mrs. Sproule to help me out of this dress?"

"Alright. I'll see you in the morning."

She touched his shoulder lightly as she started up the stairs. "Good night, Papa."

"Good night, Sarah. Sleep well."

Sunday, December 13th

On his second Sunday in Homestead, Emlyn had stayed at home when the rest of the family went to church. He wasn't going to risk another mishap with his knee or an encounter with Roy 'Bucky' Buckman.

He was grateful to have somehow muddled his way through the last two weeks of working at the mill. Now on the third Sunday, he was facing another danger: horseback riding with Sarah Oesterling.

Because of the condition of his knee and the attitude of Sarah Oesterling, he was having serious misgivings. Was she still upset about their first meeting? He thought it likely.

"I don't think I can pull up with my left knee."

At the entrance to Aaron Walker's livery stable on Fifth Avenue, Emlyn stood beside Figaro, his right hand resting on the horse's withers. Bridle in hand, Dr. Oesterling stood at Figaro's head, while Sarah, wearing a brown tweed jacket, was already mounted on Dee. Sarah wore thick leather gloves, and her hair was pulled up under a derby hat with a chinstrap. She patiently watched his struggles to get into the saddle.

"Will he dislike it if I try to mount from the right?" asked Emlyn.

"Probably not," replied the doctor. "I'll stay here and keep him calm."

Emlyn went around the opposite side, put his right foot into the stirrup, and swung easily into the saddle.

"There you go," said Oesterling, handing Emlyn the reins. "Have a good ride."

"'Bye, Papa," said Sarah, urging Dee off at a trot.

"Thank you," yelled Emlyn, turning Figaro to follow.

Figaro was a big horse, much taller than Dee. Emlyn wished he could have ridden the mare, as she was like the ponies he had known in Wales. However, he could hardly ask Sarah to ride the larger horse.

The sun was bright overhead, and a light breeze blew from the south as the two riders followed McClure Street up the hill. The horses, eager for exercise, climbed at a trot, and Emlyn quickly got accustomed to Figaro's smooth gait.

As they ascended, the clusters of houses thinned out. The farther they got from the mill, the less discolored the clapboard siding was from smoke and chemical fumes.

When they reached the top of the rise, the horses broke into a canter. They passed Anne Ashley Memorial Church and made their way between the two halves of the Homestead cemetery, Protestants on the left, Catholics on the right.

Sarah didn't say a word, but looked back now and then to see if Emlyn was still following.

Emlyn found himself staring at Sarah's back as the horses slowed, tackling the slope beyond the cemetery. He couldn't read her. She seemed friendly, at least on the surface, yet distant. Maybe he was just imagining it, but he felt she was standing in judgment. He thought it likely she was riding with him because Eirwen had deflected the invitation to him.

Emlyn looked down at his grimy hands and fingernails. Self-consciously, he tried to wrap the reins around his knuckles. At least he felt better for having clean clothes. Eirwen had washed and ironed a white shirt for him, and he was wearing heavy wool trousers and sweater. Dr. Oesterling's oilcloth riding coat topped his clothing. It felt so good to be clean, out in the air.

For the past two weeks, in the pre-dawn hours, Emlyn had dragged out of bed and limped to his post at the furnace. He returned home exhausted, but had gotten out of bed early the next day. By the time Saturday afternoon had rolled around, Emlyn was ready for a very long sleep.

The weekend time off, however, was shortened by the change of shift. Instead of getting up early the next Monday, Emlyn and Gwyn went back to work at four on Sunday afternoon. Although he was relatively rested, having slept late on Sunday, when the work dragged on past midnight, Emlyn found himself constantly fighting to stay alert.

The same workers were doing the same jobs, but this time their work was done under the cloak of night. Not that it mattered much whether it was light out or not—the incandescence of the furnaces lit up the entire mill like a scene out of the first book of *Paradise Lost*. While the molten metal was contained in the furnaces, electric lights, a recent innovation, illuminated the mill interior. Yet their faint white rays seemed to be swallowed by the immense dark space; the electric bulbs twinkled like distant stars beside the blinding suns of molten steel.

Virgil, for his part, had said nothing about the scene in front of the saloon, and acted aloof and smart-alecky, as he had before Emlyn's hiatus. Virgil resumed his routine of bossing Emlyn around and verbally abusing Joe Galik—who either didn't understand, or chose not to. Emlyn, with Joe, shoveled and pushed wheelbarrows around till he felt on the verge of collapse.

Emlyn decided to ignore Virgil, and he began talking to Joe only in German. Emlyn learned that Joe, the youngest of ten children, was saving as much as he could from his meager wages to bring Anna, a girl from his village in Slovakia, to America. He communicated with his intended via letters dictated to a priest in Braddock. After receiving a letter, Anna would take it to the village priest, who read the letter and wrote back to Joe for her.

Emlyn became increasingly appreciative of being fluent in English, and literate in it to boot. Joe, who could speak four languages, wound up in a position subservient to Virgil, a man who could speak only one.

However, Emlyn and Joe's conversations in a language he couldn't understand infuriated Virgil, who intensified his maltreatment of Joe. But instead of being demoralized, Joe relished getting Virgil's goat. He remained unflappable, while Virgil grew increasingly cross.

By Thursday of Emlyn's first week back, Virgil had become so abusive of Joe that Frank took him aside. Emlyn didn't know what Frank had said, but he deduced it was a dressing down for Virgil, who, after all, was not the boss. Virgil went into a sulk, but by the time work resumed on Monday, he had reverted to his initial low-keyed despotism.

Each morning Emlyn had come home, downed his breakfast in a haze of fatigue, and fallen into bed utterly exhausted. By three o'clock in the afternoon, he had to drag himself out of bed and start the cycle all over again.

The last fortnight at the mill had completely worn him down, but he had not gotten injured. Each workday was the same round of drudgery, relieved by brief periods of terror when the metal was shifted from the furnace into the ladles. Emlyn was getting better at making back wall, but he still trembled with fear whenever he had to follow Virgil and work beside the terrible stream of hot metal pouring from the spout of the open hearth ladle. Thankfully, he was getting better at that, too.

Emlyn's musings were interrupted when Figaro stumbled. Emlyn looked around at the jumble of hills surrounding them, noticing them for the first time. They had reached Homestead Park, at the second summit of the long hill.

Sarah reined in Dee and turned in the saddle. "How are you doing? "

Emlyn nodded. "I'm fine. It's such a beautiful day to be out."

With Sarah in the lead, they continued at a walk for another half hour through Lincoln Place, following winding paths along a creek bed, passing a couple of farmhouses and pastures.

When they reached the top of a third big hill, Sarah stopped in a clearing overlooking the valley they'd just passed through.

"This is one of the highest places in the county," said Sarah. "Papa and I like to ride out here on nice days to take in the view."

Emlyn halted Figaro beside her. Sarah pointed back to the rise of the last hill they had crossed.

"See all the smoke?"

Plumes of various colors—beige, white, black, gray—lifted into the sky behind the hill. The higher they rose, the more the colors blurred and grew faint.

"That's coming from the Homestead Works. Over here further, that's Braddock. The towns follow the twists of the Monongahela River around these hills. Over this hill," said Sarah, pointing behind them, "is McKeesport."

Emlyn's eyes skimmed the panorama. The sky above was bright blue, striped with wispy cirrus clouds. The broad hills were covered with the dark trunks of bare trees, dotted with an occasional evergreen. Small streams slashed through the valley bottoms, winding their way to the river.

The landscape was serene and golden in the slanting rays of the mid-afternoon December sunshine.

Soon, thought Emlyn, it would be winter. When was the solstice? That day? The next? He hadn't thought about the passage of time and the seasons since his arrival in Homestead.

"So lovely it is," said Emlyn wistfully. "Such a different world from the one in the towns behind the hills."

"Yes," said Sarah. "But listen. Even all the way up here you can hear the mills."

Sure enough, over the sound of the dead leaves blowing around, he could hear faint booms and crashes. And of course, the smears of dirty sky marked the locations of the various steel works.

"I've never been up here after dark," said Sarah, "but Papa has been occasionally, tending to patients. He says the glow from the furnaces lights up the whole horizon, and the display of fireworks from the Bessemer converters at Carrie Furnace makes it look like the hills are Mount Vesuvius or Etna." She paused. "In fact, there is a mill town called Etna over on the Allegheny River, northwest of here."

"No Vesuvius?"

Sarah shook her head, smiling for the first time that day. "No, too many syllables."

Emlyn grinned. "I've seen a steel works at night," he said. "Every night for the last two weeks—on the inside."

"Well, obviously, I've never been inside. I'm sure it's much more dramatic up close."

"True, at least for a while, before you get too knackered to care." He kept his gaze on the plumes of smoke.

They fell silent.

Maybe he had been wrong about Sarah; she seemed more

genial now. But if that was so, why was he afraid to keep eye contact? It was probably because of their inauspicious first meeting, he decided.

Forget it, he commanded himself. Instead, he replayed the images of her figure coming towards him, the nausea, his utter humiliation. He felt the blood rising to his cheeks. Involuntarily, his hands tightened on the reins.

Simultaneously, Figaro snorted loudly. The horse shifted his weight from one side to the other and shook his head up and down.

"I think he's getting impatient standing around," Sarah said. "I know a clean stream at the bottom of this hill where the horses can drink. Follow me."

They wound their way along a rocky path to a meadow, where Sarah pulled up and slid off Dee. Emlyn dismounted from the left, landing on both feet, and side-by-side, he and Sarah led the horses to the creek.

As they walked, Emlyn noted again that Sarah was tall, much taller than he had remembered. As they led the horses to the creek, he glanced down at her boots. Ah, elevated heels. Still, she was much taller than average, an impressive woman, but, to his perception, not exactly alluring.

"I can't believe Christmas is less than two weeks away," said Sarah, watching the horses drink from the purling stream.

"I'm looking forward to it," said Emlyn. "Gwyn says the only holidays we get off work are Christmas and the Fourth of July. It's a special day, certainly."

"The children at school are so excited. It's been difficult getting any studies done," she said. "We've been working on the pageant, and that's kept them busy."

"When is that?" asked Emlyn.

"On Wednesday evening, the last day of school before Christmas break," she said. "Thomas is in it, you know. He's a shepherd."

"I know," said Emlyn. "He's been practicing his lines for over a week."

"Will you be spending the holiday at home?" asked Emlyn.

"No. Papa and I will be going to my sister's house. We'll be home only on Christmas Eve, for the service at church. Mr. Griffiths and some of the congregation—a few immigrants from Mid-Wales—wanted to sing *plygain* last year, but it didn't work out. Some people didn't have the time or energy to stay up all night, and the rest weren't interested. We wound up doing one service in the evening."

"Eirwen mentioned that."

"I love the old carols and hymns. When Mama was alive, we used to have such splendid times singing around the piano—not only at Christmas, but all year 'round.

I'm so glad Papa has agreed to do the Twelfth Night party again. Of course we can't actually have it on Twelfth Night—that's a Wednesday, and a workday. Ninth night, Saturday, will have to do."

She pushed some stray hairs back under her hat and looked up at the sky. Emlyn followed her gaze. The high clouds were thickening, spreading; the sun was touching the dark silhouettes of the western hills.

"We'd better head back," she said.

Emlyn nodded in agreement.

Sarah glanced at him, examining his face. "Do you . . . have you. . . ?" She hesitated.

He looked at her quizzically.

"Have you had time to decide if you can play violin for the party?"

"I don't have time to do much of anything except sleep, eat, and work."

Sarah gazed across the creek.

"That's fine... I mean, I understand," she said.

"I can give you a definite answer by Wednesday. Next week we'll have Christmas Day off, and a light day on Saturday. I'll hardly know what to do with all that extra time."

Sarah smiled again.

Emlyn pulled out his watch as they led the horses across the meadow to a large, flat-topped boulder. Nearly four.

Sarah insisted that she hold Figaro's bridle while Emlyn mounted from the right. On Figaro, he held Dee's reins while Sarah, standing atop the boulder, pulled herself into the saddle.

"We have less than an hour of daylight left," she said, and started off at a good clip. Figaro's long legs easily kept up with Dee's brisk pace.

Sarah slowed Dee to a walk when they started down the hill from Homestead Park. As they passed by the cemetery, a fitful breeze came up and blew the dry leaves around the tombstones and across their path. A blank grayness crept across the western horizon, obscuring the last feeble rays of the sun.

By the time they arrived at Walker's Stables on Fifth Avenue, the sky was dark. They dismounted and handed the horses over to one of the stable hands.

"Thank you—and your father—very much for letting me ride today," Emlyn said. "And Figaro, too," he added, patting the horse's flank.

"I'm sure Figaro was glad for the ride," replied Sarah, "and myself as well." After a moment, she asked him if he was coming to the school pageant.

Emlyn thought of Thomas, eagerly reciting his three lines. "I'll try," he said.

As they had agreed earlier, Emlyn started walking with Sarah toward the doctor's office on Eighth Avenue, where Oesterling would be waiting, catching up on reading. Oesterling would accompany Sarah home from there.

They hadn't even reached Seventh Avenue when a man with a dog beside him came toward them out of the smoke and darkness.

"Papa? Is that you?" The doctor's features emerged clearly under the gas lamppost.

"Hello Sarah, Emlyn."

Tail wagging, Cerberus trotted up to Sarah.

"Why didn't you wait at the office?" she asked, bending to stroke the dog.

"I finished my book a half hour ago. At five o'clock Cerberus and I decided to walk to the stable to meet you."

Emlyn thanked the doctor and handed over the oilcloth coat. Then they started off in separate directions, Emlyn toward the tracks, father and daughter toward Eighth Avenue.

As he walked over the tracks, Emlyn remembered that he had to go into the mill again at four the next morning. He sighed.

For the first time since his arrival in Homestead, today's outing had provided an escape from the monotony of labor. He had been in town less than a month. What would this routine feel like a year from now? He blocked out consideration of the question. Whatever happened, he had a commitment to Gwyn and Eirwen to fulfill. Somehow, he would stick with it, while keeping a lookout for other opportunities.

At Sixth Avenue, Emlyn pulled his cap down tight and thrust his hands into his pockets. He had gone only a few paces when a woman stepped out of the shadows in front of him, blocking the sidewalk.

"I know you," she said in a low voice. "You're Mrs. Jones's brother, ain't you?"

Startled, Emlyn stopped. "Yes?"

"I seen you talkin' to the doc and Miss Sarah."

"So?"

"Do you want to see what you're responsible for?"

"What are you talking about?" Emlyn asked impatiently. "Let me pass."

She took a step toward him and pulled back her headscarf.

Emlyn started when he saw the woman's swollen and battered face. Under the mass of dark bruises and welts he recognized the features of Mrs. Buckman.

"You shouldn't have taken that cane to the Avenue. Bucky was real vexed at seein' you with the cane, and even more hot under the collar when he had to pay a dollar to fix the broken window. When he got home, he took the cane to me. That was nearly two weeks ago, and see how bad it is."

"I'm very sorry," replied Emlyn, shocked. "I didn't think that..."

She cut him off. "You're off hobnobbin' with the fine folk of the town, like what happens to me ain't no consideration of yours."

"You left the cane at the house. I wouldn't have used it if I'd known it was your husband's," said Emlyn, his ire rising. "I take no responsibility for this. It's too bad you're married to such a brute. Now let me pass."

He tried to go around her, but she stepped in the same direction.

"You're not gettin' off so easy."

Emlyn looked over her shoulder, seeking a way around her. "What do you mean by that?"

She smiled slyly. "I've had lots of trouble because of you."

"Your trouble comes from your husband—and your own folly, not from me."

"The beating came from the cane you took, with no thanks to me. I need recompense."

"I didn't take the cane, you left it—remember? What the devil do you mean, 'recompense'?" Emlyn demanded.

In reply, she held out her hand.

"What? Money?" asked Emlyn incredulously.

A sneer crossed her face, as she held her outstretched palm closer.

Exasperated, Emlyn exploded, "You must be mad, woman! I don't have any money. Everything I make goes to pay off my debt to my brother-in-law."

She tilted her head to one side and looked at him with one eye half-closed. "You ain't tryin' to fool me, are you? Gwyn Jones is one of the best-paid men in the mill. He needs the money less than I do."

"This is absurd," said Emlyn, again attempting to move around her.

"You have time to go ridin' around with Miss Oesterling, but no time for fixing the trouble you cause," she snarled, stepping closer.

Now he could smell the whisky on her breath.

"You've caused your own trouble; I owe you nothing. Get out of my way."

In response, she clutched his sleeve. "You and your sister think you're too good for the likes of me, don't you?"

His anger flared. "If you got money, you'd only waste it on liquor, anyway. No drunken trollop is going to extort anything from me."

She straightened, her features twisted.

"Damn you!" she shrieked, and spat in his face.

He recoiled, wiping his face with his sleeve. She leaped

at him, trying to claw at his eyes. She raked her fingers down the left side of his face. He swung his right arm and hit her backhand against the side of the head. Emitting a low moan, she swayed and collapsed sideways into the gutter.

For a moment, Emlyn stood over her, fearful and uncertain. His cheek burned where she had clawed him.

"Damn you," she muttered. Her swollen features contorted in anger, she started to stagger to her feet.

Emlyn backed into the street and broke into a half-run. As he reached the railroad tracks, he heard her shout in a hoarse voice, "You'll pay for this!"

He kept a quick pace until he reached Third Avenue. His leg was throbbing, and he was panting with exertion and fright. At the house he saw Gwyn and the two boys in the front room, and decided to go around to the back.

Emlyn hesitated at the kitchen door when he saw Eirwen setting the table for tea. Taking a deep breath, he pushed the door open.

"Em, what happened?" Eirwen asked. "Where did you get those scratches on your face? Don't tell me that you injured yourself riding."

"No, worse," Emlyn moaned, crossing to the sink to wash his face.

"What's a madder, Uncle Em?" asked Dilys from the corner where she was playing with her doll and wooden blocks.

"Oh, Dilys, it's nothing for you to worry about," said Emlyn, mustering an assertive tone. He dried his face and collapsed into a chair.

Eirwen put down the teapot and sat at the table next to him.

"Whatever could be worse?"

Emlyn looked at her, then at Dilys.

"Addie Buckman" he said. Using Welsh, he poured out

the story of his encounter with her. Because he hadn't told Eirwen of his narrow escape from Mr. Buckman two weeks previous, he had to backtrack and fill her in on that episode as well.

Eirwen looked up as Gwyn appeared at the door from the parlor.

"My ears perked up when I heard Welsh coming from the kitchen. Lord, what a situation," said Gwyn, shaking his head.

As they continued the discussion in Welsh, Gwyn became increasingly angry. As far as he was concerned, they *were* better than the perpetually drunk-and-disorderly Buckmans. Emlyn finally convinced him that the best course was to wait and see, keeping alert to any more ambushes.

Rising to his feet, Emlyn announced that he would play at the Oesterlings' party, Buckmans be damned. No one could stop him from socializing with whomever he pleased.

After making short work of the bread, cheese and baked apple Eirwen had set out with tea, Emlyn took out his violin, brought it into the kitchen and tuned it. As Eirwen cleared away the food and dishes, he played some tunes, and they discussed which would be best to play for the party.

Both had little experience with dance music, as Congregationalists in general and their father in particular frowned on dancing and fiddling. Nevertheless, their mother's father, the farmer-fiddler, had passed on some pieces he had learned over the years by listening to others play.

Emlyn tried playing some of these, occasionally fumbling with a phrase or missing a repeat. His hands, stiff from working in the mill, were initially reluctant to do his bidding. He grimaced as he watched the fingers of his left hand move over the strings. The nails were filthy, broken;

the skin was rough and stained.

In the end, Emlyn decided to play one of their grandfather's tunes, a slip jig called 'Gyrru'r Byd O'm Blaen' ('Cast the Word before Me') and three of the tunes he'd learned from the Irish fiddler on the crossing. One of the reels, 'Over the Moor to Maggie's,' was his particular favorite. At Emlyn's suggestion, Eirwen settled on the traditional 'Mil Harddach Wyt Na'r Rhosyn Gwyn,' ('Fairer Than the White Rose'), a mother singing about how precious her baby is to her.

Eirwen said that Sarah had planned a few pieces that were currently popular in America, but they would have to wait until Sunday to find out what Sarah wanted either of them to do with her selections.

The kitchen clock struck nine as Emlyn was packing up his violin. He wearily washed up and crawled into bed. In several hours, he'd be forcing himself out of bed and off to the mill for another ten-hour shift, followed by five more days of the same.

At least he wouldn't have to go through this routine next Thursday, for Friday was Christmas Day.

The week passed quickly for Emlyn. After dinner Wednesday evening, he had gone to the school pageant with the rest of the family, but had fallen asleep in his seat twice. Fortunately, he was awake to see Thomas, dressed in a striped bathrobe with a towel over his head, come to adore the infant Jesus in the manger. Afterward, seeing the crowd of people around Sarah, Emlyn decided to go home straightaway. He needed to get some sleep, for the next day was Christmas Eve.

Thursday, December 24th

"Have a very merry Christmas," yelled Frank as Emlyn packed up at the end of the shift.

"Merry Chris'moos!" Joe called out to no one in particular. He had been so excited all week anticipating the Christmas celebration he and his friends would be attending at the Slovak hall in Braddock, across the river.

Most everyone was in a holiday mood anticipating the one day out of two during the year that they had off from their usual six-day-a-week labors at the Homestead Works.

"Happy Christmas to all," shouted Emlyn, doffing his cap, and then pulling it on again.

A few flurries were swirling around under a neutral sky as Emlyn emerged from the open-hearth building. After a month working in the mill, Emlyn no longer needed Gwyn to help him find his way out of the labyrinthine steel works. The work continued to be grueling. Although he had gotten pretty good at making back wall, he grew more weary with each passing day. He didn't know how long his body would bear the strain.

Emlyn carefully picked his way through the various mill yards, finally emerging at City Farm Lane. There he picked up his pace, walking along the tracks toward the railroad station on Amity Street. He hoped the old German farmer who had been selling fir trees near the station yesterday would still be there. If so, he would buy one.

One day the previous weekend when he had come home from a walk along the river, he found Eirwen and Gwyn in a heated debate. When he entered through the front door, Thomas and Dilys were in the parlor, playing with David. From the kitchen came their parents' voices, almost shouting in Welsh.

The children, pretending nothing out of the ordinary was going on, greeted Emlyn. He took his time removing his coat and boots, trying to decide whether to go to the kitchen or to remain there.

When he realized that Eirwen and Gwyn's argument involved something about Christmas, he ventured into the kitchen. Both Eirwen and Gwyn were standing, he gesticulating at the table and she, arms crossed, at the stove. Eirwen saw Emlyn first.

"Emlyn, we didn't hear you come in," she said.

"What's going on? Why are you speaking Welsh?" he asked.

"Dwi'n casau gwneud hyn *I hate to do this,*" replied Gwyn, "ond mae e er lles y plant *but it involves the children.*"

"Mae Gwyn yn credu dylen ni gael coeden Nadolig, ond dwi ddim yn cytuno," said Eirwen. "*Gwyn thinks we ought to get a Christmas tree, and I don't,*" she continued in Welsh. "*It's enough to have given in to American ways and play Santa Claus for Thomas, and now for Dilys. I don't think we should go so far as to bring a tree into our house. Let it stay in the woods where it belongs.*"

"*It's the custom here, Eirwen,*" said Gwyn, his voice rising. "*Most of the Americans have trees. I don't see how we're going to explain it to the children if we don't have one.*"

"*We don't have to do everything the Americans do, do we?*" Eirwen replied with some heat.

"*I thought we are ourselves Americans now,*" Gwyn retorted.

There was a brief pause while they both looked at Emlyn.

"Wel?" demanded Eirwen. "Beth wyt ti'n feddwl? *Well? What do you think?*"

Emlyn couldn't help laughing. "Dyma beth yw trafodaeth dda, dadlau am ba mor Americanaidd rydych—yn yr hen iaith. *This is a fine debate, arguing about how American you are or aren't—in the old language.*"

Neither Eirwen nor Gwyn seemed to see the humor in it. They both kept looking at him. The smile faded from his lips. Emlyn pondered the question for a moment, and answered, *"Many people back home now have Christmas trees. What harm would it do?"*

Gywn shouted, "Ha!" while Eirwen threw up her hands.

And so, it was decided that they would put up a tree on Christmas Eve after the children were in bed, as the Americans did.

Emlyn had mixed feelings about the holiday because of memories of Christmases past in Wales. Christmas was a holiday, yes, but in the Phillips household, it was a sober one.

His father had often railed against the custom of singing *plygain*, as many did in chapels throughout the villages of mid-Wales. He wasn't against the singing of hymns through the night on Christmas Eve, but against the drunkenness and foolery that often accompanied it.

The family marked the holiday by a service on Christmas Eve, then again on Christmas morning. The family always had a fine dinner, with a roast fowl and plum pudding (minus the flaming brandy). And he, Eirwen, and Arthur all got little gifts—an orange, a homemade toy, a bit of candy—but from their parents in honor of Jesus' birth, not from any jolly old elf or even a saint called Nicholas.

That was over twenty years ago. Customs were changing, even if his father's views were not.

Emlyn shook his head, as if to shake off the notion of his father's stubbornness, and looked down the street. In the next block he could see a locomotive pulling a passenger train away from the Amity Street Station toward Pittsburgh. When the smoke and steam cleared, he saw the stout old farmer leading his horse and wagon over to the trees, which were leaning against sawhorses on the river side of the tracks. Another man was walking off with a small fir slung over his shoulder.

Emlyn broke into a trot.

"Hello!" he yelled, "Am I too late to get a tree?"

The farmer looked up. "Hmm, almost. I will deliver these to St. John's Church, then I go home."

Emlyn stopped in his tracks.

"You're taking them to a church?"

"Ja, our Lutheran church on Fourth Avenue. We use them to decorate around the altar."

"Do you have any left to sell me, then?'

The man looked Emlyn up and down. "How about we make a trade? You help me take these to the church, and I give you one. You get free tree, I get home sooner."

Emlyn felt the coins in his pocket. Maybe he could buy the children something. "It's a deal."

He helped the farmer load the nine scrawny firs into the wagon, and they rumbled off down Amity, taking a left onto Fourth Avenue. As they pulled up in front of the small church, the farmer climbed out and went around to the back. A few minutes later he emerged from the front doors, accompanied by a smiling, thin man in a black suit. The thin man's white shirt had a collar that Emlyn immediately identified as that of a Lutheran cleric.

At least he wasn't entering a Congregational church. Emlyn recalled his going on at length with Gwyn and Eirwen about how he would never set foot inside a church again. He glanced around. A few pedestrians were hurrying along the street, oblivious to anything but completing their errands.

The old farmer and the minister walked up to Emlyn.

"I'm Elmer Krause, the pastor here," said the cleric, extending his hand. "Thank you for helping Oscar with the trees."

"Emlyn Phillips," he replied, shaking the minister's hand. "You're welcome."

It took less than a half hour for Emlyn and Oscar to unload the trees, carry them into the sanctuary, and, with the minister's help, arrange them on either side of the altar.

Emlyn was surprised at how much St. John's looked like some Welsh chapels he'd known—spare, unadorned, rectilinear. It was an unfortunate association for Emlyn; the longer he stayed there, the more he wanted to get away. After they set up the last tree, he excused himself and practically ran outside, into the falling dusk.

He waited several minutes before Oscar appeared at the door. A pace behind the farmer was the minister.

"You leave so fast, I think you forget the tree," said Oscar.

"Oh no. I couldn't disappoint my niece and nephew."

Pastor Krause shook Emlyn's hand again. "Many thanks for helping us."

"You're very welcome," replied Emlyn.

Krause pulled a paper out of his pocket.

Here it comes, thought Emlyn.

"This is the bulletin for our service tonight. You're more than welcome to join us in worship." Krause held out the paper.

Without thinking, Emlyn held his hands out, palms forward, as if to ward off an attack.

Nonplussed, Krause lowered the paper. For a moment, Emlyn was at a loss for words. He didn't want to lie, but the truth was uncomfortable.

"I . . . I am . . . er, my family goes to the Welsh Congregational Church."

"Ah," said the pastor, a smile returning to his lips. "I see."

An inspiration came to Emlyn.

"In fact," he added, "my father is a minister back in Wales."

The pastor and Oscar nodded their approval. Emlyn felt relieved to get out of this situation without having to tell an outright lie.

"May you and your family have a blessed Christmastide," said Krause, who then turned to go back into the church.

"Thanks," returned Emlyn, touching his cap visor. "And yours as well."

"Here is your Tannenbaum," said Oscar, pulling the last fir tree from the wagon.

"Danke sehr," replied Emlyn. "Frohe Weihnachten."

Oscar looked startled, then smiled.

"Ach, sehr gut. Froehliche Weihnachten. Do you need a ride home?"

"No, thanks," said Emlyn as he took a hold of the center of the tree trunk.

He and the farmer set off in different directions.

Emlyn walked at a brisk pace to a grocery store on Seventh Avenue, but it was already closed, so he went to another. The clerks were preparing to shut up the store, but Emlyn had just enough time to buy some humbugs, licorice, and peppermints for the children.

He placed the paper bag of treats in his pocket, and awkwardly clutching his lunch pail, Emlyn half-carried, half-dragged the tree to the backyard of the house, where he hid it behind the shed.

Inside the house the mood was quite different from that of a usual Thursday evening. Gwyn was finishing dressing behind an old, torn blanket next to the stove after having bathed in the water the others had used. Eirwen was setting the table for supper, a light meal of potato and leek soup before services at church.

Dilys ran into the room crying and clutched at Eirwen's skirts.

"Mummy!" she wailed.

"What is it?" asked Eirwen, setting down a bowl.

"Thomas has one of Daddy's socks. He says I can't have the other to hang for Santa."

"I'll deal with Thomas," said Gwyn, coming from behind the blanket. "If you quarrel on Christmas Eve, Santa will not put anything in your stocking, however small or big it is. I know that for a fact."

Yanking at his shirttail with one hand, and patting Dilys's head with the other, Gwyn headed into the parlor to talk to Thomas.

"You're next," Eirwen said to Emlyn. "I've already set out your towel and some clean things from the laundry. You can use the water in the kettle to warm the bath."

Emlyn took off his coat, cap, and boots and set them by the door. He lifted the steaming kettle from the cook stove and poured its contents into the tub of bath water.

Behind the blanket, Emlyn hastily undressed and lowered himself into the tub. The water was only lukewarm and coated with soap scum, but Emlyn didn't mind. He sank into the water till only his face and knees were protruding. This was a moment to savor.

He closed his eyes.

The next thing he knew, Eirwen was calling his name. "Emlyn! It's so quiet back there. I hope you haven't drowned."

"Er, no. I must have dozed off."

"Brother, you'd better get moving. Supper's almost ready."

Hastily, Emlyn vigorously scrubbed himself, especially his rough, blackened hands and aching feet, and rinsed himself with fresh water from a pitcher. Shivering, he patted himself dry and quickly pulled on the clothes Eirwen had set out.

At supper, the children were beside themselves with anticipation. Dilys was worried that Santa might not fit down the small flue of the chimney for the parlor firebox. Thomas, however, assured her that treats had come for the last three years and certainly would come this year.

By the time the dishes were cleared away and washed up, it was nearly 7:30. Emlyn, feeling a bit guilty about staying home, insisted on putting away the pans, dishes and utensils while Eirwen got the children ready for church. The service wasn't until 10, but Eirwen had to get there early to warm up and go over her solo.

Shortly before nine o'clock, Eirwen, Gwyn, and the children headed out the door, and the house fell quiet.

Emlyn, lying on the sofa covered with an afghan, immediately dozed off.

East Liberty, 10 p.m.

George Bernhard sat on the bare parlor floor next to his father, holding a broomstick while his father drilled holes into it.

"Pa," said Kate from the doorway to the kitchen. "This is crazy. You should've let George get a real tree."

"This will do fine," said Karl Bernhard, boring a hole with the hand drill. "It was good when you were little, and it will be good for your younger brothers."

"Ja," said Susanna over Kate's shoulder. "We don't have the money to buy a tree and treats for the little ones, too. The broomstick will have to do. Come help me with the cookies, Kate."

"I don't know why you don't like the idea of us cutting down a tree from the yard of one of those fancy houses over in Point Breeze," said George, grinning.

Kate snorted in derision. "That's all we'd need—you and

John in jail for Christmas."

"Hold the stick upright," Karl directed George, who did as requested. Karl poked in a bit of glue, then shoved a thin stick into each hole in the broomstick.

Karl sat back. "Now, turn it around." George spun the broomstick slowly.

"Good! Put it in that bucket of gravel so Kate and your mother can decorate it," said Karl.

George set the broomstick into the can, working it into the gravel until it was perfectly straight.

"That's good," said Karl, as Susanna and Kate each brought a plateful of baked goodies from the kitchen. Father and son watched them as Kate hung Pfefferkuchen, German gingerbread cookies, and Susanna hung Zimtsterne, peppermint stars, on the stick boughs. Finally, Kate hung on a few candy canes and strung on garlands of cranberries.

"What do you think?" asked Kate, stepping back to admire their handiwork.

"It looks beautiful," said Susanna, "or at least it will until the boys attack it tomorrow morning."

"All that's lacking is the smell of the evergreen," Kate said wistfully.

"I can fix that," said George, jumping up and going out the front door.

"He'd better not be going to Point Breeze," Kate said, disappearing into the kitchen.

Several minutes later George came back with little sprays of spruce, which he hung over the stick branches.

"Very good. Now for a treat for us older ones," Karl said, going to the closet by the stairs, reaching up on the top shelf, and pulling out a bottle of schnapps. Susanna brought in three tumblers from the kitchen, and Karl poured a little of the clear liquid in each.

"Prost!" said Karl, holding up his glass. George and Susanna held up theirs, and they all took a sip.

"Ach, so," said Susanna, easing herself onto the sofa.

Karl saluted the broomstick with his glass. "To the tree! May it stand at least till dawn." Smiling at the broomstick tree, he began to sing:

Der Christbaum ist der schönste Baum
The Christmas tree is the most

den wir auf Erden kennen.
beautiful tree we know on earth.

Im Garten klein
In the small garden

im engsten Raum
In the narrowest space

wie lieblich blüht der Wunderbaum
How lovely blooms the miracle tree

wenn seine Lichter brennen
When its lights are burning

wenn seine Lichter brennen
When its lights are burning

ja brennen.
Yes, burning.

"Ja, Karl," said Susanna, "it is the most beautiful tree—even if it doesn't have lights. Frohe Weihnachten!"

"Yeah, Pa," said George, taking a cookie from the tree and popping it into his mouth. "Merry Christmas."

Homestead, 11 p.m.

The chiming of the kitchen clock crept into Emlyn's consciousness, and he sat bolt upright in near panic.

He went into the kitchen and retrieved the bag of candy from his coat pocket. After the children were in bed, he'd put these in their stockings. Donning his boots, cap, and coat, he went into the back yard and looked for two boards in the shed. These he nailed to the bottom of the tree, as he had seen Oscar do at the church, so it would stand upright.

Crossing his arms, Emlyn stood back to regard the tree. Even in the darkness, he could see the fir tilted slightly to one side. Who would notice? And if they did, who would care?

He looked up at the heavens. In the hours since he left work, the sky had cleared. The mill smoke stacks weren't belching the usual volumes of smoke, as production slowed for the holiday.

Now the stars twinkled brightly in the black sky. Emlyn could see Orion with his star-studded belt and sword wheeling his way through the winter sky. It was the clearest the sky had been since Emlyn had arrived in Homestead. It was the same, familiar sky he used to see in South Wales.

All is calm, all is bright.

He thought about his parents and brother so many miles away across the cold North Atlantic. Dawn would be breaking in a few hours in Wales. He saw his parents lying asleep in the front bedroom of the stone house. His mother would have all the culinary treats in the kitchen prepared for the feast after the church service. Arthur and his fiancée, Tegwen, would probably be there for service and dinner.

Did they often think of him, as he often thought of them? Would they miss his presence this Christmas at the service, at the table—this, the first year he was not in their home for the holiday?

Duw, he missed his mother. Annwyl Mam. Dear Mum. And Arthur. He felt a sudden pang of longing for his friends, his family, for the old land—*hiraeth*, as they say. Tears welled up in his eyes and blurred the stars.

He heard the pealing of the church bells—first, one, then more joining in. He instinctively reached for his watch, but realized it lay in the drawer of his bed stand.

He didn't need the watch; he knew it was midnight. Christmas was here.

Soon, the family would return. He brushed the tears aside with his cuff and went back inside the kitchen. Coming through the door, he heard the others come through the front. He quietly went back outside and fetched the tree, bringing it around to the front door. Through the window, he could see no one. They had apparently gone upstairs to put the children to bed.

Emlyn opened the door and slipped inside with the tree. He removed his coat and boots and looked around for a good place to set up the tree. It seemed that every corner and cranny of the parlor was occupied.

Eirwen appeared at the bottom of the stairs. When she saw the tree, she broke into a broad smile.

"Thanks for getting a tree. The children will be very happy."

"Nadolig Llawen *Happy Christmas!*" she whispered, coming over and giving Emlyn a tight hug.

"Nadolig Llawen," he said, returning the embrace. "How did your solo go?"

"Just fine," she smiled through her exhaustion. "The

whole service was so beautiful. I love the Christmas music."

Gwyn came downstairs humming, and after a brief consultation, the three of them moved the reading table and its contents so they could set the tree in the far corner opposite the fireplace. Eirwen went into the kitchen and brought out strings of popcorn. She strung these around the tree, and hung a few dozen paper rosettes and little ginger cookies on the front branches.

Meanwhile, Gwyn took down the two stockings from the mantelpiece and put in goodies for the children—an orange and some chocolate drops for each, a patchwork bear for Dilys and a dozen marbles for Thomas. After Gwyn had tacked the stockings back up, Emlyn threw on top the hard candy he had bought.

"Christmas Eve is so magical, I'd like to stay up all night, " said Eirwen, standing back to admire the tree.

"But," she added, flopping onto the sofa, "I'm so tired, and the children will probably be up in a couple of hours."

"They'd better not stir till dawn," said Gwyn, going over to the sofa and sliding down next to Eirwen. "I told them how Santa would be unhappy if they got up too early and happened to see him. It would be cinders in their stockings for sure."

He threw an arm around Eirwen's shoulders and closed his eyes.

Almost immediately, he opened them again and sat upright. "I nearly forgot a very important item."

He stood up, went into the kitchen, and returned a moment later with a cutout metal star.

"I made this out of some scraps at work."

He went over to the tree, and reaching up, affixed the star to the top with a bit of wire. Thrusting his hands into his pants pockets, he grinned at Emlyn and Eirwen.

"Da iawn iawn. *Very good,'* said Eirwen. "The perfect touch."

For a moment, silence fell over the room. Even the usual din from the mill was absent.

Emlyn went to the kitchen for a glass of milk before bed. He poured the milk and drank slowly, happy in the knowledge that he would not have to arise early and go to work.

At first, Emlyn thought he was imagining that someone was singing. He set down the glass. No, it was Eirwen's voice, barely audible.

Quietly, he slipped into the parlor and moved over to the window by the tree.

Eirwen was still sitting on the sofa with Gwyn, eyes closed, beside her. She was singing very softly, gazing at the star on the tree.

O deued pob Christion
O come all Christians,

I Beth'lem yre awrhon,
hasten to Bethlehem

I weled mor dirion yw'd Duw.
To witness God's love.

Hearing the old Welsh carol, despite himself, Emlyn became choked with emotion. All the memories of Christmas Eves in the chapel came flooding over him—the candles winking in the dark sanctuary, the wispy exhalations of the singers visible in the cold air.

No, it wasn't the words, nor the ideas they expressed that affected him so: it was the simple, assertive tune, so plaintive, so sweet; it was Eirwen's dear, familiar voice; it was the evocation of the irretrievable past.

For the second time that night, tears began to well in Emlyn's eyes. He turned to the window and peered out. There, hanging silently over the houses huddled by the great river, the Christmas stars twinkled.

Friday, December 25th

"'He had no further intercourse with Spirits, but lived upon the Total Abstinence Principle, ever afterwards; and it was always said of him, that he knew how to keep Christmas well, if any man alive possessed the knowledge. May that be truly said of us, and all of us! And so, as Tiny Tim observed, God bless Us, Every One!'"

Oliver clapped the book shut and leaned back in the overstuffed plush armchair.

"Indeed, God bless us, everyone!" said Carrie. "It's such a wonderful story, I never tire of hearing it."

Sarah cast a glance at Oesterling, but he pretended not to notice. He was feeling so relaxed and warm. Roast goose, chestnut stuffing, peas in cream sauce—he couldn't remember it all—followed by a flaming plum pudding. After such a sumptuous feast, he was content to sit by the brick fireplace in Carrie and Oliver's front parlor.

Carrie was resplendent in her new Christmas dinner gown of burgundy silk faille, inset with pewter-colored brocade panels in the bodice and sleeves. Sarah was wearing her only good dress, the one her mother had given her three years previous. She had pinned sprigs of holly in her upswept hair and on the shoulder as a holiday corsage.

"I'd like to propose a toast," said Oliver's brother Robert, a sophomore at Princeton.

He stood up and held the snifter of cognac before him. "To Oliver, his lovely wife Carrie, and to their beautiful new home. Merry Christmas!"

"Hear, hear," said Norton Montague, raising his glass.

"Cheers," said Oesterling, lifting his water tumbler.

The three younger men drank from their snifters.

Carrie giggled. "Thank you so much. It's so good to have you all here."

"Too bad Mater and Pater decided to remain in dirty, smelly old Chicago," said Robert. "They find it too hard to tear themselves away from Vicky and her pack of brats, I suppose."

Oliver snorted. "Mama dotes on the grandchildren so much I doubt she'll ever leave Chicago. That is, not until you or I have our own brats."

Robert laughed. "You're already ahead of me on that score."

Oliver looked at Carrie, who began nervously twisting the silk rope on her dress, and returned his glance at Robert.

"I mean," Robert hastily added, "you're already married, and I'm not."

An awkward silence filled the room. Oesterling knew that Oliver and Carrie wanted a family, but so far, after nearly five years of marriage, theirs was a childless union. It was getting to be a touchy subject with Carrie.

Oesterling looked helplessly at Sarah, then at Norton Montague. Damn it, why didn't somebody change the subject? Montague picked up the cue.

"I hear, Miss Oesterling," said Montague, "that you are quite an accomplished pianist. Perhaps you could play us something."

"Yes, Sarah, do!" exclaimed Carrie, eager to change the subject.

"Oh dear," replied Sarah, looking down at her punch glass. "I don't know if I can remember anything."

"Come on, Sarah," said Carrie, standing up and going over

to Sarah. "You know you can do it."

She took the glass from Sarah and set it on the side table.

"Alright," said Sarah, "but I won't guarantee anything."

She went over to the square rosewood piano and sat down. The piano had been an anniversary present from Oliver to Carrie two years ago. Carrie played competently, but not, thought Oesterling, half as well as her mother or sister.

"Let me see," said Sarah, her eyes on the keyboard. "I don't know any Christmas pieces—outside of what I play for church, that is. Mozart will have to do."

"Mozart," pronounced Montague, "will more than 'do'." He moved over to a chair where he could watch the keyboard and sat down.

Sarah rubbed her hand together. "This is the first movement of the G-major Sonata."

Good, thought Oesterling. That was one of his favorites, one that Margaret used to play.

Sarah started off rather too slowly, but soon accelerated into a sprightly allegro. As Oesterling listened to the bass marching up parallel to the treble, he forgot about present ills and was transported to a place of comfort and joy.

He closed his eyes. He thought of nothing, lost in the hesitating melody, alternating with the flashes of the chromatic runs, the vigorous bass. Then the andante, with the shift to C major—stately, elegant, confident.

Perhaps, he mused, Sarah was beginning to surpass even her teacher, Margaret, as a pianist. Oesterling breathed slowly, relaxing deeper into his chair. He was happy.

Then to the presto, and the call and response of the three-note chords. This was his favorite part, so exhilarating. He kept his eyes shut until the final, triumphant G-major chord.

As the last chord sounded, the group broke into applause. Sarah stood up, put her hand on the piano, and did a slight curtsey.

"Brava!" shouted Montague, echoed soon after by Robert.

"Thank you," said Sarah, returning to her place on the sofa.

"That was wonderful, Sarah. Thank *you,*" said Oliver, clapping.

Carrie moved in front of the fireplace and clasped her hands in front of her. "And now, we'd like to give all of you a little something for Christmas."

Carrie glided over to the tall spruce tree, set against the wall opposite the fire and trimmed with German hand-blown glass ornaments. She stooped to examine the wrapped boxes underneath, picked up the three smaller packages and handed them around to Robert, her father, and Montague.

Oesterling, as the eldest, got to open his first: a long muffler of soft cashmere. Next was Montague: a box of fine, deckle-edged writing paper. Robert got a copy of Arthur Conan Doyle's popular new historical novel, *The White Company.*

Each in turn thanked Carrie and Oliver for their thoughtfulness. Carrie flushed with pleasure.

"Now I have to show you what Oliver gave me last night," exclaimed Carrie. Her hand went to her throat and touched the pendant hanging there.

She stood in front of Oesterling and bent over so he could see it better.

"It's a ruby on a platinum chain," she said proudly. "Oliver picked it out to match my new gown."

Oesterling examined the pendant. The ruby was large, a rosy red stone set in a cluster of small, sparkling diamonds in platinum filigree. Oesterling could not guess its worth—probably more than he made in a month. He had often pondered how Oliver could afford such lavish gifts in addition to paying rent on this house.

"Isn't it just superb, Papa?" she asked her father.

"Indeed it is," Oesterling agreed.

She showed it to Sarah.

"Carrie, it's lovely," she murmured.

"And now," said Carrie, "last, but certainly not least . . ."

She returned to the tree to fetch the sole remaining package, a large rectangular box.

As Carrie picked up the box and walked across to Sarah, an uneasy feeling overcame Oesterling. He remembered the discussion he and Sarah had on the way back to Homestead after the last dinner party here. Now Montague shows up at their family Christmas celebration. He prayed that the package didn't contain what he thought it did.

Carrie placed the package in Sarah's lap and, smiling nervously, sat on the sofa beside her.

Sarah untied the string and pulled back the paper wrapping. She lifted the cover and pushed aside the tissue lining. For a long moment, Sarah stared at the contents.

"Go ahead, Sarah. Take it out," urged Carrie.

Sarah lifted out a dark green gown of heavy silk damask. The underskirt, collar and cuffs were of stiff wine-colored silk. The bodice was covered with a layer of black lace netting, which was gathered up in the back to form a bustle and short train.

Oesterling's heart sank. It was as he had feared.

Sarah shook the dress, and the box fell to the floor. She held the garment before her, speechless.

"Well? What do you think?" asked Carrie excitedly. "I hope it fits. I used the dressmaker who did the gown you're wearing."

Sarah lowered the dress into her lap.

"Carrie dear, I don't know what to say," said Sarah in a faint voice.

"What's the matter? Don't you like it?"

"It's exquisite, it's beautiful," Sarah said.

"Then what's wrong?"

"Where I am going to wear this dress? It's far too elegant for me."

"Nonsense," said Oliver from across the room. "You'll be smashing."

"We had it made for the Twelfth Night party," explained Carrie.

Sarah turned to her sister. "The Twelfth Night party? In Homestead?"

"Why not?" asked Carrie defensively. "We always got dressed up for the Twelfth Night soirees when Mama was here."

Sarah lower lip trembled. "Not like this."

"I don't understand," Carrie responded. "I thought you'd like it."

Sarah stood up abruptly and set the dress on the sofa.

"It's not a question of liking or not liking it. I don't *need* this kind of a dress."

"That's why we thought it would be a special gift," Carrie replied, picking up the box from the carpet.

"Carrie, why don't you understand?" said Sarah in exasperation, moving to the front window. She crossed her arms and stared out into the darkness.

"I *don't* understand. Why are you so stubborn?" Carrie folded the dress and laid it back in the box.

The four men cast nervous glances around the room at each other. The clock on the mantelpiece chimed nine.

Moving toward the pocket doors to the study, Oliver said cheerfully, "Well, gentlemen, shall we adjourn to the library for a smoke?" He held the heavy horsehair portieres aside for Robert and Montague, and pulled the pocket doors shut behind them.

Oesterling stayed put. He was more than happy to have the opportunity to escape from Oliver's entreaties that he, the doctor, invest in railroad stock that Montague had strongly recommended. Oliver was convinced that investing in these new railroads would make them rich, but Oesterling was resisting. He had been very conservative about his investments, and feared plunging into a new venture.

Oesterling contemplated his two daughters standing before him.

"Carrie," Sarah said, turning towards the center of the room. "This dress would be out of place at the party. I'd stick out like a sore thumb." Her voice was thick with emotion.

"I hardly think of this beautiful gown as a sore thumb,'" replied Carrie, hurt.

"Sarah," Oesterling said. "Wouldn't it be OK to wear the dress for the party? I thought it was a special occasion for you."

"It is a special occasion, Papa," Sarah replied, "but I'd feel much more comfortable in my old dress. What would Eirwen Jones feel like in her Sunday dress next to that?" She pointed to the box.

"Who's Eirwen Jones?" asked Carrie. "Do you mean to say that this Jones woman has only one good dress?"

"*I* have only one good dress, Carrie," retorted Sarah.

"Eirwen Jones," interjected Oesterling, "sings in the choir at church. She has one of the loveliest voices I've ever heard. She and her brother, who plays violin, will be performing with Sarah at the party."

"Oh? " said Carrie, pursing her lips. "Who is this brother? And is there a Mr. Jones?"

"Carrie, what does it matter?" replied Sarah. "But since

you asked— her brother, Emlyn Phillips, recently arrived from Wales. And Gwyn Jones, her husband, is a roller in the mill."

"You've invited common laborers to the Twelfth Night party?" asked Carrie.

Oesterling, annoyed, retorted, "Common laborers? Carrie, for heaven's sake!"

Sarah whirled to face her sister. "We've invited many of the same people who came to the other Twelfth Nights. These people are our friends. We didn't come up with a guest list based on the social register."

"I didn't mean to imply you should," said Carrie, "but nevertheless..."

Oesterling cut in.

"Carrie, the invitations are out, the music is set. Mrs. Jones and Emlyn Phillips are, in fact, coming to the house tomorrow evening to go over the pieces for the entertainment. There's no point in discussing further who is or is not coming."

"I can't believe these Welsh immigrants will be taking Mama's place at Twelfth Night," Carrie replied, throwing up her hands.

"Carrie, don't talk nonsense," said Sarah heatedly. "Our grandparents were Welsh immigrants—and so was Mama, for that matter."

"Mama was brought over as a baby," said Carrie. "As far as I..."

"Please, please!" said Oesterling, his voice rising. "Let your mother rest in peace."

"Yes, let's," said Sarah. "I don't wish to carry on this discussion further. In fact, it's been a long week and a long day and I'm going to retire for the evening."

"Sarah, please don't leave the party." Carrie's voice was almost a whine.

"Please excuse me, Carrie," Sarah replied. "Give my best to Oliver and the others."

She came over to Carrie, and touching her sleeve, gave her a light kiss on the cheek.

"Good night," said Sarah to both, and quietly went into the hallway and up the stairs.

Carrie collapsed onto the sofa and put her hands over her face.

"Oh, Papa," she wailed softly. "Why can't Sarah accept my gift? She's so stubborn!"

Oesterling pushed himself out of the armchair and went to sit next to Carrie.

He thought for a moment. He hated these spats between the sisters.

Finally, he said, "Give me the gown. I'll pack it with my things and take it to Homestead. Maybe I can think of something that will change her mind."

"Would you?" said Carrie, blinking back tears. "That would be good. Thank you so much, Papa."

Oesterling stared across at the shimmering tree. With one hand he stroked his beard while with the other he patted Carrie's hand.

How was he going to manage this diplomatic mission? Looking at the dress box next to him on the sofa, he felt very tired.

Emlyn heard the plopping of slippers on the stairs, the squeals of delight from the children, the deeper voices of Eirwen and Gwyn, but they all seemed far away. A thud or peal of laughter from downstairs occasionally brought him to consciousness, but only momentarily. He lapsed again into a deep slumber.

From afar, a soft voice: "Emlyn. Emlyn?" He opened his eyes. It was Eirwen in her best dress standing at the door. Dilys peeked around her mother's skirts, and when she saw he was awake, she came to the bed, stood on tiptoe and kissed him on the cheek. "Merry Christmas, Uncle Em." She hastened back behind Eirwen.

He sat up in bed. "Why, thank you, Dilys dear. Merry Christmas to you, too."

He looked over at Eirwen. He felt vaguely disoriented after staying up so late and sleeping so long on a weekday morning.

He rubbed his face with his palms. "What's going on?"

"Christmas dinner," replied Eirwen. "Our guests will be here in less than an hour."

"Dinner? Guests? So early?"

"Early? It's nearly one in the afternoon."

"Afternoon? I can't believe it."

"Believe it. Come on, get up." She turned to go, and Dilys ran off.

"Wait. Who's coming?"

"The Griffiths—and their little dog Albert. It's such a treat for the children."

"The Griffiths? Who are they?"

Eirwen paused a moment. "The minister and his wife and son."

Emlyn was suddenly wide-awake. "The minister?"

"Now don't be cross, Em. The Griffiths have come here for the last two Christmases. They're from the Valleys—very nice people. You'll like them." She disappeared down the hallway.

Emlyn washed and dressed in his good black suit. Downstairs, Emlyn discovered a rush of activity. The settee and Gwyn's armchair were pushed against the wall. In their place stood the kitchen table, extended by a leaf and covered with a white cloth. Thomas was setting out the dinnerware, while Gwyn carried in chairs.

Emlyn smiled and tried to look amazed as Dilys and Thomas showed him the magical tree and presents Santa had brought. However, Emlyn's thoughts were elsewhere, preoccupied with Griffiths and his wife. Would Griffiths be a valley-of-the-shadow-of-death sort? Would he be saying prayers for something or other every time he turned around? And Mrs. Griffiths—would she be a self-righteous busybody, nosing into everybody's business?

Shortly after the clock struck two, a knock sounded at the door. Thomas ran over and threw it open.

"Happy Christmas, Thomas," said a loud, high-pitched male voice outside, and in trotted a shaggy little terrier followed by a boy slightly younger than Thomas. Behind them were a plump, petite woman and a short, wiry man with bristling copper-colored hair and matching beard.

"Nadolig Llawen," said the man, removing his hat and looking around. "Oh, you have a tree. And a star on top. Very pretty." He smiled and turned to the dog.

"Now, Albert, sit up." The dog reared up on his haunches.

"Now, Albert. Do you wish everyone a Happy Christmas? If so, bark twice." Griffith nodded at the dog, which barked twice. Everyone clapped in appreciation.

Gwyn took the Griffiths' coats upstairs, and Eirwen introduced the Griffiths family to Emlyn.

The next two hours were so filled with activity that Emlyn forgot to worry about Griffiths, the church, or the ministry. Everyone gathered at the table as Eirwen set out the steaming turkey, with sage dressing, mashed potatoes, candied carrots, and a slaw of cabbage, nuts, and apples. Griffiths said grace twice, once in Welsh, and a second time in English for the benefit of the children.

During the meal, Gwyn and Griffiths dominated the conversation. Ordinarily in such a situation, Emlyn would have felt left out, but this time, he was grateful. Mrs. Griffiths turned out to be a shy, quiet woman, who seemed happy to help the children with their food, while Eirwen tended to David in his high chair. Sam Griffiths and Thomas kept slipping bits of food under the table to Albert the terrier, but their parents seemed not to take notice.

The dessert, made by Mrs. Griffiths, was the traditional Welsh Christmas fruitcake, *Teisen Nadolig,* served with several pots of strong black tea and milk.

The boys asked to be excused, and accompanied by Albert, went outside to join the neighbors' sons. Mrs. Griffiths and Eirwen carried the dishes to the kitchen sink, where Eirwen rinsed and left them to be washed up the next morning.

The women sat at the table end next to the fire and began a quiet discussion about their respective needlework projects. David fell asleep in Eirwen's arms, while Dilys played on the floor with her blocks.

Griffiths moved to the sofa on Emlyn's side of the table, and Gwyn settled into his overstuffed armchair.

"Wonderful dinner, Eirwen. Thank you so much," said Griffiths over his shoulder. Gwyn and Emlyn added their thanks.

"You're very welcome," she replied.

"Ah, this is the life," said Gwyn, stretching out his legs and loosening his tie.

Griffiths turned to Emlyn. "Eirwen told me you came over recently from Treorchy."

"Yes, I've been here about a month."

"What do you think of Homestead so far?"

Emlyn recalled his meetings with the Buckmans, but quickly banished them from his thoughts. "To tell you the truth, I don't know the town very well. Most of my waking hours are spent working in the mill. I've met only a few people—some of the fellows at work and the Oesterlings."

"How do you know the Oesterlings?"

"It's a rather pathetic story. I injured my leg during my second day on the job, and Gwyn took me to see Dr. Oesterling."

"Good man, the doctor," said Griffiths. "I trust you're better now."

Emlyn nodded. "I hear you're from the Valleys."

"Yes, I'm from Pontypridd and my wife's from Abercynon. When I got the call to Homestead, I didn't hesitate. In many ways, the towns of the Valleys seem like older versions of Homestead. Ministering to working people is what I know best, what I think God has called me to do."

There was a long pause.

"Eirwen says you went to seminary, at Brecon."

"Yes," replied Emlyn, looking down at his raw hands.

His hands would be a sight at the Twelfth Night party. He self-consciously made fists.

"And," Griffiths was saying, "you were studying at Cardiff?"

Emlyn clenched his fists tighter and nodded. He didn't like where the questioning was headed.

"I'm quite impressed," said Griffiths, easing back into the sofa. "Only the best and brightest are admitted to university."

It turned out that Griffiths knew many of the professors from the theological college. In fact, Griffiths seemed to have gone in many of same circles as Emlyn's father, although the two ministers were not personally acquainted.

Emlyn was completely taken by surprise when Griffiths asked him point-blank why he had forsaken his studies for the ministry.

"Um, well," mumbled Emlyn, "I do not have the calling, as you and my father do."

Emlyn glanced over at Gwyn, hoping he could deflect the course of the conversation elsewhere, but Gwyn's eyes were closed and he was snoring softly.

"Do you feel you've been called to work as a laborer in the mill?"

Emlyn looked at the minister sharply. "I doubt any man is 'called' to such labor."

"Do you think then," asked the minister without irony, "that some kinds of labor are more valuable than others?"

"Of course not," replied Emlyn, his voice rising. "I suppose I was called to *leave* the ministry and Wales—if you want to use such terms."

"Having left Wales myself, I can understand part of what you're saying. It just seems like such an extreme change—from the university to the mill."

"You mean to say," Emlyn said with undisguised hostility, "you think I must be a damned fool for throwing away such prospects."

Griffiths gaped at him.

"I . . . er, I didn't mean to suggest . . ." replied Griffiths, mortified.

Flushing with anger, Emlyn pushed back his chair, scraping it loudly on the floor, and stood up. At the noise, Gwyn started awake with a snort.

"Please," Griffith said, "I meant no offense."

"What do you expect me to do? Launch into an *apologia pro vita sua?*"

For a moment, Emlyn stared at the minister, trying to read if the allusion to the title of Cardinal John Henry Newman's autobiography had had any effect. Emlyn decided it had.

Griffiths sat there wide-eyed and silent, while Gwyn kept blinking, trying to make sense of the scene before him.

Abruptly, Emlyn shoved the chair back to the table. "Please excuse me."

"Emlyn, what's the matter?" Eirwen's voice behind him.

"No matter," Emlyn said in the most casual voice he could muster. "I think I need to get some fresh air."

"Please stay. Don't leave on my account," entreated Griffiths.

Emlyn didn't answer as he walked toward the door to the kitchen. At the doorway, over his shoulder he said in a husky voice, "Happy Christmas."

It wasn't turning out so happily, he thought, his anger at Griffiths rekindling. Why did Griffiths have to probe the wound?

In the warm kitchen, fragrant with spices, he seized his coat and went out the back door.

He strode to the alley and escaped into the gathering dusk. As he heard Eirwen calling out his name from the kitchen door, he quickened his pace.

Damn Griffiths! Why couldn't he leave well enough alone? The day had gone fairly pleasantly up to the point that Griffiths started in about vocation and 'calling'. Emlyn kicked a rock and sent it skittering across the street.

Truth was, he didn't know where he was headed in life. All he knew is that he couldn't serve as a clergyman, and that the only present option was for him to keep working in the mill. Perhaps in the future the path would become clearer. But he couldn't even think about the future. He was living day to day, immersing himself in the dangerous, back-breaking labor of the mill.

Somehow, some day, he'd sort it all out.

Emlyn reached Eighth Avenue and walked along the sidewalk toward Munhall. All of the shops, bars, and offices on the usually bustling avenue were dark. It was strangely quiet—no mill sounds, no traffic. He walked slowly, examining details that he hadn't the time or opportunity to take in previously.

He wandered down Ammon Street toward the tracks. Passing a storefront with a sign that read "D. Fisher Music," he stopped short. The show windows were cleared, so he peered into the interior trying to see what kind of merchandise they carried. He made out the shapes of several upright pianos, parlor organs, and racks of sheet music.

Seeing the instruments and music reminded Emlyn that he needed to practice the violin again before he and Eirwen went to the Oesterlings' tomorrow to rehearse for the party. He had so little time for anything but work and more work. Emlyn contemplated the reams of sheet music inside the shop and sighed.

"Hey there, Em-Lyn. What're you up to?"

The familiar voice made him start. He turned to see Virgil, hands in pockets, standing beside him.

"You know, they're closed."

Emlyn laughed self-consciously. "I know."

"Interested in maybe gettin' one of them pianos? Hard to steal, pianos."

"No, only wondering what kind of music they carry."

"You play?"

"Yes, violin."

"You must play the fancy kind of violin, with music written on paper. My pap played fiddle from the tunes in his head."

"Really? Do you play?"

"Yep, not fiddle but banjo."

"Banjo? I don't know anything about it."

"It's often tuned like a fiddle."

"Actually, I play both fiddle and violin—from tunes on paper and in my head."

"Hmm," mused Virgil, digesting this information.

They stood in silence for a long moment.

"Where you headed?" asked Virgil.

"Oh, I suppose I should go back to the house. I have to get up and go to work tomorrow, but at least it's only a half day."

"Yep. Many of the fellers won't be there. I thought Hunky Joe was gonna bust a blood vessel, he was so worked up about going to Braddock for the big weekend party. Right about now he's probably feeling no pain."

Emlyn nodded, envisioning Joe, amply primed with alcohol, at the Slovak Christmas celebration.

"Come Monday, though, he'll be feeling heaps of it." Virgil chuckled in sadistic satisfaction.

Emlyn shifted uneasily. Virgil never seemed to cut Joe any slack.

"What're you doin' wandering the streets on Christmas night? Don't you have kin here?'

"Uh, yes. I was just walking off dinner." He looked at Virgil. "How about you?"

"Nope. My family—what's left of it—is back on the farm in western Virginny. When my pap died, my older brother Jed took over the property. I headed north, to seek my fortune. I guess you might say I'm an immigrant myself, from Dixie."

"Dixie?"

"Yep, old times there are not forgotten, ever. The South shall rise again." Virgil laughed mirthlessly. "Pappy fought in the Confederate Army. Lot of good it did him, too. By the end of the war, he had been shot up twice and was so crippled he could barely walk. About the only thing he remembered with pride was being asked to fiddle for Marse Robert before the battle at Chancellorsville—one of them battles where he took a minié ball."

Virgil stared into the empty store window, slouched forward, hands still in his pockets. "That was before my time."

After a brief silence, Emlyn pulled out his watch. "Past seven. I'd better get going. Happy Christmas—what's left of it."

Virgil emitted a short grunt. "Yep. See you at the hellhole tomorrow."

As Emlyn made his way back to the house, he contemplated what kind of scene would await him. The Griffiths would be gone, he was certain. His thoughts turned alternately from worrying that he had unduly upset Eirwen to renewed anger about Griffiths' quizzing him about his abandoning studies for the ministry.

By the time he reached the house, it was almost seven-thirty. He entered through the back door and found Eirwen in the kitchen, preparing the children for bed.

"Hi, Uncle Em. Where'd ya go?" asked Thomas.

"Oh, just for a walk up to the Avenue and back, " replied Emlyn with feigned casualness. Should he try to explain to Eirwen, or would that make matters worse?

"I bet there weren't many people out," said Thomas.

"No, there weren't, but I did run into one of the lads from work." Recalling Virgil's loneliness and separation from his family, Emlyn felt regret for forsaking the company of Eirwen and her family.

As Emlyn hung his coat on the hook, he observed Eirwen and the children. Changed into an everyday dress, she looked so tired, so frail. The dishes were piled neatly on the sink, awaiting tomorrow morning's chores.

"Mr. Griffiths wanted me to tell you that he apologizes," said Eirwen quietly. "He didn't say what you were talking about—only that he hopes you will accept his apology."

Emlyn drew a deep breath. As he examined Eirwen's haggard face, his anger at Griffith faded. "His apology is accepted." He paused. "I beg your pardon for leaving so abruptly. I'm sure you can guess what we were discussing." Starting toward the door, he added, " I don't want to talk further about it."

Eirwen smiled sadly at Emlyn. "Your apology is accepted."

She turned to Thomas. "Now you, Master Jones, wash up and get ready for bed."

Emlyn decided to practice for a bit before he went to bed. He went into the front room, now restored to its pre-dinner configuration. Gwyn was already upstairs sleeping, even though he would not be going in to work the next day. The company wouldn't be stoking up the furnaces to full capacity until Sunday night, although the mill never was shut down completely, even for the two holidays.

Emlyn picked up his violin case and took it into the kitchen, which was still warm from the cook stove. While Emlyn tuned his fiddle, Eirwen herded the children out of the room and upstairs.

For the next hour, Emlyn lost himself in the music, first going over the tunes for the party, then playing several pieces he had consigned to memory.

After a short while, Eirwen came in, took off her apron, and poured herself a cup of tea. She eased herself wearily into a chair at the table and listened to Emlyn's playing while she sipped the tea.

When the kitchen clock struck the half-hour after eight, Emlyn lowered the violin.

"I'd better get to bed if I'm going to make it to the mill to-morrow morning," said Emlyn, standing up and setting the instrument in its case. He looked at Eirwen. "You need to get some rest, too."

Eirwen smiled. "So good it is to hear you play. Diolch yn fawr iawn."

Emlyn smiled back. "Very welcome you are."

Eirwen rose, came over to Emlyn, put her arms around him and hugged him tight. They stood there for a long mo-ment, her face against his chest, before Eirwen released him. As she stepped back, Emlyn opened his mouth to speak, but she slipped by him to go upstairs, squeezing his arm as she passed.

Emlyn poured some warm water from a kettle on the stove into a basin and washed up for bed. He pulled his tow-el off its peg and buried his face in it. Standing alone in the quiet kitchen, he bit into his lower lip until he tasted the salt of blood.

Saturday, December 26th

The morning came all too soon for Emlyn. The rest of the family was sleeping as Emlyn groggily pulled on his work clothes and went downstairs. In the parlor, he inhaled the fragrance of the fir tree before going to the kitchen and gulping down the cold tea and *teisen nadolig* that Eirwen left out for him.

At work, only a skeleton crew was keeping the furnaces

primed for when the Sunday night shift came on and started up a full heat. Perhaps because Joe Galik wasn't on the job, Virgil seemed more subdued, less testy. Directed by Frank, Virgil and Emlyn occupied themselves with clean up and maintenance. By the time they left at noon, Emlyn was only half as tired and dirty as he usually was after a full shift.

Back at the house, Emlyn found Gwyn sitting at the kitchen table, remnants of a turkey sandwich on the plate before him. Eirwen was standing by the stove, reading a letter.

"How was the mill today?" asked Gwyn. "I sure am glad I could sleep in."

"Same old mill," replied Emlyn, sliding into the chair opposite Gwyn. "Is that a letter from home?" he asked Eirwen.

"Yes, it came Thursday, but we just opened it now. It's from Gwyn's brother. Good news," replied Eirwen, handing the letter back to Gwyn.

"What is it?"

She set a heaping plate of potato and turkey leftovers in front of Emlyn. "His father has been promoted."

Gwyn's eyes quickly scanned the letter. "The Park Slip Colliery owners have rewarded Tad's honesty and skill with numbers. He has been promoted to weigher. No more going down into the slip for him. At 54, he is getting old for work underground, certainly."

"That is good news," said Emlyn, swallowing a mouthful of mashed potatoes. "How about your brother John?"

"John is still working as shift foreman at the pit. He says he's satisfied with the work, but of course he'd like to be above ground like Tad. Some day, I'm sure."

Emlyn nodded, thinking of his visit to Gwyn's family in Ton du last October. He had made a trip to the old coal and iron area near Aberkenfig by the South Wales coast to pick up items the Joneses had asked him to take to America.

Ton du—'black song'—was indeed black, but not very tuneful. The village was less than a mile from one of the first blast furnaces in Britain, Cefn Cribwr Ironworks, begun in the 1780s. In the Ton itself, the narrow lanes of low miners' row houses were clustered together a short walk from the slip entrance, a large, ugly gash in the landscape.

Emlyn had been relieved that Gwyn's parents didn't pry into his reasons for leaving Wales. Hard-working, devout people, they simply seemed grateful that he was taking two family relics, a tablecloth embroidered by Gwyn's grandmother and a small milk pitcher, to their successful son in Pennsylvania.

They had always been impressed with the Phillips family's prominence in the community, and especially with Emlyn's progress through the heady realm of higher education. Nevertheless, they accepted his choice to emigrate without comment, perhaps assuming that if Gwyn could be such a big success in the New World, so could Emlyn. Emlyn didn't share their confidence.

"John says that your parents are well. At least they were a few weeks ago when he saw them at a cymanfa in Ogmore Vale. And construction on your tad's Beulah Chapel is moving along well, or at least it was until winter set in."

"Tad is undoubtedly very pleased," said Emlyn. "The congregation is growing ever larger. Pretty soon the entire Rhondda Valley will be resounding with hymns of praise."

"Well, anyway," said Gwyn, trying to defuse Emlyn's sarcasm, "it seems the news from South Wales is good all around."

Emlyn started to say something, but Eirwen tightly squeezed his shoulder with one hand as she heaped stuffing on his plate with the other. Emlyn got the message.

As the hall clock chimed seven, Oesterling paced back and forth in the parlor. Cerberus lay on the rug in front of the fireplace, head on his paws, his eyes following his master.

Where was Sarah? He pushed the lace curtains of the front window aside and looked out onto Tenth Avenue. All he could see was the porch in the flickering light of the overhead gaslight.

He reset the curtains and resumed pacing. Breakfast this morning at Carrie's had been strained.

When they arrived home, Oesterling had been called out to tend to one of Dr. Baker's patients, a woman who had injured her ankle when her foot broke through a rotten sidewalk plank. When he had come home around four, Mrs. Sproule told him that Sarah had gone out, but that she would be home for a rehearsal for the Twelfth Night parlor concert at seven o'clock.

Sarah's opinion of Emlyn Phillips had improved after their ride, but she was still wary of him. "Anybody that quits university in the middle of his studies to come to Homestead must be touched in the head," she said.

Oesterling's lukewarm protestations in defense of Emlyn did not sway her. She would withhold final judgment until the party.

On the way back to Homestead earlier, Oesterling had begun to have second thoughts about his offer to carry the dress to Homestead. He didn't know where to begin with Sarah. In despair, he decided to ask Mrs. Sproule. He unpacked the dress and brought it down to show her.

No sooner had he entered the kitchen with the dress over his arm than Molly started to squeal. Mrs. Sproule dropped a wooden spoon and came around the table, wiping her hands on a towel. Both women gaped at the garment, eyes wide.

"What a beautiful dress, Doctor!" Mrs. Sproule exclaimed. "Is it for Sarah?"

"Yes, maybe . . ."

"How can it be 'maybe'?" she asked. "Is it or isn't it?"

She leaned closer to examine the fabric.

Oesterling held it up for them to see. "Carrie had it made for her, but Sarah thinks it's too fancy to wear to the party next week."

Mrs. Sproule snorted. "I never heard of such a thing. Sarah would look beautiful in it."

"If only someone gave me a fine frock like that!" said Molly, her eyes running over the dress.

Oesterling started as he heard the front door open. Sarah.

"Let me help, Doctor," said Mrs. Sproule, lifting the dress from his hand. "You go. Ring if you need me."

Oesterling straightened his waistcoat and pulled open the door to the hallway. Sarah's coat was hanging on the hall tree, and she was removing her hat.

"I couldn't get away from Edie's. She wanted to show me her engagement ring. Stephen gave it to her Christmas Eve." Sarah set down the hat and smoothed back her hair.

"Of course I'm happy for her. Still, I'll miss her at school when she must resign after the wedding."

Sarah looked over at Oesterling. "Is anything wrong, Papa? Oh dear, I hope Eirwen and Emlyn haven't come and gone."

Oesterling tried to manage a smile. "No, they haven't come yet. I hear you're going to rehearse some of the pieces for next Saturday."

Sarah rushed into the parlor and opened the lid on the piano keyboard. It was Margaret's piano, an upright grand, his gift to her many years ago. Sarah began rummaging through some stacks of music.

The doorbell rang, and through the leaded glass of the front door, Oesterling saw two figures standing outside.

"I'll get it," he said to Mrs. Sproule, who had started to come out of the kitchen.

He helped Eirwen to remove her coat and hung it on the hall tree. Her brother set down his violin case, shrugged off his coat, and nervously rubbed his hands.

"How's the knee?" asked Oesterling, extending his hand.

"Good, good, thank you," said Emlyn, taking it and shaking it. His hands were very cold.

Oesterling stood in the doorway while Sarah led Eirwen to the piano. Emlyn walked over to the fireplace and held out his hands to the heat.

Oesterling went across the foyer to his study, leaving the pocket doors open a few inches so he could hear the rehearsal. He settled into his worn horsehair armchair and tried to read the newspaper, but his eyes scanned the words without registering their meaning.

He tucked the afghan around his legs and closed his eyes. Eirwen warmed up, her clear voice gliding up and down the scales. Emlyn tuned the violin to the piano.

During the next hour and a half, they went over pieces, often stopping to work on a part. Sometimes he heard them talking about phrasing or interpretation. He recognized some of the pieces—a song in Welsh by Eirwen, with only violin accompaniment, then a ditty about 'little maids from school.' Ah yes, that was the Gilbert and Sullivan piece Sarah wanted Eirwen to do with another teacher and Melanie Carstens.

One group he'd never heard before, tunes played on the violin. Sprightly, happy tunes. He started tapping his foot to the beat. Dances? That's probably why he never heard them before. What was a Congregationalist minister's son doing playing dance tunes? Who knew? This fellow was an odd one. As long as nobody got up and danced, it would be OK.

The music ceased, and Oesterling stood up and went into the parlor.

Emlyn was putting his violin into its case, while Eirwen was talking to Sarah.

"...and Emlyn picked up a tree on his way home. We set it up and trimmed it after church, when the children were asleep. I made some little things to hang on it. It was so pretty. Thomas and Dilys were thrilled when they came down yesterday morning. There were not only their filled stockings, but the tree, too."

"That's the best part of Christmas," observed Sarah, "the joy it brings to the children. I can see Thomas bounding down the stairs and catching sight of the tree."

"We wouldn't even have had a tree, if Emlyn hadn't convinced me that it would be good for the children," said Eirwen.

"I used the 'when-in-Rome' argument," said Emlyn, snapping the case shut.

"I'm glad it worked," said Sarah.

"So am I," said Oesterling from the foyer archway. "I really enjoyed the concert from my study. It sounds great."

"Thanks, Papa," said Sarah. Turning to Eirwen, she added, "By the way, what time do you want to come to warm up next Saturday?"

The three younger people discussed the logistics of setting up for the concert. Sarah had watched Margaret do this for years, but she was obviously nervous about managing it herself.

"All will be well, you'll see," said Eirwen finally. "Oh! I almost forgot to mention—-As an early Christmas gift, Gwyn gave me money to get material to make a new Sunday dress. Mrs. Griffiths and I have been working on it for the past month. I had hoped it would be finished by Christmas, but there was so much else to do. It will be ready by next weekend, even if I have to work all night to complete it."

Oesterling could swear he saw Sarah's jaw drop. She glanced over at Oesterling, but he showed no reaction to the news.

"That's . . . that's wonderful," said Sarah, turning back to Eirwen. "I'll look forward to you making your debut in it."

Oesterling hesitated, took a deep breath and plunged in. "Sarah also has a new dress."

"Really!" exclaimed Eirwen. "We can make our debuts together."

Sarah turned to Oesterling. "I don't think my dress is appropriate for the party."

"Why not?" asked Eirwen. "I'd love to see it."

"It's not here," replied Sarah. "It's at my sister's house."

"Why don't you send for it? It would be such fun to show off our new frocks."

Sarah opened her mouth to reply, but Oesterling spoke first.

"As a matter of fact, you can see it. The dress actually is here."

Sarah's mouth stayed open and her eyes widened. "How did. . . ? Who?"

Oesterling went to the bell pull and yanked it twice. He was going to be in for it when their guests left.

A moment later Mrs. Sproule emerged from the kitchen carrying the dress.

"Oh Sarah!" Eirwen exclaimed. "What a beautiful dress!"

Eirwen came over to Mrs. Sproule, took the bottom hem in her hands, and stood back, admiring the dress.

"Sarah, this is such an exquisite gown. You *must* wear it. It'll look lovely on you."

She turned toward Emlyn, standing across the room. "Em, don't you agree?"

Emlyn's glance moved from Sarah, the doctor, and back to his sister. "Ah, yes," he said at last. "It is a lovely dress."

Sarah stood silently, the blood rising to her face. Oesterling cringed in anticipation of the impending storm, but she said simply, "Alright, if you both think it's good for the party, I'll wear it."

Mrs. Sproule laid the dress on the sofa and went back into the kitchen as Eirwen and Emlyn put on their overcoats and said their goodbyes.

As Sarah closed the door behind them, her lips went from smiling to tightly pursed.

"Papa, what is the meaning of this treachery? I thought I expressed my opinion clearly on the subject of this dress to Carrie. I'd expect this from her, but from *you*!"

Tears welled up and her lower lip trembled.

Seeing her pain, Oesterling felt a stab of guilt. "Well, yes, I knew you don't want a new dress, and I agree that your old one is perfectly fine. However, since the new one's already been made, I thought . . ."

He faltered, and Sarah jumped in. "I suppose Carrie put you up to this. She always insists on having things her way."

"Actually, no," admitted Oesterling. "I offered to take the dress home with me."

Sarah brushed away a tear and crossed her arms.

"To tell you the truth," continued Oesterling, "I didn't know what I was going to do with it until Eirwen said that she'd be wearing her new dress. What harm is there in asking her opinion? Your objection was that the dress would be too ostentatious for the occasion."

She glanced from him to the dress.

"That was my spoken objection to Carrie—but I told you

how much I hate these tricks of hers. Since they've moved to Point Breeze, it's gotten so much worse. You'd think she was living next to the Vanderbilts instead of some social-climbing snobs."

Oesterling looked down. "You seem to be implying," he said carefully, "that Carrie and Oliver are snobs, too."

"Well?" Sarah challenged. "The two of them take every opportunity to snipe at Homestead and the residents they see as hoi polloi. Oliver and Carrie don't, however, seem to mind living off the money they make from the labor of the unwashed masses in the mill."

Oesterling sighed. He knew it was true, but he didn't want to increase the friction between the sisters.

"Did you hear?" Sarah continued. "Carrie invited Norton Montague to the party—on her own, without consulting me. I suppose she and Oliver need someone of their own class to talk to."

"Now, Sarah," said Oesterling. "It's not going to help getting all upset over something that's already been done. Try to concentrate on the friends you invited and have a good time."

"OK, fine," declared Sarah, striding over to the sofa and picking up the dress. "I will try to do that. And I will wear the dress—but only because Eirwen wants me to."

With the dress in her arms, Sarah ran up the stairs. A few seconds later, Oesterling heard the door to her room close with a decisive thud.

The kitchen door opened and Mrs. Sproule leaned into the hallway, looking at the sofa where the dress had been placed. "Will she wear the dress?"

"She will," replied Oesterling, placing his hands in his pants pockets. "But Lord only knows what will happen when Carrie gets here."

—•●•—

For the Oesterling household, the week after Christmas brought a flurry of activity. When he was home, the doctor retreated to the study to avoid the frenzy of preparations for the party. Sarah was practically crazed. She bustled about, consulting with Mrs. Sproule, directing Molly in the cleaning of the crystal glassware and the glass fixtures of the gaslights—all this and practicing for the parlor concert as well.

1892 Saturday, January 2nd

When the hall clock struck seven, Oesterling stood looking out the front door at the light snow beginning to cover the grass. Molly and her sister Lizzie—hired for the party—were preparing to set out the punch bowl and platters of canapés on the dining room table, while Mrs. Sproule was fussing with the spruce and cedar roping on the staircase banister. Sarah was upstairs.

Oesterling put Cerberus into the back hallway and went into the parlor to stoke the coals in the fireplace grate. He was more than ready for the guests, although he dreaded a possible squabble between his daughters.

Mrs. Sproule went upstairs to help Sarah with something.

The doctor crisscrossed the parlor, dining room, foyer and study checking that all the seats had been placed at good angles for conversation and mixing. The gaslights were lit. Now to wait for the guests.

At a little past seven-thirty, as expected, the Griffiths were the first to arrive. The minister and his wife came early because they needed to leave early, the next day being the second Sunday after Christmas.

At the sound of the minister's voice in the foyer, Sarah came out of her room and started down the staircase. Oesterling barely suppressed a gasp; he hardly recognized her.

As she descended to the foyer, Sarah stood tall and straight in the dark green and burgundy dress, a black velvet ribbon around her neck. Her hair was swept up, held in place by a black Spanish comb, and she was wearing her mother's pearl earrings.

"Miss Oesterling!" exclaimed the minister, smiling broadly. "If I may say so, you look stunning this evening."

"Thank you, Mr. Griffiths." She smiled back.

Mrs. Griffiths, a fine seamstress herself, also complimented Sarah and expressed her admiration for the dress.

No sooner had Molly taken the Griffiths' wraps upstairs than the doorbell rang again.

This time it was George Johnson, a teacher from the high school, and his wife Polly. On their heels came William Williams, the superintendent of O.H.2, accompanied by Mrs. Williams. Then Eirwen and Gwyn Jones, with Emlyn Phillips bringing up the rear.

Sarah came over to greet them, and Eirwen expressed enthusiastic approval of the new dress. In turn, when Eirwen removed her coat, Sarah insisted she walk back and forth in the foyer to model her new frock. Those standing nearby applauded and complimented both Sarah and Eirwen on their handsome dresses.

Eirwen's was much more modest than Sarah's—maroon wool with lace edging and a small bustle—but to Oesterling, the dress looked quite attractive. He was thankful that Carrie was not there to aggravate Sarah.

For the next hour, the doorbell kept ringing, and one after the other, over thirty guests had arrived—people from the church, the business community, some teachers, a couple of lawyers, Oesterling's two doctor-friends and an engineer. At Carrie's insistence, Edwin and Marian Cross had been invited, but much to Oesterling's relief, had sent their regrets. One of the last to arrive was Norton Montague, but even he arrived before Carrie and Oliver, who still hadn't appeared as of quarter to nine.

"Please forgive my late arrival," Montague said as he took off his coat. "I stopped by the Potters' open house this evening and had difficulty getting away."

So that's why Carrie and Oliver hadn't come yet.

Over Dr. Baker's shoulder, Oesterling saw Montague lean over Sarah, complimenting her dress, and kissing her hand. Sarah tolerated this attention for a minute, but eventually excused herself. Montague glanced around, looking for a familiar face. Shortly thereafter, Oesterling saw him talking with Earl Wainwright, the engineer.

Oesterling circulated through the guests, chatting and moving on. He found it difficult to move freely, as guests were scattered throughout the dining room, parlor, study and foyer. Oesterling glanced out the front door. No Carrie and Oliver.

As he moved into the study, the doctor saw Jasper Goodwin take a silver flask from his suit jacket and pour something into the punch cups of himself and another attorney. Oesterling pretended he didn't see. Margaret would have been upset, but he didn't mind so long as everyone acted civilized.

The doctor retraced his steps to the foyer. The party was going well. Laughter and conversation filled the downstairs rooms. Molly had come from the kitchen three times to replenish the food and drink.

Shortly before nine-thirty, Sarah came around to announce the parlor concert would begin soon. Gwyn and Mr.

Griffiths arranged the furniture in concentric half-circles around the piano for the women and elderly guests. Ten minutes of chaos ensued, as people moved around, selecting places to hear the concert.

The sound of voices singing scales issued faintly from one of the upstairs rooms. Emlyn was at the piano, tuning his violin.

Finally, everyone was settled and Sarah stood by the piano to announce the opening piece, 'Nocturne #5 in F-Sharp' by Chopin. Oesterling noted with annoyance that Montague was standing just to one side of the piano.

As Sarah sat on the piano stool and placed her hands on the keyboard, Oesterling, standing at the back of the group in the dining room, checked his pocket watch. Nearly 10 and no Carrie.

After the Chopin piece, Jack and Melanie Carstens began singing 'É Il Sol Dell'Anima' from *Rigoletto*. No sooner had they begun than the doorbell interrupted their duet. Oesterling heard talking near the door, Carrie's laughter, whispering among the guests. When he glimpsed Carrie and Oliver pushing their way through the foyer, anger boiled up in Oesterling. The Carstens kept singing, but many heads turned toward the commotion.

At the end of a phrase, Sarah stopped playing, pivoted around on the stool, and stood. Sarah looked straight at her sister and remarked coolly, "Carrie! How nice of you to drop by for our concert."

Carrie flushed, and Oesterling headed around via the back way from the dining room into the foyer. By the time he reached Carrie and Oliver, the duet had started over again. Oesterling took Carrie's arm and led her into the back hallway. Oliver followed.

"Carrie, where were you? What do you mean bursting in on the concert like this?"

Carrie kissed Oesterling on the cheek.

"Papa, don't be annoyed. We were invited to the Potters' open house this evening, and we had to put in an appearance there."

"But it's ten o'clock," retorted Oesterling. "It must have been a long appearance."

"We're sorry to be late," said Oliver. "The requirements of the job, you know."

Oliver punched him lightly on the shoulder.

Oesterling thought of punching him back, but didn't.

Molly took their wraps, and Oesterling led Oliver and Carrie into the dining room, where he took his place behind the group. He was going to keep an eye on those two for the duration of the party.

Eirwen's solo, accompanied by Emlyn, was plaintive and moving; then Emlyn played the Welsh and Irish fiddle tunes. During Emlyn's set, Oesterling heard thudding coming from the kitchen.

He slipped out of the dining room and pushed the kitchen door open a crack. There were Molly and Lizzie, arm-in-arm, hopping around the table, and Mrs. Sproule keeping time with spoons. He was about to push into the room when the music stopped and so did the dancing. Applause followed, and Oesterling returned to the dining room in time to hear Sarah begin Schubert's 'Musical Moment No. 5 In F Minor.'

The grand finale was 'Three Little Maids from School' from Gilbert and Sullivan's operetta, *The Mikado*, sung by Eirwen, Melanie, and one of Sarah's teacher friends, while Sarah and Emlyn accompanied.

Three little maids from school are we
Pert as a school-girl well can be
Filled to the brim with girlish glee
Three little maids from school
Everything is a source of fun
Nobody's safe, for we care for none
Life is a joke that's just begun
Three little maids from school
Three little maids who, all unwary
Come from a ladies' seminary
Freed from its genius tutelary
Three little maids from school
Three little maids from school

As the trio began the sixth and final verse, Oesterling noticed that Montague had moved even closer to the piano, practically breathing down the neck of the dowager wife of a retired teacher. When applause broke out at the end, Montague's voice could be heard above the clapping, shouting, "Bravi, bravi!"

To conclude the concert, Sarah led the whole group in singing, 'Deck the Halls.' Oliver, not being one to sing publicly, stood there with a smug grin on his face. Montague, however, seemed to have no such compunctions and joined in lustily. Oesterling noted that Montague was the first to reach Sarah after she stood to acknowledge the applause.

As the clapping died away, guests began milling around, many coming forward to compliment the musicians. The Griffiths and several others came over to the doctor to say their goodbyes and thank him for the party. Oesterling watched as Carrie made her way over to Sarah. Carrie was wearing her Christmas dress, complete with the ruby jewelry Oliver had given her.

He watched as Sarah, Carrie, and Montague stood together by the piano. What were they talking about? He hoped Carrie wouldn't say anything to inflame Sarah.

His thoughts were abruptly derailed by Molly's voice. "Please, sir. May have a word with you."

Surprised, Oesterling turned around, "Is anything wrong?"

"No, sir. It's just . . . I mean we were wondering if we—that is, Lizzie and me—might talk for a moment to the fiddler, Mr. Phillip, ain't it?"

"I suppose so," said Oesterling, puzzled. "I'll ask him to come back."

"Thank you, sir," said Molly, dropping a quick curtsy, and running into the back hallway.

What was that about?

Oesterling waited until the crowd around the musicians had dwindled to two before he approached Emlyn. At Oesterling's presentation of Molly's request, Emlyn seemed dumbfounded.

"Why does she want to talk to me?" he asked twice. In the end, Emlyn agreed to speak to Molly in the kitchen, if Oesterling would accompany him.

When they came into the kitchen, all activity ceased. Mrs. Sproule turned from the dishes she was stacking and said to Molly, "Speak up, lass. They won't wait all night."

Molly and Lizzie came over and stood in front of Emlyn, who watched them as a buffalo watches encircling wolves.

Oesterling interjected himself. "This is Molly Ahern and her sister Lizzie. Molly and Lizzie, meet Emlyn Phillips." The young women curtseyed while Emlyn bowed slightly.

Molly was black-haired, rawboned, with smiling dark eyes. Lizzie had her sister's sturdy build, but her freckled face was fairer, more serious.

"Mr. Emlyn," began Molly. "I mean Mr. Phillip. Lizzie

here is getting married at the end of February, before Lent." Lizzie elbowed her gently. "Well, we heard you playing earlier. And we knew some of the tunes. And we. . . ."

Molly giggled nervously.

"Go on," prodded Mrs. Sproule.

"And Lizzie is wondering if you would do us the honor of playing for her wedding dance. We already have people to play the whistle, bodhran, and box, but we have no fiddler, and that's the most important instrument."

Emlyn stared blankly at the sisters.

Oesterling debated if he should say something.

"I don't . . ." began Emlyn haltingly. "I have never played for a dance. In fact, I've never even been to a dance."

The sisters glanced at each other, thunderstruck. Silence ensued.

"You've never been to a dance? Why in the world not?" Molly blurted out.

Emlyn turned beet-red. Lizzie jabbed Molly in the ribs with her elbow.

"I mean," Molly added quickly, "how do you know the tunes, then? I've only heard them played at dances."

"I learned them from Irish musicians on the ship coming over," replied Emlyn.

"Oh," said Molly and Lizzie. More silence.

Oesterling stepped into the void. "Mr. Phillips' family, like Sarah and myself, are Congregationalists, a denomination which disapproves of dancing and drinking spirits."

The sisters gaped at the doctor. They were apparently having a hard time digesting this information.

"We didn't mean no disrespect," said Molly to Emlyn.

"If your priest is against dancing, we understand," added Lizzie.

Emlyn flushed again.

"Yes, well, we don't have priests *per se*," he declared, clenching his fists.

He paused, eyes darting back and forth between the doctor and the sisters. Finally, he said decisively, "Maybe it is time for me to go to a dance!"

Oesterling's eyes examined the younger man. While he hadn't intended to encourage Emlyn to play, that's exactly what had happened.

"After all, I'd be playing, not dancing," Emlyn added. "I'll be happy to play for you."

"Are you sure?" asked Molly hesitantly.

"Yes, quite sure," he replied.

"Oh thank you, Mr. Phillip!" cried Lizzie, clapping her hands together.

A disturbance in the back hall turned everyone's attention to the door as it flew open. Oliver's head poked into the room.

"There you are!" he exclaimed to the doctor. "We've been wondering where you went."

"I'm coming," said Oesterling, heading out the door. "Sorry to abandon the guests."

As the door closed behind them, Oliver clapped a hand on Oesterling's shoulder and asked, "What the dickens were you and that violinist chap doing hobnobbing with the kitchen help?"

"You wouldn't want to know," replied Oesterling, pressing forward into the foyer.

In the kitchen, Lizzie and Molly swung each other around, bumping into the table and upsetting an empty cream bottle.

"Alright, Molly," said Mrs. Sproule, wiping her hands on her apron. "It's now time to get back to serving the guests. You and Mr. Phillips can discuss details later."

"Yes'm," said Mollie. Then to Emlyn, "Thank you, sir."

"At your service," replied Emlyn with a nod of the head.

He withdrew into the foyer, where he found Oesterling talking to three men. One was the young man who had hung over the piano to watch Sarah, the second was the man who had interrupted them in the kitchen, and the third was a bit older. They were obviously gentlemen, judging from their finely tailored clothing. Emlyn glanced into the front parlor, trying to find another group to join.

"Emlyn?" Oesterling's voice. "Come over here, please. There are some people who'd like to meet you."

Emlyn reluctantly joined the group.

"May I present Emlyn Phillips, Eirwen Jones's brother, recently arrived from Wales," began Oesterling.

Indicating the man who had stood by the piano, the doctor said, "I would like you to meet Norton Montague."

Emlyn took Montague's extended hand and found it cool and limp.

"Pleased to meet you. I enjoyed the concert," said Montague blandly.

"Thank you. Pleased to meet you I am," replied Emlyn.

"And this is my son-in-law, Oliver Strong. He and Mr. Montague both work for Carnegie Steel."

Strong took Emlyn's hand in an iron grip, crushing his fingers.

"Delighted. Nice work on the violin."

Emlyn tried not to wince. With a smile that verged on a smirk, Strong let go of Emlyn's hand.

"Thank you," replied Emlyn, flexing his fingers.

"Last but not least," said the doctor, "may I introduce another Carnegie Steel man and compatriot of yours, William Williams."

"Welcome to America," said Williams. "I'm very happy to meet you. I've heard about you from Gwyn and Eirwen."

"Glad to meet you, Mr. Williams," replied Emlyn, shaking his hand. "If I'm not mistaken, I'm obliged to you for finding me a place in the mill."

Strong and Montague looked at Williams.

"You're working in the mill?" Strong asked Emlyn.

Emlyn blushed. "I just started."

"In what capacity?" asked Montague, looking him up and down. "I don't recall seeing you around."

"I'm not working in the office," said Emlyn, his blush deepening. "I'm working in O.H.2."

"As a laborer?" asked Strong. "I thought the doctor had said something about your being educated."

Montague's eyebrows went up.

"Yes, that's true," stammered Emlyn. "I've only just got here, and. . . ."

Williams cut in.

"Gwyn didn't mention anything about your education when he asked if I could place you at the mill. And I didn't connect you with stories circulating at church about Eirwen's brother from the university.

Maybe we can find something more suitable for you. Why don't you stop by my office on Monday morning, so I can learn more about your background, maybe find something different for you? I can't make any promises, but we can talk. Gwyn can show you where I'm located."

Now it was Emlyn's turn to be shocked.

"Yes, of course, I'll be there," he replied, again shaking Williams' hand. "Thank you."

As his hand dropped, Emlyn felt a light touch on his sleeve.

"Papa, I'm waiting to be introduced to this fine musician."

Emlyn turned to the woman, the same attractive young woman whose entrance had interrupted the concert. His eyes quickly scanned her petite, yet shapely figure, and her opulent gown of rich burgundy. Could this be Sarah's sister? It seemed impossible.

"Emlyn," said the doctor, "this is my daughter, Carrie Strong. You've already met her husband Oliver.

Carrie, may I present Emlyn Phillips, recently arrived from Wales."

Carrie extended her right hand, palm down. Emlyn stared at it, wondering how he was going to shake it. There was a brief moment before he realized she expected him to kiss it.

Feeling foolish, he lifted her hand to his lips. This was not how introductions were concluded in the social circles he frequented in Wales. She gave his hand a slight squeeze as he let go of it.

As he stood upright, she smiled at him.

"I'm delighted to make your acquaintance, Mrs. Strong."

Tilting her head to one side, she replied, "As indeed I am to make yours, Mr. Phillips. What an enchanting medley of tunes you played on the violin. So simple, yet so charming."

Gazing straight into his eyes, she smiled again.

Self-conscious, Emlyn let his eyes drop.

"I'm glad you enjoyed my playing. They were Welsh dance tunes, you know."

Carrie laughed. "Indeed! That might be the first time dance music was played in this house."

She glanced at Oesterling.

"First, dance tunes. Next, liquor, gaming, wild women—

who knows? Papa, how did you and Sarah ever allow such sinfulness under this roof?" she asked, shaking her head and smiling.

Looking at the doctor, the others in the group shifted uneasily.

"Carrie, *really*—," interjected Oliver.

Before Oesterling could say anything, she added, "Oh, but there was no dancing, so that's of course permissible."

She turned to Emlyn and winked slyly.

Emlyn was so astonished his mouth almost dropped open.

Oesterling's features reddened.

"Carrie," said Oliver, coming over and gripping her left elbow. "I think it's time for us to head home."

She tried to shrug off her husband's grip.

"But dearest Oliver, we just got here," Carrie retorted.

"Indeed you did," snapped Oesterling. "And because of your late arrival, you missed some of the concert. Now this business about dance tunes!"

Emlyn grimaced, recalling that he had just agreed to play for a wedding dance.

"Sorry, Papa. I was only trying to be amusing."

Carrie glanced at Emlyn, then cast her eyes downward, a slight smile on her lips and Oliver's hand still on her elbow.

No one said a word.

At that moment, Sarah stepped into the group next to her father. She looked around.

"Have I interrupted something?" asked Sarah.

"No, no," replied her father. "Please join us."

"Yes, do, Miss Oesterling," said Montague. "We would be delighted to have the company of both sisters."

Carrie giggled; Oliver scowled.

"In fact," said Oliver, grim-faced, "I was just saying that we should start home. It's nearly eleven, and snow is falling."

Emlyn saw his opportunity.

"Indeed, I, too, regrettably must be heading home. Thank you for the party," he said to Sarah and the doctor. In turn, they thanked him for playing.

He bowed slightly toward Carrie, then at the three men. "I am pleased to make your acquaintance. Mr. Williams, I will see you on Monday. Good night, ladies and gentlemen."

As he turned to go into the parlor to get his violin, he heard Carrie and Oliver's voices behind him arguing in harsh whispers.

He hadn't planned to leave then, but this party was providing more strange situations than he bargained for. He quickly gathered up his violin and overcoat, and went to the door.

Outside, thick snowflakes fell, muffling the racket from the mill buildings. Pulling up his collar, Emlyn carefully made his way down the steps.

III.

A perfect mill is the road to wealth.

—Andrew Carnegie, letter to William Swin (1879)

January 4th, 1892

Emlyn sat on a metal chair in William Williams' office, fingering his cap. His right knee jerked nervously up and down.

For the past five minutes, Williams had been sitting at his desk as Emlyn, opposite him, narrated the story of his schooling in Wales.

Williams pushed back the oak swivel chair and stood. He walked around the desk and leaned back on it, facing Emlyn.

"That's a very impressive education you've got, Phillips," said Williams, "but as you're well aware, it's not tailored to employment in the steel industry. In this city of engineers, theology and liberal arts aren't of much practical application. Although of course, maybe more people should apply them to their daily lives."

Williams grinned.

Emlyn nodded, crossing his legs in an effort to stop the anxious jiggling.

Williams paused for a moment, pondering.

"Have you thought of seeking work as a tutor or teacher

in music or languages?" he asked. "That profession would fit your background well."

"I have," answered Emlyn, "but it pays so poorly that it would take forever to get out of debt. Gwyn says I have a chance of working up to a better-paying job in the mill."

"Well, you've managed to survive for several weeks working at the furnaces, and apparently you can take the heat, so to speak. It's true that you could move up in the mill, especially if you develop the kind of skills Gwyn has. However, that may take years to accomplish. How likely would that be?"

Emlyn looked down at the dusty floor. "Not very likely."

"And there's the possibility that you may grow tired of mill work, or get bored with it in a few months, or years."

Emlyn nodded, unable to deny that he already was getting worn down on the job at the furnace—although he wasn't going to admit it to anyone. He shuffled his feet, gazing at the papers on Williams' desk.

Suddenly, he had an idea.

"Sir, there's one field of my studies that might apply to work here."

"What's that?"

"Math."

"What kind of math?"

"Algebra, trigonometry, geometry, calculus. They are part of the liberal arts curriculum at Cardiff."

"I see," replied Williams, rubbing his chin with his knuckles. "Hmm, let me think about that for a bit. Maybe we can find a place where you could apply these."

A bald man wearing a vest and rumpled white shirt poked his head into the open office door.

"Mr. Williams," he said, "Swenson has located the missing manganese shipment."

"Thanks, Ernie," said Williams, standing up. "I'll be there straightaway."

Emlyn stood up as well.

"Thank you very much, Mr. Williams," said Emlyn, "for meeting with me."

"It's my pleasure," replied Williams, shaking Emlyn's hand. "I wish I could be more encouraging."

Williams paused, and added, "I'll make some inquiries in the main office and see if there's any position that might fit your background."

Emlyn thanked him again and took his time walking back to the furnace.

He was in no hurry to face Virgil again after what had happened earlier that morning when Frank had told Emlyn he was free to go to Williams's office.

Virgil had immediately started quizzing him about why he would be going to see the supervisor of O.H.2. Even though Emlyn had tried to downplay the significance of the meeting, Virgil deduced correctly the point of the interview, and it sent him into a fury.

"Gee whiz, wonders never cease!" snarled Virgil. "The rest of us drudges can bust our asses while Em-Lyn here strolls off to have a confab with the big boss—who just happens to be another Taffy. What a coincidence!"

Frank told Virgil to get back to work, an order that only increased Virgil's pique. He stalked off cursing.

As Emlyn walked away, audible from behind the furnace came Virgil's barked commands to Joe and Stanley, a new Slovak worker.

At least, thought Emlyn as he skirted a pile of debris by a mill shed, Joe knows how to ignore Virgil and his foul moods.

Now Emlyn would have to face Virgil and his envy once

again. And for what? Emlyn's prospects for getting any kind of mill job but the one he currently held seemed unlikely. In fact, as a native-born American, Virgil's prospects at the mill were probably much better than his—but try telling Virgil that.

Emlyn sighed despondently as he approached his work site. To his relief, Virgil and the others were off making back wall at another furnace. Frank noted Emlyn's return and directed him to take a couple of broken pickaxes to the shop for repairs.

Back at the furnace again, Emlyn braced himself for the onslaught from Virgil. Instead, however, Virgil worked in silence, acting as if he didn't even mark the presence of Emlyn and the others.

Joe rolled his eyes. "That Wirgil, he get all steamed up over crazy shit. Now he don't talk."

"*Verrückt*!" added Joe, tapping his right temple. "He crazy guy."

"Not so much crazy as envious," Emlyn said, picking up a shovel.

"What's that?" asked Joe.

"He thinks he wants what I have," replied Emlyn.

Joe laughed. "That Wirgil really is crazy."

"Anyway, let's not go near him."

"OK with me," said Joe, grabbing a shovel, and they went off to join Stanley and the rest of the crew in shoveling out the lining of the furnace.

Stanley knew little English, and Joe had to repeat instructions to him in Slovak.

For the rest of the shift, Virgil worked in silence, a development that Emlyn preferred over Virgil's verbal abuse of the Slovaks.

The next day Virgil went about work as before, alternately surly and jesting. Virgil had apparently decided to take a wait-and-see approach to the outcome of Emlyn's visit to the boss. Virgil resumed making cracks about 'dumb Hunkies' to Emlyn, who declined to join in the castigation of speakers of languages other than English—a group of which he was a member.

—•••—

The month of January passed with Emlyn dragging himself out of bed six days a week and returning home exhausted after each shift. The day after his talk with Williams, Emlyn gave up shaving. For the first few days the stubble on his face itched terribly, but extreme fatigue kept him from considering resuming this daily task. What was fashion to him? So what if he looked like Alfred, Lord Tennyson? Maybe people would start taking him for a poet, too.

The weekends provided some respite from mill drudgery, but Emlyn spent most of his time off doing nothing but sleeping and eating. Occasionally, he'd pull out a book, but often found himself too tired to keep reading more than half an hour at a time.

Sundays, while the rest of the family was at chapel, he'd take a leisurely walk along the riverbank. But the smoke and din from the mill diminished any small pleasure he felt from being outdoors.

His agreement to play for Lizzie Ahern's wedding had completely faded from memory—that is, until he was leaving the mill pay window on the first Saturday in February.

"Mr. Phillip! Oh, Mr. Phillip!" a feminine voice called out from the crowd of men waiting to be paid. He scanned the rows of faces, and outside the entrance, Emlyn saw Molly Ahern, red-cheeked from the cold under a rough tweed headscarf, jumping up and down and waving a handkerchief.

He waved back and pushed his way to the door.

"The doctor said you'd probably be here," Molly said as he approached. "I had a hard time picking you out with them whiskers on your face. You haven't forgotten about Lizzie's wedding dance, have ye?"

"Of course not," he lied. "When is it, again?"

"Saturday the 26th." She turned to put her hand on the shoulder of a thin, angular man at her right.

"This here's Paddy Mahoney, who plays box."

The man smiled broadly, showing a row of crooked yellow teeth. His thinning hair was turning gray, but his pale eyes twinkled.

"Right pleased to meet you, Mr. Phillip," he said, extending his hand.

"Call me Emlyn," he said, taking Mahoney's hand. "Emlyn Phillips. Glad to meet you. When can we get together and go over some tunes?"

"How about this afternoon?" replied Mahoney.

Emlyn hesitated. His fondest wish was to go home and sleep.

"Well, I . . . er," he hedged.

"As it turns out, none of us has to work," said Mahoney. "I work as a mill carpenter on day shift, and Dan O'Connor, whistle player, is a teamster. His deliveries should be over about 5."

There was no getting out of it. He had committed himself.

"Good," replied Emlyn. "Where shall we meet?"

"O'Reilly's pub, on the 300 block of Eighth Avenue. That's where the lads gather for *seisuns.*"

Emlyn looked puzzled.

"Y'know, to make music."

"It's a great load of fun," said Molly, giggling.

"That's good," replied Emlyn dubiously. "See you around five o'clock."

Emlyn plodded home, cursing himself for committing to do this job, a job Eirwen didn't even know about, and would disapprove of if she did. Why hadn't he told her and Gwyn? He had put it completely from his thoughts, that's why. Now he would have to face the music in more ways than one.

When Emlyn reached the house, no one was home. A kettle of beef stew was simmering on the back of the cook stove, and the table and floor were scrubbed and oiled. Two fresh loaves of bara brith sat on the shelf above the table, waiting to be consumed for Sunday breakfast.

The kitchen clock struck three as he took off his jacket and boots, and he considered taking a quick nap before going out. He poured hot water from the kettle on the stove into a basin and washed up, attempting in vain to remove all the grime from his hands. A bath would have to wait till later.

He set his alarm clock for 4:30 and curled up under the comforter on his bed. It seemed like only a few minutes had passed when the clock's tinny bell jangled him awake.

He dozed off and awakened with a start twenty minutes later. Emlyn pulled on woolen trousers and sweater, and ran downstairs. After grabbing his violin case from behind the parlor couch, Emlyn stopped at the desk and took out a piece of paper to leave a note.

What to say? Again, he wished he had mentioned this gig to Eirwen, but he hadn't.

Won't be here for supper. Off to play fiddle. Em

As he was locking the back door on his way out, the clock

was striking five. A cold drizzle was falling as Emlyn half ran, half walked up Amity Street in the twilight gloom. On Eighth Avenue, some shoppers were still bustling about, trying to complete their purchases before the shops closed.

Halfway down the 300 block Emlyn found the glowing front of O'Reilly's pub. Thick condensation on the windows prohibited him from seeing inside, and for a moment Emlyn hesitated at the door. A second later, the door burst open and two drunken mill workers, still in work clothes, pushed by him on their way out. He watched as they disappeared down the street, their arms around each other, singing and weaving around pedestrians.

"Don't just stand there, boyo, and let in a chill," someone yelled from the bar.

Emlyn stepped inside and took off his cap. The warm air was pungent with the odors of whisky, grease, and tobacco smoke. The interior was about half the size of the pub he'd been in that first day with Gwyn.

"'Ey there, Phillips. Over here," a voice shouted from the back of the saloon.

Emlyn peered through the smoke.

Seated at a small square table were four men, one of them Paddy Mahoney, with a button accordion resting on his right knee. Glass mugs holding various shades of amber liquid sat before them.

"We were just starting to warm up," said Paddy, pulling another chair over as Emlyn arrived at the table.

"Let me introduce Dan, the man with the whistle."

Emlyn leaned over to shake the hand of the fair, black-haired young man next to Paddy.

"*Cén chaoi 'bhfuil tú?*" asked Dan, taking Emlyn's hand.

"No, Dan," laughed Paddy. "Forget the Gaelic. This is Emlyn Phillips, who you see, is one of our brethren from the British Isles, a Welshman."

"Aha!" replied Dan. "Then in that case, 'How do you do?' Glad to make your acquaintance."

Dan pumped Emlyn's hand vigorously.

"Da iawn iawn, diolch yn fawr," replied Emlyn. "Glad to meet you."

They all laughed.

"These other lads," said Paddy, "are here to help us out a bit with the beat—Jack on the bodhran, and Tommy on the spoons."

Jack, a large man with a florid complexion, pounded a tattoo on the drum, and the two nodded. Emlyn nodded back.

Emlyn sat next to Paddy, pulled out his violin and began tuning it.

"I'm drinkin' stout. What'll ye have?" asked Dan, rising from his chair.

"I don't need anything, thank you," replied Emlyn. "I'm good for now."

He held his breath, fearing the reaction.

"Oh, that's right," said Dan, sitting down. "Lizzie said your religion frowns on liquor and dancing." Dan paused. "Well, to each his own."

Dan lifted his mug of stout to salute Emlyn and took a deep draft.

Emlyn started to say something, but stopped.

"In any case, we're glad to have you and your fiddle," declared Dan, setting down the mug. "Things ain't been the same since Liam Dahill took his fiddle and left for the wilds of Ohio last year, have they, boys?"

The others nodded in assent.

"Let's start with a few reels," said Paddy, pulling at the bellows of his accordion.

With that, the music began. Paddy would start a tune, and the others would join in. Emlyn wasn't familiar with over half of them, but he did his best to follow along.

For an hour and a half, they went from reels to jigs, slides to hornpipes, and 'round again: 'The Silver Spear,' 'Miss McLeod's,' 'The Star of Munster,' 'Tripping Up the Stairs,' 'Walls of Liscarrol,' 'The Road to Lisdoonvarna.' Emlyn couldn't recall the names of many of the tunes, but that wouldn't matter if he could keep the tunes themselves in his head.

Meanwhile, the pub was getting more crowded. Workers in dirty mill clothes were gradually replaced by others who had gone home and cleaned up for a night on the town.

The empty mugs on the musicians' table were taken away, and the barmaid kept returning with filled ones. Paddy occasionally stopped playing, pulled a pouch of tobacco from his vest and rolled a thin cigarette. He'd set the end afire, place the cigarette into his mouth, and resume where they'd left off.

As time passed, Dan started to play faster and faster, until Paddy finally lost his temper.

"For Chrissakes, Danny, how can these aged fingers keep up with such a mad rush?"

Dan blushed. "Sorry, Paddy. I get carried away, y'know."

After gulping down the rest of his draft, Paddy said, "Right. Well, let's recommence—but slower, dammit!"

Tom, the man playing the spoons, grew increasingly exuberant. At some points, he started banging vigorously on the table top for emphasis. Emlyn wondered if the barman minded that the polished wood was being battered and nicked.

At seven o'clock, Paddy set down the box and pushed back from the table.

"I don't know about you, but I'm in dire need of some refreshment. It was a long week at work for these old bones. What d'ye say we move to the back dining room, lads, and grab some vittles?"

Everyone agreed. Paddy got up and went to the bar, returning with five mugs hanging precariously from his fingers.

"Here, boys. Wet yer whistles. Food's coming soon in the back. The Aherns are there."

He pushed a mug of beer to each of his compatriots, and turned to Emlyn.

"This is cider. You can't go on without something to drink. I don't think your priest should mind about that."

Thinking of his father, Emlyn stifled a laugh. "Thanks. I really am getting thirsty. What do I owe you?"

"Nothing, nothing at all," Paddy replied. "O'Reilly gives us free drinks for showin' up and providin' some entertainment."

He lifted his mug. "Sláinte!"

"Sláinte!" said Emlyn, lifting his. The first sip tasted of fermentation. The second confirmed that the cider indeed was hard. His 'priest' would definitely disapprove, but Emlyn's thirst overpowered any guilty thoughts he had. He gulped down half the mug without taking a breath.

As the musicians picked up drinks and instruments and started for the back room, their seats were immediately filled with young male revelers.

In the dining area, a plain room without a bar, a dozen men and women, plus several children, sat at tables covered with soiled blue-and-white gingham cloths. Paddy headed for a large round table in a corner near the pot-bellied stove.

Emlyn recognized Lizzie and Molly Ahern, who introduced him to her parents, brother, Lizzie's fiancé, and another young couple at the table. They all expressed gratitude to Emlyn for agreeing to play for the wedding dance, and insisted the musicians join them at their table. The musicians obliged Lizzie with a jig.

"Thank you!" squealed Lizzie. "You sound so lively, I feel like dancin' on the table."

"You'd better hold off, Liz," said Molly as the serving maid came to the table with a tray of dishes, utensils, butter, and soda bread. Shortly thereafter she returned from the kitchen with a huge plate of bacon, cabbage and potatoes, and set it in the center of the table.

Emlyn felt the saliva swell in his mouth. He hadn't eaten since eleven that morning, and he was feeling faint from hunger.

"For what we are about to receive, may the Lord make us truly thankful," said Lizzie's father as they bowed their heads.

"A-men," the rest added in chorus.

The others at the table crossed themselves while Emlyn sat uncomfortably staring at the food.

"Let's eat!" said the brother, a lanky teenager, grabbing for the bread.

The food was passed around, and conversations began as the group started eating. The serving maid, seeing that Emlyn's cider mug was empty, replaced it with a full one. Still thirsty, he drained half of it away. As he set down the mug, Emlyn began to feel light-headed. Cider, empty stomach—not good, he thought, as he piled food onto his plate and began eating.

The women discussed the plans for Lizzie's wedding. Dan and the younger men got into an argument about whether the opening of the new U.S. immigration center at Ellis Island, New York, would make it easier or harder for immigrants, Irish people in particular, to enter the country.

Paddy, Jack, and Lizzie's father, Alf, who all worked at the mill, started talking about the labor dispute that was brewing at the Homestead Works.

"What d'ye think of Potter's request that the workers propose a new wage scale?" asked Jack. "Potter is saying that the company wants to avoid any potential strike."

"It's a crock of shite," replied Paddy. "Don't expect those greedy bastards to negotiate in good faith. I'll bet they're already plotting to nix any scale that would benefit the workers."

He paused to light a cigarette. "That snake Frick, Carnegie's man, has shown repeatedly how he deals with strikers: call in the Coal and Iron police, the Pinkertons, and the state militia to beat the workers to bloody pulp. Frick has brutalized his coke workers every blessed time they've tried to strike."

"Carnegie himself has said that he's opposed to the use of force in the settlement of labor disputes," said Alf.

Paddy snorted and blew smoke into the air. "If you believe that, you'll believe anything."

"You have to admit," said Jack, "that the workers have had it pretty good with the sliding scale in place. When profits go up, wages go up."

Paddy set down the cigarette and picked up a fork.

"Let me remind you that so far this year the price of steel has dropped from 35 to 22 dollars a ton. Profits are dwindling, so the company will want to give less to the workers. How long is the sliding scale going to last? Until the end of June when the contract expires, that's how long. Then it'll be every man for himself."

Paddy rammed a forkful of cabbage into his mouth.

"And don't forget," he continued, pointing the fork at Jack, "the Amalgamated members like yourself are the ones that have benefited most from the current wage scale. What do the rest of us have to gain by joining the AA in a strike?"

"Actually, plenty," said Jack, reddening. "If the union is broken, all the workers suffer. What other protection do we have? There's strength in solidarity."

"So Weihe would have us believe," said Paddy, referring to the national leader of the Amalgamated.

"The workers at the mill must have extensive training and skill, not only to do the work, but just to survive," Jack said. "I don't see how the company could afford to get rid of the lot of us. They'd go under. We must stick together."

"Well," replied Paddy. "I think it highly unlikely that the most profitable corporation in the country, run by the meanest lying bastards, will go under because of anything labor does."

"What's your solution then, Paddy?" asked Alf, his voice rising in volume and pitch. "Just give up? Or maybe join the anarchists?"

The men at the next table turned to see what the commotion was about.

Paddy gave them a withering glance, and they turned away.

"No, Alf," replied Paddy in a low, steady voice. "You're taking my comments the wrong way. I really do hope that the workers can get a good offer from the company. It's just I'm a mite skeptical that this will ever happen."

"You're more than a 'mite' skeptical, Paddy," said Jack, biting into a piece of bread.

Silence ensued as the men concentrated on eating.

Jack suddenly looked over at Emlyn. "Say, isn't your brother-in-law a member of the Amalgamated?"

"Yes," replied Emlyn, brushing an errant piece of cabbage from his beard. "Gwyn belongs to the union."

"What do you think about this situation with the wage scale?" asked Alf.

"We don't discuss politics around the house," replied Emlyn. "I know Gwyn is loyal to the union, and I know he's concerned about renegotiating the scale, but that's about all I know."

"What do *you* think?" asked Alf. "You must hold an opinion on the subject."

Emlyn ran his finger around the rim of the cider mug. He was having a hard time focusing his thoughts.

"I am embarrassed to say this, but I haven't thought about the situation enough to form an opinion. I'm more or less just trying to get through each day as it comes."

He lifted the mug to his lips.

"June seems so very far away."

"It does," mused Paddy, looking off into space, "but believe me, it will come."

He turned to Emlyn. "And what will you do then?"

"Support the workers," replied Emlyn. "Is there any other course? At least workers here in America seem to be better off than those in Britain. I expect that a strike here, if it comes, will assert the workers' power over the company."

Paddy shook his head. "You really are a dreamer, boyo. If a strike comes, it'll be the company, not the union, which will prevail. And with Frick involved, it will be in the most brutal manner possible. Mark my words."

"That's *your* opinion, Paddy," interjected Alf, his voice rising again.

"Indeed it is," said Paddy, stuffing a boiled potato into his mouth.

"Have you no faith, man?" Alf's voice was close to a roar.

Paddy shrugged. "Frick's coke workers were believers, and look what happened to them."

"Nothing ventured, nothing gained is what I believe," said Alf, slapping the table for emphasis.

"Let's remember we're all on the same side," said Jack, signaling Alf to lower his voice.

"Indeed we are," said Paddy through a mouthful of potato.

He washed the potato down with stout, and set the mug gently onto the table.

He looked up at the others, smiling. "Still, mark my words."

Ignoring Paddy, Jack pushed back from the table and consulted his pocket watch.

"Time to go. I told the missus I'd be home by eight, and it's already half-past."

Emlyn, seeing the opportunity, added that he was expected home soon as well.

"Could you wait a few minutes more?" asked Alf, glancing from Jack to Emlyn. "Dan promised earlier that he'd grace us with a song." He turned to Dan.

Molly and Lizzie clapped, Dan blushed, and Emlyn and Jack took their seats again.

"My voice is wee bit scratchy today, I fear," said Dan. "I don't know. . . ."

"Ah, come on, Danny," urged Paddy. "Give us a song."

Dan stood, took a sip of water, and seemed to contemplate an engraved picture of the old John Munhall farmstead on the opposite wall.

"A 'D', please," he asked Paddy, who obliged by sounding it on the accordion.

" 'The Meeting of the Waters' by Thomas Moore," Dan

announced, and began singing in a clear, strong tenor voice:

> There is not in the wide world a valley so sweet
> As that vale in whose bosom the bright waters meet;
> Oh! the last rays of feeling and life must depart,
> Ere the bloom of that valley shall fade from my heart.
> Yet it was not that nature had shed o'er the scene Her
> purest of crystal and brightest of green;
> 'Twas not her soft magic of streamlet or hill,
> Oh! no—it was something more exquisite still.

At this point, Emlyn joined in with harmony on the violin.

> 'Twas that friends, the beloved of my bosom, were near,
> Who made every dear scene of enchantment more dear,
> And who felt how the best charms of nature improve,
> When we see them reflected from looks that we love.
> Sweet vale of Avoca! how calm could I rest
> In thy bosom of shade, with the friends I love best,
> Where the storms that we feel in this cold world should
> cease,
> And our hearts, like thy waters, be mingled in peace.

As the last note faded away, everyone in the room burst into applause.

"Lovely, lovely!" exclaimed Molly. Mrs. Ahern wiped away a tear with her napkin.

Emlyn, too, was moved by Dan's soaring voice. Although apparently untrained as a singer, Dan knew how to express emotion.

Dan reached across the table to shake Emlyn's hand.

"Thanks for the accompaniment."

"It was my pleasure," replied Emlyn.

Dan bowed and sat down. A man from a neighboring table sent over another round of drinks, and the hum of conversation resumed.

Emlyn packed up his violin, thanked the Aherns for supper, and threaded his way through the crowd of saloon patrons to the front door.

Outside, the drizzle had changed to sleet. Emlyn pulled down the visor on his cap and hastened along the plank sidewalk toward Amity Street.

The three ciders he downed were making him feel tipsy, but this time it felt good. He'd had a fine time making music, his belly was full, and he was heading home to a warm bed.

Hunched against the wind and sleet, Emlyn wended his way along ramshackle sections of the boardwalk, whistling the tune to 'The Meeting of the Waters.' As he approached the intersection at Ann Street, his violin case bumped into the arm of a man going the opposite direction.

"Pardon me," said Emlyn, slowing, but not looking up.

"I say! Watch where you're going, sir!" said an irate male voice.

Emlyn stopped and faced the man. All he could see in the pelting sleet was a figure in a long dark coat and bowler hat, with a woman by his side.

Emlyn bowed, doffing his cap.

"Please, sir, accept my humblest apologies for my intrusion onto your portion of the public walk."

He didn't care if he sounded sarcastic. The way the man had reacted, one would think that Emlyn had intentionally hit him with a nine-pound hammer.

The man pulled himself to his full height, which was several inches shorter than Emlyn's.

"Who do you think you are, anyway?" he demanded.

"Only a poor musician, trying to make his way home," said Emlyn, replacing his cap. "'Tis a naughty night to swim in. And so, I bid you adieu."

He swung the violin case into his right hand and stepped into the street. At the same moment, a cry came from the woman on the sidewalk.

"Emlyn!"

He turned around. Through the gloom Emlyn managed to discern the features of Sarah Oesterling, and beside her, Norton Montague.

Sarah stepped to the edge of the sidewalk.

"Emlyn, I . . . we didn't recognize you. With the beard, and all . . ." Her voice trailed off.

"I didn't recognize you, either," said Emlyn, attempting to hide his surprise.

The three of them stood there, speechless.

"In any case," Emlyn added after a moment, "I'm sorry if this unhappy encounter has distressed you. I've been rehearsing for Lizzie's wedding dance, you see, and do desire to go home and . . ."

He knew it sounded stilted, but couldn't help himself.

"Of course," said Sarah. "We're returning from a performance at the opera house ourselves."

Montague grunted, still irate, perhaps more so now he realized who the transgressor was.

Sarah stepped back. "Good night then."

"Good night," said Emlyn pulling at the brim of his cap.

He walked quickly to Amity Street, wondering what had gotten into him to treat Montague so cavalierly. Well, the man was an ass, and he was glad he did it.

By the time he reached the back yard of the house, his

beard, coat and cap were covered in icy pellets.

Through the kitchen window he saw Eirwen putting away dishes.

He hesitated, hand on the doorknob. He'd have to tell her where he'd been. He hoped she wouldn't be too upset by the smell of alcohol on his breath.

Removing his cap, he pushed the door open.

To Emlyn's relief, Eirwen already knew about his playing for the Ahern wedding. The word had been passed from Molly through Sarah at church the day after the Twelfth Night party.

Eirwen said nothing about the hard cider, but she had a lot to say about his increasingly gaunt condition. He needed to take better care of himself, she said, and insisted that he pack his lunch pail to the brim each day before shift. Both she and Gwyn were very worried about how thin and unhealthy he was getting.

"Mam would be upset with me if she could see you now. I promised I'd watch out for you, and I will," Eirwen insisted.

Emlyn knew what their mother would think if she could see how haggard Eirwen herself looked, but said nothing.

Friday, February 12th

Dawn was breaking as Emlyn trudged through the mill yard back to the house, the dirt and cinders crunching under his worn boots. He had dragged through another week at the mill, often wondering how much longer he could do this backbreaking work.

All week long, Eirwen had stuffed Emlyn's lunch box with sweet breads, biscuits, hard-boiled eggs, and bits of cheese in addition to the usual assortment of sandwiches and leftovers.

Emlyn and Joe had started to trade food from their stashes, each intrigued by the variety of homespun foods the other brought.

Emlyn's favorite from Joe's box was the potato and cheese pierogies, those tasty little dumplings, while Joe had acquired a taste for bara brith washed down with sweet tea. For Emlyn, these were the only pleasant interludes in the long, exhausting days and nights at the open hearth.

He swung the empty lunch box into his left hand as he reached the final pass-through out of the steel works. Did he hear his name being called?

Emlyn halted. Yes, someone was yelling "Phillips! Hey, Phillips!" over the screeching of saws in the neighboring mill.

Emlyn turned to see a mill messenger boy in knickers picking his way through the clutter of bricks, steel rods, and castings.

"Emlyn Phillips?" the boy asked as he reached Emlyn. Without waiting for a reply, the boy handed him a note. "This here's from Mr. Williams. He wants you to look at it right away."

Emlyn took the piece of paper from the boy and unfolded it.

Phillips, Pls. come to my office after your shift today. Wm. Williams

Emlyn stared at the note. What on earth was this about?

"Very well," said Emlyn, ramming the note into the pocket of his tattered trousers. "Are you going back to Mr. Williams's office?"

The messenger nodded.

"Then I'll follow."

Fifteen minutes later Emlyn stood at the open door to Williams's office.

Williams was standing by the desk, examining some papers laid out on it.

Glancing up at the door, Williams said, "Come in, come in, Phillips."

Emlyn stepped inside, standing awkwardly with lunch pail in one hand, cap in the other.

"Please sit," said Williams, motioning toward a wooden chair. "Thank you for coming. I know you must be knackered coming off shift."

"I'm fine," Emlyn lied.

"I've found you a position to try out. I've been talking to Leon Schumacher, one of the engineers at the Works, and he thinks he can use you on the structural mill project."

Emlyn perked up.

"One of Schumacher's assistants was crossing the street yesterday on his way home, when a runaway team ran him down. Unfortunately, his back is broken and he has a concussion as well. The prognosis does not look good."

Williams paused.

"Another assistant who has been on the job will assume the man's duties, but they still need a second man. I've suggested that they try you in this position. The job would involve communicating with the various contractors, writing up reports, and keeping records. They expect to put your math skills to use as well. You would be working under the supervision of one of the project engineers, Joel Jansen. His assistant would give you on-the-job training."

Williams looked at Emlyn.

"Is this something that interests you?"

Emlyn gazed at him in disbelief. After a moment, he answered, "Yes, sir."

"Good," replied Williams, sitting down on the desk.

"Schumacher needs to fill this position as soon as possible. He will be at the General Office Building in Munhall at three this afternoon. Could you be there for an interview?"

"Yes, sir."

"Good. We'll see you at the office, then, at three."

Emlyn hesitated. "If this job works out, what about my job at the open hearth?"

Williams looked up. "You can't very well do both jobs, can you?" He grinned.

Emlyn blushed. "No, of course not."

"Don't worry about that," said Williams, standing. "If you're hired, they'll talk to Frank. You can pick up the wages you have coming at next payday. Meanwhile, go home and get some rest. You look like you need it."

Emlyn stood, his head swimming with excitement and fatigue. He shook hands with Williams, very conscious of how filthy his hands were, and started out the door.

"Mind the machinery," Williams said as a parting reminder.

Emlyn forced himself to stay alert as he made his way through the mill yards, and when he emerged from the works, he paid special attention to the horse-drawn vehicles moving on the street.

Gwyn was mopping his breakfast plate with a slab of dark bread as Emlyn pushed the back door open.

"Goodness, Em. Where were you?" asked Eirwen. "It's almost seven-thirty. We were beginning to worry."

Emlyn slumped into the chair across from Gwyn.

"Not to worry," said Emlyn. "I'll tell you what happened if I can get some food into my gullet. I'm famished."

Eirwen poured him tea and set before him a plate piled with fried eggs, toast, beans, and bacon, and he recounted the story about his visit to Williams' office.

"I'm so happy for you!" exclaimed Eirwen, bending to give

him a hug. "This is a wonderful opportunity."

"Em," said Gwyn, banging down his mug of tea, "that's bloody marvelous!"

Eirwen shot Gwyn a disapproving glance.

"Sorry," Gwyn said. "But it really is marvelous!"

"I haven't gotten the job yet," Emlyn reminded them. "And if I do, it's only short-term. For the moment, I don't care—anything that gets me out of laboring at the furnace! I don't know how much longer I can do that job."

"That's for sure," said Gwyn. "You are starting to look like what the cat dragged in."

"Gwyn, really," said Eirwen.

"He's right," said Emlyn. "I stopped looking in the mirror a month ago. Why do you think I grew this beard?"

He gave a tired laugh.

"You know," replied Eirwen, "It may be time to give your beard a trimming before you go to meet the engineer."

"I agree," said Emlyn. "It should resemble Mr. Frick's more than Alfred, Lord Tennyson's."

"Yes," said Gwyn. "I heard that Tennyson discovered a bird's nest in his one day last spring when he was changing his collar."

Gwyn chuckled at his own joke.

"At least he changes his collar every few months," said Emlyn, taking off his top shirt and jacket and pitching them onto the floor next to the door.

"These work clothes can go into the rag bag if I get this new job."

Gwyn gave Emlyn directions to the office, offering to walk over with him. Emlyn declined, knowing it would mean an hour's less sleep for Gwyn. Asking Eirwen to wake him at one, Emlyn headed to bed, taking the stairs two at a time.

The last four days on night turn had been endlessly tiring and dreary. He marveled that he could be brought so quickly back from the dead. At the top of the stairs, he nearly collided with Thomas, who was on his way downstairs to breakfast.

"Uncle Em!" said Thomas. "How come you're still up?"

"I may be changing my work schedule," Emlyn replied. "You'll be seeing more of me, I hope."

He roughed up Thomas's already tousled hair.

"Gee, that's swell," said Thomas as Emlyn turned to go into his room.

Emlyn, filthy with mill grime, fell into bed and pulled up the covers. He'd wash when he got up.

His alarm clock read one o'clock exactly when Eirwen's voice shouting from the bottom of the stairs interrupted his slumbers. He staggered sleepily downstairs.

In the kitchen, Eirwen had already filled the bathtub with warm water. Emlyn pulled the makeshift curtain divider, removed his clothes, and settled into the tub.

"Ah, this is heavenly," he murmured, and fell instantly asleep.

"Emlyn! Wake up! It's twenty past one. You've got to get ready."

"Sorry," said Emlyn, sitting up in the tub and rubbing his eyes. "Still sleepy."

Emlyn scrubbed his face, arms, and feet clean and shampooed his hair and beard. He examined his hands. They were red and raw, with remnants of dirt sticking stubbornly to the fingernails. He attacked them vigorously with an emery board, but they still looked rough and stained.

He dried off and put on Gwyn's worn dressing gown.

Eirwen had thought of everything. She had pressed his suit and a starched white shirt, and polished his everyday boots. A pair of sharp scissors and a hand mirror sat on the table, and old newspapers on the floor.

"First, eat," she said, setting a bowl of steaming navy bean soup on the table, and Emlyn sat down and spooned the soup into his mouth.

When he had finished, she trimmed his hair and beard, checking to make sure the sides were even. She finished off with some of Gwyn's pomade.

"There. That'll do until you can get to the barber's."

Emlyn examined his image in the hand mirror. Despite the beard, he looked neither like Frick nor Tennyson. Perhaps he most closely resembled some of the anarchists he'd seen coming out of the Russian saloons on the Avenue: long, dark hair slicked back, sable beard, pale eyes sunken into dark sockets. He could hardly see the man he was only four months ago.

Eirwen handed him Gwyn's bowler as he started out the back door.

"It won't do to wear a cap. You don't want to look like a farm hand."

Emlyn shrugged on his overcoat and walked fast, up McClure and across Eighth Avenue toward the General Office Building in Munhall.

Twenty-five minutes later, he approached its great bulk looming on Eighth Avenue across from the mill. A large, rectilinear edifice with ornamental brickwork around the soffits and half-towers at the corners, it seemed more fit to be a fortress than an office building. It faced the huge, sprawling complex of yards and industrial buildings filling the space between it and the river.

Emlyn crossed the street and walked up to the main entrance at the center of the building. He paused at the foot of the stone steps, and started up.

By habit, he looked down at his rough hands. His chest contracted, and his stomach turned over. He had to take a deep breath as he reached the top of the steps.

Emlyn pushed open the big oak door and entered the long foyer. At the end was the reception desk. As Emlyn tentatively approached the stern-looking woman at the desk, a noise down the hall attracted his attention. Williams was walking toward him, accompanied by two men.

"Hello, Phillips," said Williams. "I'd like you to meet Leon Schumacher, who is overseeing the construction on the structural finishing mill."

Schumacher, a stout man of around 50 with sparse brown hair shook hands briskly with Emlyn.

Williams then introduced him to a thickset man of about thirty-five. "This is Joel Jansen, the civil engineer on the project.

Neatly parted sandy hair framed Jansen's broad face and keen brown eyes. They shook hands.

Jansen then led Emlyn down the hall to an office. He sat at the desk, while Emlyn took the chair in front of it. Jansen asked Emlyn about his experience and education, taking notes on a pad. At the end of the interview, Jansen leaned back and said, "Your pay would be $7 a week to start. Of course, this is a probationary hire. If you fit into the job, your pay would be raised to $9 a week. Other work might be available, but there are no guarantees."

Emlyn stared at Jansen. Was he imagining this? He'd be making about the same, but he wouldn't be killing himself putting in long, backbreaking hours at the open hearth.

"So," asked Jansen, "are those terms acceptable?'

"Indeed they are, sir."

"Mr. Williams thinks you can do the job, and I think we should give it a try," said Jansen.

Jansen and Emlyn shook hands, making his acceptance of the job official.

"Let's get started by touring the site of the 35-inch structural mill, shall we?" said Jansen, rising from the chair. "That's the best way to show you what the job entails."

Jansen led Emlyn out the front door and across the street and over the steel footbridge spanning the tracks into the mill proper.

"As you see," said Jansen, as they entered a huge area cluttered with beams, struts, sheet metal, and piles of bricks, "work is about two-thirds completed on the project."

Emlyn looked around in awe. Jansen pointed to the right, where the large mill building stood. The gigantic roof of the mill rose in three tiers, each separated by a bank of windows. The vast mill yard to the west of the mill would be the staging area from which the completed beams would be shipped off by rail. The beams, said Jansen, would be used in the construction of bridges, buildings, ships, and other large structures.

"We're running at capacity in the production of armored plate. We have orders from the Navy to produce the steel for two battleships this spring," said Jansen. "In addition to making plate, this mill will add to the production of our blooming mills in making structural members. The Homestead Works will soon be, if it's not already, the most advanced, modern steel factory in the world."

Emlyn was having difficulty gauging the size of the site. The mill building was at least 100 yards long, probably longer. Through the smoky haze, the men working at the far end of the yard looked like insects crawling around on the girders.

"At the moment we're setting up the machinery inside the mill," Jansen said. "I don't think there's any need for us to go in there."

Jansen pointed toward a square two-story brick building at the end of the yard.

"Let's go over the operations building. It's not completely finished, but we're using it as the construction office. I've arranged for you to meet the man you'll be working with, Charles LaCroix."

They picked their way through the clutter of rails, ties, and piles of gravel to the brick building. As Jansen pushed open the front door, Emlyn could smell the odors of fresh plaster and drying paint. A workman was brushing gray paint onto the stairwell walls.

Jansen led Emlyn to the back room that was being used as the engineers' headquarters. Several desks, drawing boards, and filing cabinets were lined up in two rows. Architectural drawings were pinned to the walls, and every surface was covered with sheets of paper of varying sizes.

As they entered, a young man got up from a stool at one of the drawing boards and walked over to greet them.

"Emlyn Phillips, meet Charles LaCroix."

"Welcome to the project," said LaCroix, enthusiastically pumping Emlyn's hand. "Glad to have you on board."

LaCroix was about Emlyn's age, tall and gangling. His fine brown hair stuck out in all directions from the top of his head, as if he had just removed a stocking cap; his full moustache was surprisingly neat compared to his hair. His slate-gray eyes looked directly into Emlyn's. As they shook hands, Emlyn noted that the lower sleeves of LaCroix's jacket were covered with plaster dust. Emlyn immediately took a liking to him.

"We are under pressure to get this mill up and running soon," said Jansen. "Your training will be on the job, so come prepared to work hard. On Monday LaCroix can get you up to speed on what your duties will be here. I'll let you get acquainted."

Jansen excused himself and left the building.

"No one else is in the office right now because they're off working on site. Monday I'll introduce you to the people who work here. Part of your job will be to carry records and correspondence over to the clerical offices in the general office building."

LaCroix's English pronunciation was unlike any Emlyn had heard before. He spoke rapidly, through his nose, clipping the syllables short. LaCroix took him around the office, showing him plans for the project, explaining the logistics of fitting the parts together to make a functional mill.

When the office tour was completed, LaCroix escorted Emlyn back across the tracks. As they parted, LaCroix asked Emlyn if he could find his way back to the building the next Monday. Emlyn said yes, and LaCroix instructed him to be there at seven sharp.

Emlyn thanked him and started walking home on the Avenue. As he glanced at the huge hulk of the structural mill across the railroad tracks, Emlyn marveled at his unexpected delivery from O.H.2. On the other hand, it was possible that he wouldn't meet Jansen's expectations, and would be out of a job in a few weeks.

What would be, would be, Emlyn decided, thrusting his hands into his coat pockets. He trudged on, in the gathering gloom of dusk, toward the house on Third Avenue.

Saturday, February 20th

William Oesterling dozed in his tattered overstuffed chair in the study. He was exhausted from treating numerous patients with croup, colds, influenza, pneumonia, and other afflictions that always increased during winter in smoky Homestead. He had tried to catch up on the week's news, but promptly fell asleep with the newspapers in his lap.

"Papa, wake up. It's almost seven o'clock."

Oesterling started at Sarah's voice.

"Our guests will be here soon."

"Be right there," mumbled Oesterling, setting the papers on the side table and standing up. He crossed the hallway into the parlor and put more charcoal on the fire.

After the success of the Twelfth Night party, Sarah had cajoled him into trying a few social events at the house. First, she had several teachers over for a tea party in late January, then a Saturday evening for a few neighbors, and now, a dinner. The guests tonight all had some connection to the mill: William Williams and his wife, Norton Montague, and, of course, Carrie and Oliver.

Sarah bustled about, rechecking the table setting, plumping up pillows, and adjusting the gaslights. She had been excited to get out the good china and silverware, which hadn't been used at a dinner party since Margaret's death.

Oesterling was happy that Sarah was happy, but he was not looking forward to the evening. Since the Twelfth Night party, she had gone out with Norton Montague on three occasions. Sarah had been initially reluctant to have anything to do with Montague. The mere fact that Carrie had promoted him was enough to cool Sarah's interest. But Montague proved to have the money and refined tastes to make a desirable companion at plays and musical events. Sarah, who loved attending and discussing arts events, had been impressed with him.

Nevertheless, Montague, who held forth on a variety of topics, frequently irritated Oesterling. And the friction between Sarah and Carrie, although muted, continued. Sarah had been furious at Carrie's noisy, late arrival during the Twelfth Night concert. The sisters hadn't spoken for nearly a month after that. Oesterling had managed to patch things up by getting Carrie to apologize, which she had done grudgingly.

Oesterling sighed. The hallway clock struck seven as the doorbell rang. It was Montague. Shortly thereafter, the Williamses arrived.

Sitting by the fire in the parlor, Sarah, Oesterling and the guests discussed recent musical and theatrical performances in Homestead. Montague as usual offered the lion's share of the critique.

The clock struck quarter past, then half past the hour. Oesterling retreated to the kitchen and asked Mrs. Sproule to send out refills for their mulled apple juice and the canopy tray. He was becoming increasingly nervous about Carrie's absence. Would she be so rude as not to show?

Shortly after eight, a commotion in the foyer signaled the arrival of the Strongs. Carrie, her cheeks flushed from the cold and decked out in a maroon silk damask gown, bustled into the room, followed by Oliver. Oesterling almost gasped at her appearance, as her formal evening dress was out of place next to the wool dresses worn by Sarah and Mrs. Williams.

"Sorry for the late arrival," she said, coming over to Oesterling and giving him a light kiss on the cheek. Did he smell alcohol on her breath?

"We stopped over for the Crosses' cocktail hour and lost

track of the time," said Oliver as Carrie went over to Sarah and kissed her. Sarah stood rigidly, looking over Carrie's shoulder at Oesterling. In response, he gave a slight shake of his head, praying that this confrontation wouldn't escalate further.

Carrie settled onto the settee that Sarah had been sharing with Montague, and Oliver greeted the other guests. Sarah disappeared into the kitchen, and in a few minutes, came back to announce dinner was served.

As Molly set the first course of French onion soup in front of each guest, Oliver changed the topic of conversation from music to mill politics.

"You can imagine," Oliver laughed, "what the talk at the Crosses' was about."

"The company's offer to the workers?" ventured Montague.

"Yes, the $22 a ton apparently has gone over like a lead balloon with the workers," replied Oliver.

"That should come as no surprise," said Williams, "with a reduction in wages of $3 a ton."

"The workers are delusional," said Oliver. "Do they really hope to raise wages in this depressed billet market? The price of steel has gone down, and so must their wages. In my opinion, they were lucky to get offered $22."

"We'll have to wait till June 24th to see the outcome," said Montague. "Perhaps the Amalgamated will see the folly of their views by then."

A brief silence ensued.

"Why is it folly?" asked Sarah. "Wouldn't you hope to raise wages if you were a worker?"

"I'm not a worker, and it's obvious their expectations are unrealistic," replied Montague.

"'Unrealistic' by whose standards?" asked Sarah.

"Why Sarah," said Carrie, "you're starting to talk like a

member of the Amalgamated. Have you joined up?"

"Don't be absurd, Carrie," retorted Sarah. "I just . . ."

"It's true that the workers are upset," Williams interjected. "I've overheard snatches of complaints on the street and at work."

"Fortunately, there are several months ahead to iron things out," said Mrs. Williams.

"What's there to iron out?" asked Oliver. "The Amalgamated isn't going to get its way. That's a simple fact."

"Are you suggesting," asked Sarah, "that the company is inflexible about this?"

"I'm not suggesting it, I'm saying it. Mr. Carnegie might go around talking about the workers' sacred right to form trades unions, and meeting the workers halfway, but Mr. Frick is made of sterner stuff. He will not give in to the workers' demands."

"But Carnegie is the owner of the company," suggested Oesterling.

"Yes, but Frick is the one who handles the company's business," said Oliver. "Carnegie trusts him to do the job while he goes about rubbing elbows with European celebrities and planning free libraries for the illiterate workers."

"They're illiterate because they have no time to learn to read," said Sarah. "They barely have time for their families or any leisure."

"It's their choice," said Carrie. "No one's forcing them to work in the mill."

"No one but circumstances," replied Sarah. "Look at Emlyn Phillips, someone who is working as a laborer, even with years of education."

"All the more fool he," said Carrie. "No one forced him to throw everything to the winds and come over here."

"That's a . . ." began Sarah.

"He is no longer working as a laborer," Williams said.

Everyone looked at Williams.

"What happened?" asked Montague. "Was he sacked or did he quit?"

"Neither," said Williams. "He is now working on the new 35-inch structural mill project."

Montague looked stunned.

"In what capacity?" he asked.

"I recommended him for a job as a correspondent and assistant to the engineers," said Williams. "He's been on that job for a week, and so far, he is living up to expectations."

"Good for him," said Oesterling. "He seemed so miserable when I last saw him in January."

"People make their own misery," said Carrie, smoothing the napkin in her lap.

"What an awful thing to say," replied Sarah. "Most of the misery in this world has been created by the people in power, those who shove the little people around for their own profit."

Oesterling was taken aback by Sarah's defense of the workers. He had never seen her speak on the topic with such passion before.

"Surely you don't believe that," said Oliver. "You sound a bit like those anarchists who rage from street corners. The company supports the workers. They can make their own choices about spending their wages."

"For many those wages are so small," said Sarah, "especially when compared to the company's profits."

"The company owns the steelworks," said Montague. "It's the investors' money that's making money for all."

Oesterling glanced at Oliver for a reaction, but he just sat there, gazing at his empty soup bowl. Perhaps the cocktails imbibed at the Crosses' were keeping him placid.

"The workers have an investment in labor," said Sarah.

"Obviously you *have* joined the Amalgamated," retorted Carrie, smiling. "Or the anarchists."

Sarah was about to reply when Molly entered with the main course. Oesterling carefully steered the conversation away from labor politics and managed to keep it from reverting—at least till the end of the evening.

Around ten-thirty, the other dinner guests said their goodbyes, leaving only Carrie and Oliver. As Oesterling was helping Carrie with her wrap, she said offhandedly, "Papa, you really should teach Sarah better manners than to thrust herself into political discussions at the dinner table. It's vulgar and unbecoming a lady."

Sarah turned to face her sister.

"If you want to say something, Carrie, say it to me directly. You've got a lot of gall criticizing me for being vulgar when you come flouncing into dinner dressed up like a theater marquee—and late, and tipsy, on top of it."

"Oh, is that so?" exclaimed Carrie, putting her hands on her hips. "I dress properly for the occasion, in this case, for the Crosses' party. And I was *not* drunk."

"Yes, 'not drunk' as you were 'not drunk' at the Twelfth Night party, when you practically had to be carried out of here. And you *were* late, both times."

Carrie looked daggers at Sarah.

"The truth hurts, doesn't it?" said Sarah.

Carrie suddenly raised her hand as if to strike her sister, but Oliver seized it.

"Don't do anything you'll regret," he said calmly.

"Go ahead, Carrie. Hit me like a drunken fishwife would," said Sarah, thrusting out her chin.

Oesterling stepped between them.

"That's enough!" he exclaimed. "For God's sake, stop!

Your mother would be appalled if she could see you two quarreling like this."

"Very well," said Carrie, wresting her arm from Oliver's grasp. "I'll stop if she stops."

Sarah glared at Carrie for a moment, then strode down the hall into the kitchen.

"It's time to go now," said Oliver, handing Carrie her hat and gloves. Carrie put them on in front of the hall mirror, and turned to Oesterling.

"Good night, Papa," she said. She gave him a peck on the cheek and opened the door.

"Good night, and thanks for the wonderful dinner," said Oliver. He shrugged in a gesture of helplessness, and followed Carrie onto the porch.

Oesterling closed the door and stepped back into the foyer. He stared down at his shoes, which, he now saw, were scuffed in several places. How was he going to patch things up this time?

Saturday, February 26th

"That'll do it for now, lads," yelled Paddy over the din in the hall. "Time for a break."

The musicians set down their instruments out of the way of drunken revelers who might stumble into them.

Emlyn pulled out his pocket watch and noted it was almost 11:30. He rarely was up this late, even with the new job. The work was going well, and he liked it more than he had thought possible. He liked the shorter hours, the variety of tasks, the absence of backbreaking labor. Moreover, he enjoyed seeing the abstract drawings and calculations become incarnate in steel.

He had time for other things, like time with his sister's family, time for music, time for reading. He didn't need time for friends because he didn't have any. Work had taken all his time and energy. Although he had Eirwen and her family, at times he keenly missed those he left behind in Wales—Gareth, Arthur, Mam, even Tad.

There was Joe Galik, who was delighted when Emlyn had told him about his new position. And Virgil, who hadn't spoken to him since the day Emlyn came back from the interview with Williams, even though he'd seen him on the Avenue a few times. It was time to cultivate friendships, now he was always on day shift and always had Sundays free.

"C'mon, Emlyn, let's get some fresh air," said Paddy, heading for the side door.

"I wouldn't exactly call it 'fresh' outside," Emlyn replied, placing his violin in its case.

"Fair enough," said Paddy. "At least it's cooler than in here," he added, stopping by a keg to refill his mug with stout.

Outside, it was pleasant enough for an evening in late February, mild and windless.

"What do you think of the wedding dance?" Paddy asked, lighting a cigarette.

"I'm so busy playing, I haven't thought about it much. People seem to be enjoying themselves."

"Lent starts next week," said Paddy, "and many feel the need to stock up on merrymaking for the duration."

Emlyn chuckled. "Some are doing a very good job of it."

He had missed the wedding itself, earlier in the day, but Molly had told him that Dr. Oesterling and Sarah had attended. Of course, they were not at the dance.

"So, Emlyn," said Paddy, taking a gulp of stout, "what do you do for fun? You don't drink, you don't smoke, you don't dance."

"I play fiddle," replied Emlyn.

Paddy laughed.

"I see." He took a drag on the cigarette.

"Not all Welshman are like me and my family," said Emlyn. "There's plenty of carousing among some quarters back home. My father thinks it's his job to try to stop them and return them to the fold."

"Ah, that's right, your Da's a priest," mused Paddy. "Must be difficult."

Emlyn nodded. Paddy didn't know the half of it.

"Come to think of it, I haven't seen you chasing women, either," said Paddy. "Must be damned hard to do that without drinking or dancing. I can't imagine."

"We manage, somehow," said Emlyn, feeling the outsider.

"Let me introduce you to some of the lasses. Several of them have been asking about you."

Emlyn hesitated. During a break earlier, Molly had brought over a plump, dark-haired young woman to introduce to him. Her name was Maud, and she stood very close to Emlyn, her skirt brushing his pant legs.

"I love to hear ye play," said Maud, gazing straight at him. Her eyes dropped to look at the violin in his hands. Or did her eyes go further down? He thought of Addie Buckman, whom he mercifully had seen only at a distance since their last encounter. Unnerved at Maud's boldness, Emlyn had thanked her and turned away, pretending to tune the E-string.

"No, thanks," replied Emlyn to Paddy. "Perhaps after Easter..."

Emlyn watched the smoke curl skyward from Paddy's cigarette and from the mill stacks in the near distance.

"How's your new job going?" asked Paddy, serious.

"Fine. I especially like not having to switch shifts," replied Emlyn.

"What's it like inside the headquarters of the great lords of steel?"

"You mean the head office?" asked Emlyn. "It's imposing. At least the main entrance is. I've only gotten inside a few of the offices. More than half the time we're working at the building site."

"What are they saying about negotiations with the Amalgamated?"

"I don't hear much, but Gwyn says he's certain that come June 26th, Carnegie will be true to his word and negotiate a deal with the union," Emlyn replied.

Paddy shook his head.

"Carnegie talks a lot of rubbish about the rights of workers, but he doesn't believe it, not for a minute. Case in point: Frick's running the head office in Pittsburgh. Frick thinks only of profits, profits, profits for the company, that is, for himself and the other blackguards running the country."

"You could be right," said Emlyn.

"I am," declared Paddy.

Dan's head poked out of the door. "Hey, Paddy. Everyone's lining up for the Walls of Liscarrol. They're getting impatient."

"OK," said Paddy, stepping on his cigarette butt. "We're coming."

Turning to Emlyn, he added, "Anyway, keep your eyes and ears open. If you don't look out for yourself, no one will do it for you."

Saturday, March 12th

Oesterling glanced up at the mahogany clock with a carved stag head over the entrance on the wall opposite. Carrie was late, as usual. Not having seen her since the dinner party fracas in February, Oesterling was unsure of what to expect from his elder daughter.

Meeting her here in the Carnegie Hotel dining room in Munhall had been her idea, proposed when he had phoned the previous Sunday to find out how they were doing. Was Carrie was still smarting over the skirmish she had had with Sarah at the dinner party? He knew Carrie well enough to realize that she felt she had lost face, even if the imagined humiliation had taken place only in front of family members.

As he replayed the scene in his head, Oesterling looked up again at the clock over the dining room entrance. Much to his surprise, outside the archway stood Montague, and next to him, Carrie.

They were standing close together, talking. Carrie threw her head back and laughed, apparently at some remark by Montague. He pressed the back of her hand to his lips and disappeared into the foyer.

"Hello, Papa. How are things in Homestead?" Carrie asked as she came over and took the seat opposite.

He couldn't resist. "Didn't Norton tell you?"

She looked at him, startled.

"Oh, yes," she replied, smiling. "He is getting worked up about the renegotiation of the contract with the Amalgamated. Of course he's in complete agreement with Mr. Frick about what should be done."

"I thought you don't like to talk politics," said Oesterling.

"I don't," she said. "But the contract negotiations are all anyone seems to talk about, Oliver included."

She sighed, adding, "It's all so tedious."

"Maybe you wouldn't think it tedious if your livelihood were at stake," said Oesterling.

Carrie shook her head. "Papa, you've been listening to Sarah."

Oesterling was about to reply when the waiter came by and described the luncheon specials for the day.

After they ordered, Carrie said, "Speaking of Oliver and negotiations, he is leaving for Chicago tomorrow. Frick is sending him there to hammer out contracts with builders. Oliver says that when the new structural mill goes into operation, Homestead will become the main producer of steel beams for high-rise buildings."

Oesterling nodded. He had heard of Chicago's new multi-story buildings, the architectural wonder of the land at the moment.

"How long will he be gone?"

"A month, maybe longer. Of course, it's fine for him because that's where his family lives."

"Why don't you go with him, then?"

"Oh, he's going to be very busy, and I really don't want to spend such a long time with his relatives." She stared somberly at the tablecloth.

"I think I may go mad with boredom when he's gone," she added.

"I don't think it could be that bad," said Oesterling. "There must be plenty to do."

"Like what?" she asked. "Without him, I won't be invited to any parties or dinners."

"You certainly have more to do than go to parties," Oesterling said.

"Well, that's why I invited you to meet me here today. I've decided get out more, to come to Homestead to see you and my friends while Oliver is out of town."

"Good!" replied Oesterling. "Why don't you come over for dinner next Sunday?"

"Maybe we could go out for dinner some other day of the week, Friday or Saturday."

"You know those are work days for me. Sunday would be better," he said. "In any case, Sarah would like to see you, too."

Eventually, Carrie agreed to come for dinner after church the next Sunday.

Sarah said nothing when he told her about Oliver's working in Chicago and Carrie's coming for dinner. Oesterling was concerned that the sisters would snipe at each other throughout the meal, but that didn't happen.

Carrie was serene, even blasé, oblivious to Sarah's observations about her students or their parents. In fact, Carrie had nothing bad—or good—to say about the formerly reviled inhabitants of Homestead.

The weeks marched by, one after the other, for Emlyn. The excitement of working at his new position in the mill began to wear off as the end of March approached. He began to be annoyed by Jansen, who seemed very disorganized for an engineer. Jansen's instructions were sometimes not clear, and he would blame others if they were confused and didn't follow his directions. However, it definitely was better than laboring at the open hearth.

On the other hand, Charles LaCroix was a joy to work with. Charles made Jansen look good by keeping careful oversight on the progress of the project and by clarifying Jansen's instructions to the staff and workers. Yet Charles didn't resent doing these tasks, never complaining about having to pick up after Jansen.

Most days Emlyn and Charles would take their lunch break together in the project office. Emlyn learned that Charles, the grandson of French-Canadians on both sides, was from Rhode Island, as was his accent. He had come to

Pittsburgh from a job managing material control in a Newport shipyard. Anticipating that the steel industry would provide better opportunities for advancement, he had taken this job at Carnegie Steel last September.

Although his work at the mill site was going well, as March approached, Emlyn grew increasingly apprehensive about his position. He started losing sleep, worrying about having to resume work as a laborer. He couldn't do it. Not now, not after working during daylight, applying his knowledge of languages and math to the job.

On March 28th Jansen reviewed Emlyn's work and told him that Emlyn's wages would be raised $1 a week. He would remain in his present position for the time being. After the structural mill was up and running, they would assess if they had need for Emlyn beyond that.

That same day, a Friday, for the second time Emlyn literally ran into Norton Montague, this time at the mill office building. Inside, Emlyn was approaching the front entrance, carrying a portfolio of architectural plans and specs destined for the job site across the street and tracks. Coming through the front door was Montague, who was looking down at a paper he was reading. Emlyn tried to step out of his way, but Montague ran into him, knocking the portfolio out of his hands. The papers fell out of the portfolio and scattered onto the floor.

Montague stooped to pick up the papers, when, seeing Emlyn, he suddenly stood up.

"Oh, it's you," Montague said, tugging his waistcoat straight. "Williams told me you were now working here."

Emlyn hesitated, not knowing what to say.

"You should be more careful with company property," Montague said over his shoulder as he walked off down the hall.

As Emlyn watched Montague's figure disappear around the corner, he conjectured whether Sarah was going out with him. Montague seemed to embody the American toff—educated, cultured, and completely full of himself.

Pushing out the door with the plans, Emlyn wished he had half his confidence.

East Liberty, Pittsburgh. Monday, March 29th

Karl Bernhard turned the knob on the battered front door of the small clapboard house on Mayflower Street, and came into the front room. He removed his jacket and cap and hung them on a peg by the door.

"Karl, is that you?" his wife called from the kitchen in back.

"Ja, Susanna," he replied, taking off his muddy boots and placing them by the door.

"Any luck?"

Karl came into the kitchen and sagged into a chair.

"Did you get the job?" she asked, wiping her hands on her apron.

"I went over to the foundry, you know, the place that had announced an opening for a fireman. When I got there, they said the job was already filled."

"That's too bad," Susanna said, setting a cup of coffee in front of him. "That job would've been perfect for you."

"Ja, so." He sipped the watery coffee and set it down. "Then I walked over to the railroad yard, stopping at several places en route, but they all said they had no work to offer, not even day labor."

He slumped forward and put his head in his hands. His wife came behind him and rubbed his shoulders.

"You'll find something soon, I'm sure," she said.

He shook his head. "No one wants a fifty-year-old worker when there's plenty of younger men looking for work."

"But you have so much experience—and you're a veteran. That should count for something."

"I had hoped so, but it seems there's little work of any sort, let alone positions for firemen. I don't like to mention that I'm a Navy veteran, that I honed my skill as a fireman building fires for boilers in gunboats, because then they ask when. When I tell them it was during the Civil War, it only emphasizes how old I am."

"It's only been four months since you lost your job," she said.

"Only four months!" he exclaimed. "It seems like forever."

"You will find something soon. Meanwhile, we can get by on the money George and John are bringing in. It's enough to cover living expenses."

"Just barely," he replied, raking his fingers through his thin, graying brown hair

"If necessary," she said. "I'll take in laundry."

Karl looked over at his tall, rangy wife and shook his head again. "God forbid that you will have to do that. I'll find work somehow."

He knew that the common practice of taking in boarders was out of the question. He, his wife, and their six children, including their two teenaged sons, were crowded together in this humble five-room house. Even though it was less than five years old, the house was showing many signs of wear from its occupants. Taking in laundry would definitely be a last resort in their cramped living quarters—and he had to admit, for his pride.

Despair overcame him. Did he come all the way from Franconia, did he work hard all these years in America, only to be washed up, finished at age fifty?

Susanna sat down next to him and put her hand over his.

"Don't worry, Karl. We'll get through this," she said, squeezing his hand.

He managed a weak smile. He so admired her strength.

"Yes, Schatzi," he replied, returning the squeeze. "As always, you are right."

Homestead

The spring weather was growing milder and the days longer. Emlyn spent several evenings with Thomas and his friends, learning to play baseball. The odd rules of play made his head swim, but he enjoyed being out in the field, running around with the boys.

One evening, a sad, sallow-faced boy came and stood on the sidelines to watch them play. For some reason, Thomas and his friends seemed to be intentionally ignoring him. He was about to invite the boy to play when he saw a woman walk up to the lad and roughly grab his arm.

He couldn't hear what she was saying, but when she glanced up, he realized that it was Addie Buckman. The right side of her face was purple-black with bruising. She looked around at the other players and Emlyn, but apparently didn't recognize him. She walked off, dragging the child with her.

Later, Thomas told him that he and his friends stopped inviting Bobby Buckman to play with them because half the time his mother would come along in a drunken rage and disrupt the game. She seemed to take sadistic pleasure in abusing her son as her husband abused her. One time, she struck a boy who tried to intervene when she was roughing up Bobby, and that was the end of the boys wanting to have anything to do with the Buckmans.

By the end of March, Emlyn was feeling rested and more like himself. Sal the barber on the Avenue kept his beard and hair neatly trimmed. He bought himself a plain dark navy business suit for the office.

Letters from Wales brought the news that the chapel in Treorchy had been completed and was to be dedicated on Easter Sunday, April 17th. Arthur and Tegwen would be married there on the first Saturday in May. In her letters, Mam wished Eirwen and Emlyn could be there, but Emlyn could scarcely imagine what would happen if he did show up.

Gwyn's younger sister had become engaged to a widower, a collier at the Ton du slip where her father and brother worked. Gwyn's father was pleased with his job above ground, weighing the coal brought out.

Gareth Morgan wrote that he was finishing at university and waiting for a call to serve as a minister. He, too, was in conflict with his father, but for a very different reason than Emlyn: His father owned a coal mine, and Gareth disapproved of his father's business and labor practices. At nearly every family gathering, the two of them locked horns about something or other. Ultimately, Gareth hoped to find a position with a congregation in America and emigrate. He concluded with the happy news that in January he had become engaged to Jane Rowland, the eldest daughter of a prosperous farmer.

In Homestead, all was calm, but worries continued to gnaw at Emlyn. He felt uneasy about the situation at the company. The union and company management were still far apart, and both sides seemed to be gearing up for a confrontation in late June.

Returning from meetings of the Amalgamated, Gwyn said that the union members were in complete agreement about negotiations with the company. They would stand firm against Potter and Frick. After all, the company belonged to the workers, too. How could the company make steel without the many skilled Amalgamated workers? They couldn't. The union had the company in a tight spot. When push came to shove, the company would give in. Gwyn was sure of it.

These meetings had become a source of friction between Gwyn and Eirwen, for Gwyn frequently stopped at a bar afterwards to have a few drinks with Jim Duncan and other AA members. Eirwen was unhappy with this new custom, and told Gwyn so. He would defend his right to what he called a 'social life,' and so the quarrels would begin.

Emlyn was not as confident as Gwyn about the outcome of negotiations, but he said nothing. Every day he heard men at the head office talking with similar confidence about the company's position. The seemingly genial Potter was apparently resolved to implement Frick's plan to destroy the union. He pondered what would happen when June 26th rolled around. Who would back off, the company or the union?

Free of constant exhaustion, Emlyn's thoughts had turned more and more to women, or rather, to the lack of them in his life. Eirwen urged him to ask out Sarah Oesterling. Recalling his encounter on the street with her and Norton Montague, he decided against it. He didn't know what to make of her relationship with Montague.

Back in Wales, he had been so immersed in his studies that he hadn't had time for a steady girlfriend. He had had a friend in Treorchy who was a girl, but she couldn't be called his sweetheart. Likable, earnest, and sociable, Elizabeth Evans was the perfect companion for concerts, teas, and lectures. They enjoyed many evenings discussing everything from art to religion.

What ultimately pulled them apart was his departure to

seminary. Last year, before he left for America, he had heard that she had married a solicitor and was living in Cardiff.

As for lovers, he had had only one—almost. During the summer before he left Treorchy for seminary, Gladys Howells, three years his elder, had set her sights on Emlyn. Her parents ran a dairy outside town, and were part of his father's flock. Gladys clearly understood that Emlyn was out of bounds as matrimonial material, but that didn't stop her from trying to lure him into her experienced arms.

Gladys was a strong and buxom young woman. Not a beauty, she nevertheless was attractive because of her physical vigor and carefree manner.

Four days in a row, as he was returning to town from helping his brother Arthur repair the cottage he was leasing, she had been waiting by a turnstile. The third day, she engaged him in small talk while coyly pulling at her loose bodice strings. The fourth day she did the same, this time kissing him on the mouth.

"Did you like that?" she asked, slyly eyeing him. He stared at her, heart pounding. "Then meet me the same time tomorrow at the hayrick yonder." She pointed into the distance beyond the town. She kissed him again, voluptuously, lingeringly, and walked away, turning around once to wink at him.

That night he was in a quandary about whether to meet Gladys or not. Over and over, he relived the kisses. Finally, after being up half the night, he decided to meet her. The next day, as he arrived to work at Arthur's cottage, his brother asked him pointblank, "What are you doing meeting Gladys Howells?"

"What do you mean?" said Emlyn.

"You know damned well what I mean," replied Arthur.

Emlyn was shocked at Arthur's use of profanity.

"You think no one saw you talking to that trollop? Jones the Farrier told me, but I didn't believe him. So yesterday I followed you after work."

Emlyn dropped his gaze to the ground.

"Look at me. Don't you care about your reputation? Worse yet, aren't you concerned about picking up the clap or some other disease from that woman?" Arthur's voice rose. "She's serviced a half dozen men in the last month alone. You may be book smart, but you are not wise to the ways of the world."

"I guess the thought never crossed my mind," stammered Emlyn, embarrassed at his naivety.

After that, he had been wary of advances from experienced women like Gladys. If temptation came before him, he would remind himself of the shame and possible diseases that might follow an answer to the siren call.

Yet it frustrated him that he did not have a woman to go out with, let alone get engaged to. His thoughts would turn to Sarah Oesterling, but he did not act. He had seen her with Norton Montague, a rising star with the Carnegie Company, and Emlyn could not gauge her attitude toward himself. He would have to remain patient.

April 1892

As Easter approached, Oesterling became preoccupied with five cases of diphtheria among his young patients. He looked in on them every day, and four of them began to recover. One little girl, however, took a turn for the worse and died on the morning of Good Friday. It was always heartbreaking when a child died, but this case was especially sad because she was the only child of older parents who doted on her.

From their small house, Oesterling walked back to the office around noon, past the shuttered shops on the Avenue that were closed so people could attend church services. Well, thought Oesterling as he wrote out the child's death certificate at his office, the parents' holiday and probably their lives were pretty much ruined.

Traffic in the business district was light, and human noise had faded. However, in the background, the omnipresent bang, screech, clang, and boom of the mill continued unabated. Unlike Christmas, Easter and Holy Week were not official holidays at the mill. Steel making did not halt to mark the death of Jesus on the cross, nor, for that matter, the deaths of any workers inside the mill.

Oesterling put down the pen. He was not particularly looking forward to Easter. Oliver was still out of town, and Carrie was coming over for dinner, but not, to Sarah's annoyance, for church. So was Norton Montague, who had come for Sunday dinner twice before. Montague, an Episcopalian, would be attending services at St. Matthew's.

The doctor reached down and patted Cerberus on the head. At least there was one member of the family that he could count on not to make a scene with other family members.

On Holy Saturday, shoppers thronged the Avenue, getting food, flowers, and candy for their Easter celebrations. As Emlyn walked home from work, he noted that many homes had baked goods cooling on the sills.

It was a fine day, and the next promised to be even better. He would be spending the holiday alone, as Eirwen, Gwyn, and the children would be attending church, and afterward, having dinner at the Roberts', along with the Griffiths.

Recalling the episode on Christmas Day with Mr.

Griffiths, Emlyn had declined the invitation to dinner. He decided not to go more from embarrassment at his own behavior than residual anger at Griffiths. Eirwen insisted that Griffiths had brought up the subject of his seminary training just to make conversation, but Emlyn wasn't convinced. In any case, he had let his emotions run away with him, and he didn't want to risk that again.

As he reached City Farm Lane on Eighth Avenue, he saw a familiar figure approaching from the opposite direction. It was Virgil, eyes downcast, wearing overalls and a rough wool jacket and lugging a big lunch pail.

"Hello, Virgil, " Emlyn said.

Virgil looked up.

"If it ain't Em-Lyn," he said without a smile.

"How have you been?" asked Emlyn.

"Same as usual, slaving away in the hell-hole. Only good thing that's happened was my promotion last month to Frank's job when he became first helper."

"That's great," said Emlyn, relieved that he was not still on the job at O.H. 2.

"You got a big promotion, too, didn't ya?" Virgil asked accusingly. "All the way up to company headquarters."

"I'm working at the structural mill site. It's only a temporary position until the mill is completed."

"Yeah, well, we'll see about that," said Virgil. "Anyway, I'm finishing the last turn on night shift. Gotta get to work."

"Say hello to Frank and Joe and the others for me," said Emlyn as Virgil stepped around him on the sidewalk.

"Happy Easter," he added.

Without looking at Emlyn, Virgil muttered something unintelligible. Switching his lunch pail to his left hand, Virgil strode off toward the mill.

At the house, the Simnel cake that Eirwen had baked for

Easter was sitting in the middle of the kitchen table, next to a large bowl of hard-boiled eggs.

After a supper of potato soup, Emlyn played catch with Thomas and Billy, the neighbors' boy, until it got dark. Around eight o'clock, all the family took turns in the bathtub. First in were Dilys and Thomas, who spent more time bickering and splashing each other than they did scrubbing. Their turn ended when Thomas threw a cupful of water at his sister, missed, and hit Eirwen directly in the face. Ignoring Thomas's protests, Eirwen herded them out of the tub and upstairs, and the house grew quiet.

After his bath, clad in his dressing gown, Gwyn fell asleep in the armchair. At the kitchen table, Emlyn scanned Friday's Pittsburgh newspaper and found the usual reports of accidents, visits, deaths, births, and cultural events. The only national news of note was the announcement of the formation of a new company, General Electric, via a merger of Edison General Electric and the Thomson-Houston Company.

Homestead was already benefiting from the invention of Thomas Edison through the use of electric lights in the mill and company office buildings. A few newer residences of the wealthy were also electrified, although most of the fixtures were combination gas/electric in case the latter failed.

Emlyn put down the paper and picked up his copy of *The Golden Bough* by Scotsman James Frazer. Upon its publication in 1890, the book had scandalized the British public because Frazer had included the story of Jesus in his comparative study of myths. By implying that Scripture was just another version of many different legends about the sacrifice of a sacred king, Frazer had enraged many believers, Emlyn's father included. Wanting to find out firsthand what the fuss was about, Emlyn had picked up a used copy at a bookstore in Cardiff before he left Wales. At last he had the time to read it.

He was on page 49 when Eirwen came down to start her bath. At that point, Emlyn retreated to his bedroom and promptly fell asleep.

He awoke with a start several hours later. He pulled his alarm clock toward him, and saw in the dim light that it was shortly before five. He lay there for a few minutes, trying to decide whether to get up or try to fall asleep again.

He turned toward the window and watched the glow from the mill pulse against the black sky. It would soon be dawn.

Suddenly, an inspiration came to him: He would get up and walk to the top of the hill to see the sunrise. This was an old custom in parts of Wales, greeting the sun on Easter morning. He hadn't watched the sun rise for its own sake since last summer in Wales. It was time.

He pulled on his trousers and a thick sweater, and tiptoed down the stairs. In the kitchen he gulped down a glass of water, picked *The Golden Bough* off the table, and took a boiled egg from the bowl and a bun from the shelf and placed them in a small knapsack. He donned his cap and boots, quietly closed the back door, and walked swiftly towards the Avenue.

Men were returning from night shift, but few were heading towards it. Fortunately for those who wanted to celebrate it, Easter always fell on a Sunday, when there was a respite of several hours from the production of steel.

Emlyn took the same route as he had with Sarah on their horseback outing. That was the only time he had been beyond the lower parts of the hillside in town.

He climbed quickly, up City Farm Lane, beyond the main cluster of houses, toward the summit of the big hill. To his left, the eastern sky was taking on a red hue.

Rhododaktylos Eos, the rosy-fingered dawn, was opening the gates of heaven so Helios, the sun god, could ride his chariot across the sky. The rosy-red glow spread from the horizon over the great bend in the river. The sky began to turn from indigo to a lighter cast of blue.

As he reached the top of the rise, a sliver of blinding light peeked over the horizon. He consulted his watch: 5:40.

Standing on a promontory above the mill office and superintendents' houses in Munhall, Emlyn felt god-like, alone on the Empyrean heights.

Emlyn breathed in deeply. It was a glorious dawn.

A gentle south wind blew across the Monongahela River, away from Homestead. Smoke from the houses and mills streamed away in wispy tendrils toward the steep bank opposite the town. The noise from the steel works was diminished, not only by distance, but also because of the Sunday hiatus.

For the next twenty minutes, Emlyn watched the sky turn a brilliant blue. Though the sky was streaked with dusky patches of smoke in the north, Emlyn thought the valley looked beautiful.

The town started to come awake. Pedestrians appeared on the streets, most apparently headed for Easter services. Eirwen, Gwyn, and the children would soon be getting up and starting off for church in their Sunday finery. Eirwen would be wearing the straw bonnet onto which she had sewn silk daisies and a bright yellow ribbon.

Emlyn turned and walked beyond the first rise toward the cemeteries. On the upper parts of the hillside that were rarely touched by the toxic fumes from the smokestacks, the foliage and grasses were turning a tender green.

As he topped the rise, Emlyn saw a man, perhaps the minister or sexton, opening the door of Anne Ashley Memorial Church. Emlyn kept walking across the Protestant cemetery, toward a tree full of white blossoms at its southern boundary. As he got closer, he saw it was a dogwood. He went over to it and, finding a patch of moss underneath, sat down with his back resting on the trunk.

He thought of Easter back in Wales—his father in the pulpit, the congregation—imagining what the finished new chapel was like. He pulled *The Golden Bough* out of the knapsack and started reading. As the sun climbed higher in the sky, filling him with warmth, he lost track of time. At page 191, he closed his eyes, reveling in the peace of this place.

He dreamed of his grandparents' farm. It was a lovely spring day, and he was walking up the big hill behind the farmhouse. Fly the sheepdog ran ahead, eager to gather the Welsh Speckled Face sheep grazing on the other side. At his whistled command, the collie stopped and lay down. As Emlyn approached the brow of the hill, the dog ran off, out of view. He ran to the top and looked over. The expansive grazing field he expected to see had vanished, and in its place was a wasteland of black rocks. Fly was nowhere in sight. Emlyn turned around. The hillside he had just climbed was now rocky and without vegetation. In every direction spread a vast barren plain. Where was he? His heart began pounding.

He was jarred awake by the sound of voices. He opened his eyes and saw a young couple about a hundred feet away, walking past him on the path between the cemeteries.

After a moment's confusion, Emlyn sat up and rubbed his eyes. To his relief, he realized that he was in the Homestead cemetery, sitting under a tree. How long had he been asleep?

Emlyn waved at the couple in greeting, and they waved back. From their attire, Emlyn deduced that they were coming from services at Anne Ashley or another church.

He consulted his watch and saw that it was past noon.

Sitting in the sun had made him warm, and he pulled off his sweater. He took out the sweet bun and egg, and ate them slowly, savoring every bite.

—•••—

When Oliver returned from Chicago on April 20th, Oesterling heaved a sigh of relief. During her husband's absence, Carrie had made weekly visits to Homestead. Oesterling began to regret urging her to come to the house, as her presence there irked Sarah.

After the first dinner at the house, Sarah and Carrie had switched roles. Now Sarah sat grim and silent as Carrie chattered away about gossip regarding mill management and local society folk. Add Norton Montague to the mix, and tensions would subtly increase. While Carrie didn't bring up mill politics, Montague did repeatedly. Oesterling would try to change the topic of conversation, but he was not often successful. Montague liked to be sure his views were articulated, and, as he obviously hoped, accepted.

Not wanting to argue with Montague, Oesterling kept his mouth shut during what the doctor thought of as Montague's 'lectures.' Carrie would occasionally throw in a word of agreement, but Sarah said nothing.

Now that Carrie would no longer be making frequent visits, Oesterling hoped that dinners at his house would resume their former tranquility. He resolved that if Montague didn't drop politics and revert to opining on arts and letters, Oesterling and Cerberus would frequently be going for a walk after Sunday dinners.

—•••—

At the end of Lent, at Paddy's instigation Emlyn agreed to play for two more wedding dances. The first happened to be on May 7th, the same day as Arthur and Tegwen's wedding back in Treorchy. Emlyn had contributed to a gift that Eirwen and Gwyn had sent, a set of percale bed sheets with pillowcases hand-embroidered by Eirwen.

Playing at the Irish reception, Emlyn felt both self-pitying and defiant. He wished he could have been in Treorchy to serve as best man, as Arthur had wanted. But he feared that even if he had been able to attend, his father might have prevented his participation.

One thing was certain: No one would be dancing or drinking spirits at their reception, which was being held in Tegwen's parents' house.

Emlyn glanced around at the wedding guests lined up for a set dance. Only half of them were couples, the rest being parents or grandparents with children, girls with girlfriends, or any assortment of friends and family members. They were having a grand time. So much for his father's strictures against the evils of dancing.

However, on May 21st, at the second dance, Emlyn had to revise his assessment about the harmlessness of drinking and dancing.

Maud, the young woman from Lizzie's reception, had approached him again, this time when he came out the side door during a break. Emlyn drank water from a teacup, while down the alley an inebriated young couple flirted. The girl was laughing loudly at the boy's coarse jokes.

Emerging from the door, Maud came over to Emlyn. "Thought you might like to wet yer whistle after playing so hard."

She held up a mug of ale.

"Thank you, no," he replied, showing her the teacup. "Water is fine."

She laughed. "That's got to be a first, a musician who refuses beer."

He shrugged. She looked at the ale, and took a swallow.

"What part of England are yeh from?" she asked after a pause. "I myself was born in Manchester, though my parents are from County Cavan."

"I'm from South Wales, not England," he replied.

"Oh," she said, disappointed. Brightening, she asked, "When did yeh come to Homestead?"

"Last November," Emlyn replied, trying to figure an escape route.

"We've been here nearly two years," she said. When he said nothing, she asked, "Where did yeh learn to play fiddle? Ye'r such a fine player."

She smiled, taking another swallow of ale.

"Kind of picked it up," he replied vaguely.

Setting the mug on a rain barrel, she stepped closer to him, took his hands into hers, and examined them.

"Such strong, artistic hands," she said.

Lifting her dark brown eyes to gaze directly into his, she moved nearer, her skirt touching his legs. She moved closer. Holding his right hand, she suddenly pulled him away from the door, into the shadows behind the barrels stacked at the door to the hall.

Off balance, he lurched into her. Slipping her arms around him, she drew him to her and pushed him against the wall.

Before he could say anything, her mouth was on his. He could taste the beer, smell her sweat mingled with cheap cologne. She was pressing him against the side of the building, her pelvis and breasts snug against him. She moved her left hand against his crotch, rubbing, pressing her body into his. As she felt his erection, her mouth moved to his neck, his throat.

His breathing quickened. He raised one hand to her breast, and discovered her corset ended right under the breast. Through the thin fabric of her bodice he felt her ample breast, its nipple hard. She moaned softly and moved his other hand to her backside.

Mixed emotions flooded through Emlyn as once again, he simultaneously felt arousal and anxiety. Back home, girls (well, most girls except Gladys) would not dare be so forward with him, knowing his family and position in the community. She didn't know him from Adam. Yet here they were, on the verge of coupling in the alley behind the Hibernian Club.

She simultaneously pulled up the front of her skirt while struggling with the buttons on his trousers.

"This is not the place," he gasped, "Not the place for . . ."

"Shhh," she said, placing her hand over his mouth.

As the first button of his fly was undone, a loud, drunken male voice shouted out of the doorway to the hall, "Maud! Where the devil are ya, ya vixen? Here's the cider you wanted."

"Bloody hell," she muttered, pulling away from Emlyn and hastily smoothing down her skirt.

"I saw ya go out there," the voice bellowed from the other side of the barrels.

"Who's that?" whispered Emlyn, fumbling with the button on his pants.

"Hush," she hissed. "It's my man."

"Husband!" Emlyn's whisper was more like a croak.

"Not for another two months," she replied.

Then, straightening her bodice and smoothing her hair,

she stepped around the barrels and into the light coming out of the door.

"Here I am," she said sweetly. "So nice of yeh to bring me cider."

"Where the dickens were yeh?"

"Takin' a bit of fresh air," she said, laughing. "Come, let's go find the others before the next set dance."

Through the space between door and barrels, Emlyn caught a glimpse of Maud leading a muscular, middle-aged man back into the hall.

Emlyn exhaled sharply. "Jaysus, that was a close call," a man said somewhere behind him.

Emlyn peered into the dark alley. There was Paddy, sitting on a pile of crates several paces away, smoking a cigarette.

"You can say that again," replied Emlyn, coming over and collapsing onto a crate next to Paddy.

"I'll not say it again, but I will say that you obviously don't know how close you came to being broken in two."

"I hesitate to ask how."

"Her man is one Dennis Donovan, a puddler, one of the strongest men in Homestead. He was widowed two years ago and recently asked the charming Maud to be his blushing bride. "

"Good God," breathed Emlyn. "Why didn't you warn me?"

Paddy chuckled. "With things moving as fast as they were, I wouldn't be such a fool as to intrude."

He took a flask from his hip pocket and removed the stopper.

"Here, take some. You look like you need it," urged Paddy.

Emlyn took the flask, held it to his nose. He threw back his head and took a several large gulps. The whisky burned all the way to his stomach, and then spread out in a calming warmth throughout his body.

"Theirs is definitely one wedding I won't be playing for," said Emlyn, wiping his mouth with the back of his hand.

"Hey there, you slackers!" someone yelled from the doorway. "Let's have some music."

Emlyn turned to see Donovan standing in the light from the doorway. "What are you fickin' musicians doing, hidin' out here in the alley?"

"Keep your britches on, boyo," replied Paddy, winking at Emlyn. "We're coming."

Emlyn took another big swig from the flask, and handed it back to Paddy.

As they came to the doorway, Donovan threw one arm around Paddy, another around Emlyn, and escorted them into the hall.

Sunday, May 15th.
Baseball Sandlot, Allegheny City

George Bernhard faced the pitcher. He was at the full count with one out in the eighth inning and the score was tied. His friend Hans Wagner had just doubled to second base. George glanced quickly from Hans to the pitcher.

The pitcher wound up and threw. The ball was low, as George liked them. He swung, a crack sounded, and the ball sailed between first and second base.

George ran for all he was worth toward first. The crowd was screaming. As he crossed the bag, George turned to see Hans sliding into home in a cloud of dust. Safe! They didn't call Hans the 'Flying Dutchman' for nothing. Hans and his brother Albert were the best ball players in sandlot Pittsburgh, George thought proudly. George was out, but their team had now taken the lead.

Meeting on a sandlot the previous year, George and Hans

had instantly taken a liking to each other. Like George, Hans's parents were German immigrants, although from Prussia, not Franconia. The boys had been born in Pittsburgh only days apart in February of 1874.

As George walked back to the bench, Hans came up to him and punched him gingerly on the arm. "Thanks, George," said Hans. "You're a pal."

"It was nothing," grinned George, brushing at the dust on his pants.

They sat on the bench to watch the next batter.

"Say," said Hans, "has your Pa found work yet?"

"Nah," said George. "He's getting more and more upset each time he finds an opening, but doesn't get hired."

"My Pa could probably get him work in the coal mine, like he did for Albert and me," said Hans.

"Thanks, but no," said George. "Pa says he could never work underground. It was bad enough, he said, working in the boiler room of a gunboat during the Civil War."

"I understand," said Hans. "I don't much like mining myself."

"Is that why you're studying to be a barber?" asked George.

Hans nodded.

The next batter hit a high fly, easily caught by the center fielder.

"Anyway, let me know if you want me to ask," Hans added, getting up and trotting off toward his shortstop position.

"OK," said George, picking up his mitt and following him toward left field.

Homestead

As the hillsides turned green and the Earth reached the full bloom of spring, Oesterling took more outings on Figaro. With Cerberus trotting alongside the horse, he left the clamor and grit of the mill town behind and rode out to the countryside. There, he could briefly escape his patients' diseases and injuries that increased in warmer weather.

As he rode, he made a game of looking for wildflowers blooming along the path. He congratulated himself whenever he spotted phlox, milkweed, columbine or alumroot among the grasses and weeds. His favorite flowering tree was the dogwood, with its white cruciform blossoms. He liked it because it reminded him of Margaret and their rides into these same hills, for she had often remarked on its beauty.

As the end of the school year approached, Oesterling was seeing little of Sarah. It seemed she was either busy with some project at school, working on music for church, or going out with one of her girlfriends or Montague. He missed her as a daily dinner companion, but he didn't miss having Montague holding forth at Sunday dinner. Thankfully, Montague, too, had gotten busy at work and had less free time on weekends.

—•••—

By the beginning of April, final touches were being put on the 35-inch structural mill. The engineers, contractors, and construction workers were feverishly working to set up the initial runs. No one had said anything to Emlyn about future employment with the Carnegie Company, and he was afraid to ask, fearing the worst. Gwyn kept urging him to talk with Jansen, saying he should at least inquire. Finally, he got up the courage to approach Jansen, but the engineer brushed him off, saying that the first task was to get the mill into production.

In late April the first test I-beams rolled out of the structural mill. Emlyn was still on the job, assisting the engineers in trouble-shooting and working with Charles in keeping track of construction tasks. Emlyn worried constantly about losing his gainful employment, and he knew that many company workers were worried about the same thing.

A showdown between the Amalgamated and the Carnegie Company was becoming increasingly likely. The company was not budging from the offer made in January. Superintendent Potter kept reiterating that this was the best offer the company could make, given market conditions. Anticipating a strike, the company dramatically increased its output of armor plate, which it was producing on contract to the U.S. Navy.

At the beginning of June, on Frick's orders, Potter notified the union that if the members did not accept the company's offer by June 23rd, the company would shut out the union and start bargaining with workers as individuals. As if to underscore the company's threat, dozens of workmen started erecting a tall wooden fence, capped by strands of barbed wire, around company property. At intervals holes were cut in the fence. At the ends of the mill buildings, platforms were built, topped with floodlights.

Each day when Emlyn passed the growing barricade around the Homestead Works on his way to work, he marveled at the size of it. One fence completely surrounded the mills and yards from the railroad tracks to the river; a smaller fence enclosed the company office buildings and stables on the other side of the tracks. To get to the mill side, Emlyn and other employees had to pass through a security checkpoint on the office side, then cross a bridge linking the two. Charles told him that the fence, when completed, would be over three miles long.

On the weekend of June 4-5th, dramatic events in towns northwest of Pittsburgh momentarily distracted the locals from the wage dispute. The Monday papers reported that, following torrential rains, a dam had burst, sending a flood raging through Titusville and Oil City. In late morning Sunday, as people were gathered along the banks of Oil Creek, attempting to help flood victims, oil and benzene, released by the flood, ignited without warning. Another explosion followed shortly thereafter.

Witnesses estimated the wall of flame on the creek surface to be 200 feet high. The fire spread through Oil City, incinerating many who had survived the flood. Initial reports were that two hundred souls had perished in the disaster.

In Homestead, as the fence enveloped the mill, workers became outraged at the show of force by the company. Paddy was one of them. Emlyn had decided against playing for any more weddings after the incident in the alley, but on June 11th, he accepted Paddy's invitation to join him for a Saturday session at O'Reilly's.

As he pushed into the saloon, Emlyn immediately sensed a change in atmosphere from when he had been there in February. Fewer patrons were crowding the bar, and the loud talking and laughing had been replaced by more muted conversation.

"We missed you, lad," said Paddy as Emlyn approached the table where Paddy and Jack the drummer were sitting.

"It's been only a few weeks," said Emlyn, setting down his violin case and taking a seat.

"Seems like forever when we're missing a fiddler," said Jack, beating a tattoo on his bodhran. "And Danny Boy won't be here with his whistle because he's out gallivanting with his mates."

"How's it going over there in the company citadel?" asked Paddy, alluding to the main office building.

"Same as always," said Emlyn.

"What does that mean?" asked Paddy. "That Potter is still busy thinking of ways to screw the workers out of just compensation?" Paddy laughed mirthlessly. "Do the company poobahs feel safe enough now behind their fortifications?"

"I don't know what they think, although the fence's purpose is obvious," said Emlyn, plucking at his violin strings. "No one tells me anything—directly, that is. It seems like everything's in a state of suspended animation."

"Did you hear that on Tuesday the Amalgamated voted to sanction a strike, if that became necessary?" asked Jack.

Emlyn nodded. "My brother-in-law Gwyn is following negotiations closely. The union isn't prepared to make concessions, and the company doesn't seem to be, either. He thinks a strike is likely."

"I'd say it's damn well certain, given the attitude of Frick toward labor," said Paddy. "Carnegie, the tight old hypocrite, is hiding out in his castle in Scotland, pretending like he's the worker's friend. He's letting Frick do the dirty work for him."

The playing that evening was spiritless. Emlyn's thoughts—and apparently those of the other players—kept wandering back to the impending clash between company and labor. It seemed that everyone in Homestead, no matter what his or her source of income, was bracing for the strike.

Oesterling went about his daily rounds in June with fore-boding. Fewer patients were calling on his services, and those that did often had serious diseases or injuries. As production at the steel works reached peak capacity, more workers were getting hurt, and many were falling ill.

The last day of the school year had been June 8th, and now Sarah was on summer break. They'd had the school's musical pageant the week before, but it was a somber event, the children having picked up on the mood of their parents. The entire town, in fact, was apprehensive, laboring under a literal and figurative cloud from the mill. In the event of a strike, in addition to mill employees, all townspeople from merchants to tradesmen to professional people would suffer.

Carrie phoned, inviting her father and sister to their house for Sunday supper on June 12th. It would be a quiet family affair, she said. Sarah didn't want to go, but Oester-ling convinced her that they should allow Carrie to return their hospitality.

It was a lovely afternoon as Oesterling drove the buggy pulled by Figaro away from the ferry landing, even lovelier as they passed the top of Brown's Hill. The fields and yards were filled with greenery, dotted with colorful blooms un-blighted by smoke and gasses from the mills.

As they pulled up to the Strongs' house, Oesterling ad-mired the pale blue hydrangea bushes in full bloom by the entrance. Margaret had planted hydrangeas in front of their house in Homestead, but the plants didn't survive one year after her passing. In fact, little remained of Margaret's flow-er gardens that she had worked so hard to cultivate.

Oesterling took Figaro to the barn, while Sarah waited at the side door. By the time Oesterling had secured Figaro, the maid had come to the door. She ushered Sarah and the doc-tor into the small conservatory. White wicker furniture with pink-and-white chintz cushions was crowded among the riot of ferns, schefflera, and philodendrons. Oesterling was a bit overwhelmed by the tropical moistness of the room, but decided it was preferable to the choking smoke in Homestead.

As the doctor and Sarah were settling themselves, Carrie joined them. "Oliver is sorry that he won't be able to be here for supper," Carrie said as the maid set out lemonade, cheese and crackers. "He's been so busy working on the contract language, I've hardly seen him for the past three weeks." She paused to hand Sarah a glass of lemonade. "So I decided to invite Norton to join us."

"I thought you said it would be just . . ." Oesterling started to say when Norton Montague appeared in the doorway of the conservatory, a glass of amber liquid in one hand, his other in his pants pocket. His light beige summer suit set off his dark auburn hair and neat mustache.

"Cheers," Montague said, raising his glass to Sarah and the doctor. "I came from a meeting at the downtown office. Haven't seen much of you since this business with the union has heated up. How are you?" he asked, looking at Sarah while he shook the doctor's hand. He sat down next to Sarah, and after reaching over to give her hand a quick squeeze, he picked up a cracker. Sarah stared at him as if he had just dropped down from the ceiling.

"I hope you don't mind that I offered Norton some Scotch," said Carrie. Oesterling shrugged, while Sarah's eyes moved to the glass of whisky.

"After the last few weeks at work, such liquid refreshment is welcome," said Montague, crossing his legs. "Frick is anticipating trouble at Homestead, making plans to protect the mill."

"By bringing in police?" asked Sarah.

"Yes. The company is hoping that Sheriff McLeary will be able to keep the peace," replied Montague.

"He had better have a very large posse to support him, if he expects to be successful," said Sarah.

"If the sheriff can't do it, there are other options," said Montague, knocking back the rest of his drink.

"Pinkertons?" asked Sarah, as Montague poured more whisky into his glass.

Montague nodded.

"That's a wonderful idea—bring in your own private army," said Sarah. "Two years ago during the New York Central Strike, the Pinkertons shot and killed five people, including a woman. Whatever happened to talking instead of bringing in armed thugs?"

Montague snorted, and was about to answer, when Carrie came into the room.

"Supper will be ready soon," said Carrie, sitting on the settee next to Oesterling. "What are you all reading these days?" she asked. "If you have any time for reading," she added, glancing at Montague.

When no one answered, Carrie said, "I've been reading Conan Doyle's *The White Company*. It's a big disappointment."

When Oesterling asked why, she replied, "It's a silly adventure story, set during the Hundred Years' War. For the life of me, I don't know why Conan Doyle had to go and kill off Sherlock Holmes. Now, those are great stories!" She paused, and added, "Did a war really last for a whole hundred years?"

"As a matter of fact, yes," answered Montague, going to the sideboard to pour another drink. "It actually was a series of wars fought between two rival factions for the French throne in the 1300s."

"That long ago? Who cares?" said Carrie.

"I agree with you about Sherlock Holmes," Sarah said to Carrie.

"Maybe Conan Doyle will find a way to resurrect him," suggested Oesterling.

"I hope so," said Carrie.

"I've just finished Zola's latest novel, *L'Argent*, " said Sarah, "Or 'money' in English."

"Zola?" said Montague, returning to the settee. "Why in the world would you choose to read his depressing stuff?"

"For one, it helps me keep up with my French, and for another, I think he paints an accurate portrait of the times," said Sarah.

"How so?" asked Montague, holding up his glass and examining it.

"*L'Argent* is about the financial world in France during the 1860s. Zola shows the terrible effects of financial speculation and fraudulent company promotion, not to mention the negligence of company directors."

"You aren't suggesting that the criticisms implicit in this novel apply to the situation in the U.S. today, are you?" asked Montague.

"To some degree, yes," said Sarah.

"Sarah, how can you say that!" said Carrie. "You're sounding more like an anarchist than ever."

"You don't live in Homestead," said Sarah, agitated. "You don't see the people struggling to make ends meet, the deplorable conditions throughout the town."

"I hardly think of the Carnegie Company's substantial investment in the mills as speculation," said Montague.

"I agree, it isn't," said Sarah. "Zola's point, however, is that the financial system, big business, and the government are in collusion to keep the money flowing into directly into their coffers. That could certainly be said about what's going on in this country as well."

"What a ridiculous thing to say!" said Carrie. "You *are* an anarchist!"

Oesterling cut in. "Please, please! I was hoping for a pleasant dinner in your beautiful home, not a political debate."

"Sarah started it by bringing up that French writer," retorted Carrie.

"It doesn't matter how it started," said Oesterling. "Let's turn to another topic."

"Good idea," said Montague as the maid came in and announced that supper was ready.

They moved into the dining room, where the everyday dishes were set out on the table. During the meal of watercress soup and cold chicken salad, Oesterling had to keep steering the conversation away from the shoals of politics. It seemed that just about every topic from everyday life to cultural events had some aspect related to labor politics. By the time they finished the strawberries and cream, Oesterling had become irritable from the strain.

Carrie suggested they go into the parlor. "I've gotten the sheet music for 'After the Ball,'" she said. "Sarah, would you play it for us? We can all sing along."

Oesterling was glad when they got up and moved to the piano. 'After the Ball' by Charles K. Harris was the most popular song of the day, and one of Sarah's favorites, despite the fact that she'd never been to a ball.

Sarah sat at the piano and played the introduction. Carrie sang the verses, while the others joined in on the refrain.

After the ball is over,
After the break of morn—
After the dancers' leaving;

After the stars are gone;
Many a heart is aching,
If you could read them all;
Many the hopes that have vanished
After the ball.

Carrie brought out more music, and they kept singing—'Home, Sweet Home,' 'In the Gloaming,' 'Bicycle Built for Two,' 'Annie Laurie,' and several by Stephen Foster.

By then it was past eight, and Oesterling said he'd like to get going, as they needed to be home before dark. At Montague's request, Sarah played one last piece, 'The Washington Post March' by John Philip Souza. Carrie laughed as Oesterling began marching out the parlor door to the side entrance. He didn't mind playing the fool if it would fend off disputes between the other three.

The doctor asked Montague if he needed a lift back to Homestead, but he said that he had to return to Pittsburgh. He and Carrie walked Sarah and Oesterling to the side of the buggy.

Seeing Figaro, Montague asked if the horse was theirs or a stable hire. Oesterling explained how they shared expenses with the Bakers for the two horses, adding that Figaro did double duty as a riding and buggy horse. Montague said the horse reminded him of one he had in his youth in Maryland.

"Papa, I have an idea," said Carrie. "Why not let Norton take Figaro on an outing? Sarah could ride Dee."

Oesterling wasn't keen on letting Montague ride his horse. But before he could think of an excuse, Carrie turned to Sarah and asked, "Didn't you take that Welsh fellow on a ride last year?"

"Yes, I did, once," Sarah said.

"A horse ride would be a pleasant way to spend a summer

afternoon, wouldn't it?" asked Carrie, looking from Sarah to Montague.

"Maybe in July, when work isn't so hectic," said Montague. "As you know, we're reaching endgame with the Amalgamated negotiations. The Company is preparing to make its final offer on the fifteenth."

Oesterling was afraid to ask what the offer was, although it was becoming clear that the Carnegie Company was not going to meet union demands.

"I'll call you to set a day," said Montague as he helped Sarah into the buggy.

"Thank you so much for the songs," Carrie said. "You know Oliver hates these little sing-alongs. He thinks they're vulgar, but I say, fiddlesticks."

In turn, they thanked Sarah for supper, and Oesterling, slapping the reins on the horse's back, headed the buggy down the driveway.

"So that's why Carrie came in late and drunk to the party," said Sarah as they made the turn into the street. "She didn't want to do anything vulgar, like singing, in front of Oliver."

Oesterling sighed and glanced back in time to see Carrie following Montague into the side door of the house.

A week later, on Sunday morning, June 19th, instead of going to church, Gwyn went to an Amalgamated meeting at the Homestead opera house. Around noon, Eirwen was setting out lunch as Emlyn read the paper at the kitchen table when Gwyn and Jim Duncan burst through the back door.

"What happened?" asked Eirwen, setting down a plate of black bread and cheddar. She pulled out a chair, indicating a place for Duncan to sit at the table.

"Nearly every worker in the whole damn . . . I mean, darn mill was there. We could barely cram everyone in," said Duncan. "The situation ain't good."

"It's outrageous," said Gwyn. "The company refuses to negotiate further. Then they build this fence around the works. What an insult to the workers!"

"Yep, it looks real bad," agreed Duncan, settling onto the chair.

"Burgess McLuckie gave a great speech about how the workers have been betrayed," said Gwyn, pacing back and forth. "McLuckie should know, being one of the low-wage laborers."

"Betrayed how?" asked Emlyn.

"McLuckie said that the union supported the Republicans during the 1888 election, thinking that we'd be getting support from high tariffs—but instead we get high fences, Pinkertons, thugs, and the militia," said Duncan.

"Do you think it will come to that—the company bringing in armed men?" asked Eirwen.

"We hope not," said Duncan. "However, if Frick's past dealings with labor are any indication, police and soldiers definitely could be called in. What do you think them holes in the fence are for—to get a view of the beautiful scenery? It's clear that they're just the right size and height for sharpshooters."

Eirwen put her hand over her mouth, and Emlyn thought she might cry. Instead, she said, "I've got to call the children to lunch," and left the room.

During the following week at work, it became obvious to Emlyn—and everybody else in town—that the company was preparing for a confrontation. In addition to putting up the fence and watchtowers, the company had cancelled all pending orders, even though there was enough work to last a couple of months.

Gwyn and other union members were hopeful when, on Wednesday, June 23rd, a committee headed by William Roberts presented the union's contract offer to Frick at the Carnegie Company offices downtown. At their convention the week previous, the Amalgamated voted to make some concessions, lowering their scale offer to $24 a ton. However, nothing was decided at the meeting.

Although all was quiet in Homestead, a possible strike was the main topic of conversation in town. Thursday came and went with no word from the company, as did Friday the 24th, the company's deadline. Gwyn and the other Amalgamated members' hopes rose a little higher on the assumption that the company was considering their offer.

On Saturday morning when Emlyn arrived at the office, Charles rushed over to him and held up the front page of the newspaper.

"Read this!" he exclaimed, pointing to one of the articles.

Emlyn's heart sank as he read that Mr. Lovejoy, Secretary of the Carnegie Company, had told the press that as far as the company was concerned, the $23 offer was in effect, and the company was going to proceed without regard to the Amalgamated.

"That's it for the union," said Charles.

"What's going to happen?" asked Emlyn. "Will the Homestead Works actually be shut down?"

No one outside Carnegie upper management seemed to know.

As Emlyn walked home that afternoon along the fence the locals were calling 'Fort Frick,' he observed that, although it was payday, fewer shoppers were on the Avenue. Even the saloons weren't busy, and the mood generally was joyless.

Jim Duncan and another union member named Harry Smith came to the house Sunday afternoon to talk with Gwyn.

While Emlyn finished lunch, they sat around the kitchen table indulging in speculation about possible scenarios when the workweek began the next day and discussing what the unionists could do to prevent scabs from coming in.

"I hear the company's bringing in Pinkertons to man Fort Frick," Duncan said. "Come next week, they'll be shootin' at us through them holes in the fence."

"We're gonna stop them!" insisted Smith. "We're forming posses to make sure no black sheep sneak into town when we ain't looking."

"I don't know about you," said Duncan, "but I'm oiling my Remington."

"I have a rifle, too, a Winchester," said Smith. "It's old, but it'll be good enough to scare off scabs." He chuckled.

When Gwyn said he didn't own a firearm, both men offered to get one for him.

At this point, Eirwen suggested to Emlyn that they take Dilys and David outside to play, and he was more than happy to join her.

Emlyn sat on the front porch steps with Dilys and watched Eirwen helping David to walk. David's small hands gripped Eirwen's thumbs as he took steps in front of her. They went back and forth in the small yard several times, when suddenly David let go and lurched forward a few steps on his own before pitching into the dirt. Eirwen went over to help him up, but he stood up on his own, teetering back and forth, and then staggered into Eirwen and grabbed onto her skirt. David stood there for a moment, proud of himself.

Emlyn and Dilys clapped. Giggling, David let go of the skirt, took a few steps, and plunged into Emlyn's lap. They all laughed and cheered as David toddled around the yard, reeling like a drunk, intoxicated by his ability to move upright.

"I'm telling Dad about David," said Dilys, jumping up.

"Your father has important things to talk about," said Eirwen. "Let's wait till he comes out."

"Alright," said Dilys, disappointed. She leaped off the porch and began following David around the yard, helping him when he stumbled or fell. They both laughed at each misstep.

"You're a good sister and a big help to David," said Emlyn to Dilys as they went by.

Eirwen sat down beside Emlyn. "You know," she said, "I'd like to plan a party for David's first birthday this Saturday, but with this situation at the mill . . ." Her voice trailed off. "I don't know what to do."

"It'll be fine," said Emlyn, not believing his own words. "We can have cake after dinner, maybe invite a few people over."

"People are not in the mood for celebrations," said Eirwen. "I'll wait till Friday and see what happens." She stared off across the river.

"Oh, Emlyn," said Eirwen, her voice breaking. "I'm so frightened."

"Don't worry. All will be well," he said, putting his arm around her.

Emlyn watched the children running around giggling, as he and Eirwen sat silently on the steps. For the time being, at least, the children were free from the knowledge of impending woe.

The next day, the mill workers reported for the day shift, and production went on as usual in completing the remaining orders for armor plate. Everyone in town was waiting for something to happen.

The following day, Tuesday, June 28th, the company made its move: the union workers—that is, the skilled workers—coming on day shift were locked out. The open hearths went cold, and work in the armor plate division ground to a halt. A hush fell over the gigantic Homestead Works.

As he walked home that day, Emlyn saw two men whitewashing the outside of the mill fence. The stillness in the warm June afternoon was eerie, as if the town itself had become mute.

When Emlyn came into the kitchen, he saw that Eirwen had been crying. She told him that Duncan had come by with a rifle, and that he took Gwyn out to a vacant lot to practice shooting.

An hour later, as the rest of the family was seated at the kitchen table for supper, Gwyn came in the back door carrying the rifle. He greeted them, went into the pantry, set the gun inside a cupboard, and locked the door. He then took his place at the table and began eating as if nothing out of the ordinary had happened. When Thomas asked him what the gun was for, Gwyn replied, "Defending ourselves." When Thomas tried to question Gwyn further, Eirwen told him to hush. After dinner Gwyn went out again and did not return before Emlyn had gone to bed.

Early Wednesday morning, Emlyn started awake at the odd lack of noise from the mill. He had awakened a dozen times during the night, unsettled by the unaccustomed darkness and quiet.

When he went downstairs at six, Eirwen, red-eyed, was in the kitchen preparing breakfast. He told her that she didn't have to get up to prepare his meals, but she said that Gwyn was going to a big union meeting that morning and that she couldn't sleep anyway. Pouring cups of strong tea for both of them, she told him that Gwyn had been out drinking with Duncan and Smith and had not returned home until after midnight.

Gwyn had described scenes of locked-out workers gathering at the mill fence and peering through the peepholes in an attempt to see what was going on inside. The workers were concerned that the company would soon try to sneak in scabs. Effigies of Frick and Potter had been hung from telegraph poles while an angry crowd shouted their contempt.

As Emlyn walked through the quiet streets on his way to work, he saw large numbers of men emerging from houses and tenements, all heading toward the opera house, the site of the Amalgamated meeting.

At the structural mill office, Jansen called together the five remaining staff. Jansen told them that when the Homestead Works reopened, the structural mill would be put into operation with non-union workers, either former tonnage men who accepted the company's terms, or replacements. In the meantime, all construction records would be removed to the main office building, and they would be setting up operational offices for the structural mill in the building. For the immediate future, Charles LaCroix was to act as overseer for conversion of the offices. When Charles asked when the mill would reopen, Jansen said that company officials weren't sure, but no later than July 11th.

Coming home that afternoon, Emlyn found Duncan, a metal flask in hand, sitting on the back stoop while Gwyn paced back and forth. Gwyn paused when he saw Emlyn.

"What's going on the command center over there in Fort Frick?" asked Gwyn.

"Yeah, did you see any sign of scabs?" Duncan added.

"No, all is quiet. The only people I saw were the employees who normally work in the offices," replied Emlyn, removing his suit coat. "What happened at the meeting?"

"There were over three thousand workers, just about the whole damn work force at the meeting. Some men had to stand outside," said Duncan, passing the flask to Gwyn. "Everybody agrees that Frick has broken the contract with the union and is trying to put the blame on the Amalgamated."

Gwyn took a pull from the flask and held it out to Emlyn, who shook his head. Gwyn handed it back to Duncan.

"The mechanics and laborers threw in their lot with the Amalgamated," said Gwyn. "It's bloody amazing! They are not going back into the mill as long as the union is locked out. Even the watchmen are joining us. We will all stand together against Frick."

Duncan added that the eight Amalgamated lodges had met in secret session afterward and elected an advisory committee.

"In effect," said Gwyn, "the Amalgamated committee is now running the town."

Duncan went on enthusiastically about how the workers had organized a river patrol to watch for scabs arriving by water. They also were setting up telegraph connections to their headquarters on the upper floors of the new Bost Building a block from the company's office building in Munhall.

"After the meeting the Amalgamated committee took down the effigies of Frick and Potter," said Gwyn. "I suppose they don't want to inflame anti-company feelings."

"They should've left them," said Duncan, slapping his knee for emphasis. "Those bastards should be hanging for real." He lifted the flask to his lips and tipped it.

Emlyn looked up at the clear blue sky over the silent, fenced-in mill. How long would this uneasy quiet last?

Wednesday, June 29th

Oesterling sat in his overstuffed chair in the study, trying to read the paper. Carrie had called the previous morning, asking to speak with him in person—but only under the condition that Sarah would not be present. As Sarah had gone to Pittsburgh for the afternoon, Carrie had said she would come today.

Carrie was behaving very strangely, Oesterling mused. She had come over often when Oliver was away, but not once since he had returned. Now this private meeting. Could it be about the impending strike?

Twenty minutes later, Carrie came in, closing the pocket doors behind her. She kissed Oesterling on the cheek, and sat in the chair beside the hearth. She wore a white linen suit with black braid trim, one he had never seen before. Oesterling complimented her outfit, but Carrie didn't seem to notice.

"What do you want to talk about, Carrie?" Oesterling asked. "This is all so mysterious."

Carrie looked at him, then into the cold fireplace. "I . . . I want . . ." she said haltingly.

"You want?" prompted Oesterling.

Her face was very pale as she twisted her gloves in her lap.

"Papa, I may as well get to the point," said Carrie. "I am with child."

Oesterling blinked. This was not at all what he had anticipated. "Why, that's wonderful!" he exclaimed. "You and Oliver have been hoping for this. I imagine he's thrilled."

"I . . . I haven't told him yet," Carrie stammered.

"Why not, for heaven's sake?"

Carrie hesitated, blinking back tears.

"Because the baby is due in December."

"Why would that . . . ?" Oesterling stopped mid-sentence. A baby due in December would have been conceived in March. "Ah," he said slowly. "Are you certain?"

"I saw a doctor in the city last week. I didn't give him my real name. He confirmed what I suspected and calculated the baby's arrival to be in mid-December," said Carrie. Tears ran down her face.

They sat in silence, while Oesterling wracked his memory, trying to put the pieces of the puzzle together.

"I assume the father is Norton Montague," Oesterling said at last.

Carrie nodded.

Oesterling struggled to contain the conflicting emotions boiling inside him. The affair was one thing—but to have deceived Oliver, him, and Sarah, another. And a grandchild by the insufferable Montague! He could hardly bear the thought.

"I'm fearful that Oliver will figure it out," said Carrie. "During the last year he has had less and less interest in, you know, being intimate with me. I don't know what he'll do if he finds out the baby is not his. If he casts me out, I will be ruined. I recently ordered two new frocks to be made, in addition to this suit. I won't be able to pay for them."

"I should think that would be the least of your worries," he replied.

Carrie started sobbing. Oesterling contemplated Carrie, looking so forlorn in her gorgeous suit.

"You are always welcome to come back here."

Carrie looked at him reproachfully. "Come back to Homestead? In disgrace?" She renewed her sobbing.

Oesterling got up and started to pace.

"Predicting the date of a baby's arrival is not an exact science," he said finally. "Tell him that the baby's due in January."

Carrie dabbed her eyes with her handkerchief. "There's something else."

Oesterling waited.

"For the last five years, I've always blamed myself for my failure to conceive. Now I know it's not me," said Carrie.

"Oliver may be so thrilled with the prospect of having a child," Oesterling replied, "that the thought may never occur to him to question paternity. In any case, you must tell him about the baby, and let the chips fall where they may."

Carrie nodded sadly. "I'm sorry I got involved with Norton. He seemed so charming."

"Does he know about the baby?" asked Oesterling.

"I didn't tell him," said Carrie. "In fact, we broke off the liaison a few weeks ago."

"Mutually?" asked Oesterling.

"No," said Carrie, sniffing. "I broke it off. With Oliver back in town, the situation was far too dangerous."

"How long did this go on?" asked Oesterling. "Does this mean you two were using Norton's presumed interest in Sarah as a cover for the affair?"

"That's not how it started out," Carrie said, choking back tears. "When I introduced them in November, I truly thought they might enjoy each other's company, with their interest in music and all."

Oesterling stood up. "It started during your visits to Homestead?"

"Yes," wailed Carrie. "Oliver was in Chicago. I was lonely." She cleared her throat. "I never wanted to hurt Sarah."

Oesterling walked over to the window and put his hands in his pockets. "As far as I see, there is only one recourse. What's done is done, and there's no point in coming forward with this revelation. No one shall ever know this secret except you and me. You must go home and tell Oliver the good news."

He turned to her. "It is good news, isn't it? Isn't this what you both have wanted?"

"I don't know if I can face Oliver!" Carrie wailed.

"Nonsense. You can and will tell him, and he will be delighted. Everyone will be happy, and you must be, too."

Carrie blotted away the tears with her handkerchief. "Papa, I've been very stupid."

"Maybe not stupid, but foolish," said Oesterling. "Let's not talk about this again."

As he watched Carrie sitting by the fireplace, he made an effort to convince himself that all would be well. It was going to be a hard sell.

Friday, July 1st

Oesterling did a good job of acting surprised when Oliver phoned the house at 8 a.m. to tell them that Carrie was expecting. Oesterling breathed a sigh of relief as Oliver narrated how he had come home late from work, and Carrie was waiting for him with the grand news. It was too late to call, so he had waited till morning to phone Chicago and Homestead.

As Oliver described how his mother was overjoyed at the prospect, Oesterling sharply felt Margaret's absence. Perhaps if she were still alive, things would be different. He felt so much a bungler in his handling of his daughters. Both of them in their distinctive ways seemed such mysteries to him—Carrie, with her mother's figure and his coloring, Sarah, with his physique and her coloring.

Carrie got on the phone and talked briefly to him, then Sarah. After they hung up, Sarah said that she hoped the birth of the baby would turn her sister's attention to someone other than herself. Oesterling said nothing, although the comment closely reflected his own thoughts.

When Sarah brought up the ride she and Montague had planned for that Sunday, Oesterling's heart sank. At that point it began to dawn on him how difficult it was going to be for him to carry on as before, holding the secret inside.

IV.

What we think, or what we know, or what we believe, is in the end of little consequence. The only consequence is what we do.

—John Ruskin, *The Crown of Wild Olive* (1866)

Saturday, July 2nd

The company paid off all its workers and served notices of discharge. Jansen told the five workers at the structural mill office not to report to work after the July Fourth holiday. Given that the entire mill workforce had been locked out, all offices would be closed until further notice. Only professional staff and upper-level management would remain on the job. The company would notify those workers who would be called back when production resumed.

"Do you still think the mill will be running again by the 11th?" Charles LaCroix asked.

Jansen hesitated. "No, it may take longer now that both the skilled workers and laborers will have to be replaced."

Jansen had them escorted to the gate. As they walked away, Charles remarked ruefully that maybe they should pack up and start looking for work elsewhere.

As Emlyn walked home along the mill fence, he wondered the same thing. If the strike went on for more than a few weeks, every resident of Homestead would be affected for the worse. He had come to Homestead only six months previously and had managed to move up from laborer to office worker—thanks in large part to William Williams. He dreaded the thought of having to look for work again; he dreaded to contemplate what would happen to the thousands of people whose livelihoods depended upon the mill.

A letter from Gareth Morgan awaited Emlyn when he returned home. This one contained important news: Gareth had received a call to serve as pastor to Salem Congregational Church, located outside of Johnstown, Pennsylvania. Members of the congregation had heard him preach in Cardiff and were favorably impressed. He and Jane were to be married in September, and he would come over first and get their living quarters in order before she arrived. He hoped to visit Emlyn before he settled into his new home.

When Emlyn asked Gwyn about Johnstown, he said it was a good eighty miles to the east, up in the mountains. The town had been virtually wiped out in 1889 when a dam burst on a private reservoir owned by Carnegie, Frick and other wealthy Pittsburghers. Floodwaters rushed into the city, killing over two thousand people.

Amazingly, the steel mill there had been brought back into production within a year, and the town was swiftly rebuilding to its former size. Was there any place in this state that had not been touched by the heavy hand of Henry Clay Frick?

Oesterling slapped the dust off his riding hat as he walked around to the back door of his house. Cerberus's tongue was hanging out after their long ride up Streets Run.

Oesterling hung up his hat and linen duster in the back pantry and set down a bowl of fresh water for the dog. As he pushed the kitchen door, it flew open. There was Sarah, waving a newspaper, with Mrs. Sproule behind her.

"Papa, look at this article," Sarah said, pointing to a column in the paper. "The Carnegie Company is making it clear they will have no further dealings with the union."

"I don't have my reading glasses," Oesterling said. "What does it say?"

Mrs. Sproule handed the doctor a tumbler of water. Sarah read as he drank.

"Listen to this by Carnegie Secretary Lovejoy: 'Hereafter, the Homestead steel works will be operated as a non-union mill. We shall not recognize the Amalgamated Association in our dealings with the men. There will be, no doubt, a scale of wages, but we shall deal with the men individually, not with any organization.' "

"They are emphatically not negotiating further," Oesterling said. "That sounds ominous for the workers."

"It certainly does," replied Sarah. "All that people are talking about is how and when the company will try to bring in scabs. I heard a few strangers have been run out of town by workers who assumed they were company men."

"This is not good. People in town are getting worked up," said Mrs. Sproule. "There's going to be violence for sure."

"Let's hope not," said Oesterling. "Anyway, there's not much anyone can do but wait and see."

"For the time being," said Sarah. "However, if the company and the workers come to blows, you and the other doctors will have your work cut out for you."

"Jesus, Mary, and Joseph," said Mrs. Sproule, sinking into a chair. Sarah patted her shoulder while the doctor stared fixedly at the newspaper.

"Maybe I should call off the ride with Norton tomorrow," said Sarah.

"Why?" asked Oesterling.

"He's so committed to the rights of the company, it's exasperating," she said. "I don't want to discuss the situation with him,"

"Then don't," said Oesterling, relieved. He must make every effort to act as if nothing had changed with Montague.

"There will be trouble if the company tries to bring in replacements or police," said Sarah.

"I doubt if anything will happen tomorrow, Sunday, or even the next day, since it's the Fourth," replied Oesterling. "You're not going to be riding around the mill, are you?"

"I suppose it is an opportunity to get out of town for a while," said Sarah.

"Do you still want me to prepare a basket of food for you to take to the church picnic on the Fourth?" asked Mrs. Sproule.

"I'd forgotten all about that," said Oesterling.

"Yes, please," said Sarah. "We've got to keep some semblance of normalcy—even though the situation is anything but normal."

Oesterling agreed, his thoughts immediately flying to Carrie.

Mrs. Sproule was so preoccupied with her own musings that she hadn't noticed that Cerberus had come into the kitchen and was rooting through the garbage pail.

Oesterling quietly led the dog into the hallway and closed the door behind them.

Sunday, July 3rd

Emlyn walked along West Run with his boots in his hand. Coming to a small pool in the creek, he waded in. The cool, gently flowing water felt soothing to his feet so accustomed to boots. Water skippers, minnows and crayfish darted off as he waded along, stirring up the silt on the bottom. He walked up the creek until boulders blocked his way.

Sighting a shady clearing off to the side, Emlyn left the creek. From his knapsack he pulled out *Dr. Jekyl and Mr. Hyde*, a novel that Charles LaCroix had loaned him, and settled down on a grassy spot in the clearing.

The rest of the family had gone off to church in the morning, but Gwyn was not with them when they returned. Eirwen said that Gwyn was going to the Bost Building to help at strike headquarters. The afternoon before, she had been very displeased when Gwyn had gone out target shooting with Jim Duncan and did not return for supper. After dinner Eirwen cut slices of the cake she had baked and served them to the children. She covered the remaining cake and set it up on the shelf.

They had a piece with Gwyn when he returned, while he talked about the strike and the union and the gun. Tensions between Eirwen and Gwyn were escalating over Gwyn's acquisition of the Remington rifle. When Eirwen had said that she did not want a gun in the house, Gwyn had removed it from the pantry cupboard, taken it out to the shed, and put a padlock on the door.

Emlyn was happy to get away, if only for a few hours. He read for over an hour, when his eyes started to droop and he drifted off to sleep. When he awoke, the sun had moved around and the clearing was now bathed in afternoon sunshine. Emlyn put on his boots and continued his walk up West Run.

As he ambled up the slope that would take him to the cemeteries, a horse with saddle and bridle but no rider came galloping down the path toward him. The horse, a big roan, slowed and stopped about fifty feet from him. The horse contemplated him for a moment, then lowered its head and began eating grass alongside the path.

This horse definitely looked familiar. As he got closer, Emlyn saw it was Figaro, Dr. Oesterling's gelding.

Emlyn approached him tentatively, talking to him in a calm voice, "There, there. Good boy. Steady."

Figaro raised his head and snorted loudly.

What had happened? Had Figaro thrown the doctor?

He gently picked up the reins and stroked the horse's neck. Figaro had worked up some lather, but otherwise seemed uninjured. Upon closer examination, however, Emlyn discovered dark wet marks on the horse's flank. He looked more closely and saw it was blood. Someone had used spurs and a whip on him. Oesterling? The other doctor who rode him?

He heard hoof beats coming around the bend in the path.

It was Sarah on Dee.

"What happened?" asked Emlyn as she rode up. "Did your father fall off? Is he alright?"

Sarah shook her head. "Papa wasn't riding. It was Norton."

Emlyn glanced up the path in confusion. "Where is. . . ?"

"He's OK, only shaken up a bit. He's waiting on City Farm Lane, where he was thrown."

"Thrown? From Figaro?" asked Emlyn incredulously.

"Yes. I was afraid Figaro might get lost or stolen, so went chasing after him," she added in explanation. "Thanks for catching him."

"Thanks aren't needed," said Emlyn. "He came up to me."

He took the reins and held them out to her. She shook her head.

"Could you ride Figaro? Please?" she asked. "I doubt if he'll try to throw you."

Emlyn hesitated. "I don't know . . ."

"Please?"

Emlyn tied his knapsack onto the back of the saddle, and swung up onto Figaro. He was amazed at how easy it was, in contrast to his ride last December.

"Follow me," said Sarah, starting toward the cemeteries.

They rode across the boundary of the cemeteries and turned onto City Farm Lane. About a quarter mile down the hill, Emlyn saw Norton Montague sitting on a stump, holding a battered bowler in one hand and a riding crop in the other. He was covered with dust, and the right sleeve of his jacket and one of his pant legs were ripped. His glasses were sitting crookedly across his nose. As they approached, he got stiffly to his feet.

When he saw Emlyn, an expression of distaste came over Montague's dirt-streaked face.

"What's he doing here?" Montague asked Sarah, his face reddening.

Sarah ignored the question as she and Emlyn dismounted.

"I think it best if Emlyn takes the horses back to the stable," Sarah said to Montague. "I can help you walk back to the house where Papa can take a look at you."

"I'm perfectly capable of riding," he said irritably. "I'm fine."

"Perhaps," said Sarah. "But I don't think you should try to ride Figaro."

"Nonsense," said Montague, stepping towards Figaro and seizing the bridle.

Figaro jerked his head up and down to shake off Montague's grip.

"Stupid beast," growled Montague, raising the crop and bringing it down on Figaro's neck.

Figaro reared up, his front hooves pawing the air, as Montague jumped aside.

"Norton, stop it!" Sarah cried sharply.

Montague struck the horse again, this time in the face. Figaro's eyes grew wild as a gash appeared under his left ear.

Emlyn dropped his knapsack and seized Montague's arm. Montague shook off Emlyn's grip and raised the whip a third time.

Sarah cried out, "I said, stop it!" Figaro wheeled around, trying to get into position to kick Montague.

Emlyn shoved Montague aside and grabbed the reins from him. "Don't you dare strike him again," Emlyn said, standing between Montague and the horse.

"This is why you can't ride Figaro," Sarah said angrily, coming over to Montague. He glowered at the horse and Emlyn, his hands in fists at his side.

Emlyn stood between Montague and Figaro as Sarah talked soothingly to the horse, stroking his neck. In a minute or so, the horse calmed down, but not Montague, who was slapping his thigh with the riding crop, fuming.

Sarah turned to Emlyn. "Would you please take Dee and Figaro to Walker's Stable on Fifth Avenue—where we went before—and give them to the groom Junius. Tell him that I will stop by later."

Emlyn glanced uncertainly from Sarah to Montague, who was trembling with anger. "Are you sure? I can stay if you like."

"I'm sure," said Sarah decisively.

Emlyn nodded to Sarah and swung into the saddle. Sarah handed him Dee's reins as Figaro started off down the lane. He could hardly believe what had just transpired.

Dee in tow, Emlyn trotted Figaro into town and turned onto the Avenue. Little traffic was on the street. Groups of men were sitting or standing in front of the hotels and boarding houses. At Amity Street he saw a bald man and a woman standing on the corner talking. With a start, he realized the woman was Addie Buckman. As he passed, she looked up. His heartbeat quickened as he remembered their encounter near this same intersection after his last ride.

Her face was scratched, her arm in a sling. She apparently had been beaten again by her husband. Her dull eyes moved from Figaro to Emlyn. How he could have ever felt afraid of her? He looked her straight in the eye and doffed his cap. This time, she recognized him, beard and all. A quick backward glance revealed her standing there, mouth agape.

Two minutes later, Emlyn arrived at the livery stable. When Junius asked what had happened to Sarah and the other fellow, Emlyn told him that Sarah would explain everything when she came over later to check on Figaro.

Emlyn patted Figaro on the neck, untied his knapsack from the saddle, and swinging it over his shoulder, walked toward Amity Street.

—•●•—

Oesterling was reading on the front porch with Cerberus at his feet when Sarah returned to the house.

"Of all the stupid stunts!" exclaimed Sarah, throwing herself onto the wicker settee.

"What stunts?" asked Oesterling, setting down his book. "Where's Norton?"

"He walked home after Figaro threw him," she replied.

"Threw him!" said Oesterling. "How did that happen?"

"Norton thinks he's some kind of an expert with horses. I wanted him to stop here to have you take a look at him, but he refused. It's probably for the best."

Oesterling resisted the urge to comment.

Sarah explained how Montague got angry when Figaro balked as they were riding along Streets Run. Montague hit him several times with the whip to get him going. But Figaro wasn't moving fast enough for Montague, who whipped and spurred the gelding every time he slowed to a trot.

After they passed the cemetery, Figaro balked again. Despite Sarah's protestations, Montague kept digging in the spurs until blood was running down Figaro's flanks. At this point, Figaro bucked, sending Montague into the dirt. The horse then ran off, over the hill toward West Run.

"That's where Emlyn caught him," said Sarah. "By chance he was taking a walk along the creek, and saw Figaro come over the hill."

"That was fortunate," said Oesterling.

"I would not let Norton back on Figaro. One or both of them might've been seriously hurt. Emlyn took Figaro and Dee back to the stable. Norton was absolutely furious, not only about not being allowed to ride back, but to have Emlyn ride instead."

"What about Figaro? Is he alright?" asked Oesterling.

"Junius put salve on the spur cuts and the one under the ear," said Sarah. "He says that Figaro should be fine." She paused. "I'm so sorry we asked you to allow Norton to ride Figaro."

"All's well that ends well," said Oesterling, thinking of Carrie. "Did you at least manage to avoid talking about the situation at the mill?"

Sarah snorted. "Not for the first half of the ride. He, Oliver, and Carrie share the same view, namely, that whoever has the capital, has the power to do as they like, with regard to no one."

"It makes me ill," she added, shaking her head. "I'm going to wash up and change," she said, standing. She went to the screen door and threw it open. It shut behind her with a decisive bang.

East Liberty, Pittsburgh

Karl Bernhard sat on the steps of the front porch of his house, whittling a piece of wood. He planned to fit it onto one of the kitchen chairs to replace a dowel that one of the boys had broken. Susanna sat in a rocker, snapping pea pods into a bowl.

Hearing a commotion, Karl looked down the street and saw his sons George and John jogging toward the house. George had a sheet of paper in his hand and was waving it over his head, grinning. The brothers took turns trying to push each other off the sidewalk as they ran.

The boys were breathless as they came into the yard. George slid onto the stairs next to his father as John stood by.

"Why are you boys home so soon?" asked their mother. "I thought you were going off to play ball."

"We didn't make it to the sandlot," said John.

"That's because we met a guy on Liberty Avenue, passing out these handbills," added George, thrusting the paper into his father's hands.

Karl scanned the text. It was an advertisement by the Carnegie Company for replacement workers at the Homestead Works.

"I know about this. It's been all over the papers for the last week," said Karl, handing the paper back to George.

"Yes, but the man also told us that they were looking especially for skilled firemen to start the boilers," said George.

Karl took back the paper.

"Pa, this is something you could do," said George. "He said the pay for firemen is very good."

"Let me see that," said Susanna, standing up and coming over to look at the handbill. She examined it, and then fixed her gaze on her sons.

"And why is the company offering a lot of money?" she asked, hitting the paper with the back of her hand. "Because this is a very dangerous job. The papers say that thousands of people are gathering in Homestead to stop others from entering the mill."

Folding her arms, she looked down at her husband. "This is not a good time to apply for work in Homestead. I say, wait."

Karl nodded slowly. "You are right. Let's see what happens over there first."

"You boys go now and get to your game, and don't worry about your father," Susanna said.

George and John looked at each other, uncertain.

"Go!" she said, ripping up the handbill.

They went.

Homestead. Monday, July 4th

Emlyn carried David on his shoulders as he made his way around yellow puddles in the street. Eirwen was tilted to one side as she and Thomas carried the picnic basket, while Dilys padded along beside her mother. Emlyn and Eirwen carried umbrellas to ward off the drizzle.

Because of the rain, the Congregational Church's Fourth of July picnic was being held in the church's basement social hall. Emlyn had initially decided to stay home and read, but when he learned that Gwyn was off on patrol for the day, he changed his mind. Eirwen was agitated, not by the patrolling, but by the rifle Gwyn insisted on taking with him.

Other concerns were vanquishing Emlyn's grief over his estrangement from his father. As the weeks had passed, his pronouncement about never going into a church had begun to seem rather childish. His thoughts had turned from what he would not do to what he should do.

Fueled by constant rumors of invasions by scabs or police, the workers had increased the number of men guarding the mill from 350 to over one thousand. Pickets were spread out with military precision on both sides of the river for over five miles. They had set up guard posts at several points further up and down the river.

Reporters coming into town were issued badges. Any outsider trying to enter town without identification was forcefully turned away. If any invaders tried to reach the Homestead Works, the union sentries would relay the alarm back to town by telegraph or by a rider on a fast horse.

As they came to the side door, Emlyn's stomach turned over. He wasn't sure how he would be received, especially by Griffiths. Inside the hall, women were setting out food on long tables. Eirwen introduced him to some of the congregation, who turned out to be less prying than he had feared.

Emlyn braced himself as Mr. Griffiths came over to greet him.

"Welcome. So glad you could come," he said to Emlyn, extending his hand. "I'm sorry we got off on the wrong foot at Christmas."

"I was the one overreacting," said Emlyn, shaking his hand. "Please forgive me for walking out like that."

"There's nothing to forgive. I was insensitive, probing a wound," said Griffiths. "Eirwen explained to me about your father and all. I understand how difficult it must be for you."

"Let's start over again, then," said Emlyn. "I promise not to run off this time."

"Good," said Griffiths. "Stay and enjoy the picnic, get to know some of the people." He paused. "I'm afraid the occasion won't be as happy as in years past. The Fourth has been such a big holiday in town, the only day besides Christmas that the mill was shut down."

"Unfortunately, now it's shut down indefinitely," said Emlyn, taking a loaf of bread and a jar of pickled beets from the basket and setting them on the table.

"Let's pray that the strike ends quickly—and successfully for the workers," said Griffiths.

Emlyn nodded. "I certainly hope so."

As Griffiths gathered everyone around to say grace, Emlyn took up a position by the open basement door. All except the littlest children bowed their heads as Griffiths asked God to bless the food and congregation, asking especially for a peaceful resolution to the conflict between the company and workers.

"Maybe when hell freezes over," someone behind Emlyn said. He turned. There stood Paddy outside the door in the rain.

"What's the craic, Paddy? I didn't see you come up," said Emlyn.

"I was just passing by when I noticed you here," said Paddy.

"Do you think that the company and workers will come to blows?" asked Emlyn.

"You know my views: You have the meanest, greediest sons-of-bitches facing off against a few thousand desperate workers fighting for their lives," said Paddy. "What do you think?"

Glancing into the hall, Emlyn nervously stroked his beard. "The workers have lots of pickets on watch. They are well prepared to stop any scabs or deputies."

"True," replied Paddy. "Still, a bunch of workers, no matter how dedicated, may not be enough to prevent the company from getting men inside the mill." He lowered his voice. "The more volatile among us Irish are planning to fight fire with fire, if it comes to that."

Emlyn searched Paddy's face, trying to discern if he was serious. "What do you mean?"

Paddy dropped his voice to a whisper. "Let's just say that when some fool scabs do get in there and try to get those furnaces going again, they will be in for a very unpleasant surprise."

Paddy put his finger to his lips. "You didn't hear me say that."

"Of course," Emlyn replied, trying to conceal his uneasiness.

Paddy's gaze suddenly shifted over Emlyn's shoulder. Emlyn turned to see Sarah Oesterling coming towards them with a plate of sandwiches.

"Would you like something to eat?" she asked, holding out the plate.

"No, thank you. Didn't mean to intrude," said Paddy, stepping back. Turning up the collar of his jacket, he started walking toward the river.

"Who was that?" asked Sarah.

"One of the Irish musicians who played at Lizzie's wedding," he replied, picking up a ham sandwich and taking a bite.

Sarah was talking to him, thanking him for helping her

deal with Montague and Figaro. Emlyn was having a hard time concentrating on what she was saying. He smiled and nodded, chewing on his sandwich, but his mind was elsewhere. Was Paddy serious about unionists planning sabotage?

He realized that Sarah had stopped talking, and she was looking at him quizzically.

"I'm sorry. What?" he asked.

"I said, would you like some lemonade or more food?" Sarah replied.

"Yes. Please. Lead me to it," he replied, managing a smile.

They walked over to the tables, which were spread with picnic fare—salads, pickles, breads, pies, and fruits. Emlyn helped himself to some beans and potato salad and sat down at an empty table. At the moment, he didn't feel like meeting people. His appetite had been dulled by Paddy's ominous disclosure, and he sat there, looking at the plateful of food. He'd get Eirwen to introduce him to more members of the congregation once he composed himself.

Several others came and sat at the other end of the table with their food. They exchanged introductions with Emlyn, as the doctor and William Williams came to Emlyn's end.

"I appreciate your catching Figaro yesterday," said Oesterling, taking the place opposite Emlyn.

"It really was no feat on my part," said Emlyn. "He came up to me."

"I appreciate it, just the same," replied Oesterling. "I don't know what would've happened if you hadn't been there to take him back into town."

Emlyn smiled. "It was nothing."

"You're welcome to ride Figaro any time you like," said Oesterling. "Let me know, and I'll arrange things with Junius."

Emlyn nodded, unsure of what to say.

"Hello there, Doctor, Emlyn," said Williams, sitting down

next to Oesterling. The three of them discussed the unfortunate change of weather. Exhausting that line of conversation, they sat in silence.

"I hear positive reports on your work at the structural mill," said Williams at last.

"That's good to hear," said Emlyn. "Of course, no one knows if..." His voice trailed off. An awkward silence ensued, with none of the three willing to broach the subject that hung in the air like a black cloud.

"All anyone can do is hope and pray that this gets settled soon," said Williams.

"I wonder when..." Oesterling began, but was stopped short by the faint sound of shouts and screams coming from outside.

"What's happening?" asked Williams, getting up.

"I don't know," said Oesterling, as they went to the doorway.

On McClure Street people were hurrying by, heading toward the river.

"Do you think scabs have tried to land?" asked Emlyn.

"If they have, they're grossly outnumbered," said Williams.

"What's going on?" asked Eirwen, joining them at the door. "Mrs. Griffiths said she thought she heard gunshots."

"Something's going on at the river," replied Oesterling.

Emlyn squinted into the mist and drizzle. "Perhaps I should go see what's happening."

"I wouldn't advise that," said Oesterling. "Hundreds of men with guns are out there, and some of them might be trigger-happy."

Emlyn conceded the point.

They watched from the doorway, trying to make sense of the incoherent chorus of many voices coming from the river.

A few minutes later, the voices faded away.

"Whatever happened," said Oesterling, "it seems to be over now."

Eirwen stared out the door. "I wonder what Gwyn is doing," she said pensively.

The light rain and drizzle continued the rest of the afternoon. Emlyn had planned to walk to the river after they returned to the house, but as Eirwen's nerves were frazzled, he stayed with her. They sat in the parlor reading while David and Dilys played on the floor. At eight o'clock, after a light meal of picnic leftovers, the younger children were put to bed, followed by Thomas.

It was well after dark when Gwyn returned to the house, exhausted, but in good spirits. Over supper, Gwyn told them that the incident along the riverbank had been triggered by a few townspeople in a rowboat returning from a picnic on the other side of the river. A picket had fired into the air, alerting the others. The people in the rowboat were frightened out of their wits as a thousand people rushed down to the landing. The situation was soon brought under control, and the workers resumed picketing as before. Gwyn was chuckling over the misunderstanding, but Eirwen didn't find it so amusing.

After eating, Gwyn went to bed, saying he needed to be up at dawn to go on patrol. Eirwen soon followed, leaving Emlyn to himself in the kitchen. He was glad he had decided to go to the church picnic. He got to meet half of the congregation, the half that wasn't involved in strike activities. They welcomed him, making him feel more connected to the community. He was sorry he had waited so long.

He tried reading, but was too restless to concentrate. At eleven o'clock, Emlyn slipped out the front door. Now was his chance to walk to the river.

The rain had stopped, leaving only a heavy mist in the air. Emlyn marveled at how dark and quiet the town seemed without the steel works in operation. The smokestacks, barely visible through the fog and mists, were backlit by the fires from the Edgar Thompson Works at Braddock, around the bend of the Monongahela. The silhouettes of the mill buildings loomed dark and vaguely ominous against the softly glowing sky. The night air was cool and damp. Low, heavy clouds hung overhead.

At McClure Street, a block before the whitewashed fence of Fort Frick, Emlyn turned toward the river landing. He heard the voices of the pickets before he saw them. As he walked down the grade to the river, Emlyn made out forms of men clustered together on the muddy shore. As he reached the open bank, several men on the landing turned to face him. One of them held a rifle; another, a lantern.

"Who goes there?" shouted one of them.

"A citizen of the town," said Emlyn.

"Come over here and let us see you," said the one holding a lantern.

As Emlyn got closer, one of the men drawled, "Well, if it ain't Em-Lyn, formerly of O.H.2."

"The same," said Emlyn. "How is patrol going, Virgil?"

"So far, so good," Virgil replied. "Ain't seen hide nor hair of any black sheep or police trying to come ashore—not that they won't try sooner or later." He spat in the mud, then added, "How are things up there in Fort Frick?"

"I wouldn't know," said Emlyn. "They sent the office workers away last week. We have no idea what's going on with management. Your guess is as good as mine."

"I'd guess," said the man with the rifle, "that right now Frick is scheming to bring in sheriff's deputies or Pinkertons to man the Fort. We aim to stop them." He shot the bolt on the rifle to emphasize his point. "The company broke the contract, and we're going to make damn sure they comply with the law. We ain't going to be whipped into submission by any hirelings sent by Frick."

Emlyn looked out at the swiftly flowing river, where the outline of the strikers' steam launch was visible through the fog.

"It looks like you have the river well covered," he said.

"We do, and damn any mercenary who tries to come ashore," said the man with the gun. He lowered the rifle, and the group turned their attention back to the river.

"Good night," Emlyn said, starting back toward town.

"Hey, Em-Lyn," said Virgil. "I'd advise against any further nocturnal ramblings around these parts. In this soup, someone might take a pot shot at you, thinking you're a scab or Pinkerton."

"I'll be careful," Emlyn said. He walked slowly up the ramp and onto McClure Street. As he passed by a tenement building, he thought he heard someone singing. He stopped and listened. A man's low baritone voice came from the yard of the building.

I believe in being ready,
I believe in being ready
I believe in being ready,
when this world comes to an end

Oh sinners do get ready,
oh sinners do get ready

Oh sinners do get ready,
for the time is drawing near

Oh there'll be signs and wonders,
oh there'll be signs and wonders
Oh there'll be signs and wonders,
when this world comes to an end

Emlyn crept closer to get a better view into the yard. In the shelter of a porch overhang, a black man was sitting on the stoop, singing, while another accompanied him on guitar.

Oh the sun she will be darkened,
oh the sun she will be darkened
Oh the sun she will be darkened,
when this world is at its end

Oh the moon it will be bleeding,
oh the moon it will be bleeding
Oh the moon it will be bleeding,
when this world comes to its end

Oh the stars they will be falling,
oh the stars they will be falling
Oh the stars they will be falling,
when this world comes to its end

Emlyn moved closer, stopping beside a tree on the edge of the yard.

Brothers, sisters please get ready,
brothers, sisters do get ready,

Mothers, fathers do get ready,
for the time is a drawing near

Oh there'll be signs and wonders,
oh there'll be signs and wonders
Oh there'll be signs and wonders,
when this world comes to an end

"A-men, Brother," said the guitarist to the singer as they finished, raising his right hand. The other man slapped it, and they both stood up and went inside.

As Emlyn walked the remaining blocks to the house, emotion roiled in him. He had never heard a song, or hymn, or whatever it was, like that before.

Back in his room, he started to get into bed, but stopped. Instead, he lowered himself to his knees beside the bed, as he had done every night until the quarrel with his father.

Head lowered, hands folded, he knelt there, but could not formulate his thoughts into prayer. Instead, the song kept running through his mind, over and over.

Oh there'll be signs and wonders,
when this world comes to an end

Tuesday, July 5th

Oesterling sat at the table, his toast and poached egg growing cold as he pored over the Pittsburgh paper for any news about the situation in Homestead. It seemed that he already knew everything the reporters knew. He had decided it wasn't worthwhile holding office hours today, and he had posted a notice to call in case of emergency.

The strike was dramatically affecting the entire town.

Those who weren't on alert were keeping out of the way of the pickets. Everyone from striker to company management was on tenterhooks, waiting for something to happen.

The telephone rang twice, the signal for their number on the party line. Oesterling pushed away from the table and went into the hallway to answer it. Expecting it to be a call from a patient, he was surprised to hear Carrie's voice on the other end.

"Papa?"

His heart contracted. "Yes? Is anything wrong? What's going on?"

"Papa, you need to leave Homestead right away. You can come over here for a few days."

"For heaven's sake, why?"

"Oliver just left for the office. He says that Philander Knox, the head corporate attorney, gave Sheriff McCleary the go-ahead to come to Homestead and post orders for the strikers to cease their occupation of company property."

"That's ridiculous," said Oesterling. "The workers are not even on company property."

"Yes, but they're stopping others from entering it."

"I don't understand why this situation calls for us to leave town."

"Don't you see?" Carrie said. "There's going to be a confrontation soon. Oliver says it might get nasty."

"Posting handbills can get nasty?" Oesterling asked. "I doubt it."

There was a pause.

"Please, Papa, you must leave." Carrie's voice broke. "The Sheriff isn't the only one who will be coming."

"What? Even if he brings a few deputies, it doesn't . . ."

"I don't mean deputies."

Oesterling was trying to figure out what Carrie meant by

this, when a loud click came through the receiver, signaling that another on his party line had picked up.

"I must go," said Carrie. "Think about what I've said." She hung up.

Oesterling placed the receiver back on the hook, and walked out to the front porch. What did she mean, not deputies? Who was coming? His gaze moved over the mill and the town, downriver toward Pittsburgh.

Abruptly, it came to him: Pinkertons. He shuddered. Now it was more necessary than ever that he stay in town.

He looked down at Cerberus. The dog cocked his head at Oesterling and wagged his tail.

OUTSIDE YOUNGSTOWN, OHIO.

Dan Gorham was bored and stiff from sitting. Ted Martin, the college student next to him, had his head buried in a book. The older men across from them were slumped in their seats sleeping. He and the other recruits had been on the train for hours, having boarded in Chicago early that morning. The train had stopped several times to pick up more men. Now there were over a hundred of them, clicking along the tracks of the Fort Wayne Railroad. Some were young, like Ted and him. Others were professional guards, and others looked to him like toughs off the streets of Chicago.

Although the windows were open, the car was hot and thick with tobacco smoke mingled with coal smoke from the locomotive. Dan stood up, stretched, and made his way down the aisle of the swaying railroad car. Stepping over the legs of other men in the car, he made his way to the end and stood at the window, hoping to figure out where they were.

The flat farmlands of Ohio were now behind them, and the train was traveling along a river winding through a valley of broad, tree-covered hills. He deduced the train was near the border of Pennsylvania—not that he cared. An Illinois farm boy looking for work in the city, Dan had answered an advertisement in the Chicago paper to serve as a Pinkerton guard. The agency hadn't said what they would be guarding, only that it paid $15 a week and offered daily rations. Dan decided it would be a good way to make some easy money.

A few days ago he had signed up, been fitted out in a uniform, and undergone preliminary training. He was an experienced hunter and a good shot. The Pinkerton Agency seemed glad to have him, but even now, he knew he could never be a regular in the Pinkerton guards. The aspect that annoyed him was the officers' swaggering around, expecting them to behave as career Army men. He had never served in the military, and took a mild dislike to Captain F.H. Heinde, the expedition leader. Oh well, he'd be done with the job and back to Chicago in no time, his wallet full.

Dan bit off a plug of tobacco and pushed it into his cheek. He pulled out his watch: half past seven o'clock. How many more hours until they reached their destination?

Homestead

In the gathering dusk, Emlyn made his way to the Amity Street station, where Gwyn had said he would be watching for strangers entering Homestead by train. When Gwyn hadn't returned to the house for dinner, Eirwen had insisted Emlyn take some food to him in his lunch pail.

Emlyn came up on the platform, but in the dim light of the electric bulbs, could not make out Gwyn in the group of pickets there. He was about to go back down the steps, when he saw Joe Galik. As Emlyn approached, Joe saw him and grinned broadly.

"Servus!" said Joe, extending his hand.

"Wie geht's?" asked Emlyn, shaking it.

"Very, very good," replied Joe. "This morning we stop sheriff and his police guys from coming into town."

"Yeah," said a fat man in a soiled plaid shirt. "We told Sheriff McCleary and his deputies to mccleary out." He laughed, looking around to see if anyone caught the joke.

"We're doing just fine protecting the mill property without their help," said another.

When Emlyn asked about Gwyn, the fat man told him that Gwyn had gone over to the Bost Building to help fix some problem with the telegraph.

Saying goodbye to Joe, Emlyn walked along the Avenue toward the Bost Building. The shops were all closed, but men were crowded in and around the saloons, which had become gathering places for strikers, now that they no longer saw each other on the job.

By the time Emlyn reached the Bost Building, night had fallen. The building, however, was a hive of activity. Situated a block away from the General Office Building and next to the mill fence, the brick three-story Bost Building was brand new, built to serve as a grocery store with hotel rooms on the upper floors. It was the perfect location for strike headquarters, with good views of the mill, the company offices, the town, and the river from its flat roof.

From a half block away, Emlyn could see figures on the roof, some talking, some pointing, a few looking through binoculars. Many were undoubtedly reporters covering the strike. Emlyn came up to the front door, but was blocked from entering by pickets demanding AA or press credentials. He asked to see Gwyn, and was told to wait. He sat on a bench next to the building, beside two reporters in rumpled suits smoking cigars.

In about ten minutes, Gwyn pushed through the crowd by the door and came over to the bench. As on the evening before, Gwyn was in a very good mood, despite the lines of fatigue drawn across his face.

"Come, I want you meet some good men," said Gwyn, picking up the lunchbox. Gwyn led Emlyn through the front doors and to a back room on the first floor. The large table in the center of the room was covered with maps, newspapers, telegrams, coffee mugs, and empty platters. Two men were seated at one end, talking.

"Boys," said Gwyn, coming up to the men. "I'd like you to meet my brother-in-law, Emlyn Phillips. He's brought some supper." Gwyn opened the lunch pail and set the sandwich, black bread, apple, and pickled eggs on a plate.

"Thanks very much," said a thin, handsome young man whose black hair and moustache stood out in relief against his pale face. He stood up and offered Emlyn his hand.

"Hugh O'Donnell," he said.

"Pleased to meet you," said Emlyn.

"Hughie is head of the advisory committee," said Gwyn, "And this is John McLuckie, Homestead Burgess," he added, indicating the other man. McLuckie was shorter and stockier; his wire-rimmed glasses and sober expression made him look serious and scholarly.

"Much obliged," said McLuckie, saluting as he picked up the apple. "We've had a busy day."

"Glad to make your acquaintance," said Emlyn.

"Thanks to Gwyn and a few others," said O'Donnell, "we've gotten the telegraph system in fine working order."

"Anything for the cause," said Gwyn.

"Why don't you go home and get some rest?" said O'Donnell. "We'll probably need your talents for something again tomorrow."

"I think I'll be going, too, after I talk to the reporter from New York," said McLuckie, rising from his chair.

Gwyn and Emlyn said goodbye and made their way out the door and through the dwindling crowd in front of the building. As they walked down the Avenue, Emlyn thought he recognized Norton Montague on the opposite side of the street, watching the Bost Building. Montague would probably love to come over and fill the reporters full of sand about the company's rights and responsibilities. Of course, he wouldn't dare.

On the way back to the house, Gwyn talked about the preparations the advisory committee had made—setting up communications not only between each other, but also with the press corps and the outside world. Gwyn emphasized that they thought it essential to keep the public informed about what the strikers were doing and why they were doing it.

As they turned down McClure Street, Gwyn pulled a flask out of his back pocket, and held it out to Emlyn.

"Want a taste?" he asked.

"No, thanks," said Emlyn.

"Suit yourself," replied Gwyn. "More for me."

"Gwyn, do you really think hitting the bottle right now is a good idea?" Emlyn asked.

Gwyn scowled. "You sound like Eirwen," he replied. "I need a drop to sooth my nerves," he said. "Don't worry so much." He took a pull and put the flask back in his pocket.

Eirwen looked relieved when they came though the kitchen door around eleven o'clock. When she learned Gwyn had given away his supper, she made him another. As he ate, Gwyn told them about his work at the Bost Building and about all the activity going on there and around town. Then he washed up and went to bed, saying that he would be rising early again for picket duty.

After he had gone upstairs, Eirwen said in a low voice, "If and when anything happens, I'd like you to go with Gwyn."

"What kind of 'anything' are you talking about?" asked Emlyn, dubious.

"Strike breakers or police arriving in town, whatever. The sheriff came here this morning, and got the boot. The company isn't going to give up."

"What do you think I could do, shadowing Gwyn?" Emlyn asked.

"I don't know, I just feel so helpless having to stay here. Please, promise me you'll go with him if some kind of crisis develops."

Emlyn reluctantly agreed, and went upstairs to bed. He got on his knees and prayed, as he had the previous day, that the strike wouldn't turn violent, but an uneasy feeling remained.

On the Monongahela River at Glenwood.
July 6th, 2:30 a.m.

Dan Gorham had been happy when the train finally stopped and he and the other Pinkertons got off at Bellevue on the Ohio River a few miles from Pittsburgh. There they were joined by other Pinkerton guards who had come in on trains from New York and Cincinnati.

Dan had hoped they would be allowed to sleep. Instead of resting, however, the entire group of over three hundred guards was immediately transferred onto two covered barges with the curious names *Monongahela* and *Iron Mountain*. At the wharf he had talked to a patrolman who said that the barges were headed for Beaver Dam, down the Ohio River.

But they were going upstream, not down—as Ted the college student pointed out as soon as two tugs pulled the barges away from the wharf. According to Ted, they had passed Allegheny City and Pittsburgh at the confluence of the Allegheny and Monongahela Rivers, and were now going up the latter. At a lock on the river, something had happened to one of the tugs, leaving the *Little Bill* to haul both barges.

Ted had insisted they sit by a porthole, so he could look out at the bank on the right side of the barge. As they passed under a railroad bridge, Ted grew jumpy.

"Do you hear that?" whispered Ted, pulling on Dan's sleeve.

"What?"

"Listen. Do you hear them?"

Dan leaned closer to the window. The thick fog blanketing the river prohibited him from seeing anything, but the sound was unmistakable: voices of men, women, even children, coming from the bank.

Other men on the *Iron Mountain* apparently heard them, too, and a nervous murmur rippled through the barge's cavernous interior. The officers began moving through the barge, trying to calm the new recruits.

Ted suddenly sat bolt upright. "Holy Christ!" he exclaimed.

"What? What's the matter?" asked Dan.

"We're going to Homestead!" said Ted, his eyes wide with fright.

"Homestead? So what? Never heard of it."

"Don't you read the papers?" hissed Ted. "There's a big steel works in Homestead owned by the Carnegie Company, and the workers are out on strike. Some of the strikers must have seen us coming and sounded the alarm."

Fear crept over Dan. "These people on the riverbank—'you think they're strikers?"

"Who else would it be?" said Ted. "From the sound of it,

hundreds of them are preparing a welcoming committee for us at the mill."

"Shit," said Dan, looking out at the fog.

Simultaneously, the crack of a rifle shot rang out from the riverbank, followed by another.

"Good Lord, they're shooting at us!" Dan exclaimed, prompting one of the officers to come over and tell him to keep his voice down.

"Keep calm. The situation is under control," said the officer. "We'll soon be landing at a secure location, where we can disembark safely."

After the officer moved on, Ted whispered that the shots were probably a warning to strikers further up the river.

"Well, that's just as bad, if not worse," said Dan, glancing around. Many men were now at the portholes, watching and listening.

"Dan, you know what the men further up the line are saying?" a gray-haired veteran named Ben asked rhetorically.

"What?"

"They're saying that the chief muckety-muck for the steel works, a guy named Potter, is aboard the tug."

"Is that so?" replied Dan. "I wonder what he thinks of this welcoming committee."

Homestead

In the distance, the sound of hoof beats thudding on hard-packed dirt entered Emlyn's dream. A horseman was galloping toward him, brandishing a saber. As he came near, Emlyn saw that the rider was Norton Montague, his eyes flashing, hell-bent on revenge. Savagely whipping his mount, he bore down on Emlyn. The hoof beats got louder; people started yelling at Emlyn in warning.

Emlyn opened his eyes and turned over in bed. Had he really heard people yelling? He sat up. Yes, a man in the street was bellowing, "The river! The river! They're coming in barges!" The chorus of shouts was growing as more people came outside.

Emlyn grabbed the clothes he had taken off three hours earlier and hastily pulled them on. Tucking in his shirt, he lurched downstairs after Gwyn.

"This is it!" Gwyn said as he moved toward the kitchen. "They're bringing in deputies."

"I want to go with you," said Emlyn, stumbling into a chair in the darkness.

"Are you sure? This could get ugly."

"I'm sure," replied Emlyn, not sure at all.

"Alright, but first, I need to get the rifle," Gwyn said as he threw open the back door.

Eirwen appeared in the kitchen doorway. "Gwyn . . . Emlyn," she said. "Be careful."

"We will," Gwyn said over his shoulder as he dashed out the back door, followed by Emlyn.

Seconds later, he and Gwyn were running down Third Avenue with dozens of others. Men, women, and children in various stages of undress rushed through the streets of Homestead, all heading toward the river. Some carried rifles, shotguns, or handguns, while others held clubs, sticks, crowbars—whatever they could find that could be used as a weapon.

By the time Emlyn and Gwyn reached the shore by the ferry landing, they were part of a large crowd pouring onto the riverbank. In the early morning fog and darkness, Emlyn could make out an immense throng of people stretching from the mill fence downstream toward West Homestead. Many more were arriving, pushing into the crowd at the river.

Gwyn and Emlyn worked their way through the motley

assemblage toward Jim Duncan, who was standing next to the water with several AA members, including Harry Smith. Seeing Gwyn, Duncan signaled them to step into the group, and they all squeezed together to make room for them.

"What d'ye know?" asked Duncan, who was wearing a nightshirt over a pair of denim trousers.

"Not much," said Gwyn. "How about you?"

"Rumors are flying," said Smith, "but most are saying that the sheriff is returning with more deputies, this time by river."

"That's what I thought," said Gwyn. "Has anyone seen them?"

"As a matter of fact, yes," said a thin young man with a moustache. "I was at the Bost Building when a telegraph came in from a scout at the Smithfield Street Bridge saying that barges loaded with men were on their way upriver."

Emlyn was certain the man spoke with a Welsh accent.

"When was that?" asked Gwyn.

"About midnight," said the man.

"By the way," interjected Duncan. "This here is John Morris, one of your compatriots. He works in the blooming mill, also a member of the Amalgamated."

Emlyn and Gwyn shook his hand as they introduced themselves.

"Has anyone seen anything since the initial report?" asked Gwyn.

"About a half hour ago," said Morris, "a scout at Glenwood reported that although he couldn't see through the river fog, he definitely heard the sound of a steamer moving upstream. Someone at the Light Works blew the steam whistle to alert those in the vicinity. The alarm spread, and people started coming to the river."

Emlyn pulled out his watch, which he had thankfully forgotten to remove from his pants when he went to bed: 3:17.

"That's when a horseman was dispatched to ride through town and sound the alarm," said Morris. "And here we are."

"I suppose no one knows for sure who they are and when they will get here," said Gwyn, "but they're obviously up to no good."

"Well, it's for damn sure we're gonna be ready for them when they do get here," said Duncan, spitting toward the river for emphasis.

"Let them just try," said Smith.

The minutes stretched into an hour, and they did not come. The crowd at the river grew increasingly restless. Emlyn began to wonder if it was a false alarm.

Finally, at quarter past four, rifle shots rang out. A steam whistle sounded out on the river, startling everyone on the bank. Through shreds of fog, Emlyn caught sight of the strikers' steam launch. A few minutes after that, a roar erupted from the crowd: two barges, pulled by a tug, were moving slowly but steadily past them. People started shooting at the tug; a window of the pilothouse shattered.

On the shore, Hugh O'Donnell stalked back and forth, urging the crowd to stay calm. Few heeded his words.

"God damn them," Duncan shouted. "They're heading for the mill landing!"

"Stop them! Stop those rats!" someone yelled, as the crowd surged en masse toward the mill. By the time Gwyn and Emlyn reached the Fort Frick fence, strikers had already torn down a section of it, and people were scrambling through, running toward the high bank overlooking the mill landing. On the bank, Gwyn, Morris, Smith, Duncan, and Emlyn were shoved along by new arrivals until they held their ground at a vantage point upriver of the landing.

The crack of rifle shots came at random intervals. A

rangy, white-haired woman leading a pack of townswomen appeared. Emlyn stared in amazement at young women carrying babies standing beside her. The older woman waved a billy club in the air. "The dirty black sheep," she bellowed. "Let me at them!" The crowd roared their approval. People on the bank cursed and hurled threats at the men arriving in the barges. More shots were fired.

In the half-light, Emlyn made out the shapes of two enormous covered barges being towed into position at the landing by a tugboat. Hugh O'Donnell was moving along the landing, speaking to the crowd, urging restraint. His words, however, seemed to have little effect on the incensed mob. More people, many carrying guns, were spreading out along the bank and taking up positions on the Pemikey railroad bridge overlooking the landing. It was apparent the situation was far beyond anyone's control.

"Duw, there must be thousands of people on the bank," said Gwyn. "Whoever they are, how could they dare come ashore?"

"We'll soon see," said Smith.

The first light of dawn was glinting on the eastern horizon as the tug with *Little Bill* painted on its bow grounded the barge *Iron Mountain* on the bank. The men who had led the charge into the mill rushed up. As a man in a slouch hat came onto the deck, someone threw a stone at the barge. From the landing people were yelling, warning those on the barges not to land. As minutes ticked away, the threats escalated.

Tensions were reaching a fever pitch as Hugh O'Donnell made his way to the front of the crowd. He was shouting something, but Emlyn couldn't hear what he was saying. To Emlyn's surprise, the crowd quieted.

O'Donnell came to the water and called out to the men on the barges. "On behalf of five thousand men, I beg you to leave here at once. I don't know who you are or where you came from, but I do know that you have no business here." He went on, entreating them not to risk violence by trying to come ashore. "Don't attempt to enter these works by force."

At that, a man in a blue military coat with brass buttons stepped onto the deck of the *Mountain Iron*. "We were sent to take possession of this property and to guard it for this company," he said.

"Damned if it ain't Pinkertons," said Duncan. "Look at them blue uniforms."

"Ssh!" said Smith.

"If you don't withdraw," continued the man on the barge, "we will mow every one of you down and enter in spite of you."

"They will, will they? I don't think so," growled Duncan.

"Hush, dammit," said Smith.

O'Donnell was talking. "What you do here is at the risk of many lives. Before you enter those mills, you will trample over the dead bodies of three thousand honest workmen." O'Donnell turned away.

For a moment, the crowd on the bank watched in silence.

A group of men on the *Iron Mountain* brought out a gang-plank and pushed it onto the landing. The man who had spoken came to the top of the plank. Simultaneously, the leader of the militant strikers took a stand at the other end of the plank, the others behind him.

"Who's the striker at the bottom of the plank?" whispered Gwyn.

"It looks like Billy Foy, the feller from the Salvation Army," said Smith. "And behind him, Martin Murray, the heater—He's Welsh," he added as an aside to Emlyn. "And next to him is Sotak, leader of them Slovaks."

Emlyn watched in disbelief at the scene unfolding below. Men on the bank shouted warnings to the men in the barges. The Pinkertons hesitated. The officer at the front shouted out, "There are three hundred men behind me, and you can't stop us." Foy yelled something in reply.

Emlyn strained forward to see what was going on, but fog blurred the details. It looked like the officer came forward and tried to hit Foy with something.

In rapid succession, two gunshots rang out. The officer and Foy went down. Hugh O'Donnell threw up his hands and shouted something at the strikers.

From the barge someone shouted, "Fire!' and a volley of gunfire roared from the portholes. As if in slow motion, Emlyn saw several men on the riverbank crumple to the ground.

Women started screaming. The people around Emlyn began jostling each other, shifting away from the exposed position on the bank. From the riverbank came more shots.

"Take cover!" Duncan yelled. Return fire from the strikers thudded into the sides of the barges as the Pinkertons continued firing.

His heart in his throat, Emlyn sprinted toward the mill building behind them. He caught sight of a dinky engine and ran behind it. Gwyn, running behind him, tripped and went sprawling onto the tracks about thirty feet away. His rifle flew out of his hands and clattered onto the bricks.

Emlyn stood at the front of the engine, trying to decide if he should run out to help Gwyn. A bullet pinged sharply against metal, and a chip flew out of a pile of bricks beside the locomotive.

"Ricochets!" yelled Gwyn, lowering his head. "Stay where you are."

The firing continued unabated, punctuated by screams and shouts.

"Are you hurt?" yelled Emlyn over the racket.

"I don't think so. I'm going to make a run for it."

"Stay there!" Emlyn shouted. "It's not safe."

Another bullet slammed into the locomotive steam chamber with a reverberating *thonk*. Gwyn raised his head and glanced at Emlyn, measuring the distance. Swiftly, Gwyn pushed himself into a crouching position and dashed towards Emlyn. Ten feet short of his goal, Gwyn tucked his head down and rolled the rest of the way, coming to a rest against the wheels of the engine.

"Bloody hell," said Gwyn, taking in great gulps of air. "I thought I was going to get hit for sure."

"Are you OK?" asked Emlyn, bending over Gwyn. Gwyn nodded yes.

"I never saw you run so fast," said Emlyn. "Did you see what happened down there?"

"No," said Gwyn. "All I could make out was that Foy was on the plank, and the officer came toward him." He paused, gasping for breath. "Then the Pinkertons started firing. I know they hit some of the men near the barge."

Emlyn glanced out at the mill yard. Men, women, and children were cowering behind anything they could find on the exposed riverbank—bricks, piles of debris, machinery. Men with rifles were firing at the barges.

"Hell's bells," said Gwyn, pushing himself into a sitting position. "How long is this going to go on?"

"Not long, I hope," answered Emlyn.

They hunkered down behind the engine as cracks of rifle shots continuously rang out. A bullet kicked up a spray of dust in the front of the engine. The odor of gunpowder grew stronger.

"Say," said Gwyn, "what happened to Jim Duncan and the others?"

"I don't know," Emlyn replied. "I didn't look back."

Oesterling stood at his bedroom window in his dressing gown, visually scrutinizing the mill site. In the dim light of dawn, he could see only indistinct shapes of buildings.

Sarah came into the room and stood at the window beside him, a wrap pulled around her.

"What's that noise?" she said anxiously. "What's happening over there?"

Oesterling hesitated. He knew immediately what it was the moment he had been awakened by the sound five minutes earlier: gunfire. It chilled him, bringing back images of slaughter and mayhem from the war.

"I'm afraid the strikers and Pinkertons are shooting at one another over by the river," he said.

"Gunshots?" she said, pushing aside the curtain. "Are you sure?"

He nodded.

"How do you know it's Pinkertons?"

Osterling grimaced. "Because Carrie phoned yesterday to warn they would be coming."

"How? How did she know?"

"Oliver told her," Oesterling said. "She wanted us to leave town, to come over and stay with her."

"Why didn't you say something?" Sarah demanded.

"What good would that do? How could I be sure?"

The volume of shots increased, the sound bouncing off the hill on the other side of the river.

"Get away from the window," Oesterling said, pulling her aside. "A stray shot could possibly make it this far."

Sarah backed away from the window, and crouching, ran to the doorway.

"I'm going to get dressed and go to the office," Oesterling said, rummaging through the wardrobe. "There will probably be casualties."

"Papa, I'm scared," Sarah said. "It's not safe to go out on the street if it's not safe to stand at the window. Please, don't go."

"I'll wait till the firing stops," he said, pulling out a clean shirt. "I can't just sit around and wonder if anyone needs help."

He glanced at the alarm clock. Almost five.

"I'm going with you," Sarah said.

"Now, Sarah," he began, but she interrupted him.

"Don't argue. You'll need help. Besides, Mrs. Cramer might not be able to get there."

Before he could answer, she closed the door behind her.

Dan Gorham's Winchester was so hot he couldn't touch the barrel. For the last ten minutes or so, he had been firing at figures on the high bank alongside the barge. Through the porthole, he had seen Captain Heinde and two others go down in the initial round of shots.

When the order came to fire, he had been stupefied, gaping like a fool as bullets tore into the side of the *Iron Mountain*. But after he saw a man near him get clipped in the shoulder, he picked up his rifle and aimed it out the window. At first, he fired wildly, but after a minute or two, anger towards the strikers on the riverbank surged in him. Why had those crazy strikers started shooting at him and the other guards?

He carefully took aim at a man who was scrambling up the bank and squeezed the trigger. The man dropped to his knees and rolled against a large rock. As he watched the man struggling to crawl behind the rock, his anger subsided. It was the first time he'd shot a human being. He felt slightly ill. He ducked down, reloaded, and took more shots, this time aiming at nothing in particular.

Beside him, Ted was curled up, his arms held across his face muttering, "O God, O God," over and over. When the officers had handed out the Winchesters, there hadn't been enough to go around. Instead, Ted received a club, not of much use in a gun battle.

When the firing had stopped, the tug captain had come aboard the barge and taken the dozen injured guards, including Heinde, with a leg wound, onto the *Little Bill*.

"Looks like that Carnegie boss Potter is aboard the tug," said Dan, as the tug pulled away.

"He's probably decided that discretion is the better part of valor," said Ted. "Smart man."

As the tug reached midstream, Ted dug an elbow into Dan's ribs. "Look, it's completely riddled with bullet holes," he said.

They stared at the receding tugboat.

"Now, how the hell are we going to get off of this barge?" asked Ted.

The firing slowed, then stopped.

"Where the devil did Jim go?" Gwyn asked, hesitantly peeking around the locomotive. He stepped from cover and fetched his rifle from where it had landed. Emlyn moved next to Gwyn and looked around.

Around the riverbank and in the mill yard, a scene of complete pandemonium was enfolding. Strikers and townspeople, some in their nightclothes, were emerging from cover. People were shouting, crying, asking for help, calling out names of loved ones. A young woman was kneeling over a prone figure on the ground, sobbing hysterically. A little boy was running around screaming, gulping down sobs, terrified.

Emlyn watched him. "That boy," he said, pointing. "He needs help."

Emlyn started toward the child, but as he did, a woman ran over and scooped the boy up.

"Come on," said Gwyn. "We've got to find the others."

Emlyn scanned the mill yard, looking for any signs of Duncan and his companions. Puffs of gunsmoke drifted lazily around the yard. Townswomen were shouting, urging the workers to kill the Pinkertons.

"I'm going to take up a position where I can get in some good shots at those bastards," a man in an army-style cap near them said to another. He held a rifle in one hand and pointed up at the roof of the mill building with the other.

"Don't forget this," said the other, handing him a box of ammunition.

"Thanks," said the sharpshooter, sliding the box into a bulging pack at his waist. He turned and ran toward the building.

In the mill yard, Hugh O'Donnell came up to the women inciting the men to revenge, and pointed agitatedly toward the fence. "You must leave the yard—now!" he shouted. The women stood their ground.

"There they are, Jim and the boys," said Gwyn, pointing toward the mill pump house a little further upriver from where they had been standing.

As they made their way along the crest, Emlyn saw people scrambling down the bank, hastening to help those who lay there, felled by the first shots. The side of the *Iron Mountain*, now visible as the fog lifted, was pocked with bullet holes. Men in uniforms were carrying their fallen comrades back into the barge.

Near the pump house and all along the bank, men were rushing about, positioning pieces of pig iron and steel to use as shields.

As Emlyn and Gwyn approached, Duncan caught sight of them.

"Are you OK?" he shouted.

"Yes—You?" Gwyn replied.

"We're all fine," said Duncan. "Hurry! To the roof of the pump house! Help us put together ramparts before the damn Pinkertons start shooting at us again."

Gwyn broke into a run. As Emlyn raced along behind Gwyn, he glanced back. A figure holding a rifle appeared high on the mill roof, silhouetted against the brightening sky.

6 A.M.

Rays of sunlight flooded the valley as the doctor and Sarah hastened down McClure Street toward the Avenue. Cerberus trotted alongside Oesterling, who was carrying his medical bag. Sarah, wearing an old cotton dress and apron, carried a box of extra medical supplies.

As they walked downhill, throngs of people brushed past in the opposite direction, streaming up the hillside to get a better vantage point. In the business district, people were rushing about in all directions. A couple of horsemen galloped by in the direction of the Bost Building.

They had no sooner reached the Avenue, than the crack of rifle shots started up again by the river. Breaking into a jog, the doctor and Sarah moved along close to the fronts of the buildings toward the entrance of the office. Oesterling fumbled for the key in his pocket, found it, and inserting it into the lock, pushed the door open. Cerberus raced up the stairs ahead of them.

While Sarah opened the windows at the front of the office, Oesterling unpacked medical supplies. Cerberus paced around nervously, sniffed at the chairs, and went over to Sarah by the window.

"He doesn't know what to make of this," said Sarah, scratching behind the dog's ears.

"Who does?" said the doctor. "I certainly can't make sense of it."

Footsteps echoed in the stairwell, and a moment later, Mrs. Cramer came through the door carrying a basket. Her usually neat uniform and pinafore were wrinkled. Her cap was missing, her hair twisted into an untidy knot.

"Good morning, Doctor. I thought you'd be here. I came as fast I could," she said. "I see you've brought an assistant." She smiled at Sarah.

Setting down the basket, Mrs. Cramer joined Sarah at the window. Chaos reigned in the street, with people of all ages racing about. Cracks of gunfire reverberated off the facades of the buildings across the street.

"It sounds like the fighting is picking up again," said Sarah.

"Did you see all the people lined up on top of the hill?" asked Mrs. Cramer. "Our neighbor said there were several thousand."

"Why on earth would people want to watch other people try to kill each other?" asked Sarah, shaking her head.

"The Romans did that," said Mrs. Cramer, taking a large handkerchief out of her pocket and tying it over her hair.

"I can think of a more recent example," said Oesterling. "Thirty years ago, hundreds of people followed the Union

Army out of Washington to watch the first Battle of Bull Run. Spectators brought along picnics to eat while they watched."

"How stupid. What happened?" asked Sarah.

"The Union Army lost—nearly five thousand casualties on both sides—and the spectators fled in a panic," replied Oesterling.

"That's appalling," said Sarah.

"It just goes to show that people don't change," said Mrs. Cramer, leaving the window and picking up the basket. "I'm going to boil some water. Would you like some tea and a raisin bun? We may not have the opportunity later."

8 A.M.

Emlyn didn't want anything to do with this battle, but here he was, crouched on the back slope of the pump house roof, watching the barges below. Because Emlyn didn't have a weapon, the other men had wanted him to leave. Gwyn had tried to persuade him to go home, but Emlyn wouldn't budge. Maybe he would soon be able to talk Gwyn and others into leaving with him.

"Go ahead, be a pig-head," Duncan told Emlyn. "Just stay out of the way." He held out a pair of field glasses. "Here. If you're not going to stop the Pinkertons, you can at least keep an eye on them for us."

O'Donnell and some other men had finally persuaded the women in the open mill yard to leave. Now men only were positioned on the bank overlooking the river, waiting and watching. A supply of ammunition had been brought to the men on the ramparts from a hardware store on the Avenue. They were stocked up, ready to fight.

With Gwyn beside him, Emlyn trained the glasses on the *Iron Mountain*. He had been watching for over an hour, but there had been no movement. He was beginning to hope that the violence had ended. Suddenly, at the bow of the *Iron Mountain*, armed men emerged.

"Gwyn," Emlyn said, his heart sinking. "I think they're coming off the barge."

"They're disembarking!" Smith exclaimed.

Through the glasses, Emlyn saw Pinkertons start down the gangplank. A second later, someone on the high bank fired a round at the *Iron Mountain*. Return rifle fire erupted from the barge.

"Get them!" screamed Duncan. "Get those scoundrels!"

The strikers pointed their rifles through openings in the breastworks. Gunfire from the barges was answered by volleys from the strikers. Taking fire all around them, the Pinkertons on the gangplank scrambled to get back into the barge. The tattoo of gunshots rippled back and forth across the bank, accompanied by the metallic thudding of bullets striking the ramparts.

Emlyn ducked down behind the rampart, where he watched the other men shooting through it. Bullets whizzed overhead. The air was thick with smoke and the acrid smell of gunpowder.

"I think I got one!" yelled Morris. "I'm going to sneak a look." Emlyn watched him ease up to peek through an opening.

No sooner had he gotten into place than Morris grunted and collapsed. Horror-struck, Emlyn watched as Morris rolled down the slope of the roof and out of view.

"My God!" shouted Gwyn, scrambling to where Morris had gone over.

Emlyn crawled to the edge and looked over. In a ditch at the bottom of the embankment about sixty feet below lay the inert form of John Morris.

Behind the surgery screen, Oesterling was finishing bandaging up a woman who had slashed her leg on a piece of metal as she fled from the mill yard.

The entry door downstairs slammed and someone came running up the stairs.

"Miss Oesterling, is the doc here?" a young voice panted.

"He's working on a patient, Henry," said Sarah. "What's the matter?"

"It's my dad," said the boy breathlessly. "They brought him to the house. He's been shot in the hip."

"The doctor will be out in a moment," said Sarah.

Oesterling came from behind the screen, wiping his hands.

"Where is he?" Oesterling asked the boy.

The boy gave an address on Fourth Avenue.

"Just a second, son," Oesterling said to the boy, "I need to fetch something." Oesterling went over and unlocked a bottom drawer of the supply cabinet.

"Fourth Avenue?" said Sarah, coming beside him. "That's so close to the mill. Please be careful."

"Don't worry," said Oesterling, opening the drawer and pulling out something wrapped in a flannel cloth.

"What are you doing, Papa?" she asked. "What is that?"

Oesterling unfolded the cloth.

"It's a Colt Model 1860 Army Revolver," said Oesterling, turning the gun over. "I got it when I served with the cavalry during the war." He took bullets out of a box and slid them into the chamber.

"Is it loaded?" asked Mrs. Cramer.

"It is now," replied Oesterling, taking a holster strap out of the drawer. "It's been sitting in this drawer for years. I don't know why I held onto it."

"But Papa . . ." said Sarah.

"Look outside," said Oesterling, pushing down his shirt-sleeves. "There's a war on."

"Please, Doc, hurry," wailed the boy from the doorway.

"I need to go," said Oesterling, buckling on the holster strap and sliding the revolver in it. "I'll be back as soon as I can."

"Stay," he commanded Cerberus, following the boy into the stairwell.

9 A.M.

"Those strikers sure mean business," said Dan Gorham, gazing out a gaping hole on the river side of the *Iron Mountain*.

"You can say that again," said Ted, as a bullet struck the barge. "There must be thousands of them out there. Where did they all come from?"

They had been shifted to that side after the second vain attempt to disembark. During the attempt, a middle-aged guard had been shot in the upper arm, and he now lay on the floor of the barge, moaning. The officers had positioned the best Pinkerton sharpshooters at the expanded holes on the landing side of barge. They kept up a steady volley of shots, which were returned in kind.

Through one of the openings opposite, Dan could see sections of steel beams and iron that the strikers were hiding behind. From the sound of it, strikers were firing at the barge from all sides—from the railroad bridge and both banks, even from the river.

Gripping his rifle, Dan looked out the porthole. Ten minutes earlier he had fired at strikers shooting at them from a skiff on the river. They had been driven off, but who knew when they might return.

"Some of those lunatics are really good shots," said Ted, sliding to the floor. "We're trapped like rats in this barge, and I don't even have a rifle to defend myself."

"Stop worrying so much," replied Dan. "I'm sure they will soon be sending in reinforcements."

At that moment, a loud boom echoed through the valley. A moment later, an explosion, followed by the crash of shattering timber shook the *Iron Mountain*.

"What the hell was that!" Ted shrieked.

"Damn them, they're firing cannons at us!" someone screamed from the far end of the barge. Curses and exclamations filled the barge's interior.

Dan glanced nervously out the opening. Screams were coming from the barge next to them on the water.

"God in heaven, a hole has been blown out of the roof of the *Monongahela*," he declared, awestruck.

Dan cautiously shifted his position at the opening. From the top of the high, cliff-like bank opposite the mill, a cloud of smoke rose slowly into the summer sky.

A second boom rumbled from atop the bank.

Dan dropped to the floor and hastily crawled toward a nearby table. Other men were doing the same. Head down, Dan rammed into the men under the table, barely managing to get his shoulders underneath. On his hands and knees, Dan waited for the crash.

Seconds ticked by, then a minute. Nothing.

Where was Ted? Dan slid back and looked around.

Against the wall by the porthole, Ted stared vacantly into space.

11 A.M.

Duncan and two other strikers had slid down a shallow ravine to the ditch where John Morris had landed. There they found him shot in the forehead, dead.

Angry shouts erupted from the men at the pump house when Morris's body had been carried up the embankment. Word had spread rapidly along the breastworks, whipping the strikers into a fury and prompting a fresh fusillade toward the barges.

Since then, two hours had passed. First, the strikers had tried firing a cannon from the bank opposite. While the first shot had blown a hole in the roof of one barge, the second had overshot the mark, landing in the mill yard. The cannonball had blown one of strikers standing there to bits. At least one other striker was reported shot.

After that, the strikers' rage had swelled ever larger, and they were now hatching schemes to deliver a fatal blow to the Pinkertons.

The men on the pump house roof were in a huddle, discussing what kind of attack would be most damaging. The strategy favored by the majority was burning the Pinkertons out, either by land or water.

The sun was almost directly overhead, beating down without mercy from the cloudless sky. Dark stains of sweat were spreading on the underarms and backs of the men's shirts. Emlyn's beard itched. He had tried repeatedly to convince the men to stop shooting, but he had only succeeded in making them angry with him. He scratched dejectedly at his beard.

"Please, let's go," Emlyn entreated Gwyn. "What good can we do here? This violence only begets more violence."

Gwyn shrugged off Emlyn's hand. "You go, boyo. I'd hate

to have to answer to Eirwen if anything happened to you."

"Funny, I was thinking the same about you," Emlyn replied.

"I'm not leaving the fight now," Gwyn snapped. "Os nad wyt ti'n barod i ymladd, bagla hi o'ma. *You shouldn't have come here in the first place.*"

"I don't understand why the Pinkertons can't be allowed off the barges," Emlyn insisted. "Let the authorities deal with them."

"Let them off?" asked Gwyn, irate. "After they started shooting at us? After they killed John?" Gwyn glared at Emlyn. "I shouldn't have let you come."

Emlyn said nothing as Gwyn returned to the huddle. Emlyn undid another button on his shirt and sat down against the rampart. He regretted having forgotten his hat. Taking out his handkerchief, he knotted the corners and placed it on his head as a sun hat. He closed his eyes and dozed off.

Emlyn jumped as a barrage of gunfire let loose. Men were shouting, "The tug! The tug!" Gwyn and the others were peering through the breastworks.

Ducking down, Emlyn carefully peeked out. The *Little Bill*, flying the American flag, was steaming toward the barges.

"Get that tug!" screamed Duncan. "Don't let those murderers escape."

The men on the pump house joined the battery. Bullets slammed repeatedly into the already pockmarked sides of the tugboat. The windows in the pilothouse exploded in a shower of glass. Splinters of wood flew.

Emlyn strained to discover what happened to the men in the pilothouse, but it was impossible to see inside. With no one at the helm, the current slowly drew the *Little Bill* away from the barges until it began to drift downstream. The strikers continued to pour volleys into the retreating craft.

Near despair, Emlyn sank down against the barricade. The bloodlust was showing no signs of abating on either side. With or without Gwyn, he had to get out of there. Wiping his brow with his sleeve, he waited for the firing to stop.

He heard a loud metallic *ding*, immediately followed by an intense burning pain in his upper right arm. What had just happened? He touched his arm where it hurt, just below the shoulder. It felt wet. He held his hand before him in the midday glare. His fingers were red.

Someone shouted, "Emlyn's been hit!"

Gwyn dropped his rifle and scrambled over. "Where? What happened?"

"I . . . I'm not sure," said Emlyn.

"Let me have a look," said Gwyn, kneeling by his side. He ripped open Emlyn's shirtsleeve to the shoulder.

"It looks like a bullet tore open his arm," Gwyn observed. "But where did it come from?"

"A ricochet," said Duncan. "I heard the initial hit."

Emlyn held out his right elbow to see his arm better. Blood was oozing from a deep gash and running down his arm in a thin stream. "We've got to get you to the doctor," Gwyn said, snatching the handkerchief off Emlyn's head and tying it tightly above the wound.

"The villains," snarled Duncan, seizing his rifle. "Every one of them fucking Pinkertons must be called to account for this butchery."

The guards in the *Iron Mountain* were tripping and clambering over one another in a panic. Dozens were rushing toward the opening that linked to a similar opening on the other barge. Officers shouted at the men, vainly trying to restore order.

Minutes earlier, guards on the upstream end had spotted the burning raft coming toward them. Flames from the raft leaped up twenty or thirty feet, distorting the air. When the raft rammed the barge, there would be no escape.

As soon as Ted caught sight of the oncoming raft, he jumped up and tried to push himself out of a porthole. Dan grabbed him by the belt and pulled him back. "Don't be an idiot. You'll either drown or be shot out there." Ted continued to struggle. Dan slapped him across the face, and Ted went limp.

For a few minutes the chaos continued, with men rushing about, trying to figure the best way to avoid the impending conflagration. Suddenly, cheers went up from the barges. To the relief of all on board the *Iron Mountain*, just before it was about to hit the barge, the raft began to sink. As it went under, the current deflected it, and it floated harmlessly away.

"Whew, that was a close call," said Dan.

"Those strikers are homicidal," moaned Ted. "What will they try next?"

"You know, son," said Ben, the gray-haired veteran who had talked to them earlier, "we're better off in here than out there. For the moment neither the river nor the landing offers a safe exit."

Shortly after Emlyn was hit, an older man named Louie showed up at the pump house with two pails of drinking water.

Gwyn wanted to accompany Emlyn, but Louie convinced Gwyn that he knew the safest and fastest route out of the works.

Emlyn followed Louie along the tracks as they worked their way around the mill buildings. The heat in the exposed yards was stifling. Emlyn's head hurt almost more than his arm.

Louie helped Emlyn through a broken section of the mill fence, and they emerged onto City Farm Lane at Fifth Avenue. On the street people were anxiously looking toward the river. Sounds of angry voices, screams, shouts and distant gunfire reverberated against the buildings. Standing in the broiling sun, Emlyn thought he might faint.

A dozen women standing near the fence came over to them. The women crowded around, anxiously asking about the men on the barricades.

"What happened to you?" a young woman asked Emlyn.

"What's going on down by the river?" asked another.

"Please, ladies, step aside," said Louie. "This man needs to see a doctor."

The first woman burst into tears.

In the middle of the filthy lane, Emlyn stumbled and almost fell. The smell of manure and garbage made him retch.

"You don't look so good," said Louie, righting Emlyn.

"It's so hot," Emlyn murmured.

"Come on," said Louie. "The pump we're using isn't far from here. Let's go there. I can report in and you can get some water."

They walked down Fifth and turned into a shady dirt-packed courtyard on Dickson Street. Several men and women were congregated around a pump with buckets and jugs.

"Louie, what's happened?" asked a middle-aged woman, coming toward them.

"This here's Emlyn," said Louie. "He got winged in the arm and needs medical attention."

The woman focused her gaze on Emlyn's right arm.

"This here's my wife Lillian," Louie said to Emlyn.

Lillian was a short, compact woman of about fifty. Her bright blue eyes smiled at Emlyn. Tendrils of gray and brown hair curled from under her sunbonnet.

"Call me Lil," she said, leading Emlyn to the pump. She grabbed the back of the chair on which she'd been sitting and turned it toward Emlyn.

"Sit," Lil said. He did. She handed him a tin cup full of water. He took large gulps, draining it in a few seconds. She handed him another.

"Where are you going?" she asked.

"To Dr. Oesterling's office on the Avenue," Emlyn said. "But first, would you please splash me with water. I'm so hot."

"Coming right up," Lil said, pumping water into a pail.

"Hold out your arm," she directed. She carefully poured half the contents of the pail over the wound, and then poured the rest over his head and shoulders.

Emlyn closed his eyes and threw back his head. "Whew! That's better."

"You still need to get to the doctor's," said Louie. "Can you walk that far?"

"Now I've cooled off a bit," said Emlyn, "I can do it on my own."

Lil squinted at Emlyn's bloody sleeve, dripping pink-stained water.

"It's not that bad," Emlyn said.

"Looks pretty bad to me," she said. "Louie, you resume water delivery. I'll go with this young man to the Avenue."

"She'll take good care you," said Louie, winking at Emlyn.

"Come on," said Lil, gently taking Emlyn's left arm. "What's the address?"

⁂

Coughing, Dan tied the handkerchief tighter over his nose and mouth. The heat inside the barge was unbearable. Smoke from the fires and gunpowder hung in the air, trapped under the roof. The guards were packed together in the sweltering interior, many of them nearly catatonic from repeated episodes of terror.

"What will these maniacs try next?" asked Ted. "We've been bombarded by cannons and attacked with a burning raft, then a burning railroad car. They've repeatedly shot down flags of truce. What do they want?"

Dan knew the answer: the people of Homestead wanted them dead. But he said nothing to Ted, who had already tried twice to jump overboard.

"Just remember that none of the strikers' attacks have gotten to us," Dan said. "We have to be patient. It's safer in here than out there. They'll eventually return to rescue us."

It was the best lie he could manage.

"Who's 'they'?" asked Ted. "I haven't seen any rescue attempts since the *Little Bill* got driven off."

Dan rubbed his nose, trying to manufacture another answer.

Explosions suddenly rocked the barge. Guards began screaming and yelling. Dan couldn't make out what anyone was saying amid the din. He crawled to an opening and looked out. Objects were hitting the water and exploding, sending up fountains where they hit.

"God in heaven!" exclaimed Ted. "What now?"

"I think it's sticks of dynamite," Dan said.

Noon

On the Avenue a few people were dashing about. Although Burgess McLuckie had ordered the saloons closed, men were hanging around in front, as if they could think of nowhere else to gather. Heat waves shimmered off the baked street.

Lillian and Emlyn plodded slowly along the rickety boardwalk toward the doctor's office. In front of a shuttered saloon, three men stood by the door, blocking the sidewalk.

As they came toward the men, an uneasy feeling crept over Emlyn. The big man gesturing broadly looked familiar. The thin man with him watched them approach.

"Let's go around them in the street," said Emlyn.

"Nonsense," replied Lil. "You must stay out of the sun."

As they reached the men, the smaller man pointed at Emlyn and said, "Hey, Bucky, ain't that the English feller that stole your cane?"

The big man whirled around. He smiled menacingly.

"I'll be damned if it ain't the limey bastard in the flesh."

Flanked by the other men, Buckman stood in the middle of the walk, his cane extended to block their way.

"Please," said Lil. "Let us pass."

"I have a little score to settle first," Buckman said, tapping his cane on the boardwalk.

"What kind of coward would attack a wounded man?" Lil asked, stepping between him and Emlyn.

"Get out of my way, you old cow," Buckman said, shoving her aside. "This here's a company man. I seen him leaving the General Office Building more than once."

Emlyn smelled the stale sweat and alcohol fumes coming off Buckman, and began to feel nauseous. Recalling his other encounter with Buckman, he said nothing.

"That's crazy," said Lil. "If he's a company man, what was he doing at the barricades?"

Buckman pulled back his chin, looking Emlyn up and down. After a long moment, he snarled, "Because he's a spy for Frick, that's why!"

He lifted the cane, and with a quick thrust, jabbed it into Emlyn's wound.

With a loud gasp, Emlyn collapsed forward. Lil grabbed his left arm, preventing him from falling into Buckman. The pain thrilled through his arm and shoulder.

"How do you like that, you fucker?" sneered Buckman. His companions howled with laughter.

"You mean cuss!" Lil shouted at Buckman. Looking around frantically, she shouted, "Help! Help us!"

"Shut up, bitch," Buckman said, backhanding her on the side of the face.

Raising her hand to her left eye, Lil cried out and fell to the sidewalk.

"Leave her alone!" Emlyn exclaimed hoarsely, stooping to help her.

"She should keep her nose out of other people's business," said Buckman. "As for you—" he shifted the cane back into his right hand.

From behind Buckman, a man's voice said evenly, "Stop. Hold it there."

"Oh yeah? Who's going to stop me?" demanded Buckman, turning around. "You and what army?"

"I don't need an army," said the man calmly. "I have this Colt thirty-six."

Emlyn looked up. There stood Dr. Oesterling in a blood-stained white shirt, holding a large revolver.

"Whoa!" said Buckman, staggering backward.

"Move away from them and put down that cane."

"OK, OK," Buckman said, dropping the cane.

Hands in the air, Buckman backed off the sidewalk and bolted. Bumping into each other, his companions fled down the street with him.

"Thank God you showed up," Lil said to Oesterling. "I thought he was going to kill us."

Oesterling shoved the gun into its holster and bent over Lil.

"Are you alright?" he asked. "Is your eye hurt?"

"Don't worry about me. He's the one who needs help," Lil said, nodding toward Emlyn. "Can you help him get to Dr. Oesterling's office?"

"I think he can," said Emlyn, smiling despite the pain. "This is Dr. Oesterling."

On the *Iron Mountain*, the situation was beyond desperate. The heat was ungodly, the smoky air searing the lungs of those trapped inside. Wounded guards lay on the floor in spreading pools of blood. One of the recruits, a medical student named Wells, had been tending to those who had been hit by shots that one way or another had made their way through the barge's cover.

"We must get out of here," Ted moaned. "Somehow, anyhow."

"Any ideas on how to do that?" asked Dan.

"Well, no . . ." said Ted.

"It's hopeless," said the guard next to Ted with a life vest wrapped around his waist. Like Ted, he was a college student, a recruit from New York named Connors. "I'm sorry I ever heard of the Pinkertons."

"Me, too," replied Ted. "I'm even sorrier to have wound up in this godforsaken place with this deranged mob. If the heat doesn't kill us, they will."

Dan dabbed at his brow with his sweat-soaked handkerchief. "I know it looks bad," he said, "but we've got to concentrate on getting through this."

Ted shook his head. "Why bother? We're doomed."

Connors pulled up his knees and curled up tightly, his head in his hands.

"Don't talk like that," said Dan. "We're still alive and in one piece, ain't we?"

There was a muffled thud, followed by a piercing cry from Connors.

"Jesus, Connors is shot," Ted whispered.

Dan leaned over Connors as other men rushed over. Connors was screaming at the top of his lungs as blood gushed from the crease of his elbow.

Wells pushed the other guards aside and stooped down next to Connors. Transfixed with horror, Dan watched blood pulsing from the bullet hole.

"How . . . how bad is it?" asked Ted, averting his eyes.

"I think the bullet hit an artery," said Dan.

Ted's hand flew to his mouth, and he began heaving dry sobs.

"Calm down, dammit," Dan snapped.

Connors kept screaming.

"Where did the shot come from?" Dan wondered aloud.

His eyes stopped at a small opening opposite them. It had to have come through there—a lucky shot by some striker, a man with a rifle who couldn't even see his target.

For poor Connors it was an unlucky shot indeed. As Wells worked on adjusting the tourniquet on Connors' arm, the wounded man's eyelids fluttered, and he finally stopped screaming.

Eyes closed, Ted was sobbing softly.

—•••—

"Careful," cautioned Lillian, as Emlyn tripped at the top of the staircase.

"Slow and steady wins the race," said Oesterling, pushing the office door back.

On the row of chairs by the door sat a young couple and a man of about sixty. The woman cradled a young child in her arms. "Dr. Oesterling?" the older man asked, rising. His eyes dropped to the doctor's bloodstained shirt. "Are you alright?"

"Yes," said Oesterling wearily. "The blood isn't mine."

"The blood on that young man looks like his own," said the man.

Ignoring him, Oesterling walked to the sink as Sarah and Mrs. Cramer came out from behind the surgery screen.

"Papa, where were you?" Sarah asked. "Two patients have come while. . . ." She stopped short, seeing Emlyn and Lillian.

"Emlyn?" Sarah said, blinking in disbelief.

"Come straight over to the surgery," Oesterling said to Emlyn. Turning to Lillian, he added, "I'll look at your eye in a moment. Sarah, please get her a clean damp cloth."

He pulled open a drawer in the cabinet. "Where's my spare shirt?"

As Oesterling washed up at the sink, Sarah helped Lillian to a seat near a window.

"You'd better lie down before you fall down," Mrs. Cramer said to Emlyn, patting the gurney in the surgery. "Let's get that shirt off."

Emlyn lay down and Mrs. Cramer began cutting away his shirtsleeve. She then washed off the wound with surgical soap.

Oesterling came behind the screen, buttoning a clean shirt.

"This looks like a gunshot wound," Mrs. Cramer said, blotting around the gash.

"It is," said Emlyn. "I was just sitting there when a ricochet . . ."

"Never mind about that," said Oesterling. "Let's take a look." He pulled up a stool and sat down.

"Hmm," he said.

"Is that good or bad?" asked Emlyn.

"The wound is not real bad. The bullet didn't hit the bone, but cut pretty deeply into the muscle. Still, it would have been much better if that vicious drunk hadn't jabbed his cane into it," said Oesterling. "I'll have to put in a few stitches. Mrs. Cramer, get the morphine."

"Please, no morphine," said Emlyn.

"Why not?" asked Mrs. Cramer sternly. "This could hurt quite a bit."

"I need to get back to the house and check on my sister," Emlyn said. "Morphine may put me asleep."

"You'll want to be asleep for this, believe me," said Mrs. Cramer.

"Give him a half-dose," said Oesterling to Mrs. Cramer.

"No arguments from you," she admonished Emlyn, picking up the morphine bottle.

3 P.M.

Voices woke him. It was very warm and his arm hurt. His face felt sunburned. He had been dreaming that a dragon was flying over Homestead, scorching everything below. Emlyn opened his eyes. A stamped tin ceiling. A white screen. Ah, yes, Oesterling's office. The stitches. He tried to sit up, but couldn't. The shapes in the room melted together.

"It's out of the question, Norton. My father is out on a call for the second time this afternoon, and I've got to stay here."

"Carrie was hysterical when she couldn't get through at your house. Oliver left a message at the office, asking me to come here." Montague.

"I must stay here. These men are waiting to take Papa to treat an injured man. We'll call her when we get home."

"When might that be?"

"Norton, for heaven's sake! Why don't you call her yourself?"

"Oliver expressly asked for you or your father to call her."

Why doesn't he go away and let me sleep?

The sound of a chair scraping on the floor.

"Miss Oesterling, is this feller bothering you?" A deep male voice.

"I'll thank you to mind your own business, sir."

"I'll thank *you* to mind your business, *sir*." A younger male, mocking. "Miss Oesterling told you twice that she needs to stay here."

"You stay out of this. . . .Sarah, really! You're not a nurse. What difference would it make if . . ."

"I'm the nurse, and I want you to leave. A patient is recovering in the back."

"I have an important message from Miss Oesterling's sister." Montague, huffy. "I'm staying until the doctor gets back."

"Oh yeah? I think everyone in this office wants you to leave, including Miss Oesterling." The mocking man.

"You, sir, can't tell me what to do."

"Oh, really—sir?"

"If we can't tell you what to do, we'll show you." Man with the deep voice.

Scuffling.

"Take your hands off me." Montague.

More scuffling. Scraping. Grunting. Clattering down the stairs.

"And don't try to come back up." Younger man, from downstairs. The sound of the outside door closing.

"Good Lord! What's the matter with some people? As if there's not enough trouble in this world!" Mrs. Cramer, exasperated.

3:30 P.M.

The temperature in the barge was well past the 100-degree mark. Fearing getting shot through an opening, the guards were hunkered down. The majority of them had some kind of wound or injury inflicted directly or indirectly by the strikers. A few had collapsed from the heat.

Dan marveled that he was one of those who had not sustained an injury. Neither had Ted, but Dan was very concerned about Ted's state of mind. Next to him, Ted was sitting with his arms around his bent legs, staring ahead. Every few seconds, he would shiver slightly. He hadn't said anything for at least a half hour.

Wells came over to check on Connors. Despite his best efforts, Connors was fading fast. Death was near.

As Wells moved past, Dan tugged his sleeve.

"When are we going to be towed off this bank?" asked Dan.

Wells glanced at him and looked away.

"Soon, I hope," said Dan.

"I'm afraid not," Wells replied. "The officers refuse to surrender, and the strikers won't allow a tug anywhere near us."

"Why?" asked Dan.

Wells sighed. "You can see for yourself how determined

they are to sink or burn us out. If we're getting off, we'll have to disembark."

Ted's eyes flew open. He sat up at attention.

"Disembark?" exclaimed Dan. "With all those maniacs on the landing?"

"The mob that's been in control of the mill site insists on unconditional surrender," said Wells. "Apparently a union leader named O'Donnell is negotiating to get us off the barges."

"I certainly don't want to face that bloodthirsty rabble," said Dan.

"Nor I," said Wells.

Ted leaned forward. "I am not disembarking," he said. "No way." Before Dan could react, Ted leaped up and in a flash dove headfirst through the gaping porthole. The splash was barely audible.

Dan and Wells scrambled to the opening and looked downriver. On the swirling surface of the muddy water, no trace of Ted Martin could be seen.

Cerberus cocked his head, watching as Sarah and Mrs. Cramer helped Emlyn into a sitting position on the cot. Teetering to and fro, Emlyn blinked at the sunlight streaming through the windows. Mrs. Cramer reached out to steady him.

"How do you feel?" she asked.

"Ah, I feel strange," replied Emlyn, rubbing his eyes. "I had such weird dreams, and I feel sick to my stomach."

"Narcotics will do that," said Mrs. Cramer. "How's the pain?"

"Not bad," said Emlyn, examining the bandage on his arm. His trousers were dirty; the front of his undershirt was streaked with blood. "That morphine really knocked me for a loop. I can't imagine what a full dose would do."

"It was a full dose. The doctor thought you were in no shape to go onto the streets."

Emlyn blinked. "He was right," he said after a moment. "Say, what happened to Lil, the woman who helped me get here? How is her eye?"

"Luckily, her eyesight is fine. She has some redness and a little bruising on the cheek, but she's alright," said Mrs. Cramer.

"That's good," said Emlyn.

"I wonder which side those drunken fools think they're on," said Sarah.

"They're not thinking," said Mrs. Cramer.

Sarah offered him a glass of water.

"Thank you," said Emlyn. He took a few swallows, then abruptly stopped. "Eirwen! I've got to get to the house. She'll be overcome with worry if . . ."

"It's OK," said Sarah soothingly. "Papa sent someone over to the house to tell her that you're here."

"But Gwyn . . . We were both at the pump house when I was hit. He stayed behind. That was hours ago."

"There's nothing you can do about that," said Sarah. "What on earth were you and Gwyn doing there, anyway?"

Emlyn shook his head. "Eirwen asked me to go with him. He has a rifle. When the fighting started, Gwyn was shooting. I wanted us to leave, but he wouldn't. Then . . ." He winced at the memory.

"Then what?" prompted Sarah.

"Then Morris was killed."

"Killed? Who was killed?" asked Mrs. Cramer, suddenly interested in the conversation.

"A man named Morris, John Morris. He worked in the

blooming mill," murmured Emlyn. "He was hit in the forehead."

"I can't believe it," said Sarah. "I saw him and his family this past weekend."

"Lord help us, will this day ever end?" said Mrs. Cramer pensively.

"I'm beginning to doubt that myself," said Oesterling from the doorway. Cerberus trotted up to greet him.

He came over to Emlyn, trailed by Cerberus. "Feeling alright?"

Emlyn nodded. "I'm fine, but I feel a bit fuzzy in the head."

"It will pass," said Oesterling, going over to the sink. He splashed water on his face and washed his hands.

"Finally—no patients in the office, and no patients waiting at home—at least as far as we know," said Mrs. Cramer, pulling down a window shade.

"I need to sit down," Oesterling said, patting his face with a towel. "It seems like I've done nothing but go from one patient to another since early this morning." Oesterling poured a glass of water from the tap, drained it, and poured another.

Mrs. Cramer went from window to window, adjusting the shades.

Oesterling eased himself into a chair. Cerberus put his head in the doctor's lap and wagged his tail. Oesterling scratched behind his ears.

"Homestead needs to build a hospital. It's difficult to treat patients in their homes, especially such serious injuries as I've seen today." He closed his eyes as he sipped from the glass.

"Emlyn says that John Morris was killed," said Sarah quietly.

"Yes, I heard that—so tragic," said Oesterling. "I also heard that the town has gotten very riled up against the Pinkertons. O'Donnell's having quite a time trying to calm the crowd. I understand Weihe has arrived in town to talk to the strikers. To top it off, many men from South Side have been coming to town. I've seen them and some of them look like ruffians. I think it may be too late for anyone, even the head of the Amalgamated, to persuade the strikers to stand down."

Oesterling held out the water glass, examining it as if it were a crystal ball enabling him to see into the future.

"Emlyn saw it," said Sarah.

"Saw what?" asked Oesterling.

"Saw John Morris get shot," said Sarah.

"Good God," said Oesterling, studying Emlyn. "I think you've had a worse day than I have."

4 P.M.

The officers had at last agreed to surrender. They were almost out of ammunition, and the war of attrition from the shore was knocking them off one by one. Once again, the officers hung out a white flag, and this time it was not shot down.

When the officers announced the surrender to the men on the barges, one guard had said he wouldn't give in, preferring death to the ignominy of crawling ashore like a whipped cur. When an officer pulled a gun, insisting he obey orders, the man walked away. A few paces away, the guard put his own revolver to his head and pulled the trigger.

Dan thought of Ted, his body somewhere downstream in the Monongahela, half-wishing he were with him.

Preparing to disembark, the men picked up their belongings and straightened their uniforms as best they could. Many were wounded; all were weak from the heat and smoke in the barges.

But when the Pinkerton guards saw the size and virulence of the enraged mob on the landing, they balked. Men and women, thousands of them, stood on the riverbank, brandishing weapons, cursing and taunting. Dan had never been so scared in his life.

Strikers boarded the barge and began hitting the Pinkertons with fists and clubs, forcing them to the exits. Gripping his small valise, Dan joined the line of Pinkertons crowding onto the gangplank. Hundreds of men stood around the landing in the sultry afternoon heat, leaving a broad path for the Pinkertons up the steep embankment.

Dan trudged up the dusty slope. As he reached the top, his heart nearly stopped: as far as he could see, enraged townspeople lined both sides of the pathway, screaming for vengeance. He glanced down at the landing. While men set fire to the barges, looters were carrying away items left behind. The strikers were finally accomplishing what they had tried to do for hours.

He took a few halting steps forward. Two men came up to him. One struck him with a club as the other snatched away his valise. He fell facedown into the dirt and cinders. The men started kicking him, snarling, "Get up, you murdering son-of-a-bitch." Dan struggled to his feet, but before he could take even a few steps, a couple of women fell on him. "Murderer!" They clawed and kicked him. Dan put his arms over his head.

In front of him, Ben, the old veteran, was lying on the ground. "Please, don't kill me," Ben entreated the men standing over him with clubs. The women, distracted by the assault on the older man, paused momentarily.

Dan saw his chance. Gathering all his strength, he took a big gulp of air and sprinted off as fast as his legs could carry him. He ran through and around Pinkertons and strikers for nearly a hundred yards, until he encountered a group of men blocking the path.

They set upon him with fists and rifle butts, knocking him to the ground. As he tried to get up, he felt a stunning blow to the back of his head. Dan lost consciousness, only to be revived by a kick in the side. "Get up! Get up, you filthy mercenary."

Somehow, he managed to get to his feet. The pain in his head throbbed violently; his vision blurred. He plodded forward, one step, then another. Beside him, boys were spitting on another guard whom they had pushed to the ground. Women were pitching stones. One struck him in the neck, another on his shoulder.

He kept moving.

Oesterling had decided that, as no one had come for help during the past hour, there was no point in staying at the office. They all were exhausted.

While Mrs. Cramer put the office in order, Sarah hung a sign on the door directing emergency patients to the doctor's house. Oesterling restocked his medical bag and locked up the remaining supplies in the cabinet, placing the gun and holster back in the drawer.

Oesterling wrapped up bandages and handed them to Emlyn, sitting on the cot. "There's some morphine in here, too. You'll need it to sleep."

"Thank you. I appreciate all you've done," Emlyn said, taking the package. "I think I can make it back to the house now. Eirwen must be worried sick."

"Sarah should go with you," said the doctor. "Now that the fighting's stopped, there should be no danger from stray bullets."

"She needn't come with me," said Emlyn. "I'm fine."

He took a step and swayed dangerously.

"Don't be foolish," said Mrs. Cramer. "Sarah is going with you, and that's that."

"Really, Emlyn, it's no bother," said Sarah. "I'm concerned about Eirwen, too."

Sarah was shutting the windows when Cerberus started barking. A moment later, a red-faced man in denim pants burst through the door.

"Doc, please come quickly," said the man breathlessly. "So many are hurt."

"Where?" asked Oesterling, grabbing Cerberus's collar. "What happened?"

"It's the Pinkerton detectives," replied the man. "They're being forced to run the gauntlet all the way from the landing to the opera house."

"That's quite a distance," said Mrs. Cramer. "Who's forcing them?"

"The strikers, them that's been shootin' at them all day. There must be thousands of people beating on the detectives, calling for blood."

The man turned to Oesterling. "Please, can you come right away?"

A club hit him between the shoulders. Dan stumbled and fell. It was the fourth time he'd been knocked down, and he didn't think he could get up again. His head ached as though it might split open.

"Murdering scoundrel!" a middle-aged woman screamed, whacking him with an umbrella. He put his arms over his head to protect himself, but someone wrenched them off, and two men began dragging him through the street by his arms.

"For God's sake, stop," Dan pleaded. "Please. I'm just a farm boy from Illinois."

"Liar!" the woman shrieked, stabbing him in the thigh with the umbrella. "You're a murdering bastard."

The men yanked him to his feet as the woman gave him another kick.

Was this nightmare ever going to end?

To his horror, Dan saw another group of men hurrying toward them. This was it. He was going to die.

"Get back!" shouted the man at the front of the newcomers as he drew his pistol. "Move away from him." The men and woman beating him paused.

"I'll not say it again."

"He's a murderer!' screeched the woman.

He cocked his pistol and aimed it at her. "Stand aside," he ordered, as his companions ran over to Dan.

"'Looks like someone's cracked him on the head with a rifle butt," said one of them.

"C'mon," said the man with the pistol. "Let's get him to the opera house."

5 P.M.

In front of the opera house on Fifth Avenue the situation was approaching bedlam. "Kill the murderers!" people were screaming at the Pinkertons being brought to the hall. They scuffled with others who were trying to clear the entrance.

The furious crowd was trying to force its way inside, while others were trying to stop them.

"Stick close to me," said the red-faced man to Oesterling

as they approached the hall. Shoving his way through the crowd, the man walked boldly toward the entrance. Seeing them approach, men at the entrance forced back the would-be attackers, allowing them to pass through.

Oesterling's sense of relief at making it safely inside the hall immediately vanished as he contemplated the sight of dozens, even hundreds of men throughout the hall, bloody, beaten, groaning, crying. Many of them appeared to be seriously hurt or in some kind of distress. Other doctors from the town were attending to the injured.

"Good heavens," Oesterling muttered. "Where do we start?"

"Over here," said a man in a tattered Pinkerton's officer's uniform. He led Oesterling to a young guard lying in the corner. "He was just brought in."

Oesterling stooped to examine at the man. A bloody handkerchief was tied around his head. His face was bruised and cut; saliva crept from the corner of his open mouth. His eyelids flickered.

"What's the verdict, doc?" asked the officer.

"This man has a concussion," said Oesterling. "We've got to get him upright and keep him awake."

The officer and Oesterling dragged the guard into a sitting position. He moaned softly, struggling to open his eyes.

As the officer went to fetch water, Oesterling slapped the man lightly on the face. It looked like a long day was going to become even longer.

—•••—

Emlyn, his right arm in a sling, cautiously made his way across the railroad tracks on Amity Street. Sarah, carrying the package of bandages, was on his right, while Cerberus trotted in front.

The streets were thronged with workers celebrating their victory over the Pinkertons. The sounds of gunshots had ceased, but he could hear the crowd down Fifth Avenue at the opera house crying for revenge.

"This day has been such a nightmare. I wonder if Gwyn made it back home safely," said Emlyn.

"I wouldn't be surprised if he's not there. There's been so much chaos today," said Sarah. She glanced down Fifth Avenue toward the opera house. "And it's still going on. Obviously, O'Donnell hasn't been able to stop the most bloodthirsty element in the strikers."

"It's amazing to me that O'Donnell was even able to get the Pinkertons off the barges," said Emlyn. "When I was at the pump house, the strikers were hell-bent on burning them out."

"The company should have to answer for all this violence," said Sarah. "I know for a fact that Frick called in the Pinkertons to secure company property."

"Frick?" asked Emlyn. "How do you know?"

Sarah paused. "Carrie. She called Papa yesterday to warn us. Of course she wanted us to leave town—probably still does."

"Oh, so that's what the business with Montague was about this afternoon."

"You heard that? Yes. He, Carrie, and Oliver are so terribly concerned about us—and of course about the sacred rights of property owners."

Two men in dusty, sweat-soaked shirts walked by, carrying rifles.

"I do hope Gwyn is at the house," said Emlyn.

"I hope so, too," said Sarah.

Dan sat on the floor with his back against the wall. He was inside a big hall. Another Pinkerton was sitting next to him, a middle-aged man with a lean face. It was warm, but not nearly as warm as on the barge. The pain in his head was excruciating. He was exhausted. He had to sleep. He closed his eyes.

"No, you don't," said the guard next to him. "You stay awake."

Dan blinked. "What? Where am I?"

"We're in some kind of music hall. Supposedly the sheriff is trying to get us to the railroad station so we can get out of this wretched town."

Dan moaned. "I don't want to go out there again."

The guard leaned closer. "They're talking about arresting us for murder," he whispered. "The local union leader promised to press murder charges as a concession to the mob at the river."

"Us? Murderers?" asked Dan, incredulous. "You've got to be kidding."

"I'm not. They wouldn't have let us off otherwise."

"They're calling *us* murderers?" replied Dan. "After they fired thousands of rounds at us the whole blessed day? After they tried so many ways to burn us alive? After they beat us mercilessly? This town is insane."

"Yeah," said the man. "It's unbelievable. It's a miracle we all weren't killed."

Dan thought of Connors and Ted and the guard who shot himself. The throbbing in his head increased.

"I've been with the Pinkertons for years," said the guard. "I served during the New York Central strike in '77, but that was nothing compared to this. This is war." He wiped his face with his sleeve. "Anyway, I for one want to get out of here before they herd us into the slammer."

Dan sighed. "You're right. The sooner we get out of here, the better." He closed his eyes.

The guard shook him. "Stay awake. Doctor's orders."

—•••—

Sarah and Emlyn cut through the neighbors' yard to the back door. She pulled open the screen door and held it for Emlyn. Anxiously, he looked around. Dirty dishes were piled in the kitchen sink; bread, cheese, and other remnants of a meal sat on the table. The house was quiet.

"Eirwen? Gwyn? A yw unrhyw un cartref? *Anyone home?"* No answer.

Cerberus squeezed past him as Emlyn went through the door. The dog trotted into the front room.

"Cerby! How did you get in?" Emlyn heard Thomas exclaim.

Going into the parlor, Emlyn saw Thomas on the floor with Cerberus enthusiastically licking his face.

"Uncle Em!" Thomas exclaimed, jumping up. The front door flew open, and Eirwen came inside.

"Emlyn bach! Diolch i dduw ydych yma ar diwethaf. *Thank God you're safe,"* Eirwen cried, running to Emlyn and flinging her arms around his neck. He held her in a tight embrace as she sobbed into his shoulder.

"I'm here now," he said, patting her back with his left hand. "I'm sorry it took so long."

Sarah came into the room and waited quietly.

Noticing the bandage on Emlyn's arm, Eirwen released him.

"Emlyn, I'm sorry," she said. "I forgot about your arm."

"It's alright," said Emlyn.

"And Sarah," said Eirwen. "Thank you for walking over with Emlyn—and thanks to your father for patching him up." She brushed at the tears running down her cheeks.

"I was glad to help," said Sarah.

"I was afraid to leave the house for fear that Gwyn or Emlyn would come home and wonder where I was," said Eirwen. "Since the shooting stopped, I've been out front with Dilys and David watching the street." She took out a handkerchief and blew her nose.

"Gwyn isn't here then?" Emlyn asked.

Eirwen shook her head. "He hasn't been home since you both left this morning. I'm so worried."

"I'm sure he'll be back soon," said Sarah, putting her arm around Eirwen. "Things are calming down."

"I hope so," Eirwen sniffed, fighting back tears.

She looked at Emlyn. "Forgive me for being so thoughtless," she said. "Emlyn, you must get off your feet." She plumped up the pillows on the sofa. "Please, sit."

Eirwen smoothed her hair back and managed a wan smile, as Emlyn carefully lowered himself onto the sofa.

"Have you had anything to eat?" Eirwen asked, glancing from Emlyn to Sarah.

"Not since last night," Emlyn said.

"Both of you must be famished," she said, wiping her cheek with the back of her hand. "Let me see what's in the kitchen."

"I'll go get the children," said Sarah.

"Gee, Uncle Em," said Thomas, sitting on the floor with the dog. "What happened to you?"

8 P.M.

"Thanks for the ride," said Oesterling, stepping down from the buggy.

"You're very welcome," said the driver.

Oesterling plodded slowly up the steps to the front porch. As he pushed the front door open and came into the foyer, Cerberus ran circles around him, wagging his tail.

"Good boy," said Oesterling. "You're happy to see me, aren't you?"

"Papa," said Sarah, taking his medical bag, "you look completely done-in." She closed the door behind him. Oesterling went into the study and collapsed into the horsehair armchair. Cerberus put his head in the doctor's lap.

"What's the situation at the opera house? I saw the mob at the door when I accompanied Emlyn home."

"It is not good," said Oesterling, smoothing the fur on the dog's head. "Many of the Pinkertons need to be hospitalized. As I was leaving, the authorities were trying to arrange getting them on a train to Pittsburgh."

"I never thought I'd see the day in Homestead when a battle would rage for twelve hours between company police and townspeople," said Sarah.

"No one did," said Oesterling. "I haven't seen such carnage since my service in the war. I'm glad I didn't have to fire my revolver, although I did take it out once. I don't think I could've scared off those men attacking Emlyn without it."

"It's a sad day when guns rule the streets," said Sarah.

Oesterling sighed, his mind flashing back to the aftermath of the battle at Gettysburg exactly 29 years ago. "Even sadder when you start counting the casualties on both sides."

"Have you heard anything about how many were killed or wounded?" Sarah asked.

"No one knows for sure," said Oesterling. "One of the doctors at the opera house said that two Pinkertons were killed. It looked to me that maybe more than a hundred of them are wounded. I didn't see one detective who didn't have some kind of injury. I would be very surprised if there were only two deaths among them."

"How about the strikers?"

"Word is that six are dead, sixteen or seventeen wounded," said Oesterling. "Of course that does not include the people injured in other ways, like those trying to escape the fighting." Oesterling grimaced. "The bloodshed is appalling."

"So many men were walking around with firearms," said Sarah, "it's astounding that more people weren't shot."

She went to the window and looked out. "It seems relatively quiet now, except for some workers with enough energy left to celebrate."

"By the way," she added. "Norton came to the office this afternoon demanding that I call Carrie immediately. He said Oliver had gotten a message through to him at the company office."

"Norton?" said Oesterling. "I didn't think him brave enough to venture out on the streets this afternoon."

"I'd say it was more bravado than bravery," said Sarah. "He does such strange things. Half the time I have no idea what's going through his head."

"Did you call Carrie?" Oesterling asked, attempting to change the subject.

"I couldn't. I've tried several times since I got home, but the lines are completely jammed."

"Then there's nothing we can do about it now," said Oesterling, resting his head against the chair. "Tomorrow is another day."

9 P.M.

Curled up on his left side, Emlyn dozed on the sofa. Sarah had left after helping Eirwen with the dishes. After putting the children to bed, Eirwen had urged him to go to bed as well, but he had insisted on keeping vigil with her for Gwyn.

The screen door banging shut awakened him with a start.

Gwyn stood over him. "Emlyn, are you awake?" he whispered. His face was beet-red from the sun. Emlyn caught a whiff of alcohol.

"You're home," said Emlyn. Gwyn was grinning ear-to-ear.

"I am," said Gwyn, propping the rifle against the settee. "I'm very relieved to see that you're alright."

"Gwyn?" Eirwen stood at the door to the kitchen.

Beaming, Gwyn swept her into his arms, and swung her around. "Cariad, rydym wedi ennill! *Sweetheart, the workers won!* We stopped Frick's mercenaries." He hugged her tight, burying his face in her neck. "The Pinkertons are going to be arrested. Isn't that bloody marvelous?"

Eirwen pushed him away.

"What's the matter?" Gwyn asked, puzzled. "We won the battle. Aren't you pleased?"

"I'm pleased that the workers won," said Eirwen, "but I'm not pleased about waiting hour after hour with no word from you. After I heard Emlyn was shot, and you remained at the pump house, I was sick with worry." Her voice trembled. "Then I heard that you both were there when John Morris was killed."

"I'm sorry I couldn't get word to you," said Gwyn, caressing her arm. "After the fighting started, I couldn't just walk away."

Eirwen glanced at the mantel clock. "Why did it take you

so long to get home? I heard that the Pinkertons surrendered hours ago."

"Jim, Harry, and I were leaving the mill property when Hughie asked us to help control the people going after the Pinkertons."

On the sofa, Emlyn shifted uncomfortably. The pain in his arm pulsed.

Eirwen stared at Gwyn. "This took five hours?"

Gwyn dropped his eyes. "Well, no. We stopped by Jim's house and had a little celebration."

"I know," said Eirwen. "I can smell it on your breath."

"Eirwen, please," said Gwyn, throwing himself into the easy chair. "I thought you'd be happy about our victory."

Emlyn pushed himself upright. "Did they ever disperse the militants crowding the opera house?" he asked. His arm was throbbing with pain.

Gwyn nodded. "Yes, but it took some doing."

The ticking of the mantel clock seemed very loud in the ensuing silence.

"By the way, where is the morphine?" Emlyn asked Eirwen. "I think I'll take some and go to bed."

"I'll get it. It's in the kitchen," Eirwen replied, turning toward the dining room. She paused in the doorway.

"Are you hungry?" she asked Gwyn, her tone softer.

"I would like something, maybe bread and tea," Gwyn replied.

"Come on into the kitchen, then," said Eirwen, and left the room.

Gwyn put his hand over his stomach and grimaced. "That gin isn't sitting too well."

Emlyn glanced over at Gwyn. "Gin? Seriously?"

"It's all Duncan had," said Gwyn. "He made it himself."

"You're dafter than I thought," said Emlyn.

"Jim didn't want to let the Pinkertons off the barges. It was all Harry and I could do to keep him from joining those setting the barges afire. We told him if he'd help us get the detectives to the opera house to be arrested, we'd go to his house to celebrate our victory."

Emlyn contemplated his bandaged arm.

"You know," he said slowly, "after the events of this day, this whole country seems a lot dafter than I ever thought possible."

On a train east of Pittsburgh. July 7th 3 a.m.

Dan sat at a window, watching the dark countryside slide by. They were climbing into the mountains now, the locomotive laboring harder as it tackled the grade. The guard who was supposed to be making sure he stayed awake had himself fallen asleep. But Dan had gone beyond the point of sleepiness to a state of trance-like wakefulness.

He had been nervous when they had filed out of the opera house two-by-two at midnight, escorted by strikers with guns. Fortunately, few people were on the streets of that hellish town, apparently exhausted from venting their fury on the Pinkertons. To Dan's relief, they had managed to board without incident. As the train pulled away toward Pittsburgh, Dan saw the one of the strikers on the platform, holding his rifle aloft in triumph.

The rumor had been circulating that they were being taken to a hospital in Pittsburgh, but that did not happen. Instead, the train stopped only briefly at a city station before moving out.

As the train passed through the river towns east of Pittsburgh, Dan caught glimpses of men waiting at stations with guns and clubs. As the train approached a station, the crowd would press forward to the edge of the platform.

The train never slowed or stopped. Town after town, valley after valley, the train kept going eastward into the night, away from Pittsburgh, away from that wretched, infernal place called Homestead.

Thursday, July 7th

When the throbbing pain in his arm woke Emlyn, sunlight was flooding through the grimy window by his bed. Still in his filthy clothes from the previous day, Emlyn carefully made his way downstairs.

Eirwen was working in the kitchen as the two younger children played on the floor. When she saw him, Dilys jumped up. "Uncle Em," she said, hugging his legs. He returned the hug.

"Did you get a good sleep?" Eirwen asked. "It's nearly ten o'clock."

Emlyn leaned on the doorjamb groggily rubbing his eyes. "I must have, although I don't feel very rested."

"How's the arm?" she asked, pouring a cup of tea.

"It's hurting again. Woke me up, in fact," said Emlyn.

"Sit down and have some breakfast," she said. "I'll get a bath ready for you. We can change the dressings on the wound."

Emlyn methodically chewed his toast, washing it down with tepid tea.

"Where's Gywn?" asked Emlyn. "On patrol?"

"No, he went to John Morris's funeral. He and two other strikers are being buried today."

Emlyn covered his eyes, trying to erase the image of Morris tumbling off the roof.

"When Jim Duncan came by on his way to the funeral, he said that patrols have resumed to watch for more Pinkertons," said Eirwen.

"It's not likely that the company will try that again, given what happened yesterday," said Emlyn.

"Last night the workers cleared away the barricades and mended the broken parts of the fences, putting it back the way it was," Eirwen said, pouring a fresh cup of tea.

"It will never be the way it was," replied Emlyn.

Hearing banging at the front door, Eirwen went to answer it. She returned with a piece of paper.

"It's a telegram from Tad," she said, handing it to Emlyn.

"HEARD NEWS STOP IS FAMILY WELL?"

"O'r nefoedd! *Good heavens.* I didn't think the news would travel so fast," said Eirwen, sitting down at the table. "But when you think of it, what happened yesterday was . . ." She stared at the telegram.

"What are you going to do?" asked Emlyn. "You can't tell them I've been shot. Mam would be so worried—Not that Tad cares."

"Don't say such things," said Eirwen. "Of course Tad cares. I'm sure Gwyn's family is worried as well. I've got to send a reply or they might think the worst. I'll telegraph them that all is fine, and I'll mail them a letter with the whole story. That way they won't worry unduly."

"If I heard news of a battle like this taking place in Treorchy, I'd surely be worried," said Emlyn. "Let me clean up, and we'll go to the Western Union office."

Friday, July 8th

Oesterling was happy to come into the relative coolness of his house after going around checking on patients on this hot afternoon. He went into the back hall and poured a fresh bowl of water for Cerberus.

Sarah met him coming into the study. "Papa, I finally got to talk to Carrie on the phone. She insists that we come over and stay with them, but I told her you had to tend to patients in town. Of course, she didn't ask me to come without you."

"I'm glad you got to talk." Oesterling said, sitting down in his favorite chair. "She didn't say anything about her coming here?"

Sarah shook her head.

"Have you seen today's paper?" asked Oesterling. "There's a very ominous article about Frick's plans for Homestead."

"What did it say?"

"Frick told reporters that any striker who took up arms against the company would never be hired back," said Oesterling. "You know what that will mean for many workers, including Gwyn Jones."

Sarah lowered herself onto the settee. "That's horrible. Do you think Frick is serious?"

"Frick not serious? The article said that since Wednesday, Sheriff McCleary has sent repeated requests to the governor to send in troops. If that happens, it will be the end of the strike. The strikers might be able to stop Pinkertons, but the State militia—impossible."

"The strikers have repaired the damage from the battle and handed control of the mill back to the company. How could they sanction the use of troops?"

"As Carrie pointed out, the company still cannot get replacement workers on site. Frick will be doing everything in his power to get the mill re-opened. The law is on his side."

"Some law! What a travesty of justice," said Sarah with disgust.

Gwyn, Duncan and the other strikers were back on picket duty, convinced that Frick would be sending an even bigger contingent of Pinkertons to take over the works.

Despite the sorrow evoked by the deaths of seven workers, the mood of the strikers was positive. Gwyn returned home with stories of support pouring in from around the country, even from abroad. Other unions were threatening to stage sympathy strikes; Frick had been savaged in the press as a kind of Nero, calmly smoking his cigar while the battle raged. At Morris's funeral, the Reverend John J. McIlyar had held Frick accountable for the violence and deaths.

On the morning of the 8th, Emlyn walked over to the tenement building where he had met Lil. He carried a bouquet of daisies and small bags of coffee and chocolate to give her as thank-you gifts. A woman in the courtyard pointed out Louie and Lil's apartment. Lil was not home, but Louie accepted the gifts.

"Thank you both for getting me to safety," Emlyn said. "I'm so sorry she got injured doing it."

"She's fine. We were happy to help," Louie replied. He looked at the bags. "How did you know chocolates are her favorites?"

"A lucky guess," Emlyn replied with a grin.

That same day, Hugh O'Donnell, heading a delegation from the AA, took a train to Harrisburg to talk to Pennsylvania Governor Pattison about the situation. Hopes ran high among the workers that the Democratic official would help settle the strike for the union's benefit.

Sunday, July 10th 10:30 a.m.

Oesterling and William Williams stood by the door of the Congregational Church, handing out bulletins. Attendance was lower than usual. Men were out on patrol, and other church members were staying home because of the tense situation.

"Do you think that someone might confront you about the strike?" Oesterling asked Williams.

"I doubt it," Williams replied. "I manage production. I have nothing to do with the wage dispute."

"The company needs workers to do the production. Are they putting pressure on the mill superintendents to step in?"

Williams hesitated. He glanced into the sanctuary and took a step closer to Oesterling. "As a matter of fact," he said, lowering his voice, "they are. Yesterday I was called into Potter's office. There was a pile of money stacked on his desk, a lot, perhaps thousands."

"That's quite a sum. What was it for?"

"He wanted me to start the furnaces."

Oesterling's eyes grew wide. "What did you say to him?"

"I told him that I have to live in this town. No amount of money would entice me to do that job."

"Good for you," said Oesterling. "Potter must be desperate to get the plant running."

Williams nodded. "He's under a lot of pressure from the head office. Potter will get somebody or 'bodies to get the furnaces started. It's just not going to be me."

Tuesday, July 12th

Since word had come the previous evening that eight thousand members of the Pennsylvania militia were on their way to Homestead, the workers had been excited. Patrols were cancelled, and the strikers prepared to greet the troops.

In the morning Gwyn had gone off to be part of the welcoming committee for General Snowden. It was now six-thirty in the evening, and Gwyn had not returned.

"I wonder what's keeping Gwyn," said Eirwen, placing a stack of clean dishes in the cupboard. "They no longer have to protect against the arrival of Pinkertons now that the troops are here to do the job."

Emlyn was keeping an eye on David and Dilys playing on the stoop outside the screen door.

"I don't know," said Emlyn. "The troops have definitely arrived. You can see the glint of rifles and bayonets from their camps on Shanty Hill and on the other side of the river."

"I hope they get the men back to work soon," said Eirwen. "The AA's strike pay for the workers won't last forever."

"The non-union workers aren't even getting strike pay," said Emlyn. "The office workers won't be called back until the mill is running again."

"We will have to pinch pennies in the meantime," said Eirwen. "Thank goodness we have the vegetable garden."

Gwyn appeared in the doorway and came into the kitchen. Emlyn could smell the alcohol fumes from a few feet away.

"Gwyn!" said Eirwen. "We were wondering where you were. We've already had supper."

"I don't need supper." Gwyn pulled back a chair and sat down. "Our welcoming committee was not well received by

General Snowden. In fact, I'd say we were downright re-buffed," he said glumly.

"What happened?" Emlyn asked.

"Hughie brought three brass bands, and we were ready to give the General and his men a heroes' welcome. But when Hughie said to the General that we are peaceful, law-abiding citizens, ready to help protect the town, the General flatly said we are not. He said that we insulted the sheriff. He ended by telling us that he was master of the situation and that we were to keep out of his way."

"O'r annwyl! *O dear*," said Eirwen. "What does that mean?"

"It means that the military is now running the town," said Gwyn. "Hughie was gobsmacked. We all were. Troops are now setting up camp on both sides of the river."

"Then the troops certainly won't be keeping out Pinkertons or scabs," said Emlyn.

Gwyn nodded. "There's more bad news," he added. "Word is that arrest warrants are being issued for Hughie and the other strike leaders."

"On what charge?" asked Emlyn.

"Murder."

Eirwen gasped.

"This is supposed to be justice?" said Gwyn. "Frick sends in Pinkertons to shoot at us, and we're the ones being charged." Gwyn shook his head.

"What happened after the General turned you away?" asked Eirwen. "Did you and Duncan 'celebrate' again?"

"I wouldn't call it celebrating," said Gwyn defensively. "We went to another man's house. He had a bottle of whisky. We felt in need of a drink at that point."

"I suppose it did a world of good for your spirits," said Eirwen.

Gwyn glowered at Eirwen. "As a matter of fact, it did."

Emlyn stood up. "I think I'll go out in the yard with the children." As the screen door banged shut, he could hear Eirwen and Gwyn's angry voices behind him.

Saturday, July 16th

Until the mill furnaces were lighted the previous day, Gwyn and the other strikers had been optimistic. Many newspapers sided with the strikers, as did other unions around the country. Public opinion was on their side, Gwyn said.

When the workers had seen smoke rising from the mill stacks, they had rushed the works. However, militia soldiers with rifles and bayonets had made sure that they did not get into the site.

In late morning Charles LaCroix stopped by the house. He speculated that because some furnaces were now running, they would soon be called back to work. When Charles saw the bandage and sling on Emlyn's arm, he asked him what happened. Emlyn told him.

"You had better hide the injury when you go back to work," said Charles. "I read in the paper that Frick said that anyone who bore arms against the company will be blacklisted. I believe you, but others may not."

"I realize that," Emlyn replied. "I regret going with Gwyn for more reasons than just my getting shot. I had no idea that the situation at the landing would turn into an all-out battle."

"I doubt if anybody did—except maybe Frick," said Charles. "Anyway, I know the company is very hard-nosed about who they're re-hiring. Did you hear that they've mailed final notices to all former workers, signed by Frick himself? It says the company will be taking applications from individuals for employment until six p.m. next Friday. Any worker who took part in the battle will not be hired back. They've already started bringing in replacements."

"So I've heard," said Emlyn. "Gwyn and the others were furious when the tug that brought the Pinkertons' barges started bringing in scabs this week. They say that nearly one hundred of them are now behind the walls of Fort Frick. Still, I can't imagine how these inexperienced replacements will be able to keep the works running."

"Where there's a will, there's a way," said Charles. "And Frick certainly has the will."

Saturday, July 23rd

Emlyn had decided to take up Sarah Oesterling on her invitation to go for a ride. He was glad to be getting out of town, if only briefly. When Gwyn was home, he and Eirwen quarreled; when he was gone, Eirwen constantly fretted about what Gwyn was doing.

The strikers had had one piece of bad news after another during the week. The presence of the militia was everywhere in town. Camped on Shanty Hill overlooking the General Office Building, the militia had a good view of the mill and town. Soldiers walked the streets and surrounded the mill. As General Snowden had told O'Donnell, their job was to protect company property and to quell any violence—and this meant that the strikers were now powerless.

On Monday, McLuckie, O'Donnell and six others were charged with murder. On Tuesday, word got out that steelmaking was once again under way in the mill. On Friday, a tugboat carrying dozens of replacement workers landed at the mill site. On Saturday, another boatload arrived.

On Wednesday Emlyn had received a letter notifying

him to report to Jansen the following Monday. Emlyn was happy that by then, he would not need the sling on his arm.

Gwyn was agitated and angry. The strikers' attempt to stop the reopening of the mill had been stymied. The smoke from the stacks and the increasing noise level were constant reminders that production had resumed. Nevertheless, Gwyn and the rest of the workers were dedicated to holding out. The deadline for applying for their old jobs was yesterday. They would not be crawling back to the company. How could the mill produce any decent steel with ignorant scabs doing the work?

Avoiding the militia camp on the east side, Emlyn and Sarah rode west out of town from the livery stable. They had agreed not to talk about the strike on their ride. It was to be a pleasant escape from the tension in Homestead. However, putting the strike out of mind was easier said than done.

As they rode along West Run, Sarah pointed out various wildflowers, but they had little conversation. Emlyn tried to concentrate on the beauty of the woods and stream, but his thoughts kept slipping back to the workers.

After riding for over two hours, Emlyn and Sarah returned the horses to the stable. By then it was nearly two o'clock, and Sarah invited Emlyn to come to the house for lemonade. Only too happy to avoid going home, Emlyn accepted.

The Avenue was so different—more soldiers than shoppers. Groups of strikers were hanging around in front of the saloons. Emlyn thought he glimpsed Gwyn in the door of the pub where they had gone to celebrate his arrival. He hoped not. Things were bad enough between Gwyn and Eirwen.

The Oesterlings' house was cool inside, darkened by heavy draperies against the heat of the sun. Emlyn washed up downstairs as Sarah changed out of her riding clothes.

They sat on wicker chairs on the porch, and Mrs. Sproule

brought out cookies and lemonade. Emlyn was telling Sarah about the telegram from Wales when Dr. Oesterling with Cerberus came up the front steps and joined them.

"If you'd like," said Oesterling, "I could write your parents and tell them that you are recovering well. It may ease their worries."

"Thank you," said Emlyn. "Let's wait and see what they write."

The telephone rang and Oesterling got up to answer it. Five minutes later he came back, a stunned look on his face.

"Do you have to go out on a call again?" asked Sarah.

"That was Carrie," said Oesterling. "Frick's been shot."

"No!" gasped Sarah. "Was he killed?"

"No. According to Oliver, he's still at his office being treated."

"Who shot him?" asked Emlyn. "I hope it wasn't someone from Homestead."

"They think he's Russian," said Oesterling. "Oliver said that this man burst into Frick's private office and fired a pistol at him several times. Another man in the office and Frick wrestled him to the floor."

"Frick couldn't be that badly injured if he's still at the office," said Sarah.

"It is puzzling," said Oesterling. "At least one of the bullets hit him. That can't be good."

The three of them sat on the porch in silence. From a few blocks away came the sound of soldiers drilling at the camp on the hill.

Homestead was once again in the headlines of newspapers across the country and Europe. Frick's would-be assassin turned out to be a Russian anarchist by the name of Alexander Berkman. He had come on his own from New York City with the express purpose of killing the evil Mr. Frick. Although he was daring, he was not a competent assassin. At close range, he had managed to hit Frick only once, in the neck.

Moreover, he had underestimated Frick, who, after he'd been shot, had helped restrain Berkman, holding on tenaciously even after Berkman pulled a knife and stabbed him in the side, thigh, and leg. Frick refused morphine while the doctors worked on him for two hours probing for a bullet. He stayed on at the office after they completed treatment so he could put affairs in order before he went home.

Sunday, July 24rd

After supper Emlyn and Gwyn sat on the front porch, sharing the newspaper.

After reading the article about the assassination attempt, Gwyn crumpled the paper into his lap. "That Frick is one tough son-of-a-bitch. It's really too bad Berkman couldn't finish the job."

"It's probably a good thing he didn't kill him," said Emlyn. "It's bad enough that Frick's now getting sympathy from the public. The company would leverage his martyrdom."

"Bah!" said Gwyn. "He is the company, and he's already been made into a martyr."

"If you want to be angry with someone, be angry at Berkman," said Emlyn. "He's the one who's brought the bad press to the strikers' cause."

"Why couldn't he let well enough alone?" asked Gwyn. "Why did he come all the way from New York to shoot Frick? He has no stake in this strike."

"Haven't you heard about these anarchists?" said Emlyn. "They believe they can overthrow the capitalist system by a workers' revolution. Berkman apparently thought he could use the strike at Homestead to spark an uprising."

"Idiot!" said Gwyn. "How is there going to be an uprising with thousands of soldiers parading around town with rifles and bayonets?"

"I'd guess he wasn't thinking that far ahead," said Emlyn.

"Blasted dimwit," growled Gwyn. "Say, wasn't that a group of anarchists who came to town the day after the strike, wanting the workers to seize the mill property?"

"I hadn't heard that," said Emlyn. "What happened?"

"We threw them into jail, that's what," said Gwyn. "What makes these outsiders think they can come here and manage the strike better than the workers themselves?"

"I hesitate to say this," said Emlyn, "but it looks the one who's really managing the strike is Frick."

Gwyn's face turned red. He threw down the paper and stood up.

"Damn all of them—Frick, the anarchist prats, the bleeding militia," said Gwyn. "I'm going out."

He walked away, toward the Avenue.

The situation in Homestead was going from bad to worse for the strikers. As August approached, over one thousand workers were on the job at the mill, protected by the fence and militia. With each passing day, the volume of smoke from the stacks grew, as did the sounds of steelmaking.

On Sunday evening, the 24th, Gwyn returned home after supper, accompanied by Jim Duncan. The two of them, slightly tipsy, had locked horns with Eirwen as soon as they came to the house. Duncan had convinced Gwyn that if Emlyn returned to work, he was no better than a scab. It took all of Emlyn's powers of persuasion to convince them that his job had no impact on the outcome of the strike. The scabs were the ones taking the workers' jobs, he argued, not the office workers returning to their own jobs.

Gwyn eventually backed down, but both he and Duncan seethed with resentment over the strikers' jobs being taken away and about the sudden turn-around of public sympathy following the failed assassination attempt on Frick.

As he lay in bed that night, Emlyn had to admit to himself that he did feel guilty about returning to work. Perhaps Duncan was right. Perhaps he would be unintentionally contributing to Frick's breaking of the union. He decided to withhold judgment until he talked to Jansen.

The next morning, Emlyn passed through security at Fort Frick and reported to Jansen's office with Charles LaCroix. Jansen began by saying that because of the unfortunate situation with the strike, management had to take a fresh look at office staff. The two men's former jobs had been eliminated, but they could return in other capacities. They would be doing similar work, but not solely for the structural mill, which was now operational.

As Emlyn scanned the contract Jansen handed him, his eyes jumped to the salary clause: His wages had been slashed by $1.50 a week, to less than when he had started. Jansen gave them a day to consider the offer and dismissed them.

After the meeting, Charles invited Emlyn to his lodgings in Munhall to discuss the offer. Charles's salary had been reduced by about the same percentage as Emlyn's. "This is less than I had been making at the shipyard," he said. "Now I'm sorry I left Rhode Island."

The more they talked, the grimmer the situation appeared. "Will you accept the offer?" asked Emlyn.

Charles fingered the contract lying on the table. "Do you read the financial journals?" he asked.

"No," Emlyn replied, "but I'll bet you do."

"It's not just the Carnegie Company who is putting the screws to the workers," Charles said. "The companies are confident in the fact that the labor force exceeds the number of jobs available. For every man who walks out on strike, there are two to take his place."

"That appears to be the case in Homestead," said Emlyn. "Do you think the strike is doomed?"

Charles nodded. "I'd say the company can pretty much dictate terms. But there's something even more disturbing going on, a practice that brought the country financial collapse twenty years ago."

"What's that?" asked Emlyn, curious. "Do you think the economy could collapse?"

"It certainly could," said Charles. "Speculation is driving the rapid expansion of railroads across the country. A few people are making enormous fortunes at the expense of economic stability."

"As far as I know, the situation is similar in Britain," said Emlyn.

"It's very disturbing," said Charles. "Bankers like this overbuilding, as they also have their fingers in the pie. Even labor likes it, at least the workers building and operating the railroads do. Can't they see this an economic house of cards? In '73 similar speculation brought on a panic that crippled the country. A quarter of the banks in this country failed, and thousands were out of work."

"I read about that at university," said Emlyn. "I recall that the panic started in Europe and spread across to America."

They sat in silence, contemplating the contract.

"So," said Emlyn at last, "does this mean that you will be taking the company's offer?"

"I must," Charles replied, "although I will immediately begin looking for another position."

Emlyn thought for a moment, and said, "I suppose I will have to accept the offer because there is no option at present. It's infuriating that the people in power so easily exploit the situation, turning worker against worker."

"You sound a little like the anarchists," said Charles, "but it's true. The most ruthless are running the country. Remember the story of Cain and Abel?"

"I don't think you have to go that far back to find examples of rapaciousness," Emlyn replied.

They sat in silence for several minutes, listening to the racket coming from the mill.

"This is all very demoralizing," Emlyn said at last. "It disgusts me to think we are helpless before the greed of the company, backed by the power of the government."

"Maybe I'm being too pessimistic in my prognosis," said Charles.

"I hope so," said Emlyn, not feeling hopeful in the least.

"Come on," said Charles. "Let me buy you lunch. We can go to one of the cafes on the Avenue."

Emlyn hesitated. "I don't think we should, under the circumstances."

"It'll be fine," Charles said, jingling the coins in his pocket. "Unlike you, I have only myself to worry about."

Emlyn sighed. He had been out to eat at a proper restaurant only once since his arrival in Homestead—to celebrate Eirwen's birthday with the family in February.

"Alright, let's go," he said, placing his hands on his knees. "I'll resume worrying tomorrow."

East Liberty. July 25th, 10 p.m.

Karl Bernhard sat on the steps of his house reading another handbill being circulated by the Carnegie Company. This time he had taken it from a man who had been passing them out on Liberty Avenue.

Susanna came out of the house and sat down in the rocker. "What's that, Karl?" she asked.

"Another solicitation for workers in Homestead," he said. "It specifically calls for those skilled in firing industrial boilers. They are offering a big bonus—$15—for firemen. What do you think, Schatzi?"

"I don't know, Karl," she replied. "I hear that Homestead is a dangerous place for those taking the jobs of the strikers. The company keeps them inside the mill—not that they'd want to go into the town, anyway."

"The state militia is there," said Karl. "They've been keeping order."

"It's been less than three weeks since the battle," she said. "It would be best to wait a while longer, to see if the company can protect the new workers."

"I don't want to wait too long," said Karl. "What if they fill all the positions they need for firemen?"

"I wouldn't worry about that," said Susanna. "It's a big mill. It will take them many weeks to have it all running."

"OK, I'll wait," said Karl, "but only a week or two."

Homestead

Back at work inside the General Office Building, Emlyn was now in a large room with over a dozen workers toiling at desks lined up in two rows. The worst of it was that this room was down the hall from the office where Norton Montague worked. Emlyn braced for a confrontation, but Montague studiously ignored him whenever their paths crossed.

As Emlyn went about his work, he was taken aback at the bungling going on in the attempts to get the works fully operational. The replacement workers were largely ignorant of the process of producing finished steel, requiring managers and engineers to provide instruction as they went. Throughout the mill, steelmaking was a comedy of errors, an on-the-job training program of enormous proportions. Nevertheless, more workers were being brought in daily by river, and very slowly, production was resuming piecemeal at the works.

Friday, July 29th

At the end of the workday, Jansen asked Emlyn to step into his office.

"Please close the door," said Jansen, sitting down at his desk.

Emlyn did so, and stood, waiting for Jansen to speak.

"Superintendent Potter's office received a report that you participated in the violence against the Pinkertons," said Jansen. "I've been asked to investigate this alleged illegal conduct."

"It's true that I was at the landing during the battle, but as an observer only," replied Emlyn.

Jansen picked up a paper on his desk. "The report says that you received a gunshot wound while shooting at the barges. Is this true?"

"I did get shot, but I never picked up a gun, let alone fired it," said Emlyn.

"Where were you? You must have been close enough to the action to have received an injury," said Jansen.

Emlyn shifted his weight. "When the fighting started, I went onto the roof of the pump house. I did not have a gun or any other weapon. After John Morris was killed, I wanted to leave, but the battle was too heated. I was hit by a ricochet as I was sitting down, waiting for the firing to stop."

"Were there witnesses to this?" asked Jansen.

"Yes, sir, there were, but I cannot name them," said Emlyn.

Jansen set down the paper and leaned back in his chair. "I understand why you do not want to name the witnesses, but do you realize your job may be at stake? In fact, you could possibly be charged with murder."

"I don't know who filed this report," said Emlyn, "but I know for certain he was not a witness to this event. If he had been there, he would know that I had tried to convince others to leave as well. The company will have to decide whom to believe, the one making these allegations or myself."

"I see," said Jansen. "I'll send a report back to Potter's office after I do more investigating. I'll let you know what they decide."

After Emlyn was dismissed, Charles LaCroix was called in to Jansen's office. Emlyn fiddled around with papers on his desk, waiting for Charles to emerge. After a few minutes, Charles came out. "Let's walk out together," he said quietly.

"I guess you know what that was about," said Charles as they left the building. "I said I knew nothing about your participation in the battle. What did you tell him?"

"I told him what I told you—the truth," said Emlyn.

"Who would be so nasty as to try to get you fired?"

"I can think of only one such person," Emlyn replied. "He works in the comptroller's office."

"Good God, Emlyn, what did you do to make him so vindictive?" asked Charles.

Emlyn considered the question for a moment. "I rode a horse after it had thrown him," he replied.

Charles looked at Emlyn, astonished. Despite themselves, they both burst out laughing.

Sunday, July 31st

The day had started out badly. Gwyn had been out late the night before. Eirwen and Emlyn were in the kitchen, finishing breakfast when he came down. As Gwyn ate, Eirwen asked him what had happened to the food money she kept in one of the kitchen tins. The previous day, she was going to take out a little to buy a few things and found the tin empty.

At first, Gwyn turned beet-red and did not answer. Eirwen stood over him, her arms folded. At last he admitted he had taken it.

"Why?" asked Eirwen.

Gwyn's tapped his foot nervously as he looked at the plate in front of him, but he did not reply.

Eirwen stared at him hard. "I see. You took it for a 'celebration' with Duncan and the boys."

"It wasn't like that," said Gwyn. "Duncan had been buying meals and drinks for us, and it was my turn to treat."

"It was your turn to treat, was it?" exclaimed Eirwen. "You took money for your family's food to buy drinks for your worthless friends!"

"Don't worry," said Gwyn. "I'll be getting strike pay from the AA next week."

"What are we going to do in the meantime?" asked Eirwen. "The merchants are getting leery of giving credit to strikers' families, now that mill production has resumed.

I've been skimping on food purchases, trying to stretch what money we'd put away, and now we have nothing."

"Stop bothering me, woman," said Gwyn, getting up from the table. "I told you I'd make it right." He pushed past her and opened the screen door.

"Where are you going?" asked Eirwen. "It's almost time to leave for church."

"I'm not going to church," said Gwyn, stepping out the door. "I'm going out." He walked off before she could say anything.

"What am I going to do?" Eirwen wailed, collapsing into a chair. "The longer this strike goes on, the crazier Gwyn acts."

Emlyn reached across the table and squeezed her hand. "Don't worry," he said. "I'll be bringing in some money, and the union will be giving strike pay, as Gwyn said." Emlyn was glad he hadn't mentioned anything to her about Montague shopping him at work. She had enough worries as it was.

He decided to go to church with her. After talking with Griffiths, his attitude had changed. His quarrel was with his father, not the church. Besides, he had enjoyed meeting new people at the picnic and seeing those he already knew. Finally, it made him feel good to see Eirwen's face light up when he told her.

An hour later the five of them were sitting the third pew on the left, listening to Griffiths' sermon, or at least Eirwen was. Emlyn's thoughts wandered to Gwyn, to the threat to his job, to the strike. He almost forgot where he was.

When they sang the hymns, he was surprised to find that singing them felt comfortable, almost as if he had never been away. Mostly, he was happy to feel part of a community again.

To Eirwen's distress, a few people asked where Gwyn

was. The strike was putting enormous stress on social interaction in the town. Some strikers were talking about going back to work. Violent arguments, even fistfights, were breaking out between these workers and devoted unionists. What used to be a united front was no longer united.

After the service, some church members came over to greet Emlyn. The last of these were Oesterling and William Williams.

"How is it going at the office?" asked Williams.

"It's been fine," Emlyn replied, "except, you know, for production."

Williams nodded grimly. "Yes, I know."

Emlyn hesitated. He decided to plunge in. Emlyn told Williams about being called in by Jansen. He related the story of his gunshot wound as he had told the others.

"I hadn't realized that you were at the landing," said Williams. He turned to Oesterling. "Were you aware of this?"

"Yes," said Oesterling. "In fact, I treated him at the office."

"Who in the world would go to such lengths to get you fired?" Williams asked Emlyn.

"I know who," interjected Oesterling. "Norton Montague." Even saying the name was distasteful. "He probably saw Emlyn when he came by my office the day of the battle."

"The fellow who has been at your dinner parties, the one at the comptroller's office?" asked Williams.

"The same," said Oesterling.

"He took a disliking to me from the beginning," said Emlyn. "It's rather a long story."

"That doesn't give him license to bear false witness," said Williams. "Let me know if you need me to corroborate your account."

Emlyn saw Eirwen coming down the aisle toward them.

"Thank you very much," he said in a low voice, adding,

"Please don't say anything to my sister. She has enough worries already."

—•••—

As he walked home after church, Oesterling could barely contain his exasperation. However, as he could hardly tell Sarah the whole story, he struggled to calm himself. At the least, he was going to make sure that Montague never set foot in his house again.

Later that day, word spread that over 400 strikebreakers had attended services inside the mill, protected by 150 guards.

Monday, August 1st

After worrying all weekend about losing his job and possibly being charged with murder, Emlyn's meeting with Jansen turned out to be anti-climactic. As Emlyn was preparing to leave for home, he saw Jansen in the hallway.

Without bothering to call Emlyn into his office, Jansen said that management was satisfied with his report and that Emlyn was to stay on the job. Jansen made no effort to conceal his annoyance at having to deal with this distraction from his job.

On the way home from work, Emlyn saw men throwing a family's household goods and furniture into the street in front of a house half a block away from theirs on Third Avenue. The wife and five children stood outside the front door crying, while the husband, restrained by two policeman, screamed curses at the men. As Emlyn passed by, the husband was loaded into a paddy wagon and taken away.

When he got home, Eirwen told him that a striker's family lived there, and the Carnegie Company, which owned the house, was using sheriff's deputies to forcibly evict them. The next-door neighbor had told her that more than a dozen other families in company housing had been unceremoniously thrown out of their homes, left in the street with their belongings.

Wednesday, August 3rd

The press reported that Frick's infant son, born on the day of the battle, had died. The Fricks had lost a seven-year-old daughter the year before. Because of these tragedies, public sympathy for Frick swelled.

The situation with strikers was growing worse. Although workers went out on sympathy strikes at the Duquesne and Beaver Falls steelworks, these had ended in a matter of days. Production was gradually increasing. Protected by the militia, by the middle of the month hundreds of replacement workers were being lodged inside the mill. The strikers were coming to realize that they had won the battle, but were losing the war.

To the chagrin of the Amalgamated leaders, Burgess McLuckie had been making anti-tariff speeches. When Hugh O'Donnell made an attempt to dissuade McLuckie from speaking out on this issue, McLuckie flatly refused. And so another rift formed among the striking workers.

Sandlot, East Liberty. Sunday, August 7th

George Bernhard and Hans Wagner sat on the bench, waiting their turns at bat.

"How are things with your Pa?" asked Hans. "I hear that he found a job."

"Yep, he just started as a fireman at the Homestead Works," said George.

"I'll bet your ma is happy," said Hans.

"She's happy he found a job, but not that job," replied George. "The pay is very good, but there's a lot of agitated strikers wanting to get their hands on the replacements. Pa has to stay inside the mill. It's too dangerous outside in town."

Hans nodded. "Yeah, it's tough. Do you know Bill Weigand, the pitcher? His pa took a job at Homestead, too. He said it was better than working in the mines."

"My pa would agree with that," said George. "He almost punched me when I suggested it."

"Well, either way, it's dangerous," said Hans, sadly shaking his head. "Would you rather be buried in a cave-in or attacked by a mob?"

"Neither," said George. "I'd rather be playing ball."

"Me, too," said Hans, punching his shortstop's mitt.

Homestead

Gwyn spent every day away from the house. After each of the Amalgamated's solidarity meetings, Gwyn would emerge reassured that the mill could not be run without the strikers. However, this confidence was short-lived. Most days when he came home, usually after dinner, he was taciturn and smelled of liquor.

He either quarreled with Eirwen, or they ignored each other. If he had received strike pay, he never spoke of it or gave any to Eirwen. Emlyn's meager salary was going for food to augment the produce from the garden. Meals became cheaper and smaller, as Eirwen tried to stretch their dwindling resources.

At least they had food. Many strikers were nearing the end of their reserves. Emlyn heard talk of some returning to the mill, while others considered leaving Homestead for greener pastures.

When Emlyn came down for breakfast on the morning of the 20th, he found Eirwen weeping, her face in her hands. She had gone into the back garden to pick tomatoes and had found all the vegetables gone. Someone had come during the night and taken everything above ground. Only the potatoes and a few carrots remained.

"Who could be so vile as to take food from a family?" she sobbed.

Emlyn didn't know what to say. The theft was proof of how desperate the situation was getting for the strikers.

When Emlyn came home that evening, Eirwen told him how Gwyn flew into a rage when he found the vegetables gone. Without saying a word, he opened the shed and took out the rifle, examined it, and put it back. Then he took out a spade, dug up the carrots and potatoes, and put them in the root cellar. After that, he left the house.

Monday, August 15th

Karl Bernhard checked the pressure gauge on the boiler. It was ungodly hot working around the boilers and furnaces, but not much hotter than what he had experienced on the U.S.S. Gunboat Hale. The company had put out another call for workers experienced with firing boilers, and he had answered.

When he had boarded the *Little Bill* to cross the river to the Homestead Works last Monday, he didn't know what to expect. The mill turned out to be bigger—much bigger—than he had anticipated. The company had wanted him nearly as much as the U.S. Navy had when, as a new immigrant in 1863, he had told them that he had worked as a fireman in a brewery in Germany.

The Age of Steam had been going at full bore ever since. Nearly every piece of machinery in the Homestead Works, including the furnaces, required the power of a steam boiler. The Carnegie Company sorely needed men like him to get the mill up to speed and keep it running, and they were willing to pay for his expertise.

He had been at work for over a week now, and found it demanding, but satisfying. The foreman had put him in charge of a crew of four that was firing boilers throughout the mill. The other men had little or no experience as firemen, but they were eager and attentive to his directions, glad to have the work.

Karl didn't much like having to stay in the mill overnight, but he had no choice. The company was boarding the replacement workers inside the walls of Fort Frick for their safety. Beyond the whitewashed fence were hundreds of angry and disgruntled strikers, so he must bide his time until he could come and go as he liked. For the time being, he had to be content with being ferried back across the Monongahela to spend Saturday nights at the house in East Liberty.

"We're not quite there," he yelled to the men. He wiped the sweat off his brow with his sleeve. "Let's get more coal into the box," he said, picking up a shovel and moving to the firebox door. The men took their shovels and began throwing chunks of anthracite into the conflagration.

Saturday, August 27th

The day was warm and sultry. Emlyn threw his suit coat over his shoulder as he walked home along the Avenue. He was dismayed at how few shoppers were in the stores, compared to the crowds that used to go out on Saturdays before the strike. The saloons and brothels were losing business as well. Many of the streetwalkers who used to hang around the mill at the turn of shift had left town, as most of their potential customers never left the works.

The strikers were growing more desperate and feeling more helpless with every passing day. At work Emlyn had heard that most strikers' families who rented company housing had been evicted, forced to move in with friends or relatives, or move on. Rumor had it that the company was seizing these properties to rent to scabs.

After dinner Emlyn played ball with Thomas and his friends—minus the boy whose father had gone back to work in the mill. The strikers' sons would have nothing to do with the son of a scab.

Flashes of lightning lit up the western sky as Emlyn returned home at dusk. He joined Eirwen reading in the parlor. A half hour later, the sound of thunder rumbled in the distance, and a stiff breeze raked at the curtains on the front windows. Eirwen was shutting the windows when someone came to door. It was a Western Union messenger.

"It's another telegram from Tad. What could this be about?" said Eirwen, ripping open the envelope.

As soon as she read it, she shrieked and collapsed onto her knees. "O'r arswyd! *Horrors!*" she cried. Alarmed, Emlyn helped her up and onto the sofa.

"What does it say?" he asked. Eirwen handed him the telegram. "There's been a pit explosion at Ton du," she sobbed. "John has been killed."

Emlyn read the telegram. "Such terrible news," he said.

"What will Gwyn do when he sees this?" cried Eirwen. "It will be more than he can bear."

Emlyn sat next to her and put his arms around her. She abandoned herself to her grief, gasping between sobs.

Emlyn understood her fear. John Jones was Gwyn's younger brother who worked as a miner at Park Slip colliery near Ton du. Gwyn was already behaving erratically.

"You'll have to be very careful how you tell Gwyn," said Emlyn at last.

"Tell me what?"

Emlyn looked up. There stood Gwyn in the doorway to the kitchen. Eirwen looked at Gwyn, too terrified to speak.

"Tell me what?" Gwyn repeated.

Emlyn stood up. "I'm afraid there is some bad news."

Gwyn laughed mirthlessly, "What other kind is there these days?"

The smell of whisky hung heavily in the air.

"This bad news is from Wales," said Emlyn, holding out the telegram. "I'm so sorry to tell you this. John has been killed in an explosion at the slip."

The smile disappeared from Gwyn's face. He stared at Emlyn, snatching away the telegram. He read the telegraph several times, not believing his eyes.

"No!" Gwyn said in an anguished cry. He tore the telegram to shreds. He glanced around the room wildly, and went into the kitchen. Eirwen and Emlyn followed him. Gwyn picked up a teacup and hurled it against the wall. He swept a stack of dishes from the table onto the floor. "Myn diawl i! *The devil!*"

"Gwyn, please," said Eirwen. She went to him and put her hand on his arm.

"Why did John have to die?" cried Gwyn. "Isn't it enough that the strike is turning out badly? Why has God abandoned us?"

"God hasn't abandoned us," said Eirwen. "We still have each other."

"What good am I to you and the children? My work has been taken from me," said Gwyn, shrugging off her hand. He went to the pantry, reached to the top shelf, and took out the key to the shed.

"Please, Gwyn. Let's sit down and talk," said Eirwen. "I'll make some tea and . . ." Pushing past her, Gwyn went out the back door.

"Gwyn, come back!' Eirwen cried, pursuing him into the yard.

Overhead, a bolt of lightning zigzagged to the top of a mill smokestack, momentarily lighting up the back yard. Fear surged through Emlyn as he saw Gwyn go to the shed and unlock the door. A few raindrops spattered onto the dirt. Gwyn threw open the shed door and told hold of the rifle.

"Stop!" Emlyn commanded. As Gwyn reached into the box of bullets, Emlyn seized his arm. "What do you think you're doing? This rifle isn't going to solve anything."

"Get away from me," snarled Gwyn, wrenching free of Emlyn's grasp. The rain began to pick up.

"For God's sake, Gwyn!" Emlyn shouted, grabbing onto the rifle. Gwyn dug an elbow into Emlyn's ribs, but Emlyn held fast. Gwyn lifted the rifle, and pushing Emlyn against the shed, pressed the barrel against Emlyn's throat. Emlyn tried to push away the barrel from his windpipe. Gwyn pressed harder.

Lightning forked the sky overhead, followed by a tremendous clap of thunder.

Eirwen screamed, "For God's sake, stop before someone gets hurt!"

Emlyn struggled to breathe as Gwyn pinned him against the wall of the shed. In desperation, Emlyn lifted his knee as hard as he could into Gwyn's groin. Gwyn groaned and doubled over as Emlyn gasped for air.

"Sod off!" Gwyn coughed. "It's my gun."

Eirwen rushed over to Gwyn. Eyes rolling crazily, he struck her in the face. She lost her balance and fell backward into the dirt.

"No!" she cried, struggling to get up.

The men stood facing each other as the rain burst forth. Emlyn strained to see through the downpour.

Once again, Gwyn grabbed for the gun. A few weeks earlier Emlyn would have had no chance of besting Gwyn, but the liquor and lack of daily physical exertion had taken their toll. Emlyn gave the stock a twist and it slipped from Gwyn's hands. Head lowered, Gwyn lunged at Emlyn. As Emlyn jumped aside, the butt of the rifle struck Gwyn hard in the shoulder. Gwyn fell heavily sideways, his face scraping into the gravel.

"O Lord, Gwyn!" exclaimed Eirwen, stooping beside him. When she touched him, he moved and moaned softly. A flash of lightning revealed rivulets of rainwater mingling with blood running down the side of his face. Gwyn slowly sat up and tried to push himself off the ground. But when Eirwen tried to help him, he shoved her aside.

"Get away from me, damn you," he said, staggering to his feet.

He faced Emlyn. "Give me the gun," he demanded.

The rain was now a deluge, pounding a loud tattoo on the rooftops.

"Are you out of your mind?" said Emlyn. "Come inside out of the rain."

Gwyn glared at him for a moment.

"Go to hell!" he shouted. Abruptly, he turned and staggered out of view behind the shed.

Emlyn dropped the gun and ran after him into the alley. He looked up and down, but the darkness and the downpour made it impossible to see more than several feet. He ran toward the mill, stopping at McClure Street. Sheets of rain obscured every view. Emlyn turned back, splashing through the small torrents running down the alley into the drainage ditch.

By the time he reached the house, he was soaked to the skin. Eirwen was waiting by the shed, peering into the rain.

"Did you see where he went?" she shouted over the deluge.

"I'm sorry," said Emlyn, shaking his head. "He could have gone in any direction."

Lightning high in the clouds briefly illuminated Eirwen's face, contorted in anguish.

"O'r Mawredd! O *Lord!*" cried Eirwen, as the ensuing thunder rolled down the valley.

—•●•—

For the next hour, Eirwen alternately wept and prayed. "What has gotten into him?" she asked repeatedly, not expecting an answer. Finally, exhausted, she fell asleep.

Emlyn fetched the rifle from where he'd left it in the kitchen. He put on his slicker, concealing the gun under it. Although it was after midnight, the militia was always on duty. Only three regiments of infantry remained after the others left town at the end of July, but there were more than enough soldiers around to patrol the town. He didn't want to be stopped carrying a weapon.

Emlyn pulled up his hood and stepped into the rain. Splashing through muddy puddles in the dark, he walked toward the riverbank. Off in the distant east, pulses of light showed intermittently through the clouds. Behind the tall fence of the steel works, the furnaces gave off a hot glow.

He walked by the tenement where he had listened to the black man singing the night before the battle. He glanced into the dark, deserted yard.

Oh there'll be signs and wonders, oh there'll be signs and wonders

He shuddered. Turning toward the river, Emlyn passed two soldiers trying unsuccessfully to keep dry under the railroad trestle over the approach to the ferry landing. They exchanged brief greetings, and he continued to the water's edge. This was where the violence had begun on the day of the battle. He looked around. Unlike on that July day, no one was on the landing. The only sounds were the rain splashing onto the earth and the booms and crashes coming from the mill. He walked slowly downriver, the mud clutching at his boots with each step.

When he reached the landing, he scrambled up the slippery bank using the rifle to steady himself. He fell twice, but eventually made it to the top of the bank. There, for a long moment, he stood watching the black river flowing past. Then he raised the rifle and threw it with all his might into the dark, swirling waters. It made a small splash and vanished.

Oh there'll be signs and wonders, when this world comes to an end

He looked from the river to the mill, and felt overcome with despair. The smoke from the mill stacks, visible in the garish light from molten steel, billowed skyward.

V.

"Man's inhumanity to man" is not the last word. The truth lies deeper. It is economic slavery, the savage struggle for a crumb, that has converted mankind into wolves and sheep.

—Alexander Berkman, *Prison Memoirs of an Anarchist* (1912)

Sunday, August 28th

Gwyn did not return that night, or the next morning. Emlyn went out at first light, starting at the riverbank and criss-crossing the lower part of the town in search of Gwyn. He found no trace.

At breakfast, Dilys asked Eirwen where Daddy was. Eirwen said that he had taken a trip.

"I heard you in the back yard last night," said Thomas. "Dad was yelling. He said a lot of bad words."

Eirwen, startled, replied, "Yes, well, he was upset. He just needs to be away for a while."

"He sounded really mad," said Thomas. "Doesn't he like us anymore?"

Eirwen pulled him into an embrace.

"Hush, Thomas," she said soothingly. "Of course he loves us."

As she stroked Thomas's hair, Emlyn saw the pain in her eyes.

Eirwen had considered staying at the house to wait for Gwyn, but after this exchange with the children, she decided it would only upset them more. The five of them tramped through the muddy streets and took their places in the family pew. Eirwen was distracted, uncharacteristically fidgeting through the service. Emlyn's bruised throat, concealed by a high collar, throbbed with pain.

After the service Griffiths took Emlyn aside. "Don't take this wrong, but I have a proposal that I hope you'll consider."

"Of course," Emlyn said. "What is it?"

"I must go to Scranton tomorrow. My wife's mother is gravely ill, and we need to go to her."

Emlyn contemplated Griffiths, wondering how this might involve him.

"You see, I need someone to lead service next week. The retired minister who usually fills in for me is out of town himself. Would you take my place? The stipend isn't much, but to that I would add my gratitude. I know you're more than qualified."

Emlyn blinked. This is not what he had expected.

"I don't . . . er, this is rather overwhelming," he said. "Could I think about it and give you my answer later this afternoon?"

"Certainly," said Griffiths. "Stop by the house. I appreciate your considering it."

"There's something else I'd like to discuss," said Emlyn, glancing about to see if anyone was in earshot. He then told Griffiths about the telegram and Gwyn's disappearance, leaving out the part about the fight over the gun.

"Gwyn will probably be there when you get home," Griffiths said.

"I hope you're right," said Emlyn.

"If he hasn't returned by the time I get back from Scranton," Griffiths added, "I'll check into it."

Emlyn waited until after Sunday dinner to tell Eirwen about Griffths' request. She was thrilled, as he knew she would be.

"Emlyn, that's wonderful!" she exclaimed. "You are going to do it, aren't you?"

Emlyn hesitated. "It's rather short notice. I'm not sure I'm up to the task."

Eirwen seized Emlyn's arms with both hands. "Don't tell me you won't do it!"

Emlyn shook his head. "I don't know. It's been months since I made the decision to leave the path to the ministry. Tad thinks . . ."

"Tad has nothing to do with this," Eirwen said earnestly. "This is your opportunity to speak for yourself, speak to the congregation. Surely your perspective has changed since you arrived from Wales."

Emlyn closed his eyes, thinking about his work, the battle, the Pinkertons, the army camped outside of town, and most of all, about Gwyn and Eirwen.

"You're right," he said. "I'll accept."

It was worth it, he thought, if only to see the light in Eirwen's eyes and a smile on her face.

An hour later, as he walked to the Griffiths' house, he passed by the tenement where he had heard the man singing. What did the 'signs and wonders' signify? Did these signs mean the end of the world, as the song seemed to suggest? It must have felt that way to many others in dark times.

No, he decided, it wasn't the end of the great world. But it was the end of Homestead as the residents had known it.

The Monday paper carried an article about the disaster at the Park Slip colliery in Ton du, South Wales. As the miners had changed shifts on Saturday morning, there had been an explosion deep inside the mine. The large blast could be heard from a distance of several miles. Rescuers had repeatedly tried to reach the miners, but had been hampered by the presence of gases as well as rubble from the explosion. On Sunday morning, the authorities had decided to discontinue rescue attempts. 110 men and boys had died.

When Emlyn came home from work, he found Eirwen with the newspaper in her lap, sitting on the back stoop, weeping. Any residual joy she had felt anticipating Emlyn taking the pulpit had been erased by the full story from Ton du.

"It's bad enough to lose John," she said, anger pushing through grief. "Why do we have to lose Gwyn as well? Where could he be?"

"He'll come home soon," Emlyn said, sitting next to her and putting an arm around her. "If he doesn't, we'll file a report with the police."

Later that evening, Sarah stopped by the house carrying a hymnal while Eirwen was upstairs putting the children to bed. Emlyn invited Sarah into the parlor. She took a seat on the sofa while Emlyn sat down opposite her in Gwyn's armchair.

"Reverend Griffiths told me that he was going to ask you to conduct the service next Sunday. I'm glad you accepted," she said. "We should decide on the hymns. Do you know what text the sermon will be on?"

"I do," Emlyn replied, reaching for the Bible next to the chair. "It's James 1:2-4." He flipped through to a marked page and read aloud:

> My brethren, count it all joy when ye fall into divers temptations; Knowing this, that the trying of your faith worketh patience. But let patience have her perfect work, that ye may be perfect and entire, wanting nothing.

Sarah listened closely. "What attracted you to this verse?" she asked.

Emlyn considered the question for a moment before offering his explanation. These first verses of the epistle resonated with him. Paradoxically, the congregation—'brethren'—should be happy when faced with trials of faith. This testing of faith produces patience—*hupomone* in the Greek—steadfastness, constancy, endurance. Difficult times call for perseverance, which in the end will bring spiritual wholeness and maturity. "We are strengthened by enduring these trials to the end," he concluded.

Sarah nodded. "So James is writing about spiritual tests in hard times. That is something many in the congregation know about," she said solemnly. She opened the hymnal and paged through it. "I think this hymn would suit perfectly," she said at last, passing the book to Emlyn.

"Ah, yes," said Emlyn, glancing at the page. "Good choice."

They heard Eirwen's footsteps coming down from the second floor. Coming into the parlor, she said, "Hello, Sarah. I thought I heard someone come in. Are you choosing music for the service this Sunday?"

"That's right," said Emlyn. He handed the hymnal to Eirwen.

Her eyes quickly scanned the page, and looking up at Sarah, she said, "Isn't it wonderful that Emlyn will be preaching?"

Sarah agreed.

"I love this hymn," said Eirwen pensively, and without prompting, began to sing softly:

Nid wy'n gofyn bywyd moethus,
I seek not life's ease and pleasures,

Aur y byd na'i berlau mân:
Early riches, pearls or gold.

Gofyn wyf am galon hapus,
Give to me a heart made happy,

Calon onest, calon lân.
Clean and honest to unfold.

On the chorus, Emlyn joined in.

Calon lân yn llawn daioni,
A clean heart o'erflowed with goodness,

Tecach yw na'r lili dlos:
Fairer than the lily bright:

Dim ond calon lân all ganu-
A clean heart forever singing-

Canu'r dydd a chanu'r nos.
Singing through the day and night.

"That was so lovely," said Sarah. "Please, Eirwen, would you sing it solo as an anthem?"

"Of course," said Eirwen. "It would be my pleasure."

Although Eirwen was smiling, her eyes were glistening with tears.

—•••—

Gwyn did not come home the next day either, and prodded by Eirwen, Emlyn went to the police station. Emlyn gave the sergeant on duty Gwyn's name and address. While the officer filled out the form, Emlyn asked what the likelihood was of locating Gwyn.

"We've received over a dozen of these reports of men going missing in the last month," the sergeant replied. "The likelihood is that if we do locate the person, it's bad news for the family."

"Bad in what way?" asked Emlyn.

"You know, to identify the body," said the officer. "The best course is to get out the word to everyone who knew . . . I mean, knows him."

Emlyn left the station thankful that he had filed the report by himself. On the way home, he stopped by Jim Duncan's house, but Duncan was not there.

"He's probably down at the saloon," said his wife, jerking her thumb toward the Avenue. "Have you tried there?"

Emlyn started to tell her about Gwyn's disappearance, but she shut the door in his face. He walked to the Avenue to check the drinking establishments. After looking into four pubs, he went into the one they had visited his first day in town.

Jim Duncan and Harry Smith were at the bar. They expressed concern when Emlyn told them about Gwyn. Duncan said Gwyn hadn't been at the saloon since Saturday evening. They were planning to stop by to ask about him, Duncan said. Emlyn thanked them and started for the door.

He met Virgil coming in.

"How have you been?" asked Emlyn.

"Just fine and dandy," Virgil said with mock cheerfulness. "It's been such great free time, being on strike without pay—but I guess you wouldn't know about that."

As Virgil pushed past him, Emlyn, realizing the futility of a reply, held his tongue.

—•●•—

As he walked to and from the Carnegie Steel offices each day, Emlyn grew increasingly uneasy. The morning walks weren't so bad, but coming home, Emlyn passed through knots of idle men on the Avenue, on the porches of the boarding houses, in front of the saloons. Although Emlyn knew they would not mistake him for a scab, the fact that there were so many out of work discomfited him.

Putting aside worries about the strikers, each night after work, Emlyn worked on the sermon. This was his chance to express his thoughts on his crisis of faith and the trials now before the town. On Thursday he asked for Saturday off, and Jansen granted it—without pay.

Charles asked why he was taking the day off and was stunned when Emlyn said he was leading service Sunday.

"Good God, Emlyn," he said. "I didn't realize that you are a minister!"

"I am not a minister," said Emlyn. "I finished seminary, but I have not accepted a call from a congregation."

"Well, I'll be!" said Charles. "You know, my maternal grandfather was a Congregational minister back in Rhode Island."

Now it was Emlyn's turn to be surprised.

"You're preaching at the Congregational church, the one on Fifth?" Charles asked.

Emlyn nodded.

"I'll be there to hear you," said Charles. "While I admit to not attending church since I've been in town, this is a good reason to go."

"I hope you won't be disappointed," said Emlyn.

"As long as you don't preach on the evils of drinking wine, I won't."

"Good," said Emlyn. "No fear of that."

Friday, September 2nd

Karl Bernhard directed the final loading of the coal in the firebox of one of the steam boilers in O.H. 2. Mel, one of the crew, threw in a final shovelful, and closed the door.

Karl watched the pressure rise in the gauge on the side of the boiler. After lighting a dozen boilers a day, his crew was getting good at it. He mopped his brow. Stepping back from the boiler, he closed his eyes. He felt exhausted. Maybe he was getting too old for this kind of work.

He opened his eyes and glanced over at the pressure gauge. He blinked a couple of times, thinking he was misreading the gauge. But no, the pressure had shot up into the red part of the dial, far above safe levels.

Frantically waving his hands, he shouted, "Get back!" to his crew. They looked at him, puzzled. Suddenly, there was a loud hiss, followed by a blinding flash. Karl was sent flying backward, propelled by an explosive force. Searing pain wracked his body.

"What had gone wrong?" he asked himself as his thoughts dissolved into blackness.

Emlyn received a letter from his university friend Gareth Morgan, saying that he was currently in Wilkes-Barre visiting an uncle. He hoped to visit Emlyn before assuming pastoral duties in Johnstown.

He and Jane had been wed in Cardiff on August 19th. Two weeks later, Gareth had traveled by steamship to Philadelphia, sending their trunks on to Johnstown. His bride would follow in a few weeks, after he had set up home in the parsonage.

Gareth was eager to see Emlyn again and to deliver a package from Emlyn's parents. He suggested that before going to Johnstown, he might come to Homestead on the third weekend of September.

Deciding to defer telling Gareth about Gwyn, Emlyn wrote a brief reply, extending an invitation to Gareth to come visit. He closed by telling Gareth of his leading the service in Homestead the coming weekend.

Sunday, September 3rd

Emlyn was already dressed in his good black suit and sitting at the kitchen table when Eirwen came down at seven to prepare breakfast.

"Good morning. I see you're already dressed and ready to go," she said, squeezing his shoulders from behind.

"I didn't sleep well," he said. "Until last night I'd been too busy to worry much. Then it sunk in. I'm going to be preaching today. I keep wondering what Tad would think, if he knew."

"You concern yourself far too much about Tad," Eirwen said. She blew on the kindling in the stove firebox, and shoved in a small log. "Besides, I already sent a letter to Treorchy with the news."

"You did?" Emlyn exclaimed, half-accusingly. "Why?"

"I mailed it yesterday," she said. "I considered writing them about Gwyn going missing, but decided to send good news instead. Lord knows they need something positive after this tragedy in Ton du." Stifling a sob, she turned to poke at the fire.

"If Gwyn doesn't return soon," Emlyn said, "you will have to write them and his family about it."

"Yes," said Eirwen in a small voice. "I know."

9:42 A.M.

Emlyn sat in the minister's study, trying to collect his thoughts. He regretted offering to do this. He had no right to preach to these people. He had decided more than a year ago that he couldn't put on the cloth. What was he thinking plunging into this? Hearing a noise, he looked up. Sarah was standing at the open study door.

"I'm about to start the prelude," she said. "Do you have any questions before we begin the service?"

Emlyn stood up and straightened his waistcoat. "No, I'm ready," he lied.

Twenty minutes later, Emlyn felt light-headed as he entered the sanctuary. During the opening hymn, he scanned the sanctuary. Half of the pews were filled.

The first part of the service went by in a blur. As he came to the pulpit to deliver the sermon, his hands began shaking. He clenched the top of the pulpit and surveyed the congregation.

He noted the Williamses, the doctor, and Charles sitting in the pews, waiting for him to begin. His eyes lighted on

Eirwen, smiling up at him. "*A clean heart, forever singing*..." A strange calm came over him.

He cleared his throat and began to speak.

—•●•—

Later that afternoon, Emlyn met Sarah at the stables to take Dee and Figaro for a ride up Streets Run. For the first time in many weeks, he was happy.

He had felt exhilarated after the service. His sermon had been well received, although some people expressed surprise—pleasant surprise—at his taking the pulpit. Charles grinned as he came up to shake his hand. "Well done! I wish Jansen's little 'sermons' at work were half as inspirational."

Eirwen's solo on 'Calon Lan' was beautiful, her voice warm with emotion. She was delighted to hear him preach, but also upset that Gwyn was not there. No one at church that day yet knew the secret of Gwyn's disappearance. Everyone assumed that Gwyn was off on union business, as were many of those absent from service.

As they rode along the creek, Emlyn told Sarah about Gareth Morgan's impending visit.

"That's wonderful that you will get to see your friend again, after nearly a year," she said. "He will be surprised to hear that you preached today, I'm sure."

"I am looking forward to seeing him," said Emlyn, "and I would like to hear how he came to accept a call in Johnstown."

They rode in silence for a few minutes, and then Sarah pulled Dee up before a pool in the creek and slid off. Emlyn watched the water swirl around the horses' legs as they drank from the stream.

"Do you think Gareth would like to meet Reverend Griffiths?" asked Sarah.

Emlyn thought about it. "He might. Gareth seems very interested in learning about the ministry in America."

"Then plan on coming to our house for dinner on the Saturday of his visit. I'll invite the Griffiths, and I know Papa would be interested in meeting your friend, too. Of course, Eirwen, Gwyn and the children are invited also."

Emlyn looked down. "Thank you for the invitation," he said. How was he going to handle this?

"Sarah, I . . . er . . . ," he said. "I need to tell you something."

Sarah looked at him in alarm. "What's wrong?"

"Gwyn's gone missing," he said hesitantly. "It's been over a week now." He then poured out the story of the cable, the gun, and the fight.

"I'd heard about Gwyn's brother," said Sarah. "So tragic. But I can hardly believe that Gwyn attacked you. It seems so out of character."

"Extreme grief does terrible things to some men, not to mention alcohol. Eirwen's worried sick," he replied.

"Oh, Emlyn," Sarah said, laying her hand on his forearm. "Poor Eirwen. I'm very sorry to hear this. Still, it hasn't been that long. He'll return soon, I'm sure."

"I'm not so sure," said Emlyn. "You didn't see the state he was in that night."

"We must pray for his safe return," Sarah said quietly.

"Yes," said Emlyn, "and for the rest of the town. The people of Homestead could use some divine intervention."

Sarah turned to him. "That's not what you said in your sermon." She gave him a gentle smile.

Emlyn smiled back. "You're right." He paused, gazing up at the cloudless sky. "Nevertheless, a miracle would be welcome."

East Liberty. Monday, September 4th

Karl Bernhard lay on his bed, barely conscious. It was very warm in the room. Before the doctor gave him morphine, the pain from the burns was excruciating. They had put salve on the burned skin, but it did not relieve the anguish.

Susanna sat at the bedside. "Schatzi, please take some water. The doctor says you must keep drinking." She put the cup to his lips. He took a sip to please her. Their daughter Estella stood beside her mother, moving a large fan back and forth.

"Pa, it's George." Karl opened his eyes enough to see George and John standing on the other side of the bed. "We are so sorry we got you into this."

Karl shook his head weakly. "No. I chose."

"We talked to the engineer at the furnace," said George. "He said you did everything correctly. They examined the boiler and found that saboteurs had jammed the safety regulator."

Karl moaned softly. "The others?"

"Two of the other men died in the explosion," said Susanna, her voice breaking. "You and another were taken home."

Susanna dabbed his face with a damp cloth. Karl was glad the explosion was not his fault. It was terribly hard to think. The pain surged through him, threatening to break through the morphine. If only he could be free of it.

Homestead

When Emlyn arrived at work Monday, Charles LaCroix told him that the last piece of armor plate for the cruiser *Monterey* had been shipped off to the U.S. Navy. The completion of this pre-strike order seemed ominous to Emlyn. The mill was definitely getting up to speed.

Griffiths stopped by the house Tuesday. Fortunately, his mother-in-law was on the way to recovery from the pneumonia that had nearly killed her. He wanted to thank Emlyn for filling in for him and to see if Gwyn had returned. When Eirwen told him Gwyn had not come back yet, he said he would do what he could to help.

That Saturday Eirwen went to the union office and, saying Gwyn was out of town, picked up his strike pay.

As one week passed, then the next, Gwyn remained missing. On the 14th, a policeman came by the house to ask Eirwen to look at a body that had been found in the river. Eirwen trembled with anxiety as Emlyn accompanied her to the morgue. Her relief was palpable when they uncovered the body and it was not Gwyn.

When classes started at the public schools, some strikers attacked the children of former strikers who had resumed working in the mill. The militia had assumed the task of escorting these children back and forth to school.

Sarah was distressed by the increasing tension. Even in the elementary school, lines had been drawn between the children of those still striking and those of returning workers. In classes, the strikers' children ostracized the other children. The principal and teachers had to stand guard during recess to make sure fistfights did not break out between the two.

When Oesterling did the books for August, he noted his income had gone down by nearly a quarter. Some patients couldn't afford to pay, while others simply didn't seek medical attention. He had heard that the Homestead storekeepers were suffering a similar drop in income. Most were now refusing to issue any further credit to strikers' families.

Oesterling became nervous when he and Sarah were invited to Carrie and Oliver's for dinner at the beginning of the month. He hoped Carrie had enough sense to block any invitation to Norton Montague, and was relieved to find that only a young attorney from Frick's office and his wife had been invited. This man had been in the outer office when Berkman had attacked Frick, and they were all treated to a blow-by-blow description of the incident—a narrative that he had evidently told many times.

Carrie, her face slightly swollen from pregnancy, complained about having to miss most of the social season this year. In mid-November, she would be starting her confinement awaiting the birth of the baby. In response to these complaints, the attorney's wife gushed on about the joys of motherhood wiping out the inconveniences. Carrie agreed, but it was clear she was not overjoyed at the prospect.

On the way home, Sarah had wondered aloud what would happen to their family holiday, given the situation with the strike and Carrie's pregnancy. Oesterling replied that until the strike was settled, there would be few parties in Homestead. It was only September, yet most strikers and their families were enduring many deprivations. Once the cold set in, the situation would become more dismal.

Saturday, September 17th

Emlyn had taken off work so he could meet Gareth Morgan when he arrived in Homestead. He walked from one end of the train platform to the other as he waited at the Amity Street station. At 11:49 a.m., one minute ahead of schedule, the passenger train from Pittsburgh pulled in.

Only a few people got off. Gareth was last. He helped an elderly woman off the train, then looked around the platform. Emlyn immediately recognized his curly dark hair and wiry, lean form. As Emlyn approached, Gareth set down his small valise. Grinning broadly, he swept Emlyn into a bear hug.

"Emlyn! You're a sight for sore eyes," said Gareth, pushing him at arm's length to examine him. "How I missed you this last year!"

"And I you," said Emlyn. "I feared it would be years before we'd see each other. You're an old married man now."

"I don't know about the 'old' part," said Gareth. "You'll have to come to Johnstown and meet Jane. I know you'll like her." Picking up this valise, he added, "Tell me about your preaching in Homestead. What a surprise! How did that happen?"

"It's not much of a story," said Emlyn as they started walking. "Reverend Griffiths asked me to fill in for him when he was unexpectedly called out of town."

"How did it go?" asked Gareth.

"Very well, I think," said Emlyn. "At least no one in the pews jumped up and objected." His thoughts immediately went to his father, wondering if he would have.

"That's great," said Gareth. "I'd like to see your sermon. What was the topic?"

Emlyn gave a brief summary, and Gareth expressed his approval.

As they walked to the house, Gareth teased Emlyn about his beard. He described his journey from Cardiff and his visit in Wilkes-Barre. He was excited about getting the pastorate at Beulah Church in Johnstown. Located on a hill outside of town, it had escaped destruction during the terrible flood in '89. Gareth was looking forward to the challenge of rebuilding the congregation.

In response to Gareth's queries, Emlyn filled him in on the current situation with the strike. Before they reached the house, Emlyn told him about Gwyn's disappearance the day his telegram had arrived.

"Heaven help you," said Gareth. "Do you have any idea where he might have gone?"

"Absolutely none," replied Emlyn. "We've exhausted all local resources for finding him."

"Do your parents know about this?" asked Gareth.

"Not yet. Eirwen keeps thinking he will return soon," said Emlyn, "and a letter would take over two weeks to reach them. We didn't want to alarm them or Gwyn's family."

"You must do something," said Gareth. "It's been three weeks. You can't wait indefinitely."

"I know," said Emlyn, as they approached the house.

Eirwen and the children were awaiting their arrival. Eirwen had never met Gareth, having left Wales before Emlyn had gone to seminary. She welcomed Gareth and ushered him into the kitchen, where a pot of vegetable soup—made with garden produce given her by the neighbors—was simmering.

After asking for God's blessings on the food they were about to eat, Gareth added a prayer for Gwyn's safe return. Eirwen thanked him, blinking back tears.

After they ate, Gareth opened his valise and took out a package. "From Treorchy," he said, handing it to Emlyn. Emlyn peeled off the paper covering. Inside were a pair of socks for each member of the family, plus a long scarf for Emlyn, all knitted by his mother. An envelope with his name on it fell to the floor as he handed the gifts around. Emlyn picked it up and opened it.

Inside was a letter from his mother, written in Welsh.

She described John Jones' funeral and how the disaster had devastated the small coal mining community of Ton du. It had left 58 widows and 152 fatherless children. The only good news to come out of the calamity for the Jones family was that Gwyn's father and brother-in-law were not hurt in the blast. The coal company reopened the slip as soon as they could clear away debris and get to unaffected parts of the mine. The colliers were terrified to go back into the slip, but almost all did.

Emlyn's mother reported that Arthur and Tegwen were settled in their cottage, and that his father's congregation had grown, and was now nearly filling the pews in the new chapel. In the final paragraph she wrote that she and his father were proud of Emlyn's accomplishments since his arrival in Homestead. She concluded by asking him to write them about what was going on with the strike.

Emlyn read the letter and handed it to Eirwen.

"Are you going to write them?" Gareth asked Emlyn. "Do they know about your preaching?"

"Eirwen wrote them a letter about that a fortnight ago," said Emlyn. "Obviously all this happened after Mam wrote this letter. As requested, I will tell them what's going on with the strike."

"Will you tell them about Gwyn?" Eirwen asked nervously.

Emlyn frowned. "We can't delay much longer," he said. "I must write them tomorrow evening."

Emlyn and Gareth spent the rest of the afternoon touring Homestead and environs. Gareth, accustomed as he was to the bleak industrial landscape of Wales, nevertheless found the scale of the steel works overwhelming.

"How does anyone get any sleep with all this racket?" he asked Emlyn as they walked along the mill fence.

"You eventually get used to it. You should be here when the mill is running at full capacity," Emlyn replied. "The din can be deafening."

"And all this soot!" said Gareth, brushing at the flecks of carbon on his sleeve. "Just walking around here makes one look like he's been down in a coal pit."

"This is no place for anyone who is devoted to spotless cleanliness," said Emlyn. "After you live here for a while, you don't notice the dirt or the noise."

Together they watched the soot and grime raining down from the smokestacks.

"Funny," said Emlyn. "When the mill was shut down, the town seemed like an alien place. I assumed everything would go back to the way it was once production resumed. Of course, it didn't. The strike and the battle utterly changed this town. The authorities are threatening to charge the strike leaders with murder. It looks like many of the former workers will not get their jobs back. Homestead will never be the same."

"From what you're telling me," Gareth replied, "I'd say the entire steel industry will never be the same."

"That's true, at least with regard to labor," said Emlyn. "The outcome of the strike has shown who has the power in this country: big industry and the banks."

Gareth sighed. "It's the same in Britain, as you know, and that's the way people like my father want to keep it." He smiled at Emlyn. "You know, I'd trade you fathers in a second."

Emlyn stopped in his tracks. "You would?"

"He can't understand why I won't join him in the big house on the hill, with his colliery out of view. Where his workers are concerned, he has willful blindness. In my book that's far worse than refusing to read Huxley."

"You have a point," Emlyn conceded and resumed walking. "Nevertheless, he did not disown you when you chose to enter the ministry."

"That's true," Gareth said, "but I'm an only child. My mother would never have let him. She is hell-bent—pardon the expression—on becoming a grandmother."

Emlyn grinned at Gareth. "And may she soon get her wish."

6:30 P.M.

Only Emlyn and Gareth had gone to the Oesterlings' that evening. Eirwen had declined the invitation, saying that she would stay home with the children.

As they passed around *hors d'oeuvres* in the parlor, Sarah and the doctor enthusiastically described to Gareth and the Griffiths Emlyn's leading the service and the congregation's response to the sermon.

"I've heard such good things about your preaching," Griffiths said to Emlyn. "People need to hear messages of encouragement in times like these."

"Thank you," said Emlyn, shifting uncomfortably in his seat. "I'm happy my sermon was well received."

"As the word gets around," said Griffiths, "I wouldn't be a bit surprised if you got invitations to preach at other churches."

Emlyn blushed. "I don't know about . . ." he began. Gareth poked a gentle elbow against his arm as Molly came in and announced dinner would be served.

They took their places at the table, and Griffiths said grace in Welsh. As Emlyn surveyed the food spread out on the Oesterlings' table, he realized he had worked up an appetite. The roast chicken dinner seemed like a feast to Emlyn after the Spartan fare they'd been eating at home.

Gareth and Griffiths hit it off immediately. After the two compared notes on mutual acquaintances back in Wales, the discussion turned to the ministry in Homestead. Griffiths and Oesterling both confirmed that many of the town's inhabitants were suffering from the strike, and Sarah related stories about the ever-present threat of violence in the schools.

Griffiths talked about the difficulties in ministering to a congregation that was comprised of Amalgamated members, nonunion workers, and managers at the mill. When Gareth asked if he had taken sides, Griffiths said that he had, but had not said so publicly. He then recounted the story of John McIlyar of the Fourth Avenue Methodist Episcopal Church. At the funeral of John Morris, Reverend McIlyar had launched an attack on Frick from the pulpit. Although the people at the funeral had embraced the message, once word got out to other factions, McIlyar had come under fire himself. Griffiths feared that with the pressure mounting, McIlyar would soon be forced to resign.

"I think it's an outrage that Reverend McIlyar is being drummed out of the pulpit," said Sarah. "People should not have to curb their speech for fear of retribution from the company."

"Like it or not," said Oesterling, "ever since the militia arrived, the company has been running the town. Frick has been very clever in getting the government to pay for and enforce security for the mill. If you were a striker, would you throw yourself headlong against Frick and Carnegie Steel?"

"Indeed not," said Griffiths. "I've heard that O'Donnell and other members of the strike committee will be charged with riot and murder."

"One horrible thing after another keeps happening," said Sarah. "Will there ever be an end to it?"

"There will, eventually," said Griffiths grimly. "We must have faith it will turn out for the best."

—•••—

Two hours later, Oesterling opened the door for Emlyn and Gareth as they said their goodbyes.

"Thank you so much for the lovely dinner," said Gareth, taking Sarah's hand.

"We are delighted you could come," said Sarah.

Emlyn thanked the Oesterlings, and the two friends went down the front steps and toward the Avenue.

"That was an interesting discussion about the strike," said Gareth as they made their way along Tenth Avenue. "So things really are that bad."

"They are," said Emlyn.

"Is that what made you decide to return to the church?" Gareth asked.

"In part, yes," Emlyn replied. "When I first arrived, I was very angry with Tad. I was furious at his being so fixed in his views. It's been only in the last few weeks that I've attended church. I initially went to services to help Eirwen through this crisis with Gwyn, but when I got there, I saw that my quarrel was not with the church."

"Last year you were so adamant about not being up to the task of serving, unnerved by your faltering faith. As I told you then, I think that's a crisis all of us face at one time or another."

"Preaching one time is not the same as answering the call to minister. My faith is still imperfect," said Emlyn. "Why do you think I chose to preach on James I? I was addressing myself as well as the congregation."

"It's a message that apparently resonated with those who heard it," said Gareth. "Your father would have been proud if he had been there."

Emlyn shook his head. "That's unlikely. Tad and I would still be at loggerheads if we got together now."

"How can you be so sure?" asked Gareth. "I interpreted your mother's letter as an olive branch from him. Don't you think his views might have softened?"

"She wrote the letter, not he," said Emlyn. "If he were here, we'd be arguing about science versus faith. I continue to stand with Huxley, not old 'Soapy Sam' Wilberforce, in the debate about Darwin's theory."

"As do I," said Gareth. "Many of our parents' generation have struggled with this debate. I don't think one has to choose between science and faith. Only those who read the Bible literally have problems resolving the conflict."

"I hope you're right," said Emlyn. "But all of this doesn't help Eirwen through this terrible crisis."

"When did Gwyn start going off the rails?" asked Gareth.

"After the battle, before he went missing, he was away from the house most every day with his pub mates."

"Drinking?"

Emlyn nodded. "After the battle, he started going to the pub or to his drinking friends' homes daily."

Gareth shook his head in dismay. "Apparently the strike is not going well for the union," he said.

"That's true," said Emlyn.

"Do you think that Gwyn will get his job back if he does return?"

They both glanced over at the mill, smoke belching from

its smokestacks, the glow of the furnaces lighting up the clouds.

"That is becoming more and more unlikely with every passing day," said Emlyn.

"What are you going to do? Is your job secure?"

"More or less," Emlyn replied. "It will do for the time being, but it does not pay enough to support Eirwen's family. In addition, it is not a job that I would relish doing for years to come. Sometimes I feel like a traitor, working when so many are out of work. And, of course I cannot speak out about whatever inequities I find on the job. On top of that, the future of the strikers is looking grim indeed. Frick is committed to breaking the union. He's done everything in his considerable power to do that."

"This Frick seems to be made of steel himself," said Gareth, stepping off the sidewalk to avoid a collision with another pedestrian. Emlyn stepped down, too, just in time to see Norton Montague sweep by with a fashionably dressed young woman on his arm. Montague, a sneer on his face, glanced at Emlyn as they passed.

"How rude! Do you know that fellow?" asked Gareth as Montague and the woman disappeared around the corner.

"Yes, a little," replied Emlyn, going on to relate the story of the incident with Figaro and Montague's attempt to get him fired and possibly indicted for murder.

"What a nice chap!" said Gareth.

"Unfortunately, I see him occasionally at work. I try to steer clear of him," said Emlyn, "although my impulse is to punch him in the face."

Gareth laughed. "You probably aren't the only one. It's people like that who test one's Christian charity."

Sunday, September 18th

Emlyn and Gareth waited on the platform for the train into Pittsburgh, where he would catch another bound for Johnstown. Gareth opened his valise and took out a nickel pocket watch and a small envelope. He handed them to Emlyn.

"What's this?" asked Emlyn, looking at the envelope marked 'Gwyn.'

"The watch belonged to Gwyn's brother John," said Gareth. "His parents sent it with me to give to him."

"You went to Ton du?"

"Your father asked me to stop there before I left for America. I believe the letter is from Gwyn's mother."

"Tad? You saw him?" Emlyn asked.

"Yes, at his request," said Gareth. "He wrote me when he learned I had taken a call in western Pennsylvania."

Emlyn stood silent, looking down at the tracks in front of the platform.

"We didn't discuss you, if that's what you're wondering," said Gareth. "All he said was to give you, Eirwen, Gwyn, and the children his and your mother's love—and the items I brought from them."

Emlyn contemplated the watch and letter. "I'll give them to Eirwen," he said at last. "She can decide what to do."

They stood on the platform in silence.

"I can't help wondering," said Gareth at last, "if you would reconsider going into the ministry."

"What?" said Emlyn. "Me?"

"You act surprised," said Gareth. "The way the things have turned out here—the strike, the violence, the suffering—I think it a natural course for you to follow."

Emlyn shook his head. "That's out of the question, at least for now. Eirwen needs my help. My small income is the only thing keeping the family from penury."

Emlyn watched the train approaching in the distance. "You're right in assuming that going through the battle has changed my perspective. Now that Gwyn has gone missing, I don't know where to turn."

"You could turn to your parents," said Gareth. "They are very concerned about you."

Emlyn felt a rush of anger. "Tad disowned me, remember? He treated me as a reprobate, unworthy to be his son."

"That was over a year ago," replied Gareth. "His attitude toward you has softened. When I saw him last month, he was anxious for any news about you and Eirwen. Anyway, what he does or says should not affect your choices in life."

"Maybe I'm overstepping a boundary by saying this," Gareth added. "You need to forgive him, whether he's forgiven you or not." Gareth smiled at Emlyn, and gently put his hand on Emlyn's shoulder. "Remember what I said about trading fathers?"

"Of course you're right," said Emlyn, as the locomotive pulled along the platform and stopped. He straightened up and offered Gareth his hand.

Gareth shook it. "Many thanks to you, Eirwen, and the Oesterlings for your hospitality. I'm so glad we could get together."

"I am, too. Have a good trip," said Emlyn. "Give my love to Jane. I'm sorry I won't be able to be there at your ordination."

"You'll be there in spirit," said Gareth, smiling. He squeezed Emlyn's arm. "May God help you and Eirwen through these trials. I'll pray for you all."

Back at the house, Emlyn wrote to his parents, addressing the letter to both. He started by briefly outlining the situation with the strike, as requested. He then wrote the circumstances of Gwyn's disappearance, laying out the details simply and directly. He concluded by saying that the family was managing without Gwyn, and that he would send a telegram if there were any significant developments.

That night, he once again knelt beside his bed to pray. This time, he could focus his thoughts and poured out all his fears and hopes.

"Not my will, but thine be done," he said finally, and climbed into bed.

Monday, September 19th

Emlyn posted the letter to his parents on the way to work. On the way home that evening, he stopped in a barbershop on the Avenue and had his beard shaved off, leaving a full moustache. As he examined his image in the barber's mirror, he thought he looked much younger, perhaps younger than he actually was. He liked the change. It reminded him of happier times in Wales.

That evening, special editions of the papers carried the news that, after a trial lasting only four hours, Alexander Berkman had been convicted of felonious assault and other charges and sentenced to 22 years in prison. In another room of the courthouse, a grand jury had handed down 167 indictments against Hugh O'Donnell and other leaders of the Amalgamated on charges of murder and aggravated riot.

Friday, October 6th , 7 a.m.

As Emlyn walked down the hall to his office, he was surprised to see a knot of men in the hall, gathered around a young clerk. He was gesturing wildly, and talking with great excitement.

"We all could have been blown up!" the clerk exclaimed. "What will these villains do next? The police should provide protection since the militia is leaving. Without them around, who knows. . . ." At this point, Jansen stepped into the hall, interrupted the narrative, and shooed the crowd away.

After Jansen returned to his office, Emlyn asked Charles what the clerk was talking about. Charles explained that in the middle of the night, someone had thrown a stick of dynamite through a dining room window in Mansion House, a boarding residence where the agitated clerk lived. The place was rented out to nonunion workers and company clerks. Even though the owner, a Mrs. Marrow, and her forty boarders were not injured and the building remained intact, they were understandably scared.

"They obviously think it's an attack by militant unionists," said Emlyn.

"Who else could it be?" replied Charles. "Remember last month when soldiers had to escort returning workers' children to school for fear of attacks by strikers? Violent strikers no longer appear openly on the streets, but it seems that some of them are resorting to guerilla warfare."

For the rest of the day, Emlyn's thoughts kept returning to Paddy's ominous prediction of violence back on the Fourth of July. What was being hidden behind the façades of the buildings of Homestead and the walls of Fort Frick?

Monday, October 10th, 7 p.m.

George Bernhard sat on his cot inside the Homestead Works, exhausted from another long day in the machine shop. He held out a three-day-old Pittsburgh paper, scanning it for news about Homestead.

He was happy to have been taken on as an apprentice machinist at the Homestead Works, while John had been assigned to work at O.H. 1.

Immediately after their father's death on September 6th, George and John Bernhard did not dare broach the subject with their mother of working in Homestead. But a month later, facing impending financial ruin, Susanna Bernhard at last gave her blessing to their taking jobs at the Works. After all, the furnaces had been lighted, and the mill was now in operation. Workers might still be out on strike, but the replacements were safe behind the high fence.

After working for nearly a year—for pitifully meager wages—in a small machine shop in East Liberty, George had been staggered at the immensity of the steel works. The machines they were working on were as big as houses, some even larger. Even now, after being on the job here for a week, he stood in awe of the Works' physical size and the tremendous fusillade of noise the mills emitted day and night.

After their long shifts, George and his brother ate meals at the company canteen and slept on cots in dormitories erected by the company. The work was so exhausting they didn't miss going home between shifts. Besides, on Saturdays they could board the *Tide* and be taken across the river for an overnight stay at the house in East Liberty. The sandlot season had ended, so he wasn't missing that. Perhaps he'd be able to go back to playing next spring.

George crumpled the paper and set it down. The big news story was about the end of the Dalton Gang in Coffeyville, Kansas. During an attempted bank robbery, the gang had a shootout with townspeople. Only one gang member, Emmett Dalton, had survived the battle, taking 23 gunshot wounds. The paper carried nothing about Carnegie Steel and the strike.

George lay down on the cot and closed his eyes. He was glad he did not have to work near the furnaces. The saboteurs who killed his father had not been identified. For all anyone knew, they could still be working inside the mill.

He had been shocked when he first got inside the works and began talking with those who had been there through September. They told him that beginning early that month, many replacement workers had been stricken by a virulent form of diarrhea. At least twenty men had died, maybe many more.

At first mill doctors had thought it was cholera, and the company took measures to provide purified food and drinking water. However, the epidemic raged on, getting worse instead of better. Could this be sabotage as well, only a more stealthy kind?

So far, Carnegie Steel had kept a lid on reports of illnesses and deaths.

Fearing that replacement workers may bolt, the company was trying to keep word of any violence inside the mill out of the newspapers.

What was going on outside the walls of Fort Frick? A few nights before, other workmen had reported hearing a muffled explosion from outside the mill fence, but no one could confirm what it was. More striker violence, George speculated. He knew that some people in the town would gladly kill him and any others back on the job, as the people of Coffeyville had killed the Daltons. They clearly thought of them as thieves who had taken what was rightfully theirs.

George sighed. He was happy to get a position with good prospects at the machine shop. The strikers had made their choice. How could they not realize that thousands of desperate unemployed and underemployed workers were out there, eagerly waiting to take the jobs they abandoned? Carnegie Steel had never considered giving in to union demands.

He needed to push these disturbing thoughts from his mind. He turned on his side and put the pillow over his head in a vain attempt to deaden the racket.

Clutching at his rough blanket, he pulled his legs up and tried to sleep.

Ever since word had gotten out about Gwyn going missing, the Jones family had been receiving help from friends and neighbors. Although many of his congregation were strikers in similar financial straits, Griffiths did what he could, stopping by every few days, occasionally bringing a loaf of bread that his wife had baked. The next-door neighbors, who were not involved in the strike, shared produce from their large garden. Now and then Sarah Oesterling came by after school with a piece of cheese or fresh eggs.

Without their explicitly planning it, since their ride after Emlyn's leading the service, an after-church outing had become usual for Sarah and Emlyn. They would either go on a walk, or if the weather permitted, take a ride out of town.

For Emlyn, it was a good way to escape the tension at the house. Each time he tried to talk Eirwen into making a decision about what course to take, she would fall silent. She refused to discuss any plans that did not include Gwyn. He was going to return soon, she insisted, and that was that. Emlyn was becoming extremely frustrated with her refusal to face the situation.

On Thursday, October 13th, the last of the militia left Homestead. Two days later, the *Homestead Local News* reported that more than 2,000 men were at work in the mill, including 100 former workers. That Saturday afternoon, while Eirwen was out picking up a few necessities, a special delivery letter arrived from Treorchy, addressed to Emlyn. It was from his father.

The brief letter dealt solely with Gwyn's disappearance. Although Emlyn had not requested it, his father said he was wiring some cash to help the family through the crisis. If Gwyn did not return by the end of the year, he urged Emlyn to convince Eirwen to return to Wales with the children, saying that he would send money for transportation. In the last paragraph, he asked if Emlyn would consider returning to finish university, offering to pay his passage as well. He concluded by sending his love to all of them.

That evening Emlyn went to the Western Union office and picked up the $30 wire transfer, as directed in the letter. He decided to hold onto half the money for the time being and give the rest to Eirwen. Meanwhile, he would consider his options and try to develop a strategy for dealing with the financial nightmare descending on them.

He was puzzled about what appeared to be a sudden change in heart from his father. While Emlyn was encouraged by the positive response to his letter, he was annoyed that his father thought so little of his work in America that he could propose that Emlyn drop everything and return to Wales.

On their walk the next day, Emlyn told Sarah about the letter. They walked in silence for several minutes along the riverbank. Sarah stopped and turned to Emlyn.

"Do you think it will come to that?" she asked, her voice a whisper. "Isn't there any way for Eirwen and the children to remain in Homestead?"

"If there is, I don't know of it," Emlyn replied. "My wages cannot support the family in the long run. Our parents can save Eirwen from the terrible fate of some women who have had to do laundry or take in boarders to support their children." Emlyn thought also of those who had been forced into prostitution, but did not mention it.

"I hate to even think of having to make Eirwen pull up the roots she's put down here," he added, "but at some point the decision will be forced on us. We have not heard from Gwyn for nearly two months now. He may be dead—God forbid—or even starting a new life somewhere else."

"It doesn't sound like Gwyn to just go off and abandon the family, "said Sarah.

"That's true," said Emlyn. "Before the strike, even he would have been appalled at the idea. However, you didn't witness how crazy he acted the night he went missing. Until we hear word of his whereabouts, we must prepare for the possibility he will not return."

"Would you go back to Wales as well?" Sarah asked.

"I would prefer to stay here," said Emlyn, "but my prospects are limited. Tad suggested that I finish at university, but that does not interest me. There's too much to be done here."

"I can't believe this is happening," Sarah said, her voice catching. She put her hands to her face and began to cry.

"Please don't weep," he said, unsure of what to do. He reached into his pocket and pulled out a handkerchief. As she took it, he grasped her hand and gently pulled her to him. He held her face against his shoulder, smoothing her hair.

She slipped her free arm around him. "What will happen to this town, to us?"

"God only knows," he said.

They stood there in silence. Finally, Sarah lifted her head. For a moment, their faces were very close. He breathed in the faint almond scent of her hair. Emlyn gently touched the side of her face. Did her dare kiss her?

He was about to do so, when he heard loud voices approaching on the path. Awkwardly, they stood apart. To Emlyn's surprise, as they resumed walking, Sarah took his hand in hers.

That evening when Emlyn returned home, he found Eirwen in the back yard, hitting a metal strong box with a hatchet.

"What are you doing?" he asked, watching her strike at the box. "It looks like the hatchet is having a worse time of it than the box."

She set down the hatchet and collapsed onto the stoop. "Gwyn kept cash and important papers in this box. I was trying to open it to see if there might be something of value."

"Where's the key?" he asked.

"Do you think I'd be doing this if I knew?" Eirwen said.

Emlyn thought for a moment. "What about in the cupboard where he kept the key to the shed?" Without waiting for her to answer, he went inside and into the pantry. Standing on tiptoe, he felt around on the upper shelf. To his surprise, he found a key. He carried the strong box into the kitchen and set it on the table. When he tried the lock, it opened easily.

"Thank God! And thank you, Emlyn," said Eirwen, hugging him.

"Let's hold the congratulations until we see what's in here," said Emlyn. One by one, he took out the contents: Eirwen and Gwyn's marriage license, steamship tickets, visa and immigration papers, their children's baptismal certificates, an envelope addressed to Gwyn.

"There's no money, nothing of value," said Emlyn.

Eirwen was crestfallen. "I so hoped to find something. Gwyn used to keep cash in here. Every payday he'd give me some for household expenses and put the rest in here."

"Well, there's no money now," said Emlyn.

"Look in the envelope," urged Eirwen. "Maybe there's cash inside."

Emlyn opened the envelope and took out a typed letter. Dated August 15th, it was a notice from the Carnegie Company. As he read it, his hope turned to despair.

"This is very serious," he said. "I don't know how we will manage this."

"What?" said Eirwen. "What is it?"

"It's a reminder that the next balloon payment for the mortgage on the house is due November first. Gwyn probably got this the week before he went missing."

"What is the amount due?" Eirwen asked.

"Over $300," he replied.

She sank into a chair, staring at the papers scattered on the table.

"No, no, no!" she moaned, rocking back and forth.

Emlyn patted her shoulder, too angry to speak. How could Gwyn be so selfish and stupid? Gwyn had apparently taken or spent whatever cash he had put there before the strike. How would they raise such a large amount of money in six or seven weeks? The crisis he had feared was upon them.

—•●•—

Rumors began flying that the local newspaper had been bought by the Carnegie Company, rumors that were eventually proved to be true. On October 17th four strikers went to the mill office and openly applied for work. Four days later, Sam Gompers, the head of the American Federation of Labor, gave a rousing speech calling for a boycott of the Carnegie Company. Nothing came of it. The majority of the strikers, having fallen into dire financial straits, were disillusioned.

The company moved Charles M. Schwab from the Edgar Thompson Works in Braddock to replace Potter as General Superintendent in Homestead. Schwab, realizing how much the company needed experienced, skilled workers, began courting them to come back on the job. A few took him up on the offer.

Pittsburgh. Monday, October 24th

Oesterling sat at a table in the dining room of the Hotel Duquesne, waiting for Carrie to arrive. He had a difficult time concealing his irritation when Carrie had called the evening before and insisted upon their meeting here. It was another one of Carrie's mysterious requests, requiring him to cancel office hours and take the train into the city.

Carrie arrived nearly fifteen minutes late, her middle covered by a loose navy blue cloak. Her face was puffy, and she walked with the waddling gait of late pregnancy. Oesterling stood up as a waiter showed her to the table and pulled out her chair. Carrie sat down heavily, and the waiter handed her a menu.

"Hello, Papa," said Carrie. "Thank you for meeting me."

"How are you?" asked Oesterling, taking his seat. "All ready for the new arrival to the family?"

"Papa, this is such an ordeal," Carrie replied. "When I walk the slightest distance, I get out of breath, and sleep is out of the question."

"It won't go on much longer," said Oesterling. "Only a few more weeks."

In reply, Carrie winced. "Forgive me for asking you to come downtown," she said. "I didn't want to go Homestead, where I might see Norton, and I didn't want to stay at home."

"What's going on?" asked Oesterling. "Why couldn't you talk over the phone?"

"I don't want anyone listening in," said Carrie. She glanced around at the nearby tables. "We're going to move to Chicago," she whispered.

"What?" asked Oesterling. "Why are you whispering?"

"There's been a change in Oliver's fortunes," said Carrie. "For the worse. Those investments he made in railroads last year—well, he's lost just about everything he invested."

"I see," said Oesterling. "This sounds serious."

"It is," Carrie agreed.

"What does this have to do with moving to Chicago?" asked Oesterling.

"Some kind of big fair is being held there next year," said Carrie, "and Frick wants Oliver there to manage contracts involved in the construction of buildings on the site."

"Oh, you mean the Columbian Exposition?" asked Oesterling.

"Yes," said Carrie. "Anyway, Oliver says he can't refuse because it will involve a raise. I think he's secretly happy to move, to be near his family." Carrie's eyes became moist.

"That doesn't sound so bad," said Oesterling. "This world's fair promises to be an exciting project, from what I've read about it."

Carrie took out a handkerchief and twisted it in her fingers. "Moving is not the worst part. Oliver says that we will have to sell off most of our furniture—even my best dresses and jewelry—to begin paying off the debt."

Oesterling contemplated his older daughter in silence. He had long been wary of Oliver's investment schemes. Now the truth was coming out.

The waiter came by and took their orders. Carrie did not look up.

"We will be living with his parents until he finds a suitable apartment for us. He says we can't afford a house." Carrie dabbed at her eyes with the handkerchief. "How will I survive living with his mother? It will be insufferable."

"It will only be for a couple of months," said Oesterling.

"A couple of months! You don't know how awful his mother can be," Carrie exclaimed.

"When will you move?" Oesterling asked, trying to change the subject.

"Oliver says he needs to be in Chicago by the end of November. He's already looking for a household goods dealer to take the furniture."

"That's very close to when the baby's due," said Oesterling. "You can't manage a big trip at that time."

"The doctor says I'll have to remain behind in Pittsburgh until after the baby arrives."

"Then you must come to Homestead and stay with us," said Oesterling. "I can arrange with Dr. Baker to attend you."

"I don't want to come to Homestead!" Carrie wailed.

The elderly couple at the next table looked over at her.

"Please," said Oesterling, making a gesture for her to keep her voice down. "Is there any other choice? What's so terrible about Homestead?"

Carrie remained silent for a long moment. "In a word, Norton."

"You can easily avoid him, I should think."

Carrie sighed. "There's another complication. Norton, it seems, is the one who advised Oliver to make those risky investments. Now Oliver is furious with him. Last night he swore he would get his revenge on Norton."

"What kind of revenge does Oliver have in mind?" Oesterling asked. "I hope he's not planning on confronting him."

"No, that's not Oliver's style," said Carrie. "He said he'd make sure that Norton would be out of a job with Carnegie Steel, and that he'd block him from getting another position with any Pittsburgh company," said Carrie.

"Can he do this?" asked Oesterling.

Carrie nodded. "I think he can."

"Do you think Oliver suspects anything about you and. . . ?" asked Oesterling.

"I doubt it," said Carrie, sniffling. "He's so fixated on his finances, he doesn't notice much else. Nevertheless, I don't want Oliver coming to Homestead. I worry about him running into Norton, or vice versa. Lord knows what they might say to each other. It could be a complete disaster."

"Let's hope Oliver remains busy with making arrangements for the move," said Oesterling. "In December you can come over and stay with Sarah and me for a few weeks." His voice sounded much more cheerful than he felt. "I will make sure that you won't have to cross paths with Norton. Then, when you're up to it, you and the child can make the journey to Chicago."

Carrie lowered her gaze as the waiter set bowls of tomato soup in front of them. After he went away, Carrie looked up, blinking away tears.

"If only Mama were still here!" Carrie whined. "Oh, Papa, this is not how I wanted my life to turn out!"

Oesterling picked up his spoon. "Carrie," he said softly, "many people are far worse off than you. You'll see that when you come to Homestead."

"That's them and I'm me," she replied.

Oesterling contemplated this young woman, his own flesh and blood, in despair.

"My dear, I have no answer for that," he replied, watching the spoon sink into the red liquid.

—•●•—

As the end of October approached, Emlyn exhausted every possible remedy for making the balloon payment. The sum was too large to borrow from other sources. Three years previously, the Carnegie Company had built the house, agreeing to hold the mortgage for their employee. Now the final payment was due. When Emlyn inquired at the company mortgage office, he was told that if Gwyn Jones defaulted, the property would be seized and sold to one of the many workers seeking housing. All of the potential buyers were workers like Gwyn had been, people who could not buy without financing from the company. The company had them all over a barrel.

Emlyn kept this knowledge to himself, hoping to find a way to keep the house. He frequently lost focus at work, his mind wandering over possible solutions. His anger began shifting from Gwyn to the Carnegie Company, the prime mover in the ruin facing so many Homestead residents.

At the house, Emlyn was constantly reminded of the impending doom coming upon the family. He looked forward to Sunday mornings, when they all would be away from the house. Surrounded by friends, in church, Eirwen set aside her preoccupation with Gwyn. Although Eirwen would not come to choir practice, Sarah managed to get her to agree to do a solo or two.

Emlyn looked forward to Sunday afternoons with Sarah, accompanied by Cerberus, and occasionally by Thomas. If they did not walk or ride out of town, they would go to a tea or soda shop to talk. Sometimes, she would link her arm in his, and they would walk arm-in-arm, like sweethearts. He did not, however, bring up the future, too afraid to consider what might befall them. He wished he had the money to take her to concerts or plays. Thankfully, she said she didn't mind, pointing out that such entertainments in Homestead had mostly dried up in the aftermath of the strike.

He supposed they were becoming sweethearts, but he feared giving all his heart. The unknown future was rushing up on them all too fast.

In late October, Sarah told Emlyn about Carrie's coming to Homestead to await the birth of her child, a development Sarah was not anticipating with pleasure. "At least she won't be able to accompany us on these walks," said Sarah. As they walked along, Emlyn had to admit to himself that he felt the same way about his sister—not that the situations were in any way similar. It was just good to get away and be with Sarah.

November 1892

On the first of the month, George and John Bernhard moved into a rooming house in Munhall, taking living quarters vacated by two former mill workers who had left town. Although George was uneasy about the sporadic violence still afflicting the town, he was tired of living inside the mill. The terrible cholera-like epidemic that had stricken so many workers during September and October had ended, although nobody seemed to know what had caused it. George had heard rumors that the company, suspecting subversion, had brought in undercover Pinkertons. It was time to move outside the walls of Fort Frick.

The Carnegie Company was constructing one hundred houses for the replacement workers and their families. Soon, they would be the majority in town.

On Thursday, November 17th, the blow Emlyn had been expecting fell. A registered letter came to the house from the company notifying them that the mortgage was in default. They had until the first of December to pay the amount due, with interest, or evacuate the premises. If they did not comply, the sheriff would forcibly evict them.

The next day, Emlyn returned to the company's housing office to inquire about an extension on the mortgage. After arguing with a clerk in the outer office for five minutes, he requested to see the supervisor. Only after Emlyn said that he was a current employee of the company did the supervisor agree to see him.

Emlyn told the supervisor he would pay for a two-month extension on the mortgage. Gwyn, he said, was no longer in town, and he needed more time to find proper housing. When the supervisor learned that Emlyn worked in the General Office Building, he agreed to the extension.

"Mind you," said the man, "this is highly irregular. But because you are a loyal employee, we can make this accommodation. However, I need to stress that January first is an absolute deadline. If you are not out by then, we will have to involve the sheriff."

When Emlyn told her about this development, Eirwen was devastated. Until then, she had been nursing the small hope that somehow, they would be saved. Faced with the probability of being thrown into the street by sheriff's deputies, she was forced to confront the terrible truth of the situation.

By then, 2,700 workers were toiling in the mill. The company released a list of those whose role in the strike prohibited them from being rehired. John McLuckie was one of those blacklisted. Shortly thereafter, his wife died. McLuckie resigned his office as burgess and left town.

On the 18th, the nonunion laborers and mechanics still supporting the AA called for a vote to end to the strike. The Amalgamated members rejected the proposal, 224-119. After the vote, the laborers and mechanics deserted the cause en masse and went back to the mill to apply for work.

On Saturday the 19th, the first anniversary of Emlyn's arrival in Homestead, he decided to consult Griffiths about Eirwen's fixation on Gwyn. Griffiths sat at the desk in the church office and listened to Emlyn's story of the mortgage default.

"I will help in any way I can," said Griffiths. "What can I do?"

"Would you please talk to Eirwen?" asked Emlyn. "I can find lodgings for myself, but not for her and the children."

"I can put the word out," said Griffiths, "but, as you know, housing is very hard to come by in town. As soon as a family moves out, another moves in. The rooming houses are full to the seams."

"Eirwen wants to stay in town in the expectation that Gwyn will return," said Emlyn, "and I am trying to help her do this. However, my income falls short of covering even household expenses. We could raise money by selling off some possessions, but so many people are being forced to do that, the sale would bring in little. The pressing problem is the mortgage. We have no hope of raising the more than $300 necessary to pay it off."

"Do you see any way out of this predicament?" asked Griffiths.

"I have thought about this for weeks, and only one solution seems feasible: that Eirwen and the children return to Wales. My parents will pay their transportation back, and my father will use his considerable connections to help her find a way to support herself."

"It will be frightening for Eirwen," said Griffiths, "to contemplate returning to a land she left nearly ten years ago—not to mention the winter crossing they will face."

"That is true," Emlyn replied, "yet I think it the best course. Even if Gwyn does return, he will not get his job back. He might even be charged with murder, like some of the others. The mortgage still must be paid. The company owns the house. The family is completely at their mercy—which is in very short supply indeed."

They fell silent. Crashes and booms from the nearby mill filled the room.

"What about you?" asked Griffiths. "Would you go back to Wales as well?"

Emlyn gazed out of the window at the mill fence. "I honestly don't know, but I know for sure I don't wish to return to university studies at this point."

Griffiths drummed on the desk top with his fingers. "Would you consider entering the ministry? More than one person in this congregation is of the opinion that you would make a fine pastor."

Emlyn watched Griffiths' fingers on the desktop. "Gareth made the same suggestion himself when he was in town," he said at last. "I need to think carefully about this. I need to know that I am truly called to service."

Griffiths opened a drawer in his desk and pulled out a letter. He handed it to Emlyn. "Perhaps this will help you decide. This letter is from a friend of mine in McKeesport. He will be officiating at a family wedding in Cleveland on the 27th and is requesting that you fill in for him. I told him about your sermon, and he hopes you will deliver it again for that congregation."

Emlyn opened the letter. He had been so distracted by financial worries that he had put aside any thoughts of returning to the pulpit.

"A train would get you there in a matter of minutes," said Griffiths. "I know what a trial Gwyn's disappearance has been for your family. It might do you good to see what's happening in another town."

Emlyn read the letter.

"Well," said Griffiths, "what do you think?"

"I think that I have nothing to lose by doing this," said Emlyn. "Why not?"

"Good!" replied Griffiths. "I will send word to McKeesport, then."

The next day, Sunday the 20th, a vote to end the strike was again put to members of the Amalgamated. This time, the result was 101-91 in favor of ending the strike.

MONDAY, NOVEMBER 21ST

To get to the office, Emlyn had to wind his way through a large crowd of men applying for work. From their office window, Charles and Emlyn observed hundreds of former strikers standing in line to make application. Superintendent Schwab himself was there, overseeing the process that continued through the afternoon. By the end of the workday, word spread throughout the office that the company was rehiring only laborers, the lowest paid workers. The vast majority of applicants had been turned away.

When Emlyn came out of the mill and saw utter dejection marking the faces of former workers, his heart sank. He knew that this was only the beginning of their trials. Many of these men and their families would be forced, like Eirwen, to consider the unthinkable: pull up roots and move on.

On the way home, Emlyn stopped by the church to pick up information about the service in McKeesport. After Griffiths gave directions to the church, his tone turned somber as he described his visit to Eirwen at the house earlier that day. At first Eirwen became upset when she learned Emlyn had told Griffiths about her plight, but she had calmed down when she realized that he was trying to help. However, Griffiths had no success in getting her to talk about the necessity for giving up the house. Frustrated in his mission, he had left when David woke up from his nap.

As Emlyn walked the remaining blocks to the house, he observed knots of men gathered on corners and stoops. He knew they were speculating on what would happen now that the strike had been settled. Crossing Fourth Avenue, Emlyn saw Lil, the woman who had helped him the day of the battle, coming toward him. When he called her name, she looked at him and smiled in recognition.

"How are you, my dear?" she asked. "Thank you for the flowers and chocolates. You didn't have to do that."

"Yes, I did," said Emlyn. "I'm glad you liked them."

She looked at him closely. "Has the wound healed?"

"Weeks ago," he replied. "And you? I was happy to hear that your eye was not badly injured. You would not have been hurt if you had not been helping me."

"We both would have fared better if we had not run into that nasty Buckman," she replied. "Thank God that doctor came by."

"That is the truth," said Emlyn. "I was saved from Buckman once before by a man I worked with. Even now, as I pass by saloons on the Avenue, I keep an eye out for him."

"Haven't you heard?" said Lil. "You don't need to concern yourself with Buckman anymore."

"Why is that?" asked Emlyn.

"Two weeks ago he was arrested for murder."

"Murder! Whom did he kill?" Emlyn asked.

"His wife, Addie," said Lil.

"His wife?" said Emlyn, an image of her perpetually battered face in his mind. "What happened?"

"The story goes that he was drinking at a saloon. He started badgering a scab at the bar, and was thrown out," said Lil. "He tried to get back in, but couldn't. He eventually gave up and went home. He saw a man leaving his house. He came in and confronted his wife, who was also drunk. She threw a pan at him, it missed, and he picked it up and started to beat her over the head with it. The police were called, but by then it was too late. It turned out that the man was only dropping off Buckman's hat, which he had left at the saloon."

"Good Lord," said Emlyn. "What about their son?"

"He saw the whole thing," said Lil. "He was taken away by social workers, they say."

"Poor boy. I knew Buckman was mean, but I didn't think he was capable of killing someone," replied Emlyn.

"My mother used to say that more drink makes a mean drunk meaner, and she was right. It makes me grateful that we escaped without more damage," Lil said. "The Lord must have been on our side."

"He must have been," replied Emlyn, recalling the close brushes he had had with death on the day of the battle.

"You take care, my dear," she said, patting his arm. "God bless you."

"Blessings on you, too," Emlyn replied as she walked away.

Eirwen was alone in the kitchen when Emlyn got back to the house. She was very pleased when Emlyn showed her the program for the worship service he was to lead. She urged him to write their parents right away with the news.

"Tad will be so happy," she said, "and so will Mam. She has worried so since you left Wales."

"I know," said Emlyn, "but I am not doing this for them. I am doing it for myself."

"Oh, yes," said Eirwen. "It's the only reason you could do it, I know." She hugged him. "Gwyn used to say what a great preacher you would be."

Emlyn's smile faded at the mention of Gwyn. "Eirwen, we really must talk about what to do about the impending eviction."

Eirwen went over to the stove and stirred the soup she made for dinner. "Do we have to? That won't happen until January."

"Eirwen, for heaven's sake!" said Emlyn. "January is only several weeks off. We can't wait until the sheriff appears at the door. Even if Gwyn returns, full payment must be made to the company if we are to stay in the house."

"We could rent another house in town," she said.

"Good luck in finding a decent place to rent," he said. "Even if we found a place, how could we afford it? I don't think you'd like living in the kind of place we could rent on my salary."

Eirwen turned to face him. "I cannot, I will not go back to Wales!"

"Why is that out of the question? The options here are not pretty," he said. "Do you want to wind up in the stews next to the mill?"

"I couldn't stand the humiliation of going back," she said, her lower lip trembling.

"I realize how difficult it must be, " said Emlyn.

"No, you don't," she said. "How could you?"

"You forget that I left Wales in disgrace," Emlyn replied. "I'll never forget the humiliation of having the door slammed in my face, of having no money. I know how painful it is."

They stood there in silence.

"What are you going to do?" asked Eirwen. "Will you be going back as well?"

"Until today, I thought it might be an option," he said. "After seeing all those poor souls turned away from work at the mill, I know there's no future for me with the Carnegie Company. The opportunity Griffiths has given me has shone a light on an old path. If a congregation calls me, I might go."

Eirwen slammed the spoon onto the table. "So you are planning on abandoning me and the children, then?" she asked accusingly.

Emlyn threw up his hands. "I am not the one who abandoned you." He immediately regretted his words.

Eirwen's features twisted in pain. With an anguished cry, she ran out of the room and upstairs.

"Eirwen, please forgive me, " he said, following her. "That was very unkind. Please . . ."

As he caught up with her at the entrance to her bedroom, she shut the door.

He knocked. "Go away!" she cried. Through the door, Emlyn heard her sobbing.

Finally, he gave up and went downstairs, cursing himself for being so thoughtless. He had only made things more difficult. Now, how was he going to proceed?

He took out paper and wrote a long letter to his parents, telling them of his leading the service in McKeesport and describing his difficulties with Eirwen. The next morning he would post it via express mail. Eviction was looming like a black cloud.

Tuesday, November 22nd

At the office, Emlyn's thoughts kept returning to Eirwen. He had to do something, but he had no idea what. He muddled through his work, preoccupied with his personal problems. Now and then, his thoughts would fly back to the gaunt faces of the workers turned away from being rehired.

At last, the workday ended. Emlyn put on his coat and rushed out of the office building, brushing past a surprised Montague in the hall. A light rain was falling as Emlyn walked along the Avenue. With the children back from the neighbors', there had been no opportunity to talk the previous evening. He slowed his pace, wondering how to approach Eirwen when he got home.

Did he hear someone calling his name? He turned to see Sarah coming toward him.

"Do you have time to come to the house for a cup of tea?" she asked.

They stood in the cold rain as workers shuffled past on their way home.

"Well . . ." he said, glancing up the hill.

"Come on," she said, taking his hand. "Let's get out of the rain."

At the house, Emlyn and Sarah hung their damp coats on the hall tree. They went into the study, where Mrs. Sproule had a fire going in the fireplace grate. Emlyn stood before the glowing coals, holding out his hands to the warmth. "That feels wonderful."

Sarah sat on the settee in front of the fireplace, and in a few minutes Mrs. Sproule came in with a tray of tea service. "Sit down and have some tea," said Sarah, patting the cushion on the settee. "Have you warmed up yet?"

Emlyn smiled and sat down beside her. "Yes, I have," said Emlyn. He sat as close to her as he dared, their sleeves touching. Sarah filled the teacups, and they sat together, sipping the tea.

"Papa should be home soon," she said. "He likes to come in here and read before supper."

"I can understand why. It's so warm and peaceful in this room," he said, gazing into the fire.

"It won't be in another week or two," said Sarah. "Oliver's going to Chicago, and Carrie's coming here to await the baby's arrival." She set down her teacup. "There are so many changes coming, it makes my head spin," she said gravely. "The strike ending, scabs flooding into town, a baby coming, Carrie moving—and now you might be leaving as well."

Emlyn looked at her face, lit by the pulsing glow from the fireplace. "Yes, I possibly will be leaving—like many others in this town," he said. "The future is so uncertain for so many." He took her hand. "I don't know what I would have done without your company during these weeks. Our Sundays together have been the only bright spots in my life."

"I feel the same way," she said, her voice hoarse. "As you said, the future is so uncertain."

"Sarah, I..." Emlyn began, but was interrupted by a commotion in the back hall. They dropped hands as Cerberus trotted into the room, followed by Oesterling.

"Emlyn!" said Oesterling, coming over to shake his hand. "This is a pleasant surprise. Sarah tells me that you'll be preaching at First Congregational in McKeesport this Sunday."

"That's right," said Emlyn. "I'm filling in for the pastor."

"By the way," asked Oesterling, sitting in his tattered armchair, "how is Eirwen doing? Has she had any word from Gwyn?"

Emlyn sighed and shook his head. "We've heard nothing since he disappeared three months ago."

"What is she going to do?" asked Sarah.

Emlyn sighed. "I don't know. She is very distressed. She feels—rightfully—that she is a pawn in a game played by others."

"Many women feel that way, at least some of the time," said Sarah, "and for good reason. We can't vote, many occupations are closed to us."

"Women may often be at the mercy of men, but they aren't the only pawns in the game," said Oesterling. "A walk through town will illustrate my point."

Mrs. Sproule came into the room and said dinner would be ready shortly.

Oesterling and Sarah invited Emlyn to stay, but seeing that it was nearly six o'clock, he declined, and took his leave.

Outside, the rain had turned to sleet. Emlyn hurried along, thinking about Eirwen and Sarah, and what life would be like without them. Eirwen and Gwyn had been so good to him, had offered him their hospitality and assistance in finding work. Since the beginning of the strike, he had come to rely on Sarah for support and companionship. His departure from Wales was a sad occasion, and now again he was being forced to move on. He knew then what he was going to say to Eirwen.

Emlyn came through the back door and took off his wet coat and boots. Eirwen and the children had already had supper, and she was finishing up the dishes.

"Eirwen," he said softly, "please forgive me for my thoughtless words yesterday. I'm very sorry that I hurt you."

She gave him a sad, tired look. "I forgive you." She wiped a bowl and set it on the table. "You've been supporting us these past three months. I want you to know I'm grateful for that."

He went to her and put his arms around her. "Dear Eirwen," he said, "you're the best sister anyone could have. Whatever happens, wherever I go, I will stand by you. We'll find a cheaper place to live. If I leave here, you and the children must come with me. Somehow we will make it work."

Eirwen slowly shook her head. "No, that would not be fair to you. You are just starting off in life. You should not be burdened with my children and me if there is another way."

"You are hardly a burden to me," said Emlyn.

"I've made up my mind, Emlyn," Eirwen replied. "If I must leave Homestead without Gwyn, I should go to a place I know."

She reached over and took down a letter from the kitchen shelf.

"I got this today from Tad and Mam," she said, holding it up. "As you know, they want me to come back to Wales. Tad wrote that Mr. Beynon said that his cottage behind the old chapel is vacant, and that we could live there for low rent."

"I thought you don't want to leave Homestead," said Emlyn.

"I don't," Eirwen replied. "It's terrifying to contemplate crossing the Atlantic with three small children."

Eirwen sat down. She looked at the letter and sighed. He started to speak, but she waved him to silence.

"I've been thinking about this all day, and have concluded that the best course is to return to Treorchy. Tad will pay our passage and help me get situated. It's not much to my liking—and the children will like it even less—but it's the most palatable of unpalatable options."

Emlyn sat down at the table next to her.

"Eirwen, I'm so sorry it has come to this," said Emlyn.

"It's not your fault," she said sadly. "If Gwyn does try to get in touch, he knows that he can always reach me through my family." She patted the letter on the table. "By the way, Tad went over to Ton du and spoke to Gwyn's parents. They of course had no idea of what was going on here. They were devastated to learn that he has gone missing. They've suffered so much, and now this." Her eyes glistened with tears. "Yet they offered to do whatever they could for me and the children. They, too, want us to come to Wales."

"Neither set of grandparents have met the children," said Emlyn. "I know they will be happy to have them near."

"That is the one bright spot I see in all this gloom," she said, standing up. "Now, let us move on to other things." She smoothed her apron and went to the stove. "Have you had supper? Would you like some barley soup?"

"Thanks, I would," he said.

She took down a bowl, filled it, and set it on the table in front of Emlyn. She went into the front room to check on the children, leaving Emlyn with his thoughts. The crisis with Eirwen was over, but there was much work ahead. Tomorrow he and Eirwen would have to wire their parents and then begin disposing of the furniture and household goods.

He didn't want to think too much about what it would feel like when she and the children were gone.

—•••—

The next day, Wednesday, Emlyn stopped by the church to tell Griffiths of Eirwen's decision. Griffiths said he would spread the word to the congregation, asking for volunteers to help her prepare for the journey. Later, he and Eirwen went to the telegraph office and wired Treorchy. The day after that, their father wired back to make arrangements for the railway and steamer tickets.

After anguishing over it, Eirwen decided that they should leave before Christmas rather than after. It would be a dreary holiday staying in a house that was nearly empty, made intolerable by Gwyn's absence. She booked passage for the four of them from New York on December 12th. That way, she said, they would be in Wales in time for the holidays.

When she told the children about their forthcoming journey to Wales, Thomas became incensed. "I don't wanna leave!" he wailed. He didn't want to go to some strange old country where people spoke a language he did not understand. He didn't want to leave his school and his friends, he said. Then he ran off, out the back door.

Emlyn chased after him, but as it was after dark, Thomas had vanished in the maze of outbuildings behind the house. As Emlyn stood in the alley, he felt chilled to the bone recollecting that summer night when Gwyn had gone off in a similar manner.

That evening, Eirwen was beside herself with worry, glancing out the window and pacing the floor. But at eight o'clock, a cold, hungry Thomas returned home.

Eirwen gave him supper, and afterwards, Eirwen sat with Thomas on the parlor settee and read him Welsh folktales, translating as she went. At first, Thomas sat there, sullen and withdrawn, but was soon drawn into the stories of dragons, giants, talking animals, and magical transformations.

Nevertheless, that night he cried himself to sleep.

SATURDAY, NOVEMBER 26TH

When Emlyn arrived at the office that morning, Charles took him aside and asked, "What is the name of the jackass who tried to have you fired—you know, the one the horse pitched?"

"Norton Montague," said Emlyn. "Why?"

"I overheard people talking in the hall on my way in. Word is that last night he became engaged to a bank president's daughter," replied Charles.

"Poor woman," said Emlyn. "Is she from Homestead?"

"No, they say her old man runs some bank on the South Side," said Charles.

"Montague must be very popular with the ladies," said Emlyn. "I've seen him around with several women."

"Not so good with horses, though." Charles laughed.

"Horses are better judges of character," said Emlyn.

—•••—

After work that afternoon, Emlyn made arrangements for a furniture dealer to come by the house. Emlyn would facilitate Eirwen's chosen departure date by staying at the house until the end of the month, disposing of what remained after whatever she had selected was on its way to Wales. After that, he would have to find other housing arrangements for himself.

Eirwen was very grateful to Mrs. Griffiths and two other churchwomen for helping her clean out the house and pack, as was Emlyn. The company of these women would ease this difficult process for Eirwen during the next three weeks. Sarah had also helped by coming over after school to watch David and Dilys while Eirwen left the house to run errands.

Sunday, November 27th, 3:40 p.m.

Emlyn alighted from the train from McKeesport and pulled his derby down tighter as he walked away from the Amity Street Station. Even though the day was bright and sunny, strong gusts of wind blew dirt and smoke down the street.

McKeesport, like so many towns in southwestern Pennsylvania, relied on steel production for its livelihood. The largest of the mills, National Tube, manufacturer of metal tube and piping, employed several thousand workers. McKeesport, however, had not been torn apart by a violent strike. Idle workers were not lurking in front of saloons and boarding houses, muttering angry words or suspiciously eyeing passersby.

Emlyn glanced at the sprawl of mills stretching along the Monongahela River. Smoke belched skyward, smearing the cerulean sky.

He pushed open the back door, and hung up his coat on one of the kitchen hooks.

"How was McKeesport?" asked Eirwen from the doorway. "Did the service go well?"

"Yes, it was fine," said Emlyn. "The First Congregational Church of McKeesport is larger than the Homestead church, and the pews were mostly filled. The congregation was very welcoming. Many had questions about what's going on here."

"So you're glad you accepted the invitation to preach?" Eirwen asked.

"I am," said Emlyn.

"Would you like some tea and biscuits?' she asked.

"Yes, please," he replied, sitting down at the kitchen table. "I've had nothing to eat since I left here this morning."

"That's many hours ago," said Eirwen. "I hope you'll have

time to rest before going to the Oesterlings' this evening. You're much later than I had expected."

"That's because there was an unexpected development," said Emlyn.

Eirwen stopped and looked at him. "What kind of development?"

"As I was saying goodbye to members of the congregation at the door, I noticed three men and a woman standing off to one side. They waited till all the others were gone, then approached me."

"Who were they? I hope they weren't there to argue with what you said."

"No, no—just the opposite," said Emlyn. "They were a delegation from Salem Congregational Church in a town called Mount Pleasant. They were inviting me to preach there two Sundays from now."

Eirwen's eyes grew wide, and she half-dropped the plate she was holding.

"They're considering calling you to serve as their pastor?"

Emlyn nodded. "They said they have been without a permanent minister for nearly four months, since the previous one left for Hagerstown. A retired pastor is currently filling in."

"That's wonderful, Emlyn!" she exclaimed. "But how did they know about you?"

"Through Gareth. He called Mr. Griffiths to see if the search committee could hear me preach before they invited me."

Eirwen sat down at the table and took Emlyn's hand. "You're going to go, aren't you?" she asked, her voice low.

"I told them I would let them know via telegram tomorrow," said Emlyn.

"Oh, Emlyn!" Eirwen exclaimed. "This is such a fine opportunity. You must go!"

"I know nothing about this place, except that it is located south of here and is the home town of Frick. That fact in itself gives me pause."

"You should find out for yourself what it's like: go there. What have you got to lose?"

Emlyn squeezed her hand. "Very well, then. Tomorrow I'll wire my acceptance."

Oesterlings' 6:30 p.m.

When Emlyn had first seen Carrie, he hardly recognized her. Her once-petite figure was swathed in a voluminous maternity suit-dress. Her hands and face were swollen. She was miserable and had no compunctions about informing everyone of the fact.

"Papa, I don't know why I can't have a drop of aperitif," Carrie said as they sat down at the table. "I have so little appetite."

Oesterling cast an irritated glance her way. "You know very well that we don't keep spirits in this house."

"Such a pity," said Carrie. "Oliver's family has no such prohibitions, but then, they are Episcopalians."

"At their house, you can do as they do," he said. "Meanwhile, you are with us."

Oesterling cut a slice of pork roast and put it on Carrie's plate.

"That's too big," she said petulantly. "I told you I have little appetite."

"Take what you like," Oesterling said, setting down the plate.

After watching Carrie take small portions of potatoes,

carrots, and cabbage salad, Emlyn felt self-conscious about filling his plate. Sarah, however, urged him to take more, so he did. He had not had a meal this good since the last time he was at their house.

"Sarah tells me that you preached at McKeesport today," Carrie said, pushing around the food on her plate.

"Yes, I did," said Emlyn. "They made me feel very welcome." He hesitated before deciding to plunge ahead. "A pastoral search committee from a church in Mount Pleasant was there as well."

Silence ensued. Sarah looked stunned.

"Word gets around fast," said Oesterling at last. "Did you contact them?"

"No," said Emlyn, going on to explain how the congregation had heard about his preaching.

"Do you think you might accept a call?" asked Oesterling. "That would be a very big step."

"That is certainly true," Emlyn replied. "That's why I think I should go to Mount Pleasant. Whatever course I choose, I will no longer have family in Homestead when Eirwen and the children leave. That will be a big change in itself."

"Do you know that Mount Pleasant is where Henry Clay Frick hails from?" asked Oesterling.

"Yes, I heard that," Emlyn replied. "They also told me it is about 35 miles from here."

"I understand that you are currently working in the mill office," interjected Carrie. "Don't you like the work?"

"The job is fine," he said. "I was very grateful to get it last winter."

"Won't you be afraid to give it up with so many out of work?" she asked. "It must pay more than the ministry."

"Monetary compensation is not what called me to the

ministry," Emlyn replied. "Besides, those out of work are mill workers, not those with office jobs."

"That reminds me," said Sarah. "I saw Norton Montague on the Avenue yesterday with a young woman. He passed me by without speaking."

"Gareth and I had a similar experience, but in our case, he forced us off the sidewalk," said Emlyn. "By the way, have you heard that he has become engaged?"

Carrie dropped her fork. "That can't be true!" she exclaimed. "Where did you hear this?"

"At the office last week," said Emlyn, going on to repeat what Charles had told him.

Sarah shook her head and laughed. "Why, I had no idea he was such a ladies' man. Perhaps I should thank Figaro for throwing him into the dirt. It was indeed a fortunate fall."

Carrie abruptly stood up. "Please excuse me," she said, hurrying out of the room.

"What's wrong?" Sarah asked. "Is it something I said?"

"She is undoubtedly suffering from indigestion," Oesterling said, getting up. "Please excuse me while I check on her."

"Aren't she and her husband friends with Montague?" asked Emlyn after Oesterling had left.

"They were," said Sarah, "but Papa tells me that Oliver and he are on the outs because Norton urged him to invest heavily in stocks that have since crashed. I suspect it's the reason Oliver has taken this new position in Chicago."

Emlyn stared at his plate. "It's hard to believe that in only a year's time, such an enormous change has come over Homestead. So many people are leaving town, while so many new ones are coming in."

"You may soon be leaving, too," said Sarah, her voice a whisper.

Emlyn shifted uneasily in his chair. He wanted to take

her hand, to ask her to go with him, but he couldn't. He didn't know where he was going, or whether he would be called. He didn't even know where he'd be living come January when the house had to be turned over to the company.

Looking into the immediate future, he felt on the brink of Niagara, about to be swept over in the crushing current. The sensation was more troubling even than what he felt when he had been cast out by his father. Footsteps in the hallway interrupted his thoughts.

"Is Carrie OK?" Sarah asked as Oesterling came into the room.

"She'll be fine," he said, going over to the buffet. "Now I'm going to have some pumpkin pie," he said, picking it up. "Who else would like a piece?"

For Emlyn the next week went by in a fury. Eirwen and her friends had packed up the summer clothing, hand-painted dishes, and family memorabilia to be shipped off the following week. Winter clothing and items they were currently using would be put in a steamer trunk that would accompany them on the journey. The furniture dealer came by Thursday and removed some pieces; the remainder was to be taken after they had vacated the house.

Each day when Emlyn came home, he would find more items gone from the walls, cupboards, and shelves. It was already starting to feel like they no longer lived there. Moving out would be no problem for him physically. He would leave with the contents of his trunk changed very little from when he had arrived.

Thomas grew more apprehensive as the departure day approached. One moment he'd be excited about going on a big journey to see his grandparents, while a short time later he'd cry and protest being torn from the only home he'd known.

For the first time since he came to Homestead, Emlyn had trouble sleeping. He'd lie in bed awake half the night, puzzling through some arrangements for the move, worrying about Eirwen, thinking about Sarah. When he did fall asleep, he'd dream disasters: being swept away in a flood, the roof caving in, an explosion in the mill leveling the town. In the morning he'd get out of bed exhausted and drag himself to work.

By Friday, he was worn out. Saturday afternoon he worked on making some revisions to the sermon for the Mount Pleasant congregation. That evening he took Sarah to a string quartet performance in Homestead, and they went out for tea afterwards at a little café. Now that the family's finances had been put in order, Emlyn felt he could afford to take Sarah out.

Emlyn wanted to tell her how he felt, but was stopped every time by the realization that the future for him was an unknown.

Sunday, December 4th, 11:30 a.m.

As prearranged, the family met Sarah after the church service.

"You are now coming to our house for a going-away party on your last Sunday at church," Sarah called to Thomas and Dilys.

Lowering her voice, she added to Eirwen, "I'd like the children to look forward to the trip."

Sarah walked toward the children. "Come on," she said. "We're all going to my house for a little party. Mrs. Sproule has prepared some sandwiches and special cakes just for you."

Thomas, sullen, said nothing, but Dilys ran to Sarah and took her hand.

As they walked up the hill to Tenth Avenue, fear crept up on Emlyn. Next Sunday Eirwen would not be in Homestead. She, Thomas, Dilys, and David would be many miles away, en route to the land of their fathers.

And he would not be here, either.

Monday, December 5th

Jansen was unhappy when Emlyn asked for the next Saturday off. Jansen finally gave in when Emlyn told him that his sister and her children were starting on a journey back to Wales that day.

"Don't request any more days off," said Jansen with a scowl. "We're approaching full production now with over three thousand men on the job. The company can't afford to have you coming in only five days a week."

When Emlyn told Charles about Jansen's comment, Charles shook his head in disgust. "The way these company men talk, we all should be working round-the-clock."

"I'm surprised that they've managed to build up the workforce to pre-strike levels in only a few months," said Emlyn.

"Yes," replied Charles, lowering his voice, "and they've done it primarily with replacements. I saw the figures: only 400 former strikers are at work in the mill, almost all of them laborers. You know what that means."

"Hundreds are out of work," replied Emlyn.

"That's right—two thousand five hundred of them, to be specific," said Charles. "And there's something else. This afternoon I overheard two superintendents talking about the company's investigation into the cholera epidemic in the mill last fall. Remember, when so many men fell ill and some of them died?"

"Yes?" Emlyn replied.

"Well, it wasn't cholera," said Charles. "Today one of the company's detectives went before a local magistrate and charged a cook in the mill with poisoning the replacement workers."

"Lord, no," Emlyn whispered. "I wonder what else has been going on inside the mill that the company is keeping hush-hush."

"One can only imagine," said Charles. "In any case, it's going to be a very un-merry Christmas in town this year."

Saturday, December 10th

Emlyn watched the train recede into the distance. That would be the last he'd see of Eirwen and children for a long while, perhaps years.

It had taken a Herculean effort by him and Eirwen to get the children dressed and on the platform with their luggage in time for the 10:20 train to Pittsburgh. Thomas had cried from the time he awoke to when he had boarded the train. Nothing would console him or deflect his grief. His wailing set off David, then Dilys.

All three were crying as Eirwen had hustled them into the car. His last image of Eirwen was of her, dry-eyed and stoical, waving at him from the window as the train pulled away. The time for weeping was past, she had told him. She was putting her trust in Providence and pushing off into the future.

Emlyn sat down on a bench and pulled out *A Hazard of New Fortunes*, the novel that Sarah had loaned him to read on the train. In less than a half hour, his train came in. Two transfers and three hours later, he arrived in Mount Pleasant.

Sunday, December 11th, 7:40 p.m.

Sarah was waiting for him as the train pulled into the Amity Street Station. The three railway cars were full of people returning from their weekend outings. Emlyn pressed through the small throng to get to her. They briefly embraced and began walking.

"How was your trip?" Sarah asked, her face reddened by the blustery wind. "And how is Mount Pleasant?"

"Good, very good," said Emlyn. "It is a pleasant town and a nice congregation."

"Nice?" asked Sarah. "That doesn't sound all that good."

"I truly mean that," said Emlyn earnestly. "The people in the congregation couldn't have been nicer to me. Last night I stayed at the home of Joseph and Effie Powell—he's the head of the pastoral search committee. The parsonage is on the same block as the chapel. It's a small brick two-story house, very cozy. It has some furniture, odds and ends left behind or donated. Of course I couldn't stay there because it's been shut up."

"How did the service go?" Sarah asked.

"Very well," said Emlyn. "At their request, I delivered a revised version of the same sermon. This time, I was not nervous. I have practically memorized it."

"Do you think the congregation will call you?" Sarah asked.

"I can't say," said Emlyn. "Most there seemed responsive to the sermon. About a third of the members are from Wales or of Welsh extraction. I think that may count in my favor." He walked a few paces. "Or perhaps not."

Sarah smiled at his small joke. "What about the town?" she asked. "Is it *nicer* than Homestead?"

"It is," replied Emlyn. "Mount Pleasant is one of the oldest towns in Pennsylvania, but measured by British standards, that's new." He went on to describe the town, long a center for coke production and more recently, coal mining. From the town one could see the profile of the Laurel Mountain Highlands to the east. "A gigantic coke-making plant is located south of there in a town called Connellsville, and there's another one outside Mount Pleasant called the Morewood Coke Works. Both of these are owned by the ubiquitous H.C. Frick."

"I've heard of Morewood," said Sarah. "Did you know that there was a violent strike there in April of last year? It was all over the papers."

"Mr. Powell mentioned it, but did not go into details," said Emlyn.

"Many call it the 'Morewood Massacre,'"said Sarah. "The situation was similar to the one here: Frick wanted to lower the tonnage scale, the union resisted, violence and sabotage escalated. Sheriffs' deputies were called in. Finally, Frick got the governor to call in the National Guard. When the workers marched on the coke works, the guardsmen fired on them."

"That's appalling," said Emlyn. "Was anyone killed?"

"Nine workers, most of them shot in the head," said Sarah. "Many more were wounded."

"Lord in heaven!" exclaimed Emlyn. "Frick is using this same strategy in whatever labor dispute he encounters."

"It's a successful strategy. It works in Frick's favor, every time," said Sarah.

"This is maddening," said Emlyn. "Is there no escaping his influence?"

"Not in Western Pennsylvania, there isn't," Sarah replied.

They walked in silence along the Avenue. When they reached Ann Street, Sarah stopped. "Let's not go to the house," she said. "Carrie is driving me crazy with her complaining. The way she goes on, you'd think she was the only woman who has had to endure childbearing. Even Papa is getting irritated by her constant whining."

"What do you want to do?" asked Emlyn.

"Let's stop in the little café where we went last Saturday," said Sarah. "We can get a bite to eat and talk."

For over an hour, they sat at a table, talking about Homestead and Mount Pleasant, and about the long journey ahead for Eirwen and children. Finally, when their teacups were drained and only crumbs of cookies remained, Sarah asked him if he would go to Mount Pleasant if called.

"I've been dwelling on that question for a week," said Emlyn. "The irony of my situation here in Homestead pains me. I came here fleeing the ministry in Wales. I arrived with nothing, and through the kindness of my family and others, I eventually found a way to support myself.

Now Eirwen and the children are the ones going back to Wales, reliant on the kindness of others, and I am pondering returning to the path of the ministry."

"What happened to them is beyond anyone's control," said Sarah. "I would like to know if you truly want to be a minister." She unnerved him by looking intently into his eyes.

Emlyn lowered his eyes for a moment before returning her gaze.

"Yes, I do," he replied. "Six months ago the notion would have been unthinkable. But now, after the battle, after Gwyn disappeared, after what's happened to Homestead. . . ." His voice trailed off. "Even if Salem does not call me, I cannot stay at Carnegie Steel. As soon as I can find a suitable position, I will leave."

"I understand," Sarah said quietly. "I would do the same if I were you."

"My main regret is that this all is coming to a head just as we are becoming . . . ," Emlyn hesitated. ". . . as we are becoming, uh, such good friends."

"Yes, I . . ." began Sarah, but she was interrupted by a stage cough from the waitress. Emlyn looked up to see the owner turning over the 'open' sign on the door to the 'closed' side.

"We can take a hint," he said under his breath. He paid the bill and helped Sarah put on her cloak.

As they came outside, the gusty wind was blowing around powdery snowflakes. Emlyn turned up his collar against the cold as they walked up the hill. Turning directly into the wind on Tenth Avenue, they linked arms and lowered their heads. Snow pelting their faces, they ran the last half block and up the steps to the front porch.

Sarah shook the snow off her bonnet. "Thanks for the tea."

"Thank you for coming to meet the train," Emlyn said.

Her cheeks were rosy, her green eyes glistening.

"I was happy to do it," Sarah said. "Let's hope you get good news from Mount Pleasant." She gave him a wistful smile.

"Thank you," he said, looking into her eyes. He was intensely aware of her body so close to his. Impulsively, Emlyn tilted her chin toward him and kissed her on the mouth. As Sarah drew in her breath, Emlyn feared she might push him away. But she returned the kiss, tentatively at first, then assertively. They kissed again.

Hearing someone moving inside the house, they stepped apart.

"Good night," she said, kissing him quickly and going inside.

Emlyn hardly noticed the driving snow and wind as he

hurried to the house on Third Avenue. He relived the kiss over and over.

At the back door, Emlyn fumbled for the key. Unlocking the door, he came into the kitchen and lit a lamp. He glanced over to where the kitchen clock used to sit. It was gone. He pulled out his watch. Nearly 11.

He had tried to anticipate the experience of coming back to the house, but he was not prepared for the emptiness that confronted him. All the time he had lived there, every day and night, the family had been there. Now there was only a void. All the furniture had been removed but the beds, the kitchen table and a couple of chairs.

He started a small fire in the kitchen stove to take the chill off the room. That morning Eirwen had helped him carry his bed downstairs. For the next two weeks he would live in the kitchen, the only room easily kept warm. Then he would either be moving in with Charles or moving to Mount Pleasant.

Emlyn hastily washed up in a basin of lukewarm water. He said his prayers, changed into his nightclothes, and got into bed. The sheets felt icy, and he pulled the feather comforter up to his nose against the cold. As he lay in the small bed set against the wall next to the stove, his mood darkened. Things were moving so fast, he felt could not keep up with so many conflicting emotions.

The garish glow from the mill pulsed through the grimy windows. A vague fear crept upon him as he listened to the wind whistling around the eaves. He felt so alone, so desolate. For a moment, he fought off the urge to rush out of the house and seek refuge in a hotel. But he would still be alone there, surrounded by strangers. Shivering, he turned over to face the wall. At last, exhaustion overcame him and he fell asleep.

Monday, December 12th, 6 a.m.

When the alarm went off, Emlyn could barely drag himself out of bed. He threw on his wool robe and built a fire in the cook stove. He brewed a pot of tea and used the remainder of the hot water to wash up and shave. Nearly two years had passed since, as a student in Cardiff, he had followed this routine. He would have to get used to it again.

Draping his coat over his shoulders, he cut a slab of bread from the loaf Eirwen had made and sat down at the table to eat. When he reached for the sugar bowl, he noticed an envelope propped between it and the saltshaker. His name was written on it in Eirwen's hand.

Inside, something was wrapped in a piece of paper folded multiple times. He carefully unfolded the paper. It was a slender gold band with a single pearl mounted on it. On the paper was a note.

Dearest Brother,

Do you remember this ring? It belonged to Nain Davies. Mam gave it to me when I left for America. I firmly believe that it belongs in America, as do you. Now that I am returning to Wales, I pass it on to you. Give it to your bride-to-be as a memento of generations past.

May God bless you and keep you,
All my love,
Eirwen

Emlyn wrapped up the ring and put it back into the envelope. Throughout breakfast and dressing for work, he thought about Eirwen, Sarah, and the ring. He puzzled over the note, wondering if Eirwen had sensed his growing attraction for Sarah. Did Eirwen intend him to give the ring to her?

As he trudged through the thin covering of soot-flecked snow on his way to work, he kept turning the question over in his head: Should he ask Sarah to marry him? They had known each other less than a year. It would be best to wait. The situation, however, was coming to a crisis. He would be leaving Homestead sooner or later. If it was sooner, he should act.

Wednesday, December 14th, 3:30 a.m.

Oesterling pulled the blanket around his ears in a vain attempt to shut out the noises in the hallway. Since Carrie had arrived at the house, she had gotten up nearly every night in the wee small hours to wander around the house. She couldn't sleep she said, and apparently wished the same for the rest of them.

Outside his bedroom door, Oesterling heard whisperings, then, from Carrie's room, a scream. He threw on his dressing gown and opened the bedroom door. Sarah, holding a lamp, was starting down the stairs.

"Papa," she said. "Carrie's pains have started." As if to emphasize the fact, another scream came from down the hall. "I'm going to fetch some clean linens."

Oesterling, followed by Cerberus, went to Carrie's room and stood in the open doorway. Mrs. Sproule was standing by the bedside.

"Papa!" Carrie cried when she saw him. "The pains are so awful." She twisted up her face, and screamed again.

"Carrie," he said, coming into the room. "You must try to calm yourself. You need to conserve your strength for later."

"Later?" she shrieked. "It can't get worse than this! I cannot endure it."

Oesterling exchanged glances with Mrs. Sproule, who

also knew that indeed it was going to get much, much worse.

"Call Dr. Graaf," Carrie demanded. "Tell him to come over right away."

After determining that the pains were about seven or eight minutes apart, Oesterling left the room and went downstairs. He had tried to talk Carrie into using a Homestead doctor, but she and Oliver had insisted on a society doctor in Oakland. The doctor had wanted Carrie to stay in his maternity hospital to await the birth, but Oesterling suspected they could not afford the expense. Instead, the doctor agreed to come to Homestead for the delivery—for what Oesterling thought was a ridiculous fee.

He rang Graaf's number and waited nearly a minute for someone to pick up.

When Oesterling described the situation, Graaf responded irritably, "Why didn't you wait to call me if labor just started? With a first baby, labor usually goes on for many hours."

"Yes," said Oesterling, "I realize that. But Mrs. Strong. . . ."

Graaf interrupted him. "If you realize that, you should not have awakened me in the middle of the night. Call me when she's in the final stages of labor." He hung up.

Sarah, her arms full of clean sheets and towels, was standing at the foot of the stairs.

"What a rude, stupid ass!" said Oesterling.

"Who?" said Sarah.

"That Dr. Graaf, whom Carrie and Oliver think is so wonderful," said Oesterling. "He shouldn't be an obstetrician if he doesn't like being awakened at all hours."

Another scream came from upstairs.

"Lord help us," muttered Oesterling.

6:20 A.M.

Oesterling and Cerberus came through the back door after their walk to the top of the hill and back. Oesterling, frustrated that he had no role in this drama, had chosen to leave the house for a while. Mrs. Sproule and Sarah had been taking turns staying with Carrie, talking to her, trying to keep her calm.

As he took off his boots, Mrs. Sproule rushed into the back hall. "Doctor," she exclaimed breathlessly. "You must do something. I think the baby is coming."

"Are you sure?" he asked. "Labor started only three hours ago."

"I've had four children myself," she said. "Her water broke about a half hour ago and the pains are getting very close."

Oesterling followed her upstairs and into Carrie's room. Carrie had twisted the sheets into knots. Her hair clung to the side of her face in damp tendrils.

"Papa!" she screamed as soon as she saw him. "Help me, I'm dying!"

"Carrie, this is only normal labor," he said gently.

"It can't be," she insisted, rolling her head back and forth on the pillow. "Oh my God! My back is breaking." She let out a bloodcurdling scream. "Help me!" When Sarah tried to take her hand, Carrie shrieked, "Don't touch me!"

Oesterling signaled Mrs. Sproule to come into the hall with him.

"What do you think?" she asked.

"You're right. We need to get someone here right away," he said. "There's no time to call in Graaf and Dr. Baker is out of town." Oesterling pulled at his beard, wracking his brain for options.

"I know a midwife who lives three blocks away, on Ninth," Mrs. Sproule said. "I could run over there."

Oesterling considered this idea, then said, "Yes, try to get her. I will the deliver the child if there's no other option, but only *if*. Hurry, please."

Oesterling paced in the hall. As Carrie's screams increased in frequency and pitch, Cerberus deserted his master for the relative quiet of the study downstairs. After about twenty minutes, the screams were replaced by grunts and long, excruciating groans.

Sarah came into the hall. "Papa, I'm afraid," she said. "Carrie is making these terrible noises."

"Don't worry," he said. "Although Carrie doesn't believe it, this is what childbirth is usually like."

At Sarah's insistence, he went to Carrie's bedside. As a pain came on, her features contorted. She held her breath, grunting as she pushed. At the end of the contraction, she slumped back against the pillow.

"Lord, I thought I was going to faint," she said weakly.

"Carrie, you must not hold your breath," said Oesterling soothingly. "Help will be here soon."

"Where's Dr. Graaf?" she demanded. "Didn't you call him?"

"I did," said Oesterling, "but he said it was too soon to come."

She stared at her father, her eyes wild. "I hate him! I hate him! I hate all men. Damn them." Throwing back her head, she braced for another contraction. "Damn Norton for this agony!"

Sarah looked sharply at Oesterling as Carrie thrashed from side to side. They went out into the hall, in time to hear the front door open and shut. Mrs. Sproule and another middle-aged woman carrying a bag came into the foyer and up the stairs.

"Doctor, I'm Mrs. Cox," said the woman, shaking his hand. "Where's Mrs. Strong?"

"Thank you for coming," said Oesterling, indicating the door to Carrie's room.

Mrs. Cox went to the doorway, followed by Mrs. Sproule. Mrs. Cox removed her bonnet and smoothed down her graying hair.

"Good morning, dear," she said to Carrie, going into the room. "Let's bring this baby into the world." She smiled at Sarah and Oesterling as she shut the door. Within, they could hear Carrie cursing a blue streak.

"Where did Carrie pick up such language?" asked Sarah, appalled.

Oesterling raked his fingers through his hair. "Women in labor can get very inventive."

"Poor Mrs. Cox," said Sarah. "I don't envy her the task of dealing with Carrie,"

"I'm sure she has heard it all before," he said. "Nevertheless, I wouldn't relish having Carrie for a patient under the best circumstances."

"That's for certain," said Sarah.

"I'm going to the kitchen and get coffee," said Oesterling. "How about you?"

As they started down the stairs, Sarah asked, "Papa, one thing puzzles me. Why did Carrie say she hates Norton, not Oliver?"

Oesterling froze in his tracks.

"Why, she is clearly hysterical," he said. "She didn't know what she was saying. Obviously, she meant Oliver."

Sarah nodded thoughtfully. "Obviously," she said at last.

For the next forty minutes, screams and moans came from Carrie's room. At times, they could hear the women moving around. Finally, shortly after 8, a new cry was heard.

Oesterling and Sarah ran upstairs as Mrs. Sproule came out of Carrie's room. "It's a girl," she said, beaming. "A lovely baby girl."

Sarah squealed with delight, kissing Osterling on the cheek. "You're a grandpa," she exclaimed. "I'm an aunt!"

They had to wait another half hour. At last, Mrs. Cox opened the door and ushered them in.

Carrie, exhausted but radiant, was looking down at the infant cradled in her arms. "Sarah, Papa!" she said, her voice hoarse. "Isn't she beautiful?"

Oesterling came closer. The infant had reddish curls that Mrs. Cox had adorned with pink ribbons. She blinked her steel-blue eyes and yawned.

"She is beautiful," he said. "I wish your mother could be here to see her."

7:10 P.M.

Emlyn sat by the stove reading an article in the newspaper about ongoing labor trouble in the Monongahela Valley. Striking coal miners, alarmed at a big increase in replacement workers, were trying to convince them to quit and support the strike.

He sighed and put down the paper. Walking back from the café where he had eaten supper, Emlyn had seen a stark change in the town from the way it had been a year ago. With so many people out of work, even those with jobs were not in a festive mood. Drunken, filthy men lay slumped in the alleys. Desperate men and women begged passersby for money. He had seen children along the railroad tracks, picking up coal that had fallen out of tenders; he had heard that a boy had been killed by a passing train.

Emlyn leaned back in the chair and closed his eyes. If all had gone as planned, Eirwen and the children would be halfway across the Atlantic. He imagined his parents back in Treorchy, preparing the house for the arrival of Eirwen and the grandchildren.

A rapping at the door startled him. He looked out and saw Mrs. Crossley, the next-door neighbor, holding up an envelope.

"Sorry to bother you, Mr. Phillips," she said, "I thought this might be important. It's special delivery. The postman tried to deliver it this afternoon, but you weren't around. I hope you don't mind that I told him I'd give it to you."

"No, not at all," said Emlyn, taking the envelope. "Thanks very much."

Emlyn closed the door and sat down. It was postmarked 'Mount Pleasant.' With trembling hands, he tore open the envelope. Anxiously he scanned the letter, then went back and read it carefully all the way through: The congregation of Salem Church was pleased to call him to serve as their minister. The compensation was about the same as he was making in the mill office, but it included a semi-furnished house. They requested that he assume his duties as pastor on January 15th, which would serve as his day of ordination. Directions were included on how to wire a response back.

Emlyn sat down, pondering the letter's contents. Then he bowed his head and gave a prayer of thanks for this unexpected turn in his life path.

For a quarter hour, he sat by the stove, his thoughts returning to Sarah. This was it. He would definitely be leaving Homestead in less than a month. He needed to tell her about the letter, for he was going to accept the call.

He damped down the fire, put on his coat, and struck out for the Oesterlings'. He had gone only a block when it occurred to him that it might not be a good time to go barging in there unannounced. He veered off toward the Griffiths' house. He had to share this news with someone, and the minister and his wife should be the first to know.

He came up the steps and knocked. Griffiths, book in hand, opened the door and contemplated Emlyn over the tops of his spectacles.

"You don't have to say a word," he said, grinning. "It's written all over your face. Come on in, and we'll have some tea and cakes to mark the occasion."

Thursday, December 15th

On the way to work, Emlyn wired Mount Pleasant and posted letters to Gareth and to his parents. Upon arriving at the office, Emlyn was prepared to give notice, but Jansen was away for the morning. Charles did a little jig beside his desk when Emlyn told him the news. "We'll have to go out for a drink after work," he said, but seeing Emlyn's blank expression, amended the invitation to 'dinner tomorrow.'

Jansen was not as enthusiastic. After lunch Emlyn stopped in his office and told him he was leaving the Carnegie Company.

"You are?" said Jansen, raising one eyebrow. "Have you found a better position?"

"Yes, sir," said Emlyn. "I am joining the ministry."

"Ministry!" said Jansen. "My father was a minister, and he died penniless. You have a bright future with the company. Why do you want to give that up?"

"Sir, I need to leave as soon as possible to prepare for my new position."

Jansen scowled, slapping the top of his desk with a ruler. "Very well," he said. "Can you finish up your current project by Saturday?"

Emlyn said yes, probably.

"Good," said Jansen. "Do as much as you can and hand over your work to LaCroix. You can pick up your final pay next week." He stood up and offered Emlyn his hand. "Good luck," he said. Before Emlyn could thank him, Jansen sat down and gave a wave toward the door. "You can go now."

As Emlyn wrapped up work at 5 o'clock, his thoughts were racing ahead to Christmas and the New Year. He didn't have that much packing to do for the move. Whenever he was ready to leave the house, all he had to do was contact the furniture dealer and arrange for pickup of the few remaining pieces. Still, he had to catch up on his reading. He also needed to go through his study notes to refresh his knowledge of theological and biblical scholarship. As he moved along in the crowd of employees leaving the General Office Building, a smile spread on his face. He was really looking forward to this new task, this new work.

"Emlyn!" someone called out. He glanced around. Across the street he saw a green bonnet among the dark hats. "Emlyn!" Sarah called again. Emlyn worked his way across the street towards her. "Emlyn," she said as he reached her. "Reverend Griffiths told me the news. Congratulations." She kissed him on the cheek.

"Yes, I sent off my acceptance today," he said. "I just quit my job."

"There's happy news in our house as well," she said as they walked along the Avenue, arm in arm. She told him about the arrival of Carrie's baby. "She's to be christened Margaret Lydia, after her grandmothers. Carrie is not exactly blissful, but then, she rarely is." She laughed. "Anyway,

Oliver will be coming from Chicago for Carrie. He will be arriving Christmas Eve, and will accompany Carrie and the baby back to Chicago the next Tuesday."

They stopped at McClure Street. "I know this is presumptuous of me, but would you like to have dinner with us?"

"You mean now?" Emlyn asked.

"Yes," said Sarah. "I've already talked to Papa and Mrs. Sproule. Of course, for the time being, Carrie is remaining in her room with the baby. But if you have other plans . . ."

Emlyn thought of the dark, empty house on Third Street. "The only plan I have," he said, "is to eat at the café again—you know, the one we went to Sunday."

"Then it's settled," she said, and they started up the hill toward Tenth Avenue.

Oesterling greeted them at the door. "Congratulations," he said, shaking Emlyn's hand. They went into the parlor and sat in front of the fire.

Oesterling was asking Emlyn about the church in Mount Pleasant when someone rang the doorbell.

"Who could that be?" asked Oesterling, as Sarah went to the door.

A moment later, she came into the parlor and said to her father, "It's Norton. He wants Oliver's address in Chicago."

"Why did he have to come here?" Oesterling asked irritably, going into the foyer.

"Can't you get it from the company?" he asked Montague.

"They won't give it to me," Montague replied testily.

"That's curious," said Oesterling. "Did they say why not?"

Montague shifted his weight from one foot to another. "Sir, I will get to the point. Yesterday I was called into the superintendent's office and told to clean out my desk. When I asked the reason, they said that my ethics had been called into question." He bit his lip. "Now I'm finished with the company. When my fiancé learns of my dismissal, she will undoubtedly break off the engagement."

"I don't see how your firing involves Oliver," said Oesterling.

Montague snorted. "It's as plain as day: he is the complainant."

"It's not as plain as day to me," said Oesterling. "In any case, the company seems to have good reason in keeping his address private."

Montague glanced over Oesterling's shoulder into the parlor. "Oh, he's here," he said. "I should have known." He ran his eyes over Emlyn and back to Oesterling.

"Of course you won't give it to me. You—and he," he said, nodding toward Emlyn, "never liked me. You're all in it together, gloating over my ruin."

Oesterling shook his head. "None of us here has any influence over what goes on in the mill offices. It must be your guilty conscience at work over your attempt to get Emlyn fired—or worse—last summer."

"He was at the battle!" he shouted, pointing at an accusing finger at Emlyn.

"Whether I was or was not at the battle is a moot point now," Emlyn said. "This afternoon I quit my job with the company."

Montague stared at him, trying to digest this news.

The thin wail of an infant came from the second floor. Montague looked up at the ceiling.

"What's that?" he asked, stepping back and bumping into Sarah. "It sounds like a baby."

"It's Carrie's daughter, born two days ago," said Sarah. "They're staying with us for a while."

"Carrie? Her baby?" Montague said, moving toward the stairs. "No one told me that Carrie is in Homestead, let alone that she . . ."

"You've had your say," said Oesterling, taking his arm. "Now it's time for you to leave." Montague kept looking up the stairs as Oesterling steered him into the vestibule.

There, Oesterling pulled Montague close to him, their faces almost touching. "If you try to contact Carrie or Oliver," he whispered fiercely, "by God, you will be ruined in more ways than one."

Oesterling pulled open the door, and Montague stumbled onto the porch.

Oesterling came back into the parlor and sat down. "Well," he said, "he was right about one thing."

"What's that?" Sarah asked.

"I never did like that fellow," he said.

I'll only have to do this two more times, Emlyn mused as he set the alarm to get up for work the next morning. He had decided to stay in the house at least until Christmas. He had considered Charles's offer to share his lodgings, but decided against the move. Instead, he wrote Gareth, asking if he could stay with them for a week or so. He planned to move into the parsonage at Mount Pleasant on January 2nd. In the meantime, here, in the house, there were no distractions—except the emptiness itself. He could work undisturbed.

Heaving a deep sigh, he pulled up the comforter and turned to face the wall. Tomorrow Charles was taking him out to dinner. Saturday, he and Sarah were going into the city to have dinner and take in a performance of Handel's 'Messiah.' This was the first opportunity they had had to go on an outing to the city, free of the cares and responsibilities of work and family. It would be good.

Through the haze of sleep, Emlyn thought he heard a noise in the parlor. He listened, eyes closed. Inside the house was completely still. The only sounds were the noises from the mill. It must have been that, he decided, and immediately slipped back to sleep.

He came halfway back to consciousness again. The room was filled with an icy chill. In the twilight between sleep and wakefulness, he sensed that someone, a man, was standing over him by the bed. He turned over and opened his eyes to see what looked like a shadow moving towards the kitchen door.

At the door the dark form slowly took the transparent, luminescent shape of a man. His face was very pale, his expression melancholy. It was Gwyn. He was looking at Emlyn, his hand raised in a gesture of farewell. And then, in an instant, he vanished.

Emlyn blinked. Was he imagining things? He got to his feet and went to the door. No one was outside. The house felt quite empty. He was sure of that.

The hands of his alarm clock read a little past three. He got into bed, wrapped the comforter around him, and stared out the window. Snow had started to fall. He watched the flakes floating past, and felt completely at peace. He closed his eyes and fell asleep.

Three hours later the jangling of the alarm clock awoke him. He sat upright with a start, remembering the vision of Gwyn. Had he been dreaming? That was the most reasonable explanation, Emlyn thought as he got out of bed. Gwyn had been on his mind a lot these past weeks. That had to be it.

Thursday, December 16th

Emlyn and Charles examined the menus at their table in the dining room of the Sherman Hotel on the Avenue, two blocks from the office building.

"Order anything you want," said Charles. "This is truly an occasion for celebration. Do you mind if I order wine for myself?"

"No, go ahead," said Emlyn. "I don't want to send you to the poor house," he added as he scanned the menu. He chose the roasted chicken, while Charles ordered the trout.

"You don't have much longer in Homestead," said Charles, after the waiter took their order. "How does it feel to be leaving?"

"Very strange," said Emlyn. "It's been sort of eerie staying in an empty house, I tell you."

"Why? Have you seen a ghost?" asked Charles, laughing.

Emlyn hesitated. "As a matter of fact, I have. I mean, I might have."

The smile disappeared from Charles' face. "You don't say!"

"I do say," said Emlyn.

"What did you see?"

Emlyn related the story of his vision of Gwyn. "Of course," he said in conclusion, "it had to be a dream."

The waiter came over and set a glass of white wine in front of Charles. He stared at the glass, running his finger around the rim. "Are you sure?" he asked Emlyn.

"It had to be," said Emlyn.

"I'm not so sure about that," Charles replied. "My grandmother saw a ghost once."

"Of whom?" asked Emlyn.

"Her husband, my grandfather," he said. "He was the

captain of a clipper ship out of Providence that did runs to England and France. One night when he was away at sea, my grandmother awoke about two in the morning. There, at the foot of the bed, stood my grandfather in his uniform. He smiled at her, and disappeared. Two days later she got a cable informing her that his ship had gone down in a storm off Newfoundland that night, with the loss of all hands."

Emlyn considered this story for a moment. "Are you suggesting that Gwyn was saying goodbye, that he has passed on?" he asked.

"That's what I'd think if a member of my family appeared to me in that way," said Charles.

"Maybe it was a projection of my mind," said Emlyn. "I was very angry with him when he left. But I really feel he would have returned if he could. For the last several weeks, I have felt that he is gone from this earth." He paused, and added softly, "Wherever he is, I hope and pray he is at peace. He was dealt a harsh blow."

"He and many others," said Charles.

They sat in silence.

Picking up his wine glass, Charles held it out to Emlyn, "To your health, Emlyn, and success and happiness in your calling." He took a sip.

"Thanks," said Emlyn. "I have appreciated your friendship these last months."

"And I yours," said Charles. "I'll miss you at the office." He took another sip. "By the way, who is the young woman I've seen you with around town, the red head? Is she the one who is organist at the church?"

"Yes, that's Sarah Oesterling," said Emlyn, explaining the connection between Eirwen, the Oesterlings, and the church. "She's a teacher at the elementary school. We're going to Pittsburgh Saturday night for a concert."

"Is she your sweetheart?" Charles asked.

Emlyn blushed.

"Aha! She is!" said Charles.

"I have not declared my affection for her," said Emlyn. "I've known her only a little more than a year."

"That's more than enough time to fall in love," said Charles.

Emlyn blushed again. "That's been a more recent development," he said.

"I see," said Charles. "Are you going to carry her off to Mount Pleasant as Mrs. Phillips?"

"I fear that . . . that she . . ." Emlyn stammered.

"What's to fear?" said Charles. "Pop the question. Saturday night."

Emlyn looked at Charles questioningly.

"I'm serious," said Charles. "Don't let this chance slip by." He rubbed a smudge off the wine glass with his thumb. "I didn't ask my sweetheart to come with me to Pittsburgh, and I've sorely regretted it. Now it's too late. She went and married an accountant."

"I'm sorry to hear that," Emlyn said. "I will try to muster the courage."

"You can do it," said Charles. He raised his glass again. "To Emlyn and Sarah," he said. "May you live long and prosper."

Emlyn's heart beat more quickly. He wanted to do this. Somehow, he had to do this.

"Thank you," he said. "Saturday night, then." He lifted his water glass to Charles.

Saturday, December 17th

All through the performance of the Christmas music from Handel's *Messiah*, Emlyn had mentally gone over what he would say. He was going to ask Sarah to marry him, to share his life as a minister.

On the way into the city, he and Sarah had talked about his performing on violin for the Christmas Eve service. They had agreed upon 'Air on the G-String' from Bach's Orchestral Suite No. 3, as it was a piece they both knew well. They had also finalized plans for his coming to celebrate Christmas Eve and Day with the Oesterlings.

Last year he had eagerly anticipated Christmas, a day off work to spend with Eirwen's family. Now he dreaded it, for he would be leaving Homestead on the 27th. He would finish clearing out the house Monday, do final packing, and be on the train for Johnstown Tuesday morning.

Applause startled him out of his reverie. The choir had finished the 'Hallelujah Chorus.' The soloists and the conductor took their bows. The audience started filing out of the concert hall.

"That was wonderful," said Sarah. "I especially liked the alto soloist. Such a marvelous voice, it reminded me of Eirwen's."

Emlyn said nothing, his thoughts springing across the ocean to Eirwen and the children.

"I'm sorry," said Sarah. "I didn't mean to make you sad."

"No, no," said Emlyn. "It's fine. I'm just wondering how the trip has gone for them. They should have arrived in Cardiff today."

On the train to Homestead, they talked about the concert and the music Sarah was preparing for Christmas services. As they walked up Amity Street, Emlyn suggested they stop for a hot chocolate in the little café.

They settled into a booth and ordered. Outwardly composed but very anxious, Emlyn rehearsed his prepared speech in his head. As they sipped their cocoa, the minutes ticked by. It was nearly half past ten, and they would soon have to leave.

Emlyn looked over at Sarah and cleared his throat. "Sarah?" he said. She gave him a smile. "I've been wanting to say . . . I mean, ask you something." He sat there foolishly glancing from her face to the cocoa cup.

"Yes?" she prompted.

"You have become very special to me," he said. "I will cherish the moments we've had together these past months." He self-consciously cleared his throat again.

"I will, too," she said softly.

His heart pounded in his chest. He felt so awkward. "I . . . I can't bear the thought of parting from you," he blurted out. Trying to compose himself, he reached across the table and took her hand. Looking directly into her eyes, he said, "Sarah, would you do me the honor of becoming my wife?"

For several seconds, Sarah looked at him as if stupefied. His heart jumped into his throat. "I know that this is all very sudden," he stammered, withdrawing his hand. "I understand if you can not . . ."

"Yes," she interrupted, taking back his hand and squeezing it. "Yes, Emlyn, I accept."

It was his turn to be stunned. "You do?" he asked.

"I do," she said.

He lifted her hand and pressed it to his lips.

"Dearest Sarah," he said. "I love you so much."

"I love you, too," she said.

As they walked up the hill to Tenth Avenue, he held her tightly to him. Emlyn asked her when he should ask her father for her hand.

"I think tomorrow after dinner would be good," she said. "The only sad part of this is leaving Papa alone in the house. First Carrie, then Mama. Now me."

"When did your mother pass on?" he asked.

"It will be four years in April. I was away at school. Papa came home from work to find Mama lying on the floor of the parlor. At first he thought she had fainted, but soon discovered that she was gone. He couldn't revive her. They think she died of a stroke shortly before Papa came home."

"How horrible for him," said Emlyn, "and for you."

"I know he misses her every day," said Sarah. "Fortunately, his practice keeps him busy."

They discussed when to have the wedding, and decided it should be in June, right after school let out for the summer. They walked over Tenth Avenue in silence, lost in their own thoughts.

"I don't know how I'll get through the next six months without you," said Sarah as they came onto the front porch.

"We've been through some difficult times and somehow we'll get through the waiting," he said.

He pulled her gently to him and took her face in his hands. He kissed her eyes, her forehead. She slipped her arms around his neck and kissed him on the mouth, tentatively at first, then fervently. His pulse quickened as he hungrily pressed his lips against hers a second time.

Emlyn heard the door to the vestibule creak, and reluctantly broke the embrace. The front door swung open, and there was the doctor, holding a newspaper.

"I thought I heard someone on the porch," he said. "How was the concert?"

"Wonderful," said Sarah. "Such beautiful voices."

"Would you like to come in for a cup of tea?" the doctor asked Emlyn.

Sarah and Emlyn exchanged glances. "Oh, it's getting late," Emlyn said.

"Why don't you come in, just for a moment?" said Sarah,

casting a meaningful look his way.

They went inside. Sarah went into the kitchen to make tea while Oesterling ushered Emlyn into the study, where a fire was blazing. "I never seem to finish the newspaper before I doze off," said Oesterling, easing into the armchair. "It doesn't matter, as it's mostly bad news, anyway."

Emlyn pulled himself to attention on the edge of his seat. "Sir, I'd like to speak to you about something," he said. Again, he felt foolish, unsure about how to proceed. He hadn't even thought beyond his proposing to Sarah.

Oesterling looked at him, puzzled. "What's wrong?" he asked.

"Nothing," said Emlyn, his voice quavering. "Nothing is wrong."

He looked into the fire, trying to gather his thoughts. He turned his attention back to the doctor.

"Sir, I would like your permission to take Sarah's hand in marriage," he said earnestly. "I have asked Sarah to be my wife, and she has accepted. Would you give us your blessing?"

The doctor returned the gaze, but said nothing.

"I will not make a great deal of income as a minister," Emlyn added nervously. "But it's enough to support her and, if we are blessed with them, children. It's a more humble life than she has known, but, as you know, she is not afraid of work."

A grin spread across Oesterling's face. "Indeed, I know Sarah isn't afraid of much, including work. Why, of course, I give you my blessing. I would be delighted to have you as a son-in-law." He reached over to shake Emlyn's hand. Simultaneously, Sarah came into the room carrying a tea tray.

"So we'll be having yet another addition to the family," Oesterling said to her as she set down the tray.

"Yes, Papa," she said, coming behind his chair and putting her hands on his shoulders. "I'm the most fortunate woman in the world to have you two in my life."

She threw her arms around his neck and hugged him.

"I think we are the fortunate ones," said Oesterling, patting her hands.

"I'll second that," said Emlyn.

—•••—

Emlyn didn't stay much longer at the Oesterlings'. The three of them talked it over and decided to make a formal engagement announcement on Christmas Eve, but begin telling close friends and family right away. As Emlyn and Oesterling knew before she articulated it, Sarah wanted a simple, small wedding.

After he got into bed, Emlyn stayed awake for a long time, his mind running over plans for preparing for his work as a minister, closing up the house, packing and moving, leaving his friends in Homestead. He had only eight more days, and he needed to make the most of them.

Monday, December 19th

Emlyn put more wood in the cook stove and set the kettle on top. Wearing his thick wool sweater, he went over the notes he was preparing for his ordination sermon. Books and notes were stacked on one end of the table; his violin case was set on one of the chairs by a pile of sheet music.

When the kettle whistled, he poured boiling water in a teapot and left it to brew. Shoving aside the notes, he sat down and took a fresh sheet of paper. He needed to write three important letters: one to his parents, one to Eirwen, and one to Gareth. The main message would be the same in each, to tell of his engagement.

As he was sealing up the envelopes an hour later, someone knocked at the front door. It was a messenger with a cable from Treorchy: "Arrived safely." Emlyn smiled, imagining all the members of his family together for Christmas. The smile vanished when he thought of Gwyn. Might he show up at some point? In his heart of hearts, Emlyn thought not. The Phillips and Jones families would be together, without Gwyn, and he would be with his new family here in America.

Later that afternoon, Emlyn, carrying his violin, was returning from practicing at the church, when he saw Paddy standing by the door of O'Reilly's Pub, watching him approach.

"Hey, there, Emlyn," said Paddy. "Haven't seen you for weeks. What's the craic?"

Emlyn told him about his decision to join the ministry and his engagement to Sarah.

"Whew!" said, Paddy, screwing up his face and scratching behind his ear. "Now that's a bit of news that takes some digesting. You're going to become a priest, and you're going to get married."

"We don't call our priests 'priests,'" said Emlyn.

"I knew that," said Paddy, clapping Emlyn on the shoulder. "The lasses will be wailin' for sure when they hear that you're getting married." He extended his hand. "Congratulations!"

"Thanks," said Emlyn, taking his hand. "What are you up to these days?" he asked.

"Not much," said Paddy. "Six weeks ago, I gave up and went back to my job as joiner for the company. Many of the lads who worked in steel production didn't get their jobs back. I told them all along that Frick was not to be trusted, but they held out false hope to the bitter end—and I mean, bitter."

"I know," said Emlyn, thinking of Gwyn. "Many terrible stories are sequels to this strike."

"Some of these poor buggers are thinking that because Grover Cleveland defeated Harrison in the presidential election last month, things will turn around for labor," said Paddy. "Did you ever hear of such fantasy? Just because the Democrats are in won't suddenly bring deliverance to us workers rowing in the galleys. Things go on as before. The rich keep getting richer." He put his hand on the pub's door handle. "Well, that's enough gloom," he said. "Would you join me in a farewell drink?"

Before Emlyn could answer, Paddy exclaimed, "Oh, that's right, sorry." He glanced down at Emlyn's violin case. "Maybe you'll join us in playing a few tunes. Can a priest play if he doesn't drink?"

Emlyn laughed. "Some of the faithful would say no, but I don't see the harm."

Paddy opened the door, and, with a dramatic flourish, ushered Emlyn inside.

Wednesday, December 21st

The wind drove the cold rain into Oesterling's face as he rode along West Run, returning from a house call to see a young patient with whooping cough. Cerberus ran ahead, staying close to the trees for protection against the wind. Oesterling pulled up his collar in an attempt to stop the water from running off his hat and down his neck.

He and Dr. Baker had compared notes and concluded that the number of patients had diminished substantially since July, despite the fact that disease was running rampant in town. Many had either moved away or were too poor to pay for treatment. He treated his destitute patients anyway, telling them they could pay him later. These poor souls couldn't afford food or fuel—which made them more susceptible to illness. It was a vicious circle.

Kaufmann Brothers department store was sending books and boxes of candy to workers' children, and workers from McKeesport had donated a thousand turkeys to devastated families in Homestead. But what would happen when the holiday passed? The long winter lay ahead. He shivered.

He was growing more and more irritated with Carrie's constant whining about being cooped up in the house, alternating with expressions of loathing about moving to Chicago. At times he wished he hadn't offered to have her stay with them.

After he had more or less thrown Norton Montague out of the house the previous week, he had had a dickens of a time getting Carrie to calm down. She had heard their conversation from her room, and had become hysterical with anxiety. Oesterling had finally slipped a light sedative into the milk she took at bedtime, and she soon fell asleep.

This morning had been especially difficult. Sarah was preparing to leave the house for the last day of classes before break, when Oliver called from Chicago. He was so sorry, he said, but pressing business prohibited him from making it to Pittsburgh for Christmas, as he had planned. Instead, he was sending a nursemaid the next weekend to escort Carrie and their daughter to Chicago.

After she hung up the phone, Carrie had a tantrum, screaming about being abandoned. She did not want to spend

Christmas in cheerless, smoky Homestead. When Sarah had said that Oliver's company was the party responsible for making the town cheerless, Carrie had burst into tears and shut herself in her room.

Oesterling tipped his hat to the side to deflect the rain collecting on its brim. How did it happen that he and Margaret produced offspring with such different temperaments? However it happened, he was glad that this Christmas would be celebrated with Sarah and Emlyn. Next Christmas, only he and Cerberus would be at the house. He sighed. He'd cross that bridge when he got to it. Who knew what the coming year would bring?

Saturday, December 24th

Emlyn counted his final wage payment for the second time as he walked away from the General Office Building. Thinking he heard his name being called, he looked up. In the sea of men pouring out of the mill gate, he saw Joe Galik waving at him.

"Joe!" he called out as Galik worked his way through the crowd toward him.

"Hallo!" said Joe, seizing Emlyn by both arms. "Wie geht's?"

"Good," said Emlyn. "How is it going with you?"

"I now Big Cheese in O.H. 2," said Joe, grinning. "Other guys are new, don't know which end is up, so I tell them."

"What about Virgil?" Emlyn asked.

"Wirgil not at furnace," said Joe. "The company not give him job. He get real mad, yell at me, Stanley." Joe shook his head in disbelief. "He crazy guy."

"That sounds like Virgil," said Emlyn. "Do you know if he's still in town?"

"I see him two weeks ago," said Joe. "He say he go back to

family farm in Wirginia." Joe shifted his weight. "Say, how your job going?"

Emlyn told him about his leaving to become a minister, and his engagement.

"Very, very good!" exclaimed Joe. "I get married next year, too. I send for my Anna, and she comes in May."

"I'm very happy for you," said Emlyn.

"Merry Christmoos," said Joe. "I happy for you, too."

As Joe walked away, Emlyn thought of the more than two thousand Homestead former strikers, now facing a new year without work. He pulled his scarf over his mouth, and plodded back to the house.

As he stood on the deck of the ferry crossing to the north bank of the Monongahela, George Bernhard patted the pocket containing his wages. He was happy to have found a place as apprentice machinist for the Carnegie Company. He loved his job, loved seeing how the machines fit together and how they worked.

George was proud to hand over most of his pay to his mother, who was understandably devastated by the loss of her husband and breadwinner in September. His mother was stoical—he had seen her cry only once, when they brought his father home after the explosion. But despite her stony expression, George could see the suffering in her eyes. His pay, coupled with his brother John's, would be more than enough to support her and his younger siblings.

On the way back to the house in East Liberty, he was going to pick up the goose he had ordered for Christmas, as well as oranges and hard candy for Santa to bring the two youngest children. He was determined to make it a happy holiday.

The ferry hit the landing, and George waited patiently as the gangplank was thrown down. He ran down the plank, and struck off at a fast walk up Brown's Hill.

Sunday, December 25th

Oesterling sat at the head of the table, the Christmas feast spread before him.

Sarah, wearing her old green dress, sat opposite. Sarah had sold the dress Carrie had given her last year, saying that she would never have occasion to wear it again. Some of the proceeds from the sale had gone into a fund for unemployed strikers, with the remainder set aside for trousseau items.

Emlyn was at Oesterling's right, and Charles LaCroix at his left. Sarah had suggested inviting LaCroix for dinner when she had heard that he would be spending the holiday alone. Carrie was upstairs, shut in her room with the baby.

It was taking all of Oesterling's self control to contain his exasperation with Carrie. She complained about everything—Mrs. Cox, whom he had hired to help Carrie with the baby, Mrs. Sproule's cooking, Oliver's absence, Cerberus's presence, and the lack of a tree. What had upset her most was his decision to suspend the giving of gifts among the family. He was glad that Carrie hadn't been there to witness Emlyn giving Sarah his grandmother's pearl ring.

"It's really a gift from Eirwen," Emlyn had said, explaining how she had given it to him.

Although Carrie didn't say it outright, Oesterling suspected she did not approve of Sarah's choice of a husband. "He's going to be a minister? Why, you'll be poor as church mice," she said when Sarah told her of their engagement Sunday morning.

"We'll be rich in other ways," said Sarah.

Carrie sniffed. "I don't see why you have to bother yourself in the kitchen, hanging about with Mrs. Sproule."

"Good grief, Carrie," said Sarah. "I think it generous of Mrs. Sproule to show me how she manages the kitchen and food preparation. Mama cooked when we were young, and I will be cooking after I'm married. Not everyone can afford servants, you know."

Carrie made a face. "It's so unseemly."

Sarah pursed her lips, exasperated. "Look at yourself!" she cried. "You and Oliver have been blessed with a child, with material wealth, but you are not happy. What would satisfy you?"

Carrie's lower lip trembled, and she was on the verge of tears.

"That's right. Feel sorry for yourself—again!" exclaimed Sarah, and stalked out of the room.

When Oesterling had told Carrie yesterday that Charles LaCroix would be their guest, she turned up her nose. "So now we're inviting clerks to share our family celebration?"

Anger swelled inside him. "Would you prefer to have someone of your own class here—Norton Montague, for example?"

In response, she gave him a stricken look.

He regretted saying that. He didn't want to hurt her. Nevertheless, as he sat at the table with Sarah, Emlyn, and Charles, he had to admit that he secretly rejoiced when Carrie had said she would not join them. He was tired of her scenes, weary of the melodrama.

"That was an absolutely gorgeous piece you played last night," Charles said to Emlyn. "What was it again?"

"Bach's 'Air on the G-String,'" said Emlyn.

"Ah, yes," said Charles. "I almost cried. So embarrassing! Say, would you consider playing it again, after dinner? I promise not to cry."

Sarah laughed. "It's OK if you cry. Emlyn, are you up for it?"

Emlyn said yes, and after dinner they moved into the parlor. Oesterling and Charles sat on chairs near the piano, listening attentively. At the end, they clapped.

"Should we keep going?" asked Sarah. "Would you like to sing a few carols?"

"A splendid idea," said Charles.

They started with 'Once in Royal David's City,' and then, 'Hark, the Herald Angels Sing.'

"You have a fine baritone voice, Charles," said Sarah. "I'll have to recruit you for the choir."

"Thank you," said Charles. "I would be happy to serve." He bowed, and they went on to 'It Came Upon the Midnight Clear.'

After they sang the last verse, Emlyn played the tune on the violin.

Oesterling took out his handkerchief and blew his nose. He always associated that carol with Margaret and the many Christmases they had sung it around the piano. It got him every time, especially the third verse. *Oh rest beside the weary road, and hear the angels sing.*

"That was beautiful," said Oesterling at the end.

"I agree," Carrie said from the doorway. They all turned around. Oesterling contemplated his older daughter, her eyes red, the baby in her arms.

"May I join you?" she asked.

"Of course," said Oesterling. He introduced her to Charles and helped her settle on the sofa with the baby.

"Please continue," Carrie said. "I just love singing the old carols."

Sarah began 'I Heard the Bells on Christmas Day,' and they all joined in. As they sang, Oesterling's thoughts went back to Christmases during the Civil War, when Longfellow had written the verses.

> Then pealed the bells more loud and deep:
> 'God is not dead, nor doth he sleep;
> The wrong shall fail, the right prevail,
> With peace on earth, good will to men.'

Oesterling wished he could feel half as optimistic as Longfellow. He looked at Carrie, cradling little Margaret on one side, holding a hymnbook on the other, singing. It struck him that it was first time in many days that he had seen her content.

At the end, Carrie asked, "Could we sing, 'O Little Town of Bethlehem'? It's my favorite."

"Mine, too," said Charles, and they began singing. Oesterling shut his eyes and listened to his daughters, his son-in-law–to-be, and Charles, singing in harmony.

> Where children pure and happy
> Pray to the blessed Child,
> Where misery cries out to thee,
> Son of the mother mild;
> Where charity stands watching
> And faith holds wide the door,
> The dark night wakes, the glory breaks,
> And Christmas comes once more.

Oesterling cast a surreptitious glance at Carrie. She was singing with great animation, her eyes intent on the page.

At the end of the verse, smiling down at her daughter, she kissed her ardently on the forehead.

Oesterling took a deep breath as they began the last verse. Maybe there was hope for the future, after all.

Tuesday, December 27th

Emlyn set his things by the front door and went through the house a final time. The furniture dealer had taken away the last pieces that morning, and he had turned over all the keys but one to the company. They had told him that another worker's family would be moving in next week.

His footsteps echoed in the cold, empty house as he went from room to room. His steamer trunk was already on its way to Mount Pleasant. Sarah had wanted to see him off at the station, but he had requested that she did not. He could not bear another parting beside the tracks.

Instead, he had gone to their house for breakfast, and after the doctor and Carrie had discreetly withdrawn to the study, he and Sarah had said their goodbyes in the foyer. He held her tightly in his arms for what seemed a long time, not wanting to let go. She and the doctor were coming to his ordination in Mount Pleasant, but after that, they would see each other only once or twice before the wedding. They had promised to write each other every day.

Emlyn stepped out the door, and pulled it shut. He locked it, and set the key on the lintel. He cast one long, lingering look at the house, the street, and the mill looming large in the near distance.

Carrying the violin in one hand and bag in the other, he strode off toward the Amity Street Station.

EPILOGUE

1893 The murder trials of three strikers end in acquittals. Strike leader **Hugh O'Donnell**, cleared of charges, is blacklisted in the steel industry and shunned by labor for the rest of his life. He ekes out a living as a journalist.

Within a year of the end of the strike, at the Homestead Works wages for skilled workers, like rollers and heaters, are reduced by half. Wounded by the outcome of the strike, the **Amalgamated Association of Iron and Steel Workers** goes into a slow, protracted decline.

In the aftermath of the strike, the press, church leaders, and politicians in the U.S. and Britain vilify **Andrew Carnegie**. He never regains his pre-strike prestige. In his autobiography, Carnegie writes: 'No pangs remain of any wound received in my business career save that of Homestead. It was so unnecessary.'

The real, historical **William Williams** continues as a mill superintendent until his death in 1905.

1898 The Carnegie Library of Homestead, located on the hill overlooking the battle site, opens its doors. It is the second public library funded by Carnegie, and features a music hall, athletic center, and swimming pool. Frick anonymously donates a concert grand piano.

1899 Carnegie and **Henry Clay Frick** have a bitter falling out. Carnegie forces Frick's resignation as Chairman of the Board of Carnegie Steel.

1900 The real, historical **Hans (Honus) Wagner** joins the Pittsburgh Pirates as shortstop. He wins his first batting championship with a .381 mark and also leads the league in doubles (45), triples (22), and slugging percentage (.573).

1901 Carnegie sells Carnegie Steel to banker J.P. Morgan for the staggering sum of $48 million. Morgan establishes the United States Steel Corporation, the first corporation in the world with a market capitalization over $1 billion.

1902 After wandering to the Southwest, and then to Mexico, former burgess **John McLuckie** finds work as a repair superintendent for the Sonora Railroad.

The real, historical **George Bernhard (George W. Busch)** becomes superintendent of the Homestead Machine Shop #2. He is instrumental in establishing baseball teams representing the various mill shops.

1904 The **Welsh Congregational Church** in Homestead is closed.

1906 Completing a 14-year sentence for the attempted murder of Frick, **Alexander Berkman** is released from prison.

1917 Berkman is convicted under the Espionage Act of conspiracy to induce persons not to register for the military draft.

1919 On his deathbed, Carnegie sends a request to meet Frick, whom he hasn't seen for two decades. Frick's famous reply to the messenger: 'Tell him I'll see him in Hell, where we both are going.'

On August 11, Carnegie dies of bronchial pneumonia at age 83. On December 2, Frick dies of a heart attack shortly before his seventieth birthday. That evening, on the eve of his deportation to Russia, Alexander Berkman, asked to comment by a reporter, says that Frick has been 'deported by God.'

1936 The Baseball Hall of Fame inducts Honus Wagner as one of its first five members, along with Ty Cobb and Babe Ruth.

1937 The entire neighborhood north of the railroad tracks is razed to make way for the expansion of U.S. Steel's Homestead Works, displacing 8,000 residents. George Busch retires as superintendent of the Homestead Machine Shop.

1942 The United Steelworkers union is established by a convention of representatives from the Amalgamated Association of Iron, Steel, and Tin Workers and the Steel Workers Organizing Committee.

1976 In July *The Pittsburgh Post-Gazette* runs a commentary on the 1892 strike, 'Homestead's Worst Day.' No locals talk about the strike; the unions do not comment.

1986 U.S. Steel closes the Homestead Works, which at one time produced nearly a third of all the steel used in the United States.

1988 U.S. Steel sells the Homestead Works to the Park Corporation, which demolishes the industrial structures on the 430-acre site.

1996 The Rivers of Steel National Heritage Area is established by Congress.

1999 The Waterfront shopping complex opens for business on the land previously occupied by the Homestead Works.

TO THE READER

This story of the 1892 Homestead Strike has been many years in the making. It can be told from a number of perspectives, and indeed has been in histories and documentaries. I, however, wanted to tell my own story, or more accurately, a narrative suggested by the family stories handed down to me.

My father, G. Edward Busch, had a lifelong fascination with the Strike, writing his senior paper on it at the University of Pittsburgh. During my childhood, he recounted the story many times over of the death of his grandfather John Paul Busch (Karl Bernhard) in the mill two months after the workers fought Frick's Pinkertons. Union saboteurs had set a boiler to explode when my great-grandfather and his crew were firing it up. All four men died of the burns they received.

The conclusion of the story was always the deathbed scene in the house in East Liberty, which begins with John Paul saying that, despite the outcome, he is glad to have left Germany. "Stand by America," he tells his wife and eleven children gathered at the bedside. His dying wish is that his sons take the names of American patriots as a tribute to his adopted homeland. Thus my grandfather, George, the eldest, became George Washington Busch, John Paul became John Paul Jones Busch, and Benjamin became Benjamin Franklin Busch. (This scene does not appear in *Darkness*

Visible because it seems too allegorical for historical fiction. However, I did include other Busch stories—the broomstick Christmas tree, for example.)

After his father's death, my grandfather took a job as machinist at the Works, and about ten years later became shop superintendent. Dad showed me crumbling sepia photographs of the Homestead Works Machine Shop #2: his father and the machinist crew in 1898; a very young Eddie and his father standing by the general superintendent's automobile; early 20th century shots of his father with gigantic pieces of machinery; his father with the mill shop baseball teams that he helped organize.

Another one of Dad's stories about his father was George's friendship with baseball legend Honus Wagner. Born in the same year, 1874, Honus and George met on Pittsburgh sandlots and developed a close friendship. Although they rarely saw each other as adults, both had a lifelong devotion to baseball, Wagner in his professional career, my grandfather through organizing mill and community teams in Homestead.

As an adult, after a decade of studying and teaching, in the 1970s I embarked on genealogical research. Dad took me around to the Pittsburgh sites related to his family: his paternal grandmother's house in East Liberty, his maternal grandmother's grave in Allegheny Cemetery, John Paul's grave in the Lutheran Cemetery, and the house where Dad was born on Hays Street in Homestead. I sent for the record of John Paul's service in the U.S. Navy during the Civil War. And I looked up John Paul's death certificate, which corroborated Dad's story of his grandfather dying of burns in September of 1892.

These stories and images piqued my curiosity about my grandfather and the huge role the Strike and Homestead

Works had played in the course of his life and his family's. Dad's take on the Strike was that the villain of the piece was H.C. Frick. He let Andrew Carnegie, his father's employer, off the hook.

Strangely enough, I can remember only one occasion during my youth when I discussed the Strike with someone outside my family. My friend Joyce Bergert's steelworker father was a roller, a skilled position, and a member of the union. Her family was much more anti-Carnegie than mine. It surprised me to find that some did not think Carnegie a good guy, despite his gifts to the community after the Strike.

After my father's death in 1998, I started thinking about putting together my story of the Strike in the form of an historical novel. It seemed the only way to weave together the stories in the history books with the folklore. I knew that I couldn't do this while Dad was alive, as he took a proprietary interest in the Strike, and I would have to negotiate my way through his stories.

It wasn't until I began researching the Strike that I discovered why nobody in twentieth-century Homestead talked about it: the residents were mostly descendents of scabs, not strikers. Ironically, these workers were by then unionized, a feat that took nearly four decades to accomplish.

The Strike, however, had created so much survivors' guilt that the conspiracy of silence continued for a century after the Strike. By then, the Homestead Works was gone, and the younger generations had no memory of the mill, nor of those who had toiled there.

About the same time as I sought background about the Busches, I also began a search for my grandma Annie Edwards Busch's relatives in Wales, using online databases, visiting Wales, and even hiring a Welsh researcher. I found my great-great-grandparents' house in Froncysyllte, but never did track down family members. Instead, something just as wonderful happened —I found many friends (some of them now surrogate family) in Wales.

As my book predates the arrival of my mother's parents in Homestead by two decades, their experiences are not directly relevant to the story. Nevertheless, my mother became a partner in the writing enterprise, telling stories about her childhood in Homestead and stories my Busch grandparents had told her, reading early drafts, and discussing histories of the Strike (which she borrowed from the Homestead Library).

I recall one time in particular when we were talking about Leon Wolff's *Lockout*. When I said that I was appalled at the violence visited upon the Pinkertons after they got off the barges, my mother responded by exclaiming, "The workers were fighting for their lives!" Although Mum had helped run the family business, Katilius Furniture, she definitely identified with her customers, the workers.

In 2000 I began researching the book by reading just about everything written about the Strike, interviewing friends and relatives, and revisiting the locales I had chosen as settings for the book. Once I fell into the groove so reminiscent of graduate school days, I easily could have gone on researching indefinitely. I had to force myself to begin writing. This was a difficult transition, for although I'd written many feature and opinion pieces, I had no experience writing a long work of fiction. However, I had the historical events, fleshed out by the research, and these provided the framework on which to fit my fictional characters.

When I learned that the Welsh pretty much ran the prestrike mill, both as skilled union workers and management, I decided that my story's striker family would be Welsh immigrants. Naturally, my Grandfather Busch's family would represent the scabs. (The substitute name, "Bernhard," is the surname of John Paul's grandmother.) I used the Welsh connections I had made in my search for my own relatives to create my fictional Jones and Phillips families.

For me, the exciting part of writing was putting the pieces of research and family folklore together. This process gave me insights into the background stories that previously had been inscrutable. In one case, for example, someone I interviewed provided an important character in the novel. Jack Fix, a Pittsburgh native, recounted the story of his great-grandfather William Williams's experience during the Strike. It is essentially the same one as the fictional Williams tells the doctor: how Superintendent Potter had offered him a huge sum of money to start the mill furnaces.

After hearing this story, I understood why my unemployed great-grandfather, experienced in starting industrial boilers, would risk going into the Works: the company was willing to pay handsomely for his skill. Thus a fictionalized version of Williams made his way into my story, along with my paternal great-grandparents, grandfather, and five of his ten siblings.

In focusing on the plight of the workers, both strikers and scabs, I have of necessity had to leave out significant episodes of the Strike story, the Iams court martial, for instance. My goal from the beginning has been to tell a story that could be told no other way but through the vehicle of the historical novel. My hope is that in my recreation of 1892 Homestead in words, I have succeeded in being faithful to the narratives of those who were witness to and those who documented these terrible events.

ACKNOWLEDGEMENTS

I would like to express gratitude to those who encouraged and assisted me in this project.

In the research phase: to the staff at Rivers of Steel National Heritage Area, notably Ron Baraff (Director of Museum Collections and Archives), Tiffani Emig (Curator of Collections), Julie Williams, and Susan Lineback; to the Saint David's Society of Pittsburgh, in particular, Jack Fix, Garnet Roth and Rev. Richard W. Davies; to John Asmonga, Peter Oresick and Ernie Spisak; to fellow Munhall High School alums who shared their family immigration stories, namely Joyce Bergert Becze, Dennis Duda, Mike Veslany, Ray Matuza, Gloria Powell Hardington and Gwen Phillips; to my cousin Grace Jack Krepps for family stories, and to her husband Phil Krepps, who provided invaluable information about steel production in the Homestead Works; to John Martine for descriptions of workers' houses; to Steven Potach for background on Slovak immigrants; to Rev. Joseph Corbin for explaining the ordination process; to Carol Johnson and Tom Tollman, librarians at Normandale Community College; to the reference librarians at the Carnegie Library of Homestead, the Carnegie Library of Pittsburgh in Oakland, and the New York Public Library.

And those across the Atlantic: in Wales to Rev.Vivian Jones for background on Welsh Congregationalism; to Dr.

Bill Jones of Cardiff University for information on the Ton du mine disaster; to Emyr Morris, who guided me around South Wales; to Ann Morris, for providing dialogue in Welsh; and in Germany to my cousin Hanne Pösch (Busch) Heuer for checking my translations.

In the writing phase: to Joyce Becze, Jay-Louise Weldon, and Grace Krepps for reading and commenting on drafts; to Mary Morris Mergenthal, Jack Brondum, and Brian Sharkey for editing and commenting on near-final drafts; to Ruth V. Jones for proofreading the final draft; to Mike Ferguson for listening to my ongoing struggles; and to Bob Taylor and Pat McGowan for providing background to the social economics of the late nineteenth century.

I am especially grateful to my daughter Ceridwen Christensen and son-in-law Richard Mueller for steering me through the publishing process. Additional thanks go to Ceridwen for proofing the typesetting and to Richard for his help with marketing and for his evocative cover design. Finally, special thanks are due those who gave suggestions and encouragement throughout this project, from beginning to end: Joyce Becze, Jay-Louise Weldon, and my daughter Morwenna.